The Intimate Beginnings of Taylor

A Sapphic Romance

Lavender Quinn

Copyright © 2024 by Lavender Quinn

All rights reserved.

No portion of this book may be reproduced in any form without written permission from the publisher or author, except as permitted by U.S. copyright law.

This is a work of fiction. Names, characters, places, and incidents either are the products of the author's imagination or are used fictitiously. Any resemblance to actual persons, living or dead, businesses, companies, events, or locales is entirely coincidental.

Cover Design by Christine Marie (IG: @capt.christine).

Line Editing by Astrida Schaeffer.

Contents

By Lavender Quinn

Hotel BED Series Duology #1
The Intimate Beginnings of Taylor
Suite Enemy

Blurb

Her rival's girlfriend. The most important lesson of her acting career: love is a fantasy and fantasies are made to break you.

When Taylor pauses her acting dreams to explore life as a single, bisexual college student, she never expects trouble to follow.

But old rivalries never die and Taylor learns it's not always the jealous co-star you have to worry about. Sometimes, it's her girlfriend.

Gabriella, the girlfriend of Taylor's arch nemesis, is a master at sabotaging the prospects of young actors, especially those deemed a threat to her girlfriend's career. With Taylor's most intimate secrets at Gabriella's disposal, Taylor battles two enemies simultaneously, while living out her darkest fantasies anonymously, to maintain her pristine reputation.

With the stage now abandoned for the war they rage behind the velvet curtain, Taylor and Gabriella race against time to secure their freedoms, at the risk of exposing the one secret that may destroy them both.

Author's Note

TAYLOR CAME TO ME in a dream. It was during a time when I was realizing more and more every day that I was, in fact, bisexual. There was a girl living in my head, who had met her first girlfriend in college, and I couldn't stop thinking about them. As their relationship grew, so did their friendships, and soon, the story of the Five was born.

The Five are a group of frenemies who come together one summer to build upon a dream to open a black, queer-owned erotic hotel in Las Vegas. Each member of the Five brings their unique skill set, their sexual desires, and memories of failed dreams.

We start with Taylor, an actress who decides to temporarily leave Hollywood behind to explore her sexuality with a girl she met on the internet, unaware that her former co-star–and her former co-star's girlfriend–are keeping a watchful eye.

Each member of the Five is special to me. I think, in part, because each represents a piece of me. Like Taylor, I have an undeniable desire to explore more about this special side of me that has stayed hidden for so long, which is why I wrote this book.

I hope you have as much fun reading about her as I have dreaming about her.

Content Warnings

Taylor's story is not dipped in Modge Podge and coated with glitter. Please take care of yourself. This book contains graphic sexual scenes, dubious consent, knife play, cutting (self-harm), threats of suicide, domestic abuse (not between the main characters), biting, cheating (not between the main characters), exhibitionism, and role play.

This one's for you.

Chapter One
Taylor

"First, Taylor, I want to congratulate you on everything you've accomplished in such a short amount of time. You've portrayed a beloved character on an award-winning television series and have proven to be such an inspiration for young children of color and of the LGBTQ+ community. What do you say to your critics who told you that coming out at such a young age would ruin your career?"

I'm expecting the question. My coming out at seventeen warranted a front page cover story in one magazine and an in-depth interview in half a dozen others. It was a big deal, orchestrated by my public relations team to quiet another brewing scandal.

"Gina, I am just so blessed to have such supportive fans and family members who have rallied behind me to tell me they love me for who I am. And who I am is an unapologetically black, queer woman, who isn't afraid to be herself." I'm sure my large smile shines in the lights rigged in my living room. The interview is meant to be personable, an intimate discussion about me leaving Hollywood behind for college dreams and the search for a normal life.

Except the university I'm going to is quite local and as several young actors will all be joining the same performing arts program as me, there will be no leaving Hollywood behind.

"How do you see your relationship with Sara Aguilar moving forward as you both start these new life chapters?"

My lips close over my teeth, though I maintain the smile. Sara fucking Aguilar. The biggest pain in my ass. My arch nemesis. We've been battling it out for acting roles since we were in diapers. We even landed in one together, a bouncing baby commercial where the babies took over the world, only to be lulled to sleep by a moderately priced singing electronic device.

And then, at eleven, we were cast on the same kids' television series, *Sunny and the Dreamers. Sunny and the Dreamers* was very successful in its demographic. We lasted three seasons, which was typically the norm for young actors cast in children's programming.

After our series ended when we were fourteen, I was offered another role as Piper Paige, a smart, confident, young aspiring paranormal investigator with a knack for getting into trouble, solving mysteries, minor crimes, and offenses around her neighborhood.

It had a great premise and the show won many awards for outstanding teen drama series, but now the show is over. I've officially aged out of children's programming and am looking forward to the break.

Rumor had it Sara learned about the role months before they offered it to me and campaigned hard for it. The part was mine without an audition because the executive producer said I was the only one he could picture in the role.

Sara scored her own show, though it never reached the same level of viewership as *The Paige Society*.

Behind the scenes discourse and turmoil is not usually mentioned until years after a show has already ended, unless of course, an actor wants to get out of a contract, but that's with adults. With kids, being perceived as someone difficult to work with is career annihilation, which is exactly what Sara tried to do to me when a social media post of hers went viral.

She waited until the series finale aired to post it. After three seasons, the show was finally ending, and instead of thanking the crew for their hard work and the fans for their support, she sent her vapid fanbase after me. While I was being crucified, Sara continued to post cryptic messages about strength, healing and forgiveness.

My team convinced me that the magazine spread about acceptance would be the best thing to counter the negative image Sara was trying to stick me with. My family already knew about my sexuality. My dad called me out on it at fourteen. When I didn't deny it, he said to me, "There's no reason for you to hide from us. You be who you want to be and love who you want to love. If anyone has a problem with it, you tell them to speak to me." I cried then, first in relief, and then in security. The show ended a few months later.

The day my article was published, my parents each posted on their own social media accounts how proud they were of me. I had given the masses an answer to their questions. Now, instead of being inherently cruel, I was only mean because I was struggling with being in the closet and concealing my sexuality. Again, not true, but the truth doesn't sell headlines, or satisfy hungry internet mobs.

Sara followed up my announcement with a different black and white image, one of her looking adoringly into the eyes of a girl with the caption: "*Finally, I'm free,*" and attached every emoji you could associate with queer love. That's when the other rumors flew.

TWO YOUNG TV STARLETS
SECRETLY IN LOVE?

The narrative had changed again. Now Sara and I were carrying on a secret romance that ended badly. The theory of why our romance didn't work was actually very kind. "The stress was just too much."

Fans gushed about the possibility. Fanfiction was written about us. I couldn't bear to read any of it, though my best friend, Nicole, who co-starred on our show while starring in her own, read it obsessively.

She knew the truth about Sara, having crossed paths with her almost for as long as I had. Sara was the true mean girl. She'd torture us mercilessly, all under the guise of pranks and harmless fun. But none of it was funny.

Sara was the real evil. The rumors of her toxic behavior followed her from set to set for years, but so did her daddy's money, which she never talked about. If she talked about that, she couldn't avoid the other topics, like her last name changing from Richards to Aguilar, her mother's maiden name.

I've gone back to that photo of her and her girlfriend more times than I care to admit. She posts her often, always with her face shielded from view, covered by her voluminous curly hair. That's one thing that didn't come out of my queer declaration. I'm still as single as ever.

Although I was seventeen when I made the announcement, I wasn't ready to date then. Last year I considered dating a guy who showed an interest in me, another young actor who worked on Nicole's show, but I'd decided against it, not wanting to be linked to anyone before going off to college to start my "new chapter" as

Gina Thomas, from *Rise and Shine L.A.*, phrased it.

"It's been a few years since Sara and I have been able to sit down and talk with one another. Now that we're going to attend the same school, and maybe attend the same classes, I'm hopeful it'll be a positive experience for the both of us, and a new way for us to connect."

The segment ends as Gina wishes me the best of luck on my new endeavor and calls the show back to her in-studio colleagues before the field producer calls "Cut." She surprises me with a hug after we're both unmic'd, her hands brushing just underneath the coils of my low ponytail.

"You were great. You are always so classy and you show so much grace. People will love everything you've said here today." She leans in closer, her hands firmly planted on my blouse-covered shoulders. "But do yourself a favor. Stay the hell away from that damn girl."

That's exactly what I plan to do.

I'm probably one of the few who doesn't entirely blame Sara for her behaviors. I kind of get it. Being a popular actor so young can be hard. People keep track of our friends, our fashion, our habits and analyze any superficial change we make.

It's hard to be yourself, especially in an industry where your closest confidants could also be your biggest competition.

Creaking open the door to my closet was more than a strategy, it was a relief. Being able to talk about who I was and who I've always been gave me the confidence I needed to finally explore new things.

While college is the first step, I plan for so much more.

It takes a while for the crew to load up their equipment to leave. They've been here before. You stay in the industry long enough, you run into the same production teams continuously. Mama feeds them snacks and small meals because that's what Mamas do to show they're polite and know how to raise respectful children.

I try my best to not make it too obvious I'm trying to escape to my bedroom. I sit on the bottom step first and then, after a few minutes of listening to them talk, I edge up one step, then another. I continue the entire process until I'm too far up the stairs for the lower kitchen ceiling to give me away.

I only need one finger to swipe away the screensaver on my cell phone, concealing the messages underneath.

Daisy [7:00 p.m.]

Are you home yet?

We talk at the same time every day. It's been that way for the past two years.

I created an online account a few days after the magazine published my announcement. My publicist and my parents only kept telling me positive things.

"People love it."

"Everyone's being so supportive."

"Don't worry. Everything's going to be okay."

I didn't believe them. Not because I thought they were lying, but because I knew they loved me and would keep the truth from me, especially if it hurt.

I scrolled through dozens of gossip sites, reading comments I was not supposed to read. My parents hadn't lied completely. There were some encouraging comments, but then there were others spouting off about an *agenda* and continuously spreading false rumors about grotesque industry behaviors. None of which were true for me.

So, I went off. I made an account I wasn't supposed to make

and cussed them all out—anonymously, of course. Some people accused me of being a member of my PR team. Others rooted me on.

That's when I met Daisy. After she revealed she lived in California, like me, I told her I used to live in California, but moved to Canada a few years ago.

I had just completed filming a cable TV movie in Vancouver, and since I hadn't planned on continuing the discussion beyond a few days, lying didn't seem too bad.

After a while, the many internet searches I had to do to make sure I was being true to the Vancouver weather forecast got too daunting. I announced one day I was moving back to California, chose one of the L.A. suburbs I felt I could describe well and left it at that. Shockingly, the only response she had was, *"Glad your parents came to their senses."*

We're supposed to be the same age. Though there's no way to verify this. I thought long and hard about that one, but in the end, it would be much harder to act older. So far, so good.

At first, I told her my name was Tinsel, an old nickname from my frequent gigs on the holiday circuit. Tinsel Townes, they called me. No one but those who know my industry history would guess that Taylor and Tinsel were connected. Daisy didn't buy it.

"Even if I wanted to believe your parents weren't on something when they named you that, I could never do that to you. Can I call you Emmy?" She has never explained where the nickname comes from and I've never asked.

Lately, the name has felt different. Whenever it pops up on my screen, I feel...excited. That's something I've never expected to feel before.

Relationships are bad in my business. As a public figure, everyone feels entitled to know everything about you. It's hard to keep anything free of speculation and intrigue. I have no plans to commit to a relationship, but Piper Paige also can't be seen leaving some girl's apartment early one Sunday morning.

I have a reputation to protect and a body dying to be set free. Every conversation with Daisy feels like opening the door another inch.

It's scary to think of changing the dynamic of something you've built with someone else. What if we meet in person and it's not the same? Sometimes we stay up talking for hours. What if, in person, we don't even last a few minutes? I can't imagine us meeting over something as boring as coffee when we talk about traveling the world together.

We've built a good friendship over the years. There are things Daisy knows about Emmy that no one knows about Taylor.

As stupid as that sounds.

Emmy [7:03 p.m.]

Here! Just got in.

Daisy [7:03 p.m.]

Good. Finished my list today. Are you excited?

A flutter of butterfly wings erupts through my belly. The list. It's a consequence of one of our latest games. A reminder for me of what happens when I become too honest.

Emmy [7:03 p.m.]

Nooooo. I'm so scared!

Ok. *Half* honest. Scared probably wouldn't be the correct

word to use. Excited. Nervous. Secretly dripping in anticipation. I probably should be afraid. Meeting anyone on the internet is a risk.

Daisy [7:04 p.m.]

> *Don't be scared. I know you can do it. I'm always rooting for you. Did you do yours?*

There were only two sexual fantasies that came to mind when she first asked about it. Our conversations had detoured from friendly chatter to steamier discussions over a year ago.

At first, I lied about my sexual experience, but she quickly caught on.

"It's okay if you haven't. I like knowing no one has touched you."

The fire. The burning, sizzling, cracking flame that blazed through my pajamas had me telling all my secrets.

And from then we formed a plan to meet in secret. No one can know what we're about to do. It'll be a hard thing to juggle, but I'm hoping freedom comes with age.

"Taylor." My heart jumps in terror. I slam my phone face down on my desk. Mama creaks the door open slowly, giving me time to adjust.

"You did great, baby." Our knees brush when she sits on the edge of my bed. My desk is conveniently next to it for easy access. I am almost ashamed of how quickly I reach for my laptop whenever I hear the signature chime. I've made it a habit to switch between my laptop and my phone when talking with Daisy. If I'm on my phone too often, they'll ask questions. Research is easier to fake on a computer.

"Zara called. There's an offer she thinks you should consider."

My head is shaking before she finishes her sentence. I am semi-retired. The benefit of working on children's shows is their shelf life. Aging out of your demographic is both a blessing and a curse. You're happy to move on with your life, but also worried about leaving behind a stable income and consistent shooting schedule.

I, for one, am looking forward to no longer being Piper Paige. Piper was a great role model and model citizen. I'm Taylor and while I can be both things, I'm not only those things. The rest I need to figure out and I can't do that in the spotlight.

"Before you start, this is not an acting gig. It's being a host." I blow out a much needed breath for a little too long.

"Hosting is still pretending, Mama. I still have to be happy even when I'm sad. I still have to act excited when all I want is to take a nap. I don't want to pretend anymore. I just want to be." Be myself. I just want to be myself.

"She thinks it'll be important for you to do some smaller gigs in between your breaks. That way, people don't forget about you. You know how hard it is to leave and come back. I don't want you to make things harder for yourself."

I know what she means without her need to say it. When they stack the odds against you, work ten times as hard.

"Ok. I'll talk to her and see what it's about."

She plants one kiss on my forehead before leaving my bedroom, closing the door behind her. I give the chair a slight push and send myself gliding across the floor. The lock makes a small clicking noise before I slide back over again.

My eyes land on the rows of text Daisy has already sent through. I devour the black lines at the same time I remind myself to swallow from the increasing wetness of my mouth and contain the movement of my hips against the bottom of my chair.

This is one of my favorite games. We've been playing it nearly every day for the past two years. As we've gotten older, they've gotten more detailed and less innocent.

Until now, we've opted to keep our communication on screen. We've shared no photos of each other or sent any voice messages. I'm worried about revealing my identity. It's hard to believe Daisy could be someone else, but I can't leave that to chance.

I told her I was too self-conscious to send pictures. I only felt bad when her response of, "*You're perfect*" appeared on my screen. Still, she agreed that when the time came, we would continue it anonymously.

Now is the only time I have to explore without prying eyes. If people were to find out, whether they root for us or against us, it would only end in disappointment. Daisy isn't forever. She can't be. She can only be what I need right now.

The rules I put into place are there to protect me. It's easy to be hurt by people in this business. People who don't know us think we'll recover quickly because we're *famous* and have seemingly unlimited resources. People who do know us are usually only out for themselves.

Daisy can never know who I am. Relinquishing that power to her might be detrimental to my career and to my family's well-being. How would I ever be able to look my family in the eyes once they found out everything Daisy knew about me? Daisy knows unspeakable things I can only utter in the dark underneath the covers.

I'm the one who chose the spotlight. Becoming an actor wasn't something my parents had ever pushed me to do. Cute baby commercials were one thing, but nonstop auditions, lessons, agents, meetings, travel and a complete loss of privacy—they didn't ask for that. I know they've supported me throughout all the chaos because they love me. The least I can do is keep the dark sides of me hidden.

Maybe after I'm done with Daisy, I'll live a normal life, like Eryn. She followed in my parents' footsteps and chose a normal career as a teacher. As far as I know, Eryn doesn't have any unspeakable sexual fantasies she needs to keep hidden. She's been in the same adored relationship for years.

Eryn's boyfriend has never been barred from knowing what she looks like or what her voice sounds like. They have never had to meet up secretly, veiled by darkness to keep their identities concealed.

Even giving Daisy my phone number was an anxiety-filled hurdle, but being on the site all the time was impossible with my schedule. She promised she wouldn't search it and I believed her. As a show of mutual trust, I didn't search hers either. Though I doubt she has as much to lose as me.

Emmy [7:10 p.m.]

Yeah. It's all done. It's pretty short. Only 2.5 things.

Daisy [7:10 p.m.]

2.5?

With Daisy, I never know when she's teasing me or genuinely curious. She's never said anything bad or done anything hurtful, but I still find myself on guard.

Emmy [7:11 p.m.]

2 for certain and 1 I'm not sure I want to do.

The last one isn't the most recent and maybe not even the most taboo. I think about it just as often as the others.

Daisy [7:11 p.m.]

Tell me.

A small smile creeps onto my face when I imagine her pouting. Daisy hasn't revealed any physical characteristics about herself for me to envision her accurately. I have my own image of her. One I've adjusted over time to reduce any tempting appeal.

I can't get too close.

Emmy [7:11 p.m.]

You already know the first one.

Emmy [7:12 p.m.]

Touch me.

The heat rising in my body spreads to a place I've only allowed myself to explore late at night when everyone else is sound asleep.

Daisy [7:12 p.m.]

Where?

Oh God. Not now. Sexy talk is only allowed after dinner. When I've parted from my family for the night, and there's less chance of interruption. If we start now, I won't be able to finish for hours.

Emmy [7:12 p.m.]

Not now.

My eyes shoot at the door on instinct. It remains closed.

Daisy [7:13 p.m.]

(◕_◕) Fine. What's the second?

A laugh threatens to accompany the smile. I push it back down by smoothing out my lips and clearing the hump in my throat.

Emmy [7:13 p.m.]

Watch me.

She already knows this. Many of our late night games have been about her watching me do...things. I haven't been brave enough to do all of it. Some positions she has had me place myself in have elicited weakening results. Like when she tells me to lie with my breasts flat on the bed with my ass in the air and my hand between my legs.

I like that one the best.

I always imagine her standing behind me, watching every place my fingers go. It's possible I could blame her for the modification I made a few months ago by having my ass face my window instead of my bedroom door. I argued it would be catastrophic for one of my parents to walk in on me and that be the sight they see. Even though I triple-check that I locked my door before Daisy's first message even comes through.

Emmy [7:15 p.m.]

What about yours?

We mostly talk about myself. *Talking* is a bit of an exaggeration. We tell stories together. I start them and she finishes. It's been our primary connection from the beginning.

Daisy [7:15 p.m.]

I only have one.

I can probably guess based on what has happened when we play together. She can be bossy. It's why I laugh at the image of her rolling her eyes at me. I bet she does that a lot. In my mind, instead of it being an annoying trait, I find it alluring—challenging.

Emmy [7:15 p.m.]

Ok. What is it?

I spin in circles while I wait. My toes tap the carpet to continue the momentum. Through blurry vision, more words appear. I grip the base of my desk to steady my movement. My skin digs deeper into the wood once my eyes dance across her words. I remind myself to keep breathing and shake off the feeling that habitually makes its way into my heart.

Daisy [7:16 p.m.]

You. Everything I want to do. I only want to do to you.

Chapter Two
Daisy

THE SQUEAKING SOUND OF my sneakers pulling away from the linoleum flooring is a routine comfort. Whatever covers the dark flooring has been there since I can remember. I've been working at Diego's since I was sixteen, too young at the time to legally serve alcohol. Now, at nineteen, my paycheck is deposited into my account with a specified amount going to the government before I ever have the chance to spend it.

It's probably for the best. It wouldn't be mine to spend, anyway.

Loud chatter fills the back room, lit with fluorescent lights and filled with cigarette smoke. I swing my backpack into my locker, picking up on the various conversations happening amongst the women, both in English and Spanish.

Roxie holds her cell phone inches from her face, screaming into it. It's an argument I've heard many times before. Her long nails twist with the curling iron that wraps around her thick blonde dyed hair.

Bambi prances around in her heels, glancing back towards her reflection in the cheap, plastic sheets that pass as wall-length mirrors. She changes her thong bikini to match the shoes she plans to wear tonight. Bambi is the most stylish of the girls here. As an aspiring fashion designer, she prides herself on creating her outfits.

London watches her from the corner of her eye. It's harmless hate. She'll stare at her, roll her eyes and maybe even mumble a snarky comment or two, but nothing will ever come of it. I've warned her a few times already.

"You forgot how to speak?" I take my time acknowledging Star. As the oldest of the women here, she often tries hard to garner respect, especially from me. Sometimes I'm in a better mood to give it than others.

I send out the last few text messages to Emmy, wishing away residual feelings I can only describe as pointless. It's complete insanity to allow myself to feel anything for any girl, especially one as different as she is.

Emmy talks about life like she read about it in a fairy tale. Fairy tales wrapped in plastic used to repel the sticky fingers of children. Emmy's pages have pristine edges, no markings, no dog ears, no cracked spines. Those types of books don't exist for me.

I slide my phone onto the small shelf right above where I leave my jacket hung before slamming the door shut. The loud noise does nothing to deter the loud talking.

Star waits for me to approach. She hands me the brush I need to finish her hair and wiggles the nearly empty hair spray at me before setting it on the table. I do the job I've been instructed to do. The bristles glide through her salt and pepper strands without a single snag. Her hair shines with the right amount of moisture, despite the poor lighting in the room.

"How's your mom, Mija?"

"She's fine."

I answer her question quickly because not only is Star bossy, she's also nosey. She retired from the stage long ago. Rumor has it she used to have a relationship with the old boss, who struck up a deal to keep her on staff when the new boss took over.

"What does she say about you still working here?"

"Nothing at all."

I twist the sections of the front of Star's hair before pinning them and dousing them with hair spray. I hate how she always talks about me working at the club as if I've been working here for twenty years instead of three. I started off working in the parking lot as security. Many people wouldn't suspect a sixteen-year-old in that position, which was the point. Luis wanted to run as clean of an establishment as possible, and it was my job to communicate with him when I thought something unsavory was going on.

After preventing a few potentially devastating events from playing out, I got promoted to kitchen staff; unloading the truck, stocking the pantry and running any last minute errands the cook needed me to.

The plan was to work my way up to server by the time I turned eighteen. The law allowed for serving alcohol under the age of twenty-one, as long as I didn't make any drinks myself. That was all fine with me since I've never developed a taste or excitement for the stuff.

According to Emmy, we could say the same for her. She's never sipped alcohol, done no drugs, legal or otherwise, and is always home in time for curfew.

My life is closer to a ghost story than a fairy tale. I don't drink because I need to function. I don't do drugs because I need to make money and I don't have a curfew because I need to work. Curfews are for the unemployed.

After I leave Diego's tonight, I'll have five hours before I have to go to work at Nova's diner. I don't need Star trying to talk to me about what my parents may or may not think of me working at Diego's. It's not like they don't see my empty bed or the stacks of clothes I keep in my car. The coffee they drink every morning doesn't make itself and the breakfast my sisters happily gobble up isn't swished together by a magic wand.

"What time are you meeting with Luis?" I look down at the watch on my wrist, the only nice one I have ever owned. It's an enormous improvement from the plastic pink and purple ones I used to wear as a kid. And the price? Oh, it cost much more than money.

"Right after this." She nods her head while glancing across the room. I already know she doesn't like the current roster of dancers.

"Demasiado perezosa," she mutters under her breath, so only I can hear. She's said it more than once. They're too lazy. Never on time. Too stiff on stage. Not aggressive enough. Not pretty enough.

She's mumbled it as they've performed, shouted it from the audience, whispered it into their ears as an insult and has complained to Luis a countless number of times. Enough for him to throw his hands up and walk away before she even forms her lips to say the words.

I like that about Luis. I like that he doesn't bend easily to criticism. He took over the club after his father retired, which I guess is how things are supposed to go. Older staff members still whisper about the good ol' days when rules weren't as strict and there was more respect.

I've never been able to figure out the respect aspect. How much respect is someone expecting out of a strip club? I thought the appeal was its representation of lawlessness. You're supposed to think strip clubs don't follow the rules, even if it's untrue.

Star observes my handiwork in her small tabletop mirror before dismissing me with a slight smile. She's great at demanding respect. She's never been good at reciprocating it or mildly displaying gratitude.

I make my way out of the room into the semi-fresh hallway,

following the black walls leading to a single black door. My knuckles tap against the painted surface with force in competition with the booming bass from the dj booth.

Luis is alone in his office when the door swings open. It's not as bad as one would think. There are no naked pictures of women hung on the walls. No gaudy furniture, bright colors or weird erotic sculptures. It's not as small as a custodial closet or packed with overstuffed filing cabinets.

The only ring Luis wears is his wedding band. And as far as I can tell, all of his teeth are real. His clothes are always perfectly pressed. His bald head freshly shaven and beard neatly trimmed. "Everything good?" He shuffles through the multiple piles of paper on his desk.

"Yeah. Everyone's here except for Tina." I've trained my eyes to take attendance once my feet cross over the threshold of the dressing room. Tina is barely older than I am. She's shorter too, with a bark as big as a rottweiler and a bite the size of a chihuahua. She's a top earner at the club, but has a spotty attendance record. Star is always mumbling about how the old boss would have fired her by now.

Luis shakes his head and sucks his teeth, letting out a sigh. "Tina. Tina. Tina." He finds the paper he was looking for, makes the necessary markings and then sets it aside.

"Do you plan on changing?" His smirk tells me all I need to know about his remark. I pull at the hem of my black joggers to show the ripped jean shorts underneath.

"Better. Much better." He doesn't ask me what's underneath my matching black hoodie or try to lecture me about the lack of makeup on my face.

He didn't care about how I dressed when I worked outside, but once I was stationed inside the club, he desired a certain aesthetic.

He's backed down from the makeup argument after I showed up too many times without a streak of foundation on.

I can give him fancy chapstick or fancy lip gloss. Maybe eyeliner.

Lucky for me, my natural jet black curls work overtime to present as *done* even if I just rolled out of bed. And if all else fails, a messy bun never hurt anyone. "We have a couple of big parties today. I need you to make sure they're treated well."

With no further instructions, I leave Luis to his business. The logistics of how the club operates doesn't matter to me. I'm good at doing what I'm told and I don't need more on my plate than I already have.

I stop and correct Coco's outfit while she stands behind the stage. From the gaps in the curtain, I can see the house is packed. There is not one empty chair at any of the tables or booths. The VIP seats closest to the stage are all occupied. I bet there's a line out the door, which probably means Luis has ordered only a limited amount of drinks to be served to free the space.

I tug at a few of Coco's lazy knots and retie them so they're more likely to slip from tension and not by error. "Need anything?" She barely answers me while she sways to the music in anticipation of her set. "Girl, this ain't my first day." It's not. It's her second.

My Nikes slide back out of the spotlight when the curtain careens open. The greeting the audience gives Coco is expectedly loud. Last night was her first night, but Diego is the third club she has danced at and she has earned herself quite the following.

Star likes to whisper about that, too. The idea of a dancer being recruited to work at a strip club is blasphemous to her. Dancers should want to work at Diego's. They should be honored to walk through the heavy steel doors at night and slink back through them at the crack of light.

Jade's son, Ross, is waiting for me in the dressing room when

I get back. We start work on his presentation board first. Last night, Luis ignored me while I printed out what he needed for his dinosaur presentation on Monday.

Ross is good at following instructions, gluing the words and pictures in the exact spot I tell him to. When he practices his speech, he does so with his chest puffed out, pointing at the big, colored words with authority. I give him all the smiles I can muster while listening for the end of each girl's song and watching as they rotate out of the room.

Jade has two performances tonight. It's after the second, when Ross is asleep in my arms, and I follow her to the car and watch as she secures him in his car seat that she passes me the $20 bill. "Thanks, girl."

I used to refuse the money, arguing I already have to be in the dressing room. And Ross is such a good kid. I'm good at multitasking and as the oldest of three, I'm an expert at keeping kids busy. Somehow, the money would find itself in my locker, slipped into my back pocket, or slammed on the table in front of me, with Jade's feet scuttling away. When she started having Ross hand me the money directly, I started accepting it from her myself.

Once security ushers the last patron out the doors at closing, I slide into my car. This time of night when the dark streets are silent and the only sign of life is stray cats and raccoons are undeniably the best. It's when I breathe. Following the white blocks across the intersections, I take a breath in and then breathe a long breath out. I continue the red light practice until I turn into the driveway of the beige one-bedroom home.

My knuckles tap against the white door, softer than at Diego's. A small face pokes out of the window off the right side of the porch. She places one finger to her lips. Seconds later the click of the lock, dislodging from its hold, echoes in the stillness.

Tina's short frame steps out onto the porch. The door pulls in behind her. "It's not what you think." If it had been daytime, it might have been harder for me to hear, but now, where there's barely a rustling of leaves, her voice is clear.

"My grandma is sick. I couldn't come in." My eyes narrow at her admission. "It's true. I promise. I had to take her to the hospital last night. We just got back about an hour ago." I scan her face, free of makeup and other markings that would force me to believe she was lying. Tina helps by extending her neck, arms and kicking out her legs.

"Ok. Call me next time."

"I will. I promise." She leaves the porch only after my headlights grace the edge of her driveway.

A single car occupies my driveway. I park in front of the pink house with white shutters. The heaviness of my eyelids takes over. I pop the trunk open, pulling the pillow and comforter out before slumping into the backseat. If I go in now, I may never sleep. I might decide to tidy up the living room, prepare breakfast early or fold clothes from the never ending pile of laundry.

The time on my phone says I have about three and a half hours left to sleep. The red notification over my messages icon nudges at me. It could be one of those phishing scams, telling me to call a number for a service I've never used or claim money that's never been owed to me.

Emmy's icon pops up underneath my fingerprint.

"Hey. I know it's late. Just wanted to tell you I was thinking of you. I know it's weird. You can ignore me now. Sleep tight. Hope I didn't wake you."

Sleep tight.

More proof she dreams in fairy tales even when she's not asleep. Still, it's hard to ignore the brightness that fills my chest at her words. This isn't the first time she's sent a message like this unprovoked, unexpected and completely unnecessary.

That's the other thing I don't like. The hidden chapters in her book of fables. The ones printed on red paper with invisible ink read once, then ripped from the spine to disguise the truth. The truth is, our relationship is nothing but a transaction. She offers me a distraction and I offer her an alternative. Where bodies are draped in rope instead of ball gowns. Where happy endings don't mean forever and where, by the end, she'll be begging me to leave.

To stay would be too much.

I consider myself to be a good liar. I've had a lot of practice. There have been plenty of times I could have told Emmy I didn't like talking to her. And they all would have been lies. She can be confusing and unsure of what she wants, but that makes the game fun. With how shy she can be sometimes, it's easy to assume that I'm the reason we ended up here. But it was her. She was the first to turn our game of make believe into a steamy affair.

I remember the first tale exactly. We boarded a train in London only to find there was only one seat left. The empty seat was next to a window. For whatever reason, the woman seated next to it decided she preferred the aisle instead. She politely shifted her legs to the side, so I could get by. Emmy joined me on my lap. No one batted an eye. Girls could do that — sit on each other's laps with no one thinking anything nefarious is going on.

But they didn't know who they were crammed on a train with. My hand slipped underneath her dress, pushing her panties to the side. The tote bag she moved from her shoulder down to her elbow kept us from view. There were a few suspicious glances when she let out a breath too loudly or couldn't control her body's reactions to my concerted efforts on her most sensitive area. The suspicion only emboldened her. She spread her legs wider. Leaned back farther and came before we reached our last stop. And then we just sat there. Less suspicious with calmed heart rates and slightly cooler bodies. Once off the train, she licked my fingers free of her while everyone watched from the windows.

And it was all in her head. I was only a participant in her fantasy.

When she says she's thinking about me. I know what she means. She's not talking about my health or personal safety. When she says she's thinking about me, she means she's thinking about what I can do for her.

Emmy is a princess trapped in a castle built by bricks she laid herself. Every night she flings open the door and runs upstairs to her bed, tripping at the threshold, falling onto the carpet and crawling slowly underneath the frame, only to forget to pull that last piece of her foot behind the bed's skirt.

She waits for me to capture her by the ankle and pull. She does scream, but her screams come from a place lower than her throat. It's the same place that tingles when she's dragged across the rug. The same place that drips on my black gloves after I throw her onto the bed and her legs open for me automatically. Her screams mean nothing to either of us.

And when I leave for the night, she locks up behind me and plans a new spot to hide for the next time.

If she's in the kitchen, she'll hide in the pantry, leaving the door cracked open just enough to see me coming. She'll plead then, too, dressed only in a thin white nightgown, her ass covered in white flour that spills onto the floor. Her nails will scratch against the dark wood table, swearing she didn't mean to do whatever she decides her offense is at that time. And I'll sit in a chair right behind her, feasting on her, enjoying the feeling of her ass pressed against my cheeks while my tongue delves into the place she swears she doesn't mean for me to reach.

It's the same in the living room when she hides behind the couch, the one right in front of the mirror that always gives her position away. And don't even get me started on the garden adorned in lights or when she falls asleep in the bath that barely has any water in it.

The truth for both of us is she loves being chased and I have no problems chasing her. If the villain in her fantasies is the one who knows all of her secrets and the person she can never possibly escape, I'll chase her all night.

I'm good at making hard choices. People count on me to do the things they're unable to do themselves. Emmy is no exception. She's too afraid to feel. She needs me to push her to do it. She needs someone else to drag her from underneath the bed and find her standing behind the thin lamppost. She's too afraid to take off her own clothes and demand what she really wants.

Our fantasies are intertwined. I'm good at what I do. She rocks. I push. She opens. I fill. Soon I'll command and she will obey. That's where we're destined to be. Instead of running up the stairs, one day she will sit by the door and wait. Rather than hide in the pantry, she'll be the one to set the table, first feeding me from her breasts before taking her own meal, never complaining of being full.

One day, her castle will burn to the ground and she'll have no place to hide. There'll be no door for her to lock and no roof for her to run to and wait for a savior. I won't come swooping down from the sky on my dragon or come riding in on a horse.

People like me are only useful for a certain amount of time. Either the danger passes or we're replaced. Emmy is no exception to that rule. The day she runs out of places to hide is the day she will no longer need me to find her.

When that time comes, I don't know if it'll be her covered in gasoline, or me.

Chapter Three
Gabriella

THERE IS NOT ENOUGH caffeine in the world to prepare me for early morning shoots. If there was some kind of hustle and bustle to my role, then things would be different. But on mornings like this, when I'm left to stare at women running on the beach when the sun is barely up and it's so cold my teeth clatter against each other, it's tough.

I try to stand in the only spot on the sand that glows yellow and isn't being shadowed by gray clouds. We've been out here for about half an hour.

Two other models, both blondes, flank Sara. Sara's annoyance and irritation don't reveal themselves in the photographer's lens. I can tell by the way she positions herself to stand in between them with one knee bent to make space for the edit.

This swimwear campaign is one of the first for her. She's had an easier time securing modeling contracts than she had booking acting roles. Which for me, means she needs me less often than before. If you ask me, she should stick to campaigns, but Sara is hungry for the spotlight and no matter what I do and how high she climbs, it never seems to be enough.

The group disperses after some instruction from the photographer. I hold the towel up for Sara to change into the next bikini set. She does it quickly, looking like a true professional. She bounces back over to the photographer at the ready.

The other girls aren't as quick. They round the set of beach chairs and lift heaps of towels from off the sand.

"Did you see where I put my bag?" one of them asks.

I look at her innocently.

"No, sorry. Nothing was here when I sat down."

I remember the two girls came together. They probably met up on some promise of living the L.A. dream and took their chances on being roommates. They arrived in the same car, with matching hair, matching bags and almost the same matching nose.

"I thought it was here, but I must've left it in my car. I'll be right back." She swipes the keys off the chair next to mine and takes off to the parking lot. Her friend, having not found her bag either, runs after her.

The photographer throws his hand up in exasperation. "Are you ready?" Sara doesn't miss a beat with her response. "Of course."

He snaps away. Her body moves into the different poses our extensive research told us are the most appealing for swimsuit photos. Sara is the only reason I'm allowed to set foot on any set, whether for a commercial, photo shoot or TV show appearance.

When we were younger, most people thought I was one of Sara's friends. To justify my existence, her dad once referred to me as her emotional support companion. I was there to help Sara remain calm when she was anxious on set. Even though they were there to film her, she was always worried about what they were thinking of her behind the scenes. Eventually, my role evolved into silencing the critics.

"My car's gone!" I look over to see blonde number one, the one with the clanging car keys in her hand, running back toward us. She might as well be yelling into the void with how slowly the photographer and Sara stop to acknowledge her crisis.

"Someone stole my car with all my stuff in it." The tears in her bulging eyes spill out and over onto her cheeks. Her friend's hands wrap around her upper arms. Blonde number two's eyes turn down to her toes covered in sand. She's not crying. Her face is free from moisture, but her knees shake like the San Andreas fault has just ruptured.

The photographer responds nonchalantly. "Did you call the police?"

"No...no. The pieces you gave us were in there. We didn't want them to get dirty. We put them in the bags to keep them safe, but..."

"You're saying you're going to reimburse the brand for lost property?"

I know enough to know that the photographer is more than likely an independent contractor and not in-house with Suly Zapata's swimwear line. Still, he will probably have to explain why he was sent three models to photograph, but only returned with one model showcasing the line.

"How much will that cost? I can't afford that." The two friends shake their heads at each other, affirming their precocious financial reality.

"This is not my problem." He waves his hand, turns his back and instructs Sara to move closer to the water in her new set. I watch her crawl on her knees in the wet sand, tossing her hair from side to side, waiting for the wind to catch it at the right time.

The blonde friend, the one with the dry face and sad eyes, approaches me from the side. "Are you sure you didn't see our bags? It's just I remember leaving them right here." She places her hand on the back of the lounge chair to my left.

I glare at her. The intensity of my gaze sends her scrambling backward into an old payphone no longer equipped with the telephone needed to serve its outdated purpose.

"Are you accusing me of something?" The wind whips her hair across her face.

"No. I wouldn't do that. I was just wondering."

"Go wonder somewhere else. You're bothering me."

She walks as fast as the sand will let her to join her friend on the other side of the beach. By the looks of their wild hand gestures and panicked faces, they've either called their parents to rescue them, or the police.

Sara's shoot wraps as the sun blesses me with its warm rays. The photographer is chattier than when we first arrived. He showers Sara with compliments and praises her professionalism while waving his hands dismissively at the other models.

We pass them and two officers. Sad eyes glance at me before turning away. I steer Sara's car out onto the busy street filled with beachgoer traffic.

"How was it?" Sara asks when we drive by the Range Rover I jumped into, drove and parked down the residential street, along with their bags and the missing pieces for the shoot.

"Eh... It was fine."

Sara doesn't drive a Range Rover. She drives a Mercedes Benz S Class, which is still eons better than my Honda, which she refuses to even sit in. Bought used, it was never new enough for her or nice enough for her to ride in.

"They'll be happy to know you cared enough to make sure they didn't get a ticket."

Sabotage is what I do for Sara's benefit. Maintaining her status is work she can't be caught doing herself. A few years ago, Sara came up with a plan to take down one of her biggest acting competitors: Taylor Townes. The Taylor slander had been risky and once Taylor came out as bisexual, Sara had to cease all fire. Her dad yelled at her afterward, even though he co-signed the posting weeks before she did it. He's like that. Inconsistent and unpredictable.

I am neither one of those things. It did not thrill me to swipe the earrings off that one model, so she'd lose the job to Sara, but it made Sara happy. I returned them, sliding them underneath a light stack of papers on a desk. But the damage was already done. They labeled the model as someone irresponsible, reckless and untrustworthy. Sara secured a two-year-long contract for Cassandra Rivera's jewelry line that day with ads printed on billboards, magazines and streaming on various social media platforms.

She secured the make-up line after I gave her competition the wrong directions on how to get to the studio where the shoot was taking place. I only take partial credit for that one. She should have known to double-check with her team instead of taking instructions from me after running into her at a Starbucks.

"I can't believe they changed the shoot to a location in The Valley. The 101 is going to be awful."

I recently saw her playing the corpse of a teenage hitchhiking victim on one of those cop shows. I'm glad to know she's still working. The goal isn't to ruin lives, it's to divert them.

Stealing the keys was one of the easiest things I have ever done. At most, it'll cost them a few hours today to realize the car is parked close by. That car told me all I needed to know about them. They're not anywhere near short of resources.

It's the same problem Sara has with Taylor. I wasn't initially involved in Sara's plan. If I had been, it would've been successful. Sara's post was created out of pure emotion with no strategy behind it. There was no way she was going to turn the tide against Taylor with such a small accusation. Everyone loves watching a star's downfall as much as they enjoy a comeback.

Taylor is well liked and well resourced. No one has ever uttered a bad word about her.

"She's the nicest," they say.

"She's the sweetest," they think.

Kiki Thompson, the latest singing and dancing child sensation, said in an interview Taylor had been a "mentor" to her. She's a true princess. A squeaky clean, morally conscious type everyone claims to love.

Except it isn't true.

Sara can barely talk about what Taylor has done to her in the past. One mention of it and she flies into hysterics. Taylor's actions have had lingering effects Sara continues to battle with to this day. I'm proof of that.

Our plan to take Taylor out of the spotlight has been in the works for years. Most of the other actors were not well-known or well liked and were easier to get rid of or defame. Taylor is different, which is why Sara's previous plan didn't work out. We have to have concrete evidence of her true nature. We have something now, but we're going to need a lot more if we want this to stick.

I've been following her around these past few weeks. Her parents have lived in the same home since before Taylor was born and despite her success, Taylor has never moved. On the outside, her life is pretty simple.

She's an early riser and leaves her home around eight in the morning for a jog, which often always turns into a brisk walk. She's one of those girls who buys expensive and trendy workout gear for style, not exercise. Sara hates girls like that. She works out diligently with her personal trainer three to four times a week.

Her fandom calls themselves the *Daydreamers* after her character, Dream Daniels. They openly feud with Sara's fandom, though they do it by touting Taylor's accomplishments and spouting fake positivity.

Sara's dad's white Mediterranean home comes into view. With no other car in the driveway, it's clear we're on our own, as usual. Lately, her dad seems to be gone more often, a shift Sara began to complain about around the same time I started to stretch the breaks between jobs. It didn't take her long to notice when my calls became less frequent and her bed emptier. At least of me.

Our relationship has never felt more complicated than after what happened a few months ago. I've always played my role well. I've traveled with her, supported her and defended her. I've kept all her secrets and her family's secrets. All at a cost. After all these years of being together, I didn't even know I could feel pain. I can't say Sara broke me, but there's a crack there I'm not sure she can fill with Hollywood access.

I hand Sara her car keys before walking to my car parked on the quiet suburban street.

"You can't be serious, Brie." She's the only one who's ever used that name to address me. Everyone else calls me Gabby. I might've even gotten Ella a few times, but not from anyone significant.

"I have somewhere to be."

"I'm supposed to meet with Bonnie in two days. You know how important that meeting is to me. You need to be here." It feels like we've had this same conversation a million times. When we were younger, I went to every meeting, audition, table read, walk through—you name it.

"I'll see you after your meeting." I know the answer isn't good enough for her. The glare she gives me shifts to the left. Angel, the neighbor's daughter, home from school for the summer, stands there in a bikini top and blue jean shorts. Sara ignored her presence until the day she saw her dad flirting with Angel across the hedges. That was the last week I spent the night.

"Are you sure you don't want to stay?" I try to ignore the small ping in my chest. I've spent weeks trying to figure out how it got there and when it bloomed enough to have the nerve to cause me heartache.

The click of my car doors unlocking is the only response I bother with. Angel is no longer by the brick driveway entrance when I turn around and catch the last of Sara's scolding. "... make sure you do it right this time."

I've done a lot for Sara over the years and rarely have I ever regretted any of it. She would argue the same. Our relationship hasn't come without perks. I should be grateful–and I was in the beginning. Things have never been simple.

We started in a blur. One day I was a high school sophomore complaining about the school's dress code and the next day I was sitting at my parents' dining room table, looking at Sara on the other side. Her dad, her attorney and my parents huddled in the middle, saying words back and forth I didn't understand.

I didn't have to worry about the school dress code again for another two years. And didn't hear from that attorney again until I disappeared a few months ago. The email I got from him was a reminder of the conditions of my contract. I knew this meant Sara's dad knew what happened and wanted to make sure I knew my place.

And I do. I know it well. I know it well enough to know that despite what Sara had done, the few weeks I got to spend staring at the bedroom wall that I hardly saw for the past few years was the only opportunity I was going to have to cry. And I blew it. I tried to cry, but never could. I mostly felt exhausted. The time I spent staring at the wall eventually turned to sleep.

I've given up a lot for Sara. The only reason I even have friends outside of her is because they refuse to let go of me.

Despite the long time away from home or the periods between communication, they always answer when I'm able to call and will hang out even if I only have a few hours of freedom to spare.

My brightest moments haven't been as Sara's enforcer. Some of them were easier than others and like I said, I don't regret them. They'll all be fine. People will forget the mishaps eventually and they'll bounce back. Most of them. I have one last thing on my list before I can truly count the days to freedom.

If shoving Misty Shields into a broom closet was the first job I had ever completed for Sara, then neutralizing Taylor as a threat will be the last.

Chapter Four
Taylor

"WHAT ABOUT THAT ONE?" Nicole has been pointing out potential women for me to date for the past twenty minutes. I haven't quite figured out my type. I don't really know if I need to, but I'd rather not say it aloud and then be held to expectations that may change in the future.

We sit at the outdoor patio area of the coffee shop, where anyone walking by can bear witness to Nicole's inappropriate behavior.

I lower Nicole's index finger, giving her a stern look. I recognize the girl from an opposing children's channel to the one Nicole and I worked for. They drilled it into us as young talent not to associate with the kids from the other network. I am older now and fully capable of making my own decisions, but I'd like to start my dating life on a clean slate and not drink—or eat—from a tainted well.

"Stop pointing at people. You're going to make it so obvious." My sexuality is public, but we can't know the sexuality of every woman who walks past our table. Nicole is straight with extremely Christian parents. We share the same lack of experience. Despite my coming out, her parents remain friends with mine and never try to keep us apart.

"I just think you should at least talk to some of them. I read it is really hard to tell if a girl is gay. Especially the girly ones like you. Oh, that reminds me." She rifles through her purse, pulling out a small drawstring bag. Once opened, she dumps a rainbow tennis bracelet in my hand.

"Aw, Nicole." She fastens the bracelet to my wrist. An odd feeling fills my chest. I have avoided buying anything rainbow, afraid I would be judged by doing so. I don't want to seem like I'm putting on an act of pride or pandering. The thought of that sends my heart crumbling into the pit of my stomach. So instead I dress like I always have, not altering a single thing about me.

"Thank you. It means a lot." A voice interrupts Nicole's affirming hand pat. A voice that sounds sweet and cheery, attached to a light brown face, with a splatter of freckles across her nose.

Freckles. Why don't I know I'm attracted to freckles?

"Excuse me. Is anyone sitting here?" I look around at the crowded tables both inside and outside the cafe. Nicole and I are a table of two with one extra seat.

"Oh, no. You can take it. No one's sitting there." I expect her to take the chair and drag it away. Instead, she turns it enough to make space for her legs to fit through the gap before taking her seat.

My eyes find Nicole, who silently screams *OH MY GOD! OH MY GOD!*, while using the same finger I admonished earlier, to point at my tennis bracelet.

If Nicole could speak, she would tell me the copious amount of research she has completed on my behalf tells us this girl is gay. There are no rainbows or carabiners (OK. Maybe I researched a bit also). The black ripped jeans are easy to dismiss. They're tight and not baggy, but the gray t-shirt, flannel in July and the snapback....

Why did I not know I'd appreciate a snapback on a pretty face? And the rings. One on just about every finger. I'd argue for clearer lines of distinction, but I just got here. I don't get to propose new rules.

"Do you want me to move?" Our panicked silence forces her to look at us with worry.

"Never."

The word slips from my lips too fast to swallow it back down whole. Her eyebrow raises in a question her quivering smirk already knows the answer to.

"I'm sorry. I've had too much coffee." I laugh off my explanation, knowing it's not coffee in my cup. I've never developed a liking for the stuff and besides, hot chocolate tastes a lot better.

Nicole knowingly bites the nail of her thumb, damaging her perfect manicure. I don't know if she's more nervous or if I am. *Get it together, Townes.*

My eyes roam over the coffee shop, suddenly wary of catching any recognizable faces or recording devices. There's a reason Nicole and I meet here for lunch. It's only a block away from the lot we frequented so often to film our shows on and my manager's office is only a few blocks from here. When our parents decided we were old enough, they'd let us leave and explore the street, although there were plenty of places to eat closer to the set. Leaving made us feel like grownups and gave us freedom.

The girl returns to her work. I was so distracted by my analysis of her I failed to notice the sketch pad she balanced on her lap, almost hidden underneath the table.

"That reminds me. I forgot to tell you about Monique." My eyes swing back to Nicole in confusion. My forehead scrunches at Nicole's words. "You remember Monique. The girl you said you never wanted to hear about again?"

If we're thinking of the same Monique. I never said that. I haven't seen Monique in years, not since we were in a Christmas play together in second grade.

I toss my head back and roll my eyes, letting out a long,

exasperated sigh. "Don't tell me you saw her."

Nicole throws her hands up in defense. "If you don't want me to tell you about it, I won't." She takes her thumb and index finger and runs them across her lips. But before she can carry out the act of throwing away the key, I protest.

"You've already started, so you might as well finish." Nicole takes the action of tucking the imaginary key into her purse.

"I didn't see her, but I heard she recently broke up with her girlfriend." Nicole stares directly at our non-participating diner. My heart hammers in my chest. The girl's pencil continues to glide across the unseen page.

"Really? Do you know why?" I continue the dialogue in hopes the imaginative world will help calm my beating heart.

"They didn't say." Nicole's eyes never waver from her target. "But last night she sent me a message asking if you were single." My hand can't grip Nicole's wrist hard enough to stop her mouth from moving.

"And you told her 'no', right?" Nicole is completely unphased by my nails digging into her skin. I stretch my eye sockets wider to emphasize my point. *You're not helping.*

"Of course I did." Nicole looks at me with a smile. My grip loosens out of attack mode. The muscles in my back give way. "But I feel really, really, bad for lying."

My eyes flick to the girl and nearly miss the way her eyes meet Nicole's before traveling over to me. Me, with my hand clasped over my best friend's wrist. The same hand that bears her gift, announcing my sexuality to the world.

"Can I borrow your phone?" I can only nod at the surprising question. All sense of allowing strangers to borrow my personal property evaporates from my mind, eviscerated by Nicole's betrayal.

She stares at the phone in front of me when I don't move to unlock it. I do it quickly, handing her the phone in a rush, grateful she enters the cafe instead of running away down the street. "Nicole! Why did you do that?"

"Well, you weren't going to. A girl practically fell into your lap and you were just going to let her sit there and *doodle*." She flips her straightened dark brown hair off her shoulders.

"You're supposed to be my best friend. Not my matchmaker."

She flutters her eyelashes repeatedly with one hand over her chest. "I am multi-talented. I can do both."

The girl emerges from the cafe before I have the chance to stand and wrap my hands around Nicole's throat. She slides my phone back over to me without a word. Her sketch pad and coffee cup are in her arms seconds later.

"It was nice to finally meet you, Nicole." Nicole seems momentarily caught off guard by the greeting. She corrects herself quickly to wave goodbye like a beauty queen contestant.

The girl gives me one last look. She looks different to me now. Not as cheery and airy. Her expression is much harder to discern from a smirk or a smile. We watch the girl walk down the hedge-manicured path and disappear behind tall bushes.

I swipe and unlock my phone to find the message icon lit up. There's a message from Mama reminding me to call her after I meet with Zara. Messages from Daisy, I've been too distracted to realize she sent, and a new message from an unstored number. I click the descriptive body of the message and just as quickly slam my phone into my lap.

"What is it?" I shake my head at Nicole, tugging back when she tries to take the phone from my hand. She can't see this. This is private. This is messy. This is shocking.

Because the girl in the ripped jeans and snapback. The girl who barely said ten words while she sat here, just showed me everything she was hiding under that flannel, and if I see her again, research says she's probably going to ruin my life.

The courtyard of Zara's office always reminds me of the spa. The Mediterranean Village is equipped with sounds of chirping birds, outdoor seating and many trees.

The door to Zara's office easily opens when I push. She has almost as many plants inside as outside. A minty green rug covers the gray carpet. Photos of her family and some of me and her other clients line the walls.

It's not like Angel, my agent, to send Zara information about a job before sending it to me. Technically, I'm her boss, but I take Zara's opinions about everything seriously and rarely make a big decision without consulting her first.

I've always looked at Zara as more of an auntie than a manager. The hug we share ends in a quick kiss on the cheek. I slide her cup of real coffee across the desk. She grabs it immediately, smelling and nodding in gratitude. "So what's the gig?"

She takes a few seconds to sip her coffee. "No gig. I only told your mom that so she wouldn't be suspicious."

Mama is as close to Zara as I am, maybe even closer. It's odd Zara would try to keep information from Mama. Unless she knows it's something I wouldn't want her to hear. My only secret right now is Daisy. I wait for Zara to finish taking a few more sips before asking my question.

"What is this about?"

"It's about Sara—and Bonnie Silvers." It's the mention of Bonnie that piques my interest. Bonnie was ahead of my time. A legend in her own right, she began acting in her twenties and quickly became involved in a scandal. Back then, there was no social media or constant photo and video recordings. It was all whispered rumors, only to be confirmed later by insiders.

Or until someone wrote a memoir, like Bonnie. She admitted her rise to fame wasn't without help. She was often cast in movies as the main male character's love interest and was more known for her looks than her talent. At least that's the overwhelming opinion of her. I disagree. If every actor needed to be dominating and dramatic, the media would be boring. We all have our roles and Bonnie was amazing at being sultry and silent. A flutter of her lashes. A sexy smirk. She didn't have to do much to steal a scene and in an industry that was so heavily dominated by men—and still is in a lot of ways — that's talent.

"Turns out Bonnie is going to be a mentor in the program you're starting. A bunch of the old big timers are doing it. Paying it forward is a big deal these days and Bonnie is looking to cash in on the revitalization of her image."

It makes sense. It's not the first time I've heard of established actors searching through programs to find their next protégé. Some believe it to be their calling. If I think about it, our program, filled with proven successes, is a more sound investment.

To give the program the greatest amount of success, the school targeted already up-and-coming stars entering their college years. Our presence undoubtedly propels the program into popularity and makes it more competitive for future students, increasing its prestige.

"She's very interested in you and Sara and is very invested in the improvement of your relationship." Zara's stare forces me to ponder the message behind her words.

"She wants Sara and me to make up?" Zara nods in the affirmative. "And she wants to...take credit for it?"

"She specifically said she wants 'the world to witness two young women, coming together to fight against the forces that have tried to pit women against each other from the dawns of time.'"

"I see."

"Yup." Zara's lipstick leaves stains on the mouth of her coffee cup. She nods in gratitude with each sip, thankful for whatever the caffeine is doing for her.

"Is that all? Be nice to Sara?" Not that I've ever done anything to Sara to begin with. Bonnie has the right idea about us being friends, but she's wrong about forces pulling us apart. Sara did that all on her own.

"I know I don't have to tell you that. Be yourself. It's the first time in a long time you two have been in a room together and there are a lot of rumors flying around about what happens lately when you dare to share a stage with Sara. Stay on your guard."

Rumors like what happened with Becka Singer, who was up for the lead role in a new drama. She had already been cast in the pilot and filmed the first couple of episodes when, after one drunken night, she woke up with chunks of her hair missing. Becka was devastated, and we all knew the rule: never change your hair. Major hair changes for female actors during a show's run have tanked TV ratings in the past. They tried salvaging the show with Sara as the lead instead, but the damage was done. The show didn't complete its first season.

"I'll try my best." I don't need Sara to like me by the end of this, but it would be beneficial for Bonnie to think fondly of me. You never know who you're going to need in the future.

I leave Zara's office less anxious about my decision. It will please

Bonnie Silvers that tonight, I might follow in her footsteps.

Chapter Five
Taylor

WHO KNEW CHOOSING A hotel could be so hard? Too cheap and I send the message this is just a hook-up, a one time, one night thing that means absolutely nothing. Too nice and I'm asking a stranger to spend the rest of her life with me. A boutique hotel seems like a good bet. They're relatively unknown, with no preconceived expectations.

I opt for one in Hollywood, somewhere I would normally stay away from because of the traffic, noise and insane amount of people walking the streets. But for this, it feels appropriate. The music-centered hotel embodies a party atmosphere. It's fun enough to feel casual, but at $300/night this place is serious enough to not feel like a fling, but also cool enough to stomp down the urges for marriage.

It's a silly thought to have. At least that's what I keep telling myself, except then I'm reminded this is *the first*. The first person who's going to see my grown, adult body naked. My breasts, hips, thighs and—the word feels too heavy to say. She will be the first person to touch me. And the first woman I have ever touched. This is a big deal. For me.

From the way the receptionist doesn't narrow his eyes at me, raise his eyebrows or ask too many questions, I know my disguise is working. Like a Hollywood personality trying to remain incognito, I wear black sunglasses. My kinky coily hair is braided underneath the wig I ordered online.

My hair has been the same my entire career. It has been braided, twisted and pulled into a bun occasionally, but I have not altered my texture for the sake of my job. As far as I'm aware, I've been fired from one job because of it. Mama loves to tell the story about telling off the casting director when they commented on my hair not being a "good fit."

The news didn't spread fast enough before I booked my next role on the soap opera, *The Loved & The Wicked*, as Bianca Baisley, a recurring role I still play today.

The lobby of the hotel is exactly what you would expect, with walls painted with murals and splashes of bright red everywhere you turn. A singer is playing a guitar in the lobby, probably a local. I wouldn't be surprised if she's the owner's daughter.

The shelves behind the bar house a mixture of glasses, vinyl records, and bottles filled with alcohol. Posters, portraits of musicians, and eclectic sculptures line the halls.

My early arrival guarantees my ability to carry out the first part of my plan. I order the pizza from the record-themed restaurant and then proceed to my room. A queen sized bed and a blue L-shaped couch separate the suite. The bathroom is small, but has a tub for me to soak my anxiety away.

I'm undecided about the smaller things. Do I bring out candles? Should they be scented? A massage isn't on my list, so oil is out. I wanted to smell nice, but not too overwhelming, so I packed the buttery shea butter instead of the scented lotions.

I set everything I think I'm going to need on the counter in the bathroom. It's hard for me to eat the pizza in peace without checking the time every five minutes. Every digital number change sends my mind crashing deep into my world of make believe. This could be a terrible idea. One I may live to regret.

I brought a lavender scented bubble bath for the soak. The candles that line the tub are not scented. They glow yellow in the darkness with the swish of water, the only sound filling the room.

I make sure the hair on my legs, arms and armpits is gone. I trim the curly black strands that will sit on display for someone else for the first time.

My belly button ring was a heart before I changed it to a butterfly. My other piercings are all adorned with flowers to complement the theme. She may not notice or care about the significance for me.

Tonight, I fly free.

A T-shirt is all I wear to wait for the confirmation of her arrival. It comes after I test out every couch cushion, unmake, then remake the bed and decide at the last minute to spray perfume in the air. The candles move from the bathroom to the nightstands. My body has been soaked and buttered. I'm worried and excited. I want to jump into the air and hide under the covers at the same time.

The message comes through with a soft chime on my phone. I would have barely heard it if I wasn't listening so hard.

I place the now empty pizza box in the hallway with the spare keycard inside. The door closes loudly behind me. My naked ass sits on top of the comforter. I lift the hem of the gray t-shirt and then pull it down again. I'll let her remove it instead.

I lower the black sleep mask over my eyes, blocking out the tiny slivers of light from the outdoors.

And I wait.

The knock on the door pounds in the same rhythm as my heartbeat. I pull the comforter into my fists.

Here we go. It's showtime.

The electronic click of the door and the creak of the hinge send shivers through me. My folded knees shake against me. Briefly, I think if I stretch the muscles, the quaking will lessen, but I'm too afraid to move. So I sit frozen at the sound of bags hitting the floor, the rustling of keys, the soft sound of a zipper and the swoosh of clothing hitting the carpet.

A soft clinking rattles in my ear. Jewelry, I think. They clatter against another surface I envision in my mind to be the deep brown coffee table.

The touch of her finger against my chin causes my neck to stretch upwards. I've never felt a jolt of electricity that strong before. I breathe a sigh of relief at the confirmation. Her hands are too soft to belong to a random man walking down the hall hungry for a leftover slice of pizza.

Her finger continues to trace my jaw with one tip. I clench. Now grateful that the hem of the t-shirt is long enough to hide the place I clench at.

The other hand starts at the knee folded in front of me. It traces the curve up my thigh slowly. The path to my hip propels her hand up my sides, forcing off the t-shirt.

The breeze from the AC hits me and when I shake, I blame that instead. Not the tingles on my skin from her fingers on my breasts in her hands. I don't blame the soft squeeze she gives them. Not even when the softness becomes firm. The breath caught in my chest is forced out once I remember to keep breathing. My core muscles tighten at the pinch and tug on my nipples. I bite down on my lip. To let out even the slightest moan could reveal who I am. I have to stay strong.

When she sits her ass in my lap, my folded knees cradling her in place, my hips rise just a little. Her laugh stops at the first echo. She remembers, too. Her solution is to fill her mouth with me. My breasts are covered in her. The middle of them tucked between her teeth and then amended by the swipe of her tongue.

I've never felt this before, though I've imagined this hundreds of times. My mouth waters at the image of the reverse, my neck bent at her breasts, my mouth full of her. Biting has never crossed my mind. But sucking—sucking and kneading and licking sounds like the most delicious treat I have ever had. And I know that's probably because I haven't had the other piece of her, yet. The part of her that's probably dripping the same as mine.

If I reach between us, then I'll know. I'll know how badly she wants me to uncross my legs from my trapped ankles. For now, I wait for her to finish her meal. Still clutching the white comforter underneath me. Still trying in vain to control the movements of my hips. Still clenching in the dark.

This is the assignment. To explore me. To make me feel things I have never felt before. A fantasy written out electronically for me to enjoy personally.

Her attempts to halt the usage of her vocal cords end. Her moans vibrate through my skin. Through the mask, I can't tell if her eyes settle on mine or not, but I imagine they do. I imagine her looking up at me with puffy cheeks and wet lips. Lips for me to suck later. Cheeks for me to fill. The confidence I have in the dark is intoxicating.

My breasts bounce at their release. It's the first time I notice my back has arched to serve her. Her ass lifts from my lap in a hover. Her body, a shadow over me. She kisses the bottom lip first. Behind the mask, my eyes squeeze together. The soft pecks land a few times, each lingering longer than the last. When her full lips cover mine, I push forward. The sound of our lips meeting is quiet at first. With each new greeting increasing the pace. The longer the kiss, the more hungry we become.

My hands ache to touch her. With everything we've talked

about, every plan we've put in place, every fantasy we've described that led us to this point, they feel like they know her. My fingers twitch with a desire to inch closer and trace every line we've ever imagined.

Daisy.

It was never supposed to be like this. My heart isn't supposed to feel this big for this person I barely know and still have never seen. She's a complete mystery to me. And now I'm so lost in our kisses, I don't know how I'll untangle myself from this dream.

My fingers roam from her knee, up her thigh, around her hip and up her sides. Her laugh interrupts our kiss. I travel back the way I came for the same effect. She kisses me through it, smiling against my lips and then traveling towards my ear. Her breath tickles against me, sending waves through my belly.

"Stop it before I punish you." It's not the rule breaking that causes me to lose my breath. The words she whispers produce the most vivid image of us in the same room as we are now. Except in this alternative, where she is the one in charge, I do everything she says to earn her forgiveness.

I contemplate mumbling out an apology, but stop myself. *Am I in trouble now?* The possibility of what that could mean causes me to keep the words from bubbling forward. If it's trouble she wants, I can do that.

Emboldened by rebellion, I place both hands on her lower back, moving slowly downward, unsure if she will step in and stop me. When I find my target, I pull hard, forcing her into my lap. No longer is she hovering above me in daring temptation. I'm in charge now.

My lips blindly land on her shoulder. I play nice. My lips spread from her collarbone up to her neck. Her shaking body and piercing nails in my back tell me I've found another delicate spot to use. I stay in place, kissing and licking and sucking the same as she did my breasts, when I was too afraid to touch her.

And now I own her.

With one final suck, she snatches away, sending a loud pop reverberating across the room. My lap is empty without her. The place where I sit, sticky and wet and warm. My blind eyes search beneath my eyelids for color it won't find. I listen as hard as I can for any sign of what's coming next.

She places one hand on my neck and uses the other to grab my hair. My parting lips make way for startled air to escape. Instead of kisses from full lips, I feel sharp teeth. She nips at my lips, imprints my cheeks with her fury and entraps my delicate earrings against her tongue before whispering words too dirty for me to repeat. They're filled with possession, a picture so forbidden it should never be allowed to leave my imagination. Her goodbye is swift and filled with promises made true tonight with the only pair of lips I have ever kissed.

And somehow, through all her sweet threats, another mystery builds. I never knew I could want something so bad. Or miss someone so much. After months of planning and rules. She came for what felt like seconds, only for me to want to keep her for a lifetime.

My phone vibrates from somewhere in the room. Without hesitation, I snatch off the blindfold and roll from my warm spot to search the floor. I find it lodged in between couch cushions. The display instantly lights up at my touch.

Daisy [11:41 p.m.]

I'm going to get you for that.

My forming smile ends in a wince. I spend the few seconds I have to walk from the couch back to the bed to decide on my response.

Emmy [11:43 p.m.]

What am I supposed to do now that you're gone?

The last sentence quakes out of my fingertips onto the screen. She left a mess. Though my heart rate has slowed, what's left between my legs still needs to be dealt with. My hips can't quite stop rocking against the sheet underneath me. I still feel the lingering kiss on my skin. My body shakes at the memory of it. Of her.

Daisy [11:43 p.m.]

Why do you make rules for yourself that go against what you really want?

I didn't think I would be ready for more. Telling Daisy this feels immature. A lot happened tonight that I wasn't expecting to happen and a lot of what happened, I didn't know I would like. I didn't know I would like her hands pressed against my throat or my hair in her hands. That feeling of surrender. That sense of vulnerability. I didn't know I'd like the idea of being punished. There's a difference between fantasizing about something and it finally becoming real.

I try to rewind her words in my mind. With every replay, her soft voice becomes more distant.

In my silence, she sends a new message, this one with

instructions. I read and re-read until I'm sure what I'm reading is correct. Maybe it was foolish or naïve of me to think that her response would be something simple, like "take a shower" or "go to sleep." Those two things, I can do.

Still, in my disbelief, I find my hand moving down my stomach to the place she told me to touch. I've only ever done it for her. I sit and wait in anticipation as one line becomes two. Every sentence brings a different movement and new sensations swirling through me. I learn to breathe through each additional step when it feels overwhelming. She urges me through my pauses, somehow knowing I'm not strong enough to continue on my own. I continue for her, becoming fully coated in my arousal, my fingers sticky with need. And yes, I want it. But it's not really for me.

It's for her.

Chapter Six
Daisy

THE EARLY RISING SUN of summer is both a blessing and a curse. I hate it because it pierces through my car and bedroom windows with little effort, forcing me to wake up earlier than I intend to. I like it because it means when I arrive at Nova's before 6 a.m. the sun is already out and shining. In the winter and spring, the shopping center parking lot is dark and dreary, with one light blinking slower and slower each day.

The cooks are already here and ready for the morning rush. I do the routine I'm so accustomed to. Even before working here, Nova's was the place my family went to for breakfast when no one was in the mood to cook. Besides that, Nova's is owned by my best friend's family and I spent many nights hanging out in the back booth before the restaurant closed.

The morning consists of the regulars. The Magallanes', an old married couple, have the same yogurt parfait and egg whites that they always do, reminding me of their doctor's orders about eating healthy. They're always dressed in a set of those shiny tracksuits from the 90s or maybe it was the 80s. You can see them coming from a mile away.

Mr. Jackson arrives with his youngest daughter in tow. From his drooping eyes and ruffled clothing, I always get the impression he's just coming off a long night at work. His daughter, Keyanna, with her perfectly braided hair in a unique design, is always chipper, despite the early morning. He always orders a cup of coffee—black. She always orders a cup of hot chocolate with whipped cream on top. She prefers omelets over pancakes and a side of fruit over home fries.

Krystal takes over for me in the afternoon. She never bothers to change into casual clothing on Sundays, choosing to keep on the same clothes she wore to church. The only practical thing she ever does is change shoes. Krystal's church services go two to three hours. I have never attended a mass service for longer than an hour. And I'd like to keep it that way.

She shares the latest congregational gossip with me while helping me to clear the table when she pauses, her eyes glued to the door.

"Speaking of the devil."

The look on her face at our newest customer is less than holy. I haven't had many girlfriends. Mostly because I started dating one girl in high school and never quite stopped dating her. Each one of my friends has a differing opinion of how awful they think she is; sometimes or almost always.

"Please don't tell me you're still speaking to her."

Still, because our last breakup was the second one. I purse my lips and say nothing.

It's complicated.

Our relationship is one of those you don't understand until you're in it. She's always been a beautiful whirlwind of chaos. Like when someone pulls the string on a confetti cannon. At first, there's a start, but then a pleasant surprise at all the pretty pieces of paper falling from the sky. And yet, no one ever stops to think about the person who has to clean all that shit up.

For Sara, that person is me.

Her sunglasses are suitable for the weather. She doesn't need to hide her face here. Since she's considered a local, her framed headshot hangs on the back wall. She signed it years before we became a couple after Nova spotted her in a commercial.

Krystal sucks her teeth at me once I straighten my back, release the hold on the rag I have balled into my fist, and follow Sara to her usual booth, which used to be our usual booth. Now I avoid it and only sit people there who aren't in my section.

Sara tugs at Keyanna's braids as she passes by. Keyanna giggles and swings her head to the side, forcing them to tap against her cheeks. Sara secretly hates kids. She hated kids when she was a kid, hated them as a teen, and has no interest in a future where they exist to disrupt her daily routine. Sometimes I feel the same way. Other times I don't. There was a time when I thought it may eventually become an issue, but then other issues became a problem instead.

"I feel like this is the only way I can ever get you to truly talk to me." She orders a coffee with enough room for cream. I know her order by heart; six creamers and four artificial sugars. Depending on where we are, she'll also add a few sprinkles of cinnamon.

"I don't know what you keep wanting to talk about." What's done is done. She wouldn't go back and change any of it if she could. For Sara, everything needs to have a purpose. Everyone is a pawn even when they're not playing the game.

"I want to talk about what happened. You need to understand why I did it." I blamed myself the first time. I should have been more sympathetic to the fact that she was an unusual student. Going to school on set wasn't the same as going to a traditional school. Of course, she wouldn't have the same study habits as the rest of us. Of course, she would struggle.

Most of her homework was completed by me—usually the essays. Sara was pretty good at swinging the rest of it. They adored her during group projects. No one ever complained about her doing the least amount of work, although I was sure all she did was add her name to the assignment. I was mildly surprised when she told me she was going to college. She enrolled late, which I guess when you're famous with a rich daddy, you're allowed to do shit like that. Considering she's not a fan of the mornings, I selected my classes hoping our schedules would not overlap.

"Are you still seeing her?" I know the answer, but I've built a habit of creating space so Sara can lie to me. It's a bad habit I've been trying to break. I guess you can't be perfect all the time.

Her eyes squeeze closed at my question. "Yeah, I *see* her. But not like that."

"Not like what?" A dent in the wooden table occupies my attention as she takes her time to respond.

Sara huffs as if I'm the one who barged into her job and started sprouting off vague answers in a conversation I didn't even ask to be engaged in.

"We're friends."

I don't ask about the benefits of such a friendship. She won't tell me the truth, anyway. The way I look at it now, Sara and I are together when we're next to each other and broken up when we're not. It's the way she sees it too, except when she double-books me with someone else.

"You're more important to me than she is." For the moment. Until there's a problem I can't solve and she needs to find someone who can. She's not unlike Emmy in that way. Emmy needs someone to share an experience with away from prying eyes. And when she's done with that, well, Nova's is the last place she'll be.

"Maybe if you made more time for me, things would be different." She tears open the first small creamer and pours the contents of it into her mug. I've heard this part before. It displeases her that I make my own money. "Sometimes it feels like you're trying to erase me." She adds another.

It has felt that way for me for a while. The conversation always seems to go the same way every time she brings it up. It's better when we just sit in silence and pretend that the first time was the last. The first time hurt...I think. It was a shock to our normal and the first time I had ever questioned my place. I never thought as far as forever, but I also never thought it would be *that*. It's funny when you think you're the only one who truly knows someone only for them to loan out the exact book. Feeling dependent and expendable at the same time is unnerving.

"...you won't even need to move any of your stuff. The apartment is ready." Whatever Sara was droning on about, I didn't hear. It was probably more of the same as usual; promises to take care of me. She always says I never have to worry about anything as long as we're together. I think I missed the part about worrying that there's another woman in my bed. Again. But if I say that now she'll call me dramatic. Once she said I was shortsighted because there is nothing Sara does without an ulterior motive.

"I told you I'm not going to be moving in this year. Maybe next year." Living with Sara would be the easiest thing to do, but the only reason I've been able to have any sort of separation from her is because we don't live under one roof. The moment I walk over a shared threshold with her is the moment I lose more than my freedom.

The familiar grating noise she had been making with her spoon circling against the beige ceramic mug stops. Her eyes narrow. Her jaw tightens. Her nails scratch the surface of the table.

"What time do you get off?"

Now.

"Not for another few hours."

"I want you to come home." The word home drops into the pit of my stomach like an anvil dropped into the depths of the ocean. She's never felt like home to me.

"Why are you doing this?" I ask her the same question I ask myself each time she shows up in a place she shouldn't be. For a second, I think she's going to cry. Her eyes drop into her lap and her hands ball into fists. The small crack I thought I heard in her voice is gone by the time her eyes meet mine again.

"It's fine for now. You need some space. I can give you that. Just consider that you would be a lot less stressed and busy if you spent more time on me and our goals and less time–" she flicks one hand in the air, dismissively "–elsewhere."

She leaves the cash on the table to cover her half-drunk coffee. She leans over the table and slides her hands through my hair, pulling me in for a kiss. I don't resist. Sara needs to look like she's in control, even when her world is falling apart around her.

I stay an extra hour after she leaves, not bothering to stop Krystal from calling her every name in the book. There was a time when my friends knew better. They used to smile in front of Sara, but now they roll their eyes. Sometimes they completely ignore her if she arrives somewhere unannounced, which has become more frequent.

The sun is still too bright when I finally step back into the parking lot in my black dickies that I wish were shorts. Nova's technically doesn't have a dress code, but I have to be in the mood for shorts and that's not usually at five in the morning.

It takes me over two hours to drive to my next appointment. I end my training at Craft, the new restaurant I'll be working at once school starts, with enough time to get home to eat and shower before having to work again.

Emmy [5:37 p.m.]

"Are you busy?"

Emmy's text comes sooner than it should. We usually talk in the evening, before my shift at Diego's.

Daisy [5:39 p.m.]

Not at all. Is everything okay?

It most likely is. Nothing is ever wrong in her world.

Emmy [5:39 p.m.]

Yeah. Are you alone?

My little sister sits on the bottom bunk in our room with her earbuds lodged into her ears, tapping away at the keypad on her cell phone.

"Hey."

When she doesn't respond, I take the heart-shaped sequin pillow on the foot of my bed and throw it at her. Her slow head turn is a deliberate attempt at rage, though even in all her teenage angst, she's never angry for too long.

"Can I have the room?"

The roll of her eyes is exaggerated and drawn out. She takes her sweet time lifting herself from the bed and walking across the room to the door. She swings the door fast in a slam, before catching it and pulling it into a slow click.

At this point in my young life, I am far from a prude, but trying to hide my nightly activity from my family members is ridiculously uncomfortable. I like it best when I'm alone in my car. Sometimes, if I'm home late at night, I'll lock myself in the bathroom to re-read them. Isolating myself is hard to do when everyone is home.

Daisy [5:41 p.m.]

Yeah

Emmy [5:41 p.m.]

I did something bad.

Things have changed since that night. I was slightly worried the address wouldn't lead to where it should, even though I checked and rechecked the online images repeatedly. When I hadn't ended up at a false location, I thought there was no way I'd get in the door. The text message would probably go unanswered. But then the key was exactly where she said it would be.

I knew it was real when the door opened and there she sat in the middle of the bed, bathed in candlelight. My teeth sink into my bottom lip and my hips twist against the blanket beneath me at the memory. Confessions have become her favorite. The rules are to not ask questions outside of the experience. Her rule. Not mine. She seems to have forgotten them since I saw her last. Every day she thinks of something new to tell me.

"Oops, I forgot to wear a bra today."

"Oh no. My last pair of panties is this black lace thong."

"Crap. Do you think people will notice I'm not wearing any underwear today?"

The problems come fast and at odd hours. Almost always out of our usual schedule.

Daisy [5:42 p.m.]

What did you do?

It could be anything at this point. The themes repeat, but the settings are often different. I don't mind. She's provided me with much more than entertainment over the years.

Emmy [5:42 p.m.]

What time are you coming home tonight?

I shove away the sticky feeling that slips its way into my belly. Coming home to her would be...nice. I think. The image of that makes my heart tingle in anticipation and hope. But none of that can be real.

Daisy [5:42 p.m.]

That depends. What did you do?

The picture that flashes on the screen is a surprise. We've never sent pictures to each other before. That's against the rules. She took the picture from a distance. It's cropped to show the very top of her ass and her naked back with her hair pinned up into a knot.

Emmy [5:43 p.m.]

I forgot to close the curtains before I took a shower.

The summer sun still shines bright outside, leaving the

neighbor's home lit up perfectly through her window. She's not standing too close to it to be noticed by anyone. She knows that because by now, she knows better. She must know I know that, too.

Daisy [5:43 p.m.]

That's one finger for trying to be sneaky.

At the end of the first night we met in person, I made her call me. For the first time, she performed solo, naked as instructed, with her hand between her legs. Audience of one. Still, she was hesitant to go *deeper*. I was lenient since it was her first time, but now she's pushing me.

She never says anything whenever we talk on the phone. It's against the rules. Not that I need her to. Even without the photographic evidence, I believe her. I believe that she's listening to every word I say. She groans at the instructions she doesn't like. When she follows through anyway and is surprised at what she likes, she gasps. It's that breathless gasp she does when she forgets how to breathe properly. It drives me nuts.

I've noticed her whimpers have gotten louder. I hear those when she's at the perfect spot at the perfect rhythm, but that's also when she's most likely to disobey and interrupt the activity because she says it's too intense. If she doesn't resume like she's supposed to, I add on a punishment for the next in-person experience.

Emmy [5:44 p.m.]

:o I don't think I can.

But she will. It's what she really wants.

Daisy [5:45 p.m.]

You should have thought about that before you tried to break the rules. Call me at midnight. Better set an alarm in case you fall asleep. If you miss it, I'll add a finger.

I wait a few minutes before tucking my phone underneath my pillow. A nonresponse from her can mean many things I won't allow myself to get too wrapped up about.

I still owe her a punishment for marking me. It sparked raised eyebrows and gossip at Diego's and Nova's. It invites questions I don't need to worry about providing answers to.

Emmy skips our usual time to chat. She's either upset about her punishment or building up the nerve she needs to complete it. Neither matters to me. I'm sure I'll be fine if she stops speaking to me altogether. Talking to her would be a habit I would need to break, but I have other ways I can entertain myself.

In the beginning, Sara thought there was nothing I could do without her. It would've been easier for me to allow my privileged girlfriend to do everything for me. She has for years and I'm still not sure I have anything to show for it. Working sucks, but freedom is everything.

The sound of a wailing baby stops me at the threshold of the dressing room. Tina, half-dressed and missing a false eyelash, walks back and forth patting the back of the screaming infant.

"You're okay. You're okay."

A glance around the room reveals annoyed expressions. Star's repulsed, scrunched-up face makes it clear how she feels about small humans encroaching upon her territory.

Tina is tossing the thing in my hands before she even has a chance to greet me.

"When did you get one of these?" While it's not uncommon for girls to have children young, it is extremely unlikely she cooked a baby in her uterus, danced on stage every night, and no one noticed.

The excessive crying sounds more like struggles for breath. His little face is covered with red and glistening with tiny baby tears. I look around at Jade's empty station, remembering she has the night off. *Dammit.*

"Okay! Okay!" I resume the walk abandoned by Tina. After more wailing, I change tactics, placing the belly of the baby on my forearm and rocking him wide. The adjustment in pace sparks an instant calm.

"Oh, thank God!" London's reaction joins the agreements of the other women.

"Tina." My voice is measured, but stern. Surprising us with a baby on such a busy night is unacceptable. She should have been better prepared and communicated about what was going on.

"It's not my fault, okay? It's my sister's baby. She can't take care of him right now." The reprimand dies in my throat. The desperation and hopelessness in her voice feel all too familiar. Not that we've ever sat down and had a therapy session together, but from the pieces of what I've heard, Tina's story is not unique. It sucks being the kid carrying the responsibility of your entire family. Tina is the breadwinner, caretaker, babysitter, nurse, gardener, chauffeur, cook, maid, and emotional support system for everyone who shares her bloodline. I can relate.

My sisters are still young, so not too many consequences of their personal choices fall on my shoulders. In many ways, my teenage years being sacrificed made it possible. Everything was so much calmer when I began dating Sara. There was more money. More time. More space. My parents stopped fighting. My mom didn't need me to console her as often anymore. That shift is why I've stayed for as long as I've needed to and why I've done everything I could to make her happy. But I guess I didn't do enough.

Tina wheels over the stroller to me and then returns to finish applying her makeup. The stroller is fine. It's not the kind I imagine Emmy having for her baby one day. She'll probably fuss about the brand and the ergonomics. And have arguments about safety testing and which way is the best way to install a car seat.

Woah.

The baby kicks his little legs at my impersonation of an airplane. A diaper bag appears on the floor at my feet once Tina's song plays. She shoots me a wink and walks out the door into the dark hallway.

I spend the rest of my night with the baby whose name I didn't bother to learn. He drinks a bottle, nibbles on a few of my knuckles, and tries to strangle me with my necklace. For the first time, I realize the restrooms for the dancers are not equipped for babies. I lay one of those white baby receiving blankets on the floor to change him. The damage isn't so bad. He manages not to pee on me in the process and his baby onesie remains free of poop stains.

I develop a new appreciation for solo bathroom breaks when every dancer refuses to watch him for me and I end up using the stroller to prop the door open, so he sees I haven't gone too far. Everything is suddenly a rush. I have never pushed out pee so fast and have never hated the sound of the hand dryer so much.

Luis' office is empty when I knock. I make myself comfortable in his plush office chair and use the springs at the base of it to rock the little guy with a fresh bottle. He looks around for a few minutes before his eyes close. Putting him in his car seat in the back of Tina's car is seamless.

"Thank you. Thank you. Thank you." I know her appreciation is genuine. I saw the huge wad of bills she stuffed in her bags after she finally finished dancing. She stayed longer than she usually would have and spent more time out on the floor than usual, too.

Luckily for me, everything else worked out for the night and I didn't need to put out any fires. Still, my arms ache from the baby's weight and my lower back hurts more than I ever remember it hurting before.

I dip out before anything has the chance to go wrong. The drive for me is silent. The streets are just as empty as all other nights. Going inside to rest in a bed instead of in the back of my car is an easy choice.

But first...

I toss my phone on the middle console and watch as the minutes click up. Midnight. Emmy's name flashes across the screen.

Good girl.

Chapter Seven
Gabriella

BONNIE SILVER'S OFFICE LOOKS like she hired an interior decorator to design it. Considering she's not a permanent member of the staff and is a mentor on a volunteer basis, it's a bit much. Light pink furniture accents the painted green forest. A portrait of her, about 20 years younger, hangs on the wall behind her chair. Her white desk has a single piece of white paper on top with one of those fluffy-ended pens placed next to it.

I sit alone at the long white table on the right side of the room. It's impossible to lean back in the pink barrel chairs she had me order. Still, I'm grateful they're not the ones with the childish back shaped like a bow or those hideous velvet wingback dining chairs.

I check and recheck the stacks of paper in front of every seat. Almost every place is identical to the others, except one. I maintain focus on my task even when the knock on the door sounds. It comes again when I'm fluffing the couch pillows and then again while I run the vacuum over the carpet one last time.

The phone on Bonnie's desk rings. She thought it would be cute to have one of those old-fashioned landlines, made famous in the 1920s, as a showpiece. It made sense for her considering those were the roles she often took on when she was relevant, and since it worked well with my plan, I didn't fight her on it. The phone is gold and white instead of pink and has buttons instead of a rotary dial.

I wait a few more rings before picking up the handle and placing it to my ear.

"Hello. Bonnie Silver's office."

The voice on the other side sounds well rested and confident, a compliment considering I scheduled for them to arrive at 8 a.m.

"Good morning. My name is Taylor. I have a meeting with Bonnie today. It was supposed to start a few minutes ago, but I'm not sure if anyone is in the office."

"Good morning." I mimic the sweetness in her voice. It must've taken her years to learn how to hide her frustration, even when justified. She's probably not used to being inconvenienced and is unusually understanding.

I place her on hold, setting the gold handle on the desk. I take two slow laps around the room before opening the office door.

Taylor turns sharply, her face caught in a mix of surprise and confusion. She's dressed for the first day of school like a normal college student. Her trademark hair is up in a bun instead of hanging down past her shoulders, probably because she thinks it'll help her blend in more. She's wrong. Her hair did nothing to hide her face. Sure it was big, but her features are striking. Her eyebrows are a perfect thickness, but still shaped and appropriately manicured. Her nose is original. It's something she's gotten hate and praise for throughout the years. I remember her once quoted in a magazine that her nose was her father's and therefore a part of her Mississippi lineage that she had no interest in replacing.

It was an article celebrating natural beauty, which later got flack for judging women for what they did with their bodies. Eh, sometimes you can never win.

It's not until she asks me to move from in front of the door with a soft and courteous "excuse me" that I do it. She places her backpack in the back of the first chair closest to Bonnie's. I guess it's the natural thing to do. One would assume that you should sit close to the person you plan to meet with.

"Is this okay?" She asks, her hands remain on the straps.

"It's fine."

She declines my offer of a cup of coffee, briefly glancing at the complicated-looking machine. I place a muffin on a small, white napkin. She accepts it gracefully with a large smile, pulling off a small piece and placing it into her mouth.

She stands silently with her back against the chair she claimed. Her eyes roam around the room. Her expression offers nothing more than a few twitches to convey her opinion about the decor. It didn't take Sara more than a few sentences to convince Bonnie to accept me as her intern. Bonnie was nodding her head as soon as the word girlfriend slipped from Sara's lips and since work-study is a part of my financial aid package, I'm free labor. My first task was finding the crew who could put it all together before school started.

"Do you know what time Bonnie will be in?" She hasn't shown an ounce of frustration since she got here. No loud sighing or impatient leg bouncing. No exaggerated stretches or constant clock checking.

"You're early. She won't be in until nine." The muffin is out of her hands and on the table, replaced by her cell phone in seconds.

"I could have sworn my email said 8 a.m." It did. I know because I wrote it.

"Oh, shit. I'm sorry. I must've made a mistake." I try my best to look like an insecure intern. I cast my eyes down at my shoes and shake my hair slowly, so my ponytail brushes across my shoulders.

Taylor's eyes appearing underneath mine surprises me. With a wide smile and soft voice, she places one hand on my wrist. "It's okay. The professor in my first class used to be my acting coach when I was little. I'll just text him and let him know what's going on." Of course, she will. Because, of course, someone who met her as a small child would adore Taylor.

A glance at my watch tells me I'm running out of time. "Are you sure? I will feel terrible if you're dropped from the class for missing your first day." She dismisses my concern with a wave. She barely notices when I grab her free hand just as she uses the other to slide her phone into her pocket. The pink couch cushions bounce softly as we land on them.

The more Taylor tries to reassure me, the closer I bring her hand to my chest, sandwiching them into the valley of my breasts.

"It...it's really...it's okay." She places one hand on my pleading wrist. A gold rainbow ring is stuffed on her index finger. It looks like an identical matching piece to the rainbow bracelet she wears on the wrist I'm clutching.

Her words stop and though I feel a slight tug, she doesn't wrestle away from me. "I've been meaning to ask you something." Her eyes flutter to mine, away from the hold I have her locked in. My hand grasps the side of her face and pulls her closer. She follows, her heart rate increasing the beats against my palm. I fight the urge to pull any of the rings that decorate her ear with my teeth. "How many times have you touched yourself while looking at my photo?"

She holds her breath in for a beat too long. Her brown eyes never leave me as she answers.

"That would be inappropriate."

It's not the response I expect.

"Excuse me?" Her hand slides from between my breasts. It makes a soft thud in the space separating us.

"I don't even know you. It would be rude of me to use your

photo in that way without asking permission." Almost how wrong it was of me to take a half-naked photo with her phone without asking first. The reason I took her phone wasn't for the photo. That was a bonus.

"You need my permission to touch yourself?" I know it's not what she was saying, but I enjoy the twitch of her neck all the same.

"No." She elongates the word as if I'm a toddler who doesn't understand why I can't wear my Halloween costume to school in July.

"We don't know each other."

"Are you saying you haven't looked at it since?"

"I'm not saying that."

"Are you admitting to masturbating?"

Her response is quick.

"If I didn't, you'd call me a liar." I would.

"There could be other explanations for why you wouldn't."

"And none of them you would believe. Not from me." I don't respond to her assertion. We're past the point where I pretend I don't know who she is. The entire world waits for her to go on a drug binge, date some abusive loser; either another actor or musician—perhaps a basketball player — and ruin her life. I'm supposed to be the first one in line to take the photo—the documentarian of her downfall.

She's being oddly nice to someone she feels violated by. She used very pretty words, but that's what she means. This is one piece of her that Sara finds insufferable. She's never direct.

"What did you think about it? The photo?"

"You mean after I got over my panic?"

"Sounds dramatic. Even for an actress."

"It's not *dramatic*. I've never had a photo of a girl on my phone before. Not like that. What am I supposed to do with it? What if someone sees it? I felt oddly careful about it, like I needed to secure something precious. Even deleting it felt wrong."

She pulls out her phone from her back pocket and drops it into my lap. "Since you're here, you can delete it." Her lips melt into their respective corners like butter sliding across a warm baking sheet.

It only takes me a second to decline. "I like the way you look at me." I hope it sounds more menacing than yearning.

I get it. I do. When you're the one she focuses her brown eyes on, it feels like you're the only one in the room. That's what her fans are so captivated by. It's why they defend her so ferociously with rhinestone-embellished daggers and hang on to her honey-coated words. Nothing she ever says will upset them.

And it's why we have to make her do what they think can never be done.

She doesn't move an inch when I move closer, brushing our cheeks together. "I like it when you look at me like *that*." I ignore the displaced heat that rises some place it shouldn't be. Not now. Not here.

I await the snarky retort that never comes. Taylor's warm eyes meet mine before falling to my lips. My smirk is evident. A sort of dare I had intended to put into motion much earlier than this. But she had been so quiet. So patient.

Her lips part to speak just as the door opens. My own lips graze the corner of her lower one before sliding down to her chin. She sits frozen in panic, her eyes stuck on the two figures who have just entered the room.

"Did you just kiss my girlfriend?" Bonnie's head snaps up from her cell phone. Her hands juggle her need to stay up to date with current news and also handle the small yappy dog she holds in her arms.

Taylor's eyes jump from Bonnie to Sara. Sara's doing a good job of playing the jealous girlfriend. As the girlfriend in question, she's never played that role.

"No, of course not." Taylor breathes out a small, awkward giggle. A hand falls over her chest. "I moved so fast I must've bumped my head into yours. I'm so sorry." The tapping of her palm against my arm shocks me. If I didn't know my own ruse, I'd think she was being genuine.

"It was my fault. Don't be mad at -" My name gets lost in my throat.

"Brie," Sara answers on my behalf.

Taylor's shoulders visibly fall with each added breath she allows to escape.

"Well, now that we've got that cleared up. Let's get started, shall we?" Bonnie shuffles into the rest of the room after her declaration. She's dressed in all white, covered in a perfume that travels from miles away. Her small dog, whose name I only nodded at and didn't bother to remember, finds his water and food tucked into a corner behind her desk.

Bonnie sits at the head of the white table with Sara and Taylor occupying the seats closest to her. I take my place next to Taylor, opening up the notebook I placed there earlier.

Taylor makes no complaints as Bonnie takes her time deciding on which pen to write with for the day. She decides on a leopard-printed one, stating she has been neglecting it as of late. Taylor's smile is gentle and encouraging, like one you may give an elderly person who has told the same story to you for the hundredth time.

Sara places her hands in front of her. Her spine is straight. Eyes focused. Taylor's hands wedge between her crossed knees. Her chair swings in small half circles from side to side.

"I have good news." The dance Bonnie does in her seat does nothing to inspire the rest of us to move, though Taylor lets out a small sound of acknowledgment.

"The college is going to put on a big back-to-campus event and I volunteered you girls to host." Bonnie drops her leopard pen like she just nailed her act during an open mic night. "I said to the Dean, 'Who's better than my girls?'" This is not news to me or Sara. I, of course, told Sara when Bonnie told me.

"What does the host do, exactly?" Although she's been polite, Taylor has expressed little excitement about the news. I could think of a million other things I could be doing myself, but wherever Taylor is, is where I must be, unfortunately.

"You'll introduce the musical guests and walk around welcoming everyone to campus. I already have a photographer booked to take photos of you two playing games and eating some of the food."

Taylor nods slowly while Bonnie continues to list the ideas I helped her curate a few days ago. Sara interrupts when Bonnie remembers the names of the celebrities she's already invited to the event. A sad look of understanding covers Sara's face as she addresses Taylor. "It's okay if you don't want to do it. I know how much you were looking forward to retirement." Bonnie looks up in alarm.

Taylor shakes her head. "Oh. No no no no no no. It's fine. Sounds like a lot of fun." Her reassurance is enough for Bonnie to dismiss Sara's concern.

"Questions?" Without bothering to look at one another, Sara and Taylor shake their heads in denial. Sara is the first to stand up once Bonnie gleefully ends the meeting. Taylor, with all her patience, slowly pushes out her chair and slides it back in, her backpack once again strapped to her.

"So you're the one?" She replaces her courteous expression with a more playful one.

"I don't know what you're referring to."

With a slight shrug of her shoulders, she responds, "Of course you don't." A smile stretches onto her face again, though not as big. It stops before her cheeks have the chance to rise and keeps her lips from pulling back to reveal her teeth.

I push back against the electric sensation my body zips into with every second her eyes take examining me. They start from my shoulders and transfer down my arms to my wrists. Once satisfied with her inspection, she releases her back from the edge of the table and walks to the door Sara and Bonnie have already exited through, calling out, "Take care of yourself, Brie."

Chapter Eight
Taylor

THE FURTHER AWAY I get from Bonnie's office, the faster I walk, dodging unaware students and large social gatherings as I go. I find Nicole in front of the theater, chatting with Melissa Kane, the former president's daughter, on Wednesday nights. They have limited her role in the show since her TV father's impeachment. She spends most of her time on social media, posting the latest dance trends.

She doesn't look too annoyed with me when I pull Nicole away. Her phone, which was already firmly placed in her palm, is in her face in an instant.

"Are you okay?" Nicole's chipperness mirrors my mood this morning, even with waking early. I was excited to start school today. While meeting Bonnie didn't excite me, I wasn't bummed out about it. I was fine when I thought she was running late and also fine when I thought her intern made a mistake.

The memory scrolls through my mind like a damaged piece of film. I recognized her when she opened the door and decided it was some weird coincidence conjured up by the universe. She looked only a little different. Her clothing was less masculine and more casually feminine today. Regardless, she was still pretty, and I fell right into her trap.

I am not okay. My hands have just done something they've never done to another person before. Not even to Daisy, whom Nicole knows nothing about, and who I thought was the person I was going to do everything with. And now I feel terrible because I did something with someone else, but I shouldn't feel bad because me and Daisy are just—a moment. We're not supposed to mean anything, so actually me touching Sara's girlfriend is fine. Except she's Sara's girlfriend, which is not fine.

I have to explain at least half of this to Nicole. She doesn't need to know anything about Daisy to share my outrage about Sara.

"Look over there."

My hands cradle Nicole's face to steer her eyes in the correct direction. Still, she takes a while to notice Sara and her girlfriend walking toward us.

"Do you see who she's with?" Now free of my hold, Nicole's head shifts from side to side. "Picture her wearing a snapback and ripped jeans." Nicole's eyes narrow at my instructions.

"Oh! Oh! Oh! She was so cute before." Nicole pouts at the realization that the girl she was desperately trying to set me up with before is the same girl we've heard so many rumors about, but had never had the displeasure of meeting, until today.

I disagree with her implying that Sara's girlfriend is less attractive because she's dating Sara. Sure, her morals are questionable, but Sara wasn't always an acquired taste.

"I know. And she works for Bonnie." Sara and her girlfriend stop and chat with a few other students, none of whom I recognize. Sara does most of the talking, while her girlfriend looks around the lawn with mild interest. "I don't think meeting her that day was a coincidence."

Other than the attempts to paint me as a mean girl, Sara has never made me her primary target, partially because we haven't been on-set with each other in years. The rumors of her terrorizing didn't start until after our show wrapped.

"Weird, she's never shown her face. You'd think she'd want to show her off." We continue to watch Sara interact with the group. Once they pull out their cell phones, it's clear they're fans. I doubt Sara was veiling her identity to protect her, considering the things they're rumored to have done together.

Sara's girlfriend looks like she doesn't care. She was the same once Bonnie walked into the room. Once the meeting started, she sort of just faded away.

"What's her name?"

"Oh, shit." I think back to the morning. Bonnie kept calling her Darlin', which I'm pretty sure isn't her name and Sara kept calling her–

"Brie. Her name is Brie."

"This makes sense." Nicole's eyes remain on Brie and Sara. Other people have approached Sara and asked for photos. Nicole and I are very much aware of the sly cameras pointed at us. It comes with the job and you get used to it after a while. Most of the time, if you look busy, people are polite enough to not interrupt you.

Sara and Brie arrived together, but also separately. It's easy to see how people miss the two of them as a unit so often.

"At the cafe, she knew my name. I've played that moment over and over in my head ever since and knew you hadn't said my name." Nicole bites on her bottom lip.

"What do you think it means?"

"Other than Sara's been talking shit about us? Nothing."

Sara's girlfriend doesn't go to the same class as the rest of us. I'm guessing that means she's studying to be in a completely separate field. We ignore Sara's presence as best as we can. I don't see Brie again until later in the afternoon. Sara is nowhere to be found. Instead, she sits at a table with two other girls. The sketch pad from the day at the coffee shop sits underneath her arm.

I thank the barista for my smoothie, ignoring all the cell phones that secretly record me as I do it. People have already tagged me on several posts depicting my morning; walking with Nicole, having lunch, sitting in class and even going into the restroom. The restroom is where I sent the text I had been writing and rewriting in my head all day.

Emmy [1:15 p.m.]

A girl tried to kiss me today.

It wasn't just any girl. The girl who almost kissed me is a girl I've only heard about through whispers. Sara's girlfriend has made her rounds, ruining the prospects of other actors, and it looks like she's coming for me next. Not like this is anything Daisy would know or care about. I'm just curious about how she would react to knowing someone else almost got that close to me.

I think about my follow-up to her outrage. *And she sent me this picture. Weird, right?* It was weird. Still, I haven't deleted it. If Brie's goal is to make me uncomfortable, she's going to have to try much harder than that. I have to admit there's something about Brie that I like. Something is challenging and captivating about her. I like how she smirks when she looks at me like she's daring me to defy her. Few have tried and I have no reason to. I am no threat to Sara and whatever gig she's going after soon.

They're too busy talking to notice me. I smile at everyone else I walk past and keep the smile on my face when Brie's eyes and mine collide.

"Hey, Brie."

All conversation at the table ceases. One of her friends, a

beautiful girl with dark brown skin and long, straight black hair, flinches.

"Hey, Brie? Who are you?" Her face scrunches up in annoyance, an expression that forces her already thin eyebrows to arch higher. I'm not exactly incognito. I only stopped because I thought Brie would give me something entertaining to tell Daisy later. Outright lying doesn't feel good and isn't as fun.

I ignore her friend. Asserting my relevance is one of my least favorite things to do. By the sound of the girl's constant mumbling, gasps, and other sounds of audacity, she isn't too pleased. Her theatrics force Brie to look in my direction.

"Yes?" Brie shifts just enough to rest her chin in her palm and droops her eyes closed. It's rich coming from her. I was interesting enough for her to accidentally-on-purpose meet at a coffee shop and incorrectly schedule my meeting with Bonnie, but now I'm the most boring person in the world. She and Sara deserve each other.

I take a few seconds to sip more of my smoothie. "I forgot to ask you earlier, what's your major?" I don't claim to know all of Hollywood. There are actors who are also models, actors who are musicians, and actors who only take on indie projects for ethical and spiritual reasons. I am not that actor, but Brie looks like she could be. Her energy screams unbothered, even when she's annoyed, like now.

"You forgot to ask me something that isn't your business?" She raises that one eyebrow, just like back at the coffee shop. I thought it was cute, then. She's making it more complicated than it needs to be. Most people know how to have a simple, polite conversation. Even Sara can fake it.

"I'm asking because we're clearly going to be working together a lot." She pauses to consider my words and while her eyes never leave mine, the gaze of her friends bounces between us. The one friend, the very pretty one with the thin eyebrows, shifts in her seat.

"I'm a writer." I peep over to her notebook and notice drawings, but no words.

"Comic Books?" Brie's face morphs into an expression I have a feeling is rare. Rather than be offended by my question, she's amused. Her friend responds before Brie has a chance to."

"Head Writer. Showrunner. Probably your future boss."

Her friend talks too much. As I'm almost certain Brie is the reason behind Sara's reputation, I doubt she needs guard dogs as friends. And this one seems eager to pounce. The other girl, just as brown and just as pretty, but with much better eyebrows, is mostly quiet. I ignore them both and give my full attention to Brie.

"Can I read it?" I hold out the palm of my expected hand. The amusement on Brie's face widens. Whatever Brie is working on isn't really of any interest to me. It takes years to get a show off the ground. Hopefully, we won't know each other that long.

Daisy would be proud of me, I think. If she were Brie, she'd think of a way to make me apologize. And since we're meeting tonight, she'd be in luck.

Brie traces the edge of the notebook with the pencil she's holding. "This one's too mature for your audience. I'll let you know when I write a family comedy."

I walk around the table and wiggle my body between Brie and her nice friend. The nice friend makes space for me. Brie stares at me with what I hope is contempt. "That's funny. I don't remember seeing your girlfriend's titty spread." Posing nude for a magazine is a proven strategy for propelling child stars into adult roles. Zara begrudgingly passed on the offers to me shortly after my eighteenth birthday. They started rolling in before then. I declined them all. If in my thirties, I'm still able to play a teenager, I'll take the compliment. There were a few of us who believed Sara would accept any offers sent to her. None materialized.

"Sara's not–"

The talkative one's words are cut short by Brie's stare. It's unnecessary. I already know what she's going to say. And she's wrong. Sara *is* like that. Whatever decision she made to not pose for the salacious magazines was because her dad forbade her from doing so, or it was for strategic purposes. It has nothing to do with morals or ethics. If she's ever asked about it in an interview, she'll say it's because she's a role model to young girls. And it'll all be bullshit.

"Listen." My voice is more forceful than I mean it to be. Brie turns her attention back to me. The anger that formed because of her friend's outburst remains. "I can pass on that photo I have of you, if you want. I'm sure it'll get you some well-deserved attention." The corner of her mouth pulls up into a smirk. I try to maintain my defiant expression as her hand, shielded from view, snakes its way up my thigh.

"If *you* want, I can arrange for your private shoot. I'm sure Sara won't mind if I chaperone." Her face is too close to mine for me to breathe properly. She probably does this a lot, tease and disparage. Of course, Sara would approve. Everything Brie does is to her benefit.

Not wanting to back down, I lean in. Our mouths make the softest impact, with our upper lips pressing together like two soft clouds. My stomach twists. *I won't be telling Daisy about this.* "No, thank you. I already have a handler." I back away and remove myself from the seat I wedged into. Her grip on my thigh loosens the farther I go.

Each step I take sheds away the boldness I mustered to meet

my goal. For Daisy. I type out my question to her, gearing up for tonight's meetup. The last one remains unanswered. She's probably busy. After this one, I'll be more patient.

Emmy [1:26 p.m.]

What are the rules about touching?

"Are you sure about her?" The Pretty One's voice echoes behind me. She didn't seem like the whispering type before. There's no reason for her to pretend now. I can't hear Brie's response to her question. But I don't need to. I already know the answer.

She has no idea.

The hotel Daisy picks for us differs from the one I chose before. While I think my pick conveyed ambiguity about our present situation, hers screams hook-up in ugly beige letters.

The seclusion of the hotel makes me anxious. The entrance is dark. The receptionist is bored and nearly unpleasant. I almost walk away from his dark, sunken eyes until he tells me the room is already paid for.

The dimly lit hallway with brown carpeting and sand-colored walls makes me cautious about touching anything. This is Daisy's night. This is the moment for her fantasy to come to life. I scold myself for being judgmental. She did exactly what I asked of her and more. I will do exactly as I'm told. Just as she taught me.

I've had to come to terms with what I learned about myself after just one night together. It wasn't what I thought it was going to be. I thought Daisy was going to be sweet. The things she did, she never talked about before. Yes, things were heated before we met, but the commands. The punishments. Those were the surprises I think I liked. Almost every night since then has involved semi-mute phone conversations with the only noise being made are the ones she commanded from me.

I open the brown door to the hotel room and peek inside from the hallway. The queen-sized bed is dressed in one of those floral comforters I'm sure my mom has crammed in a closet somewhere, convinced it'll come back in style one day.

I neatly fold my clothes into the bag I bring with me and place them out of sight. The wig I plan to wear tonight is missing. A brief flashback of me setting it on the desk in the bedroom flashes across my mind on repeat. Shit. The sleep mask will have to be enough.

In nothing but my bra and panties, my knees settle onto the rough, scratchy carpet and I wait. The sound of the door creaking open and then slamming shut causes my bones to quake beneath my skin. It's a little cold on account that I wasn't able to figure out exactly how to turn off the ancient air conditioning unit.

The shivers only intensify when her lips brush against my earlobe and her words float through my ear. "You're late."

I fight the urge to call bullshit on that one. Yes, I may have circled the block to make sure I was where I was supposed to be, but I left early to give myself enough time to not be reprimanded for it later.

The directions did not say to head straight toward the group of sketchy looking men loitering in the parking lot and once you pass them, turn right at the dark courtyard where you'll find even more sketchy men hanging around. The burnt butts of their cigarettes will be the only thing available to use in a lineup after the police discover my body.

The hand she places around my throat is soft at first. Her hold tightens as she grips me, drags me to my feet, across the room, and slams my face against the bed.

The mattress springs creak beneath me. The cold, steel blade shocks me out of my fight. It trails up the inside of my thigh, keeping flat to one side. A warning. She could cut me, but she's trying not to.

"Even good girls have to be punished sometimes." My ears strain to catch every word. Her voice is too soft to hear properly. The blade continues to graze against me and flips upwards when she reaches for the bands of my underwear. The fabric tears easily, falls away from my skin and hangs loosely at the side.

I hear a click and feel a second blade cut away at the other end, robbing me of my shield. The first blade trails over the exposed folds of my vulva. I hiss at the contrasting cold against my warmth. A blade's spine sliding through the heat between my thighs has never been a dream of mine.

Daisy's fantasy colors in the lines of what I already thought I knew about her. The first time we were together, she followed my script, even if it was at a quicker pace than I imagined.

The second blade cuts at the straps of my bra. First the shoulders, then behind. A small push on my lower back sends me a new message. I lift myself from the knife underneath to settle my knees on the bed. She wraps what feels like rope around my wrists before pushing me down to my back and secures them to the bed frame above my head.

I arch slightly as she winds more rope around my waist before pushing each calf against my thighs, binding them together. The position pulls at my muscles almost uncomfortably. Small moans escape from my lips. I take a while to understand that while I fear her now, the thought of me being viewed from her perspective, spread apart by her threads, is more beautiful than I could have ever thought.

It's not like she knows who I am. I can walk away from this experience tonight and pretend it never happened and there would be no one who could tell me it did.

A cluster of ropes across my clit brushes against me. I try to pull away.

When something smooth and round chases my retreat, I can't stop my scream from belting out as my hips tilt forward. She twirls it around in a circle, securing it in its place between me and the ropes she created. I pant breathlessly. My wrists twist against my restraints. Her fingers continue turning whatever she's using to steal the air from my lungs. I hear a small click and a whirring sound come to life at the same time as the rotating shake.

I raise my hips in response to the vibration, gliding against the slick softness easily. My hips lower as intense pressure in my belly builds. My breath is light and ragged. Another button clicks. The vibration intensifies. "Oh!" I call out, biting my lip to stop the rest of the words from tumbling out. My movements quicken as my need increases. My clit hums against the ball when my hips lower.

I don't hear her press the button the third time. The vibration changes as my hips buck harder and move faster. The sounds I have been trying to conceal pour out of me in shaky, hushed tones. "Oh, please... Fu...Ah..."

My panic rumbles underneath the building heat. The unmistakable swooshing sound of the balcony door being pulled open pierces through. "D-Did yo...?" The wave breaks up my words. My protest is more lost and passive than what I mean to say. I can't focus on the pleasure she's forcing out of me and the thought of her exposing this moment to someone else at the same time.

The familiar feelings of an incoming orgasm surface. Normally, this would be when I stop. When I decide there has been enough excitement, enough breathless moments and enough temptation to satisfy me until another time.

But I can't. She has wrapped me in a web I have no idea how to get out of. Others can hear me now. She has given strangers access to our intimacy. And the thought of it is so thrilling, it scares me. I envision people pausing their TVs and turning down the volume of their music to listen in. I am now their main attraction. Their songstress. Their entertainment.

My wrists pull at the restraints with different intentions. The harder I pull, the tighter they become, burning into my flesh. And the harder I pull, the closer I press against the weapon she has lodged against me.

Closing my thighs is futile. Every movement only serves to aid my arousal. There is so much moisture between us I can hear the light splashing sounds against the vibrations. I'm soaked.

Feeling the urge to give in, I move against it, enjoying the powerful sensations that flow through me.

I feel courageous.

I feel adventurous.

I feel challenged.

I lower my hips, clenching when it nestles against my clit. My breath fills my chest until my will for survival kicks in, forcing me to breathe.

I gasp, allowing my hips to rise again. My wild panting fills the room. For a moment I have a shameful thought about what's happening. My breaths have been too big to keep concealed. My whimpers. My pleading. The tone of the toy, although I'm sure advertised as whisper quiet, buzzes through me and out into the open air. It's too late.

I ride the wave of ecstasy by sliding against the head of the device slowly and then at a faster pace, always keeping to the rhythm my body needs to reach the inevitable.

When it comes, it's too much. My clit spasms and pulses, beating against the bulb as more moisture creams out of me. The sounds of it rotating against me are louder now. The comforter is damp and my skin glistens with exhaustion.

"Please! Please! Please! Please!" I call out. The whirling against my now sensitive clit continues. It's excruciatingly delicious and overwhelming. She pushes it closer against me, holding me down along with it. I shake uncontrollably. My clits throbs harder against the pressure. My lower muscles spasm at a rate I've never been able to produce myself. I scream out sounds I didn't know I could create. I move my hips even though she's left no room for them to go.

She pulls the toy away and I think I'm saved. A forceful tap comes back down and smacks against the wetness. I yelp. She does it again. I jerk in my restraints. Each tap sends my body into a different movement I have no control over. I lose count of how many times she does it. The toy has stopped vibrating, but that hasn't stopped her from wielding its power.

She glides the head of it up and down my sticky wet lips and presses against the place only my finger has gone before. Just one. I haven't gotten into enough trouble for two, yet. I pant against her assault. Temporary gratitude appears whenever she pulls it away from me, but then longing settles in until she resumes the punishment. I can feel how wide she's spread me. The evidence of what we've done flows out to my inner and upper thighs. I wait for her to continue, half dreading, half wishing for more.

The sharpness of a blade slides against my skin for the third time. She tugs and the ropes loosen from around me. When she frees my wrist, my arms drop to my sides without the strength to hold them. I wait for her hands to tear at my skin without care. Maybe this time she'll bite my nipples until I beg her to stop. Maybe she'll force me to clean her torture instruments with my mouth and tongue. She'll grip my hair and not care about how badly the tension pains my scalp. She'll watch in glee as the tip of my tongue dangerously trails up her knife over and over until she decides that it's clean. And she still won't be done punishing me.

I hear nothing but silence. With hesitation, I remove the sleep mask and find the room empty. Pieces of red rope and a hot pink sex toy sit at my feet. They're either meant as gifts or insults. The sliding door is still open. The curtains blow inside from the faint summer wind. I leave it the way it is. She could still be outside, listening. This could be a test. Tonight, I'll show her how good I can be. Tomorrow, we'll see. Despite Daisy's victory, I don't feel defeated.

I feel relieved.

Chapter Nine
Daisy

OBEDIENCE LOOKED GOOD ON her tonight. It took a lot more effort than it should have to fight the urge to take control of her. By the end, I wanted nothing more than to snatch the toy away, giving her seconds of relief before rubbing it against her again.

Cutting away her bra and panties wasn't a part of the plan, but she made me do it. At least I left her other clothes intact, but if she tries to play games with me again, I'll cut those up, too.

My genuine regret, though, is the nipple clamps forgotten in the bottom of my tote bag. I meant to attach them as payment for what she did to me last time. The feeling of her nipples stretched into a tube and the fact that other people were listening to her whimper, moan and plead for mercy would have been amazing.

She tried to hide it, but she loved every second. I could tell by the way she bucked her hips and bit her bottom lip. Not once did she demand I close that patio door and keep our secrets to ourselves. She never noticed the people who came by for a closer listen. They never made themselves visible. Their curtained shadows were the only way to see them and she had no way of knowing they were there. If she knew, she probably would've screamed louder.

I didn't leave when she thought I did. Instead, I waited in the closet and watched her go. If I had left, there was a possibility someone else would come in and try to seize the opportunity to replace me. Sure, they could listen to her. It's what she's always wanted, but they could never touch her.

By the time I make it home, it's well past midnight. I send the last message of the night to Emmy before I unlock the front door. *You're only allowed to wear yellow panties from now on.* Yellow compliments the undertones of her brown skin. Red works, too, and I bet she looks just as good in blushing pink, but for our purpose, we'll keep it simple—yellow only.

I'm surprised to find my mom sitting in the kitchen stirring a spoon in her coffee cup. She glances up at the clock on the wall and then back at me again. I move slower across the room, aware she's holding something back she's dying to say.

"So, who's the girl?"

My mom's hip-length hair looks exactly like my own, except I would never allow mine to grow that long. My sisters feel the same way. Maricela complains her back is itching if her hair grows too far past her bra strap and Araceli demands a haircut as soon as it rubs against her shoulder blades. If she doesn't get one, she'll do it herself—no problem.

"Don't do that."

"Don't do what? If you were working at Diego's, you wouldn't be home 'til later. There's only one reason a girl—who likes girls like you — would be out late at night." At my lack of response, she continues, "I don't want you to feel bad about it. I've told you for years. Leave if you're not happy. You don't owe anyone anything."

She *has* told me this for years and every year it feels like a lie. Taking care of the family has been my responsibility since I was old enough to walk. If I stop fulfilling my role, they'll all fall apart. The only reason she's able to use her coffee cup is because I load and unload the dishwasher every morning and night.

In some circles, I may be lucky to have Catholic, immigrant

parents who didn't bat an eye once they noticed my attention didn't travel in the hetero-normative directions.

I had my first crush in kindergarten. We told each other we were best friends, and maybe to her, we were. We played hopscotch together, rode tricycles together, played store together and I became very good at playing the dad when we played house.

Throughout the day, I gathered up whatever barrette, bead or pompom that fell out of her hair and twisted them back in before her mom picked her up. If I missed one, I'd barter one from another kid.

Mom caught on quickly and wasn't shy about requesting for her to come over to my house and play with me. It devastated me when she moved right before Christmas. My mom's solution to my pain was to take me to my first live performance, inadvertently introducing me to my first love, blowing my kindergarten crush out of the water.

I've spent years since then working to pay for everything I think I need to have a successful career in the movie industry, starting with my college tuition.

My mom worked hard to open her own business and has a lot to take care of. For as long as I can remember, my dad has worked late nights. Their incompatible work schedules often left me home to do the other work. Some things changed when I turned fifteen, but not everything.

"It's okay if you think that. Be careful about saying it aloud," I warn her. That could be catastrophic for all of us. I have a plan in my mind that keeps changing every time I interact with Emmy. The plan was stable for as long as we communicated through words on a screen, but the in-person meetups muddle the lines and the sound of her breaths on the other end of the phone blurs out the entire blueprint.

"This will all have been for nothing if my girls are not happy." Her piercing glare tells me she wants me to believe her, and I do. Isn't that what all immigrant parents want?

"I know, Mom. I promise I won't fu–" I catch myself before using the word. My correction lessens the outrage that built behind her eyes, "mess everything up."

We sit in silence as she continues to sip and stir her tea. It takes longer than it should. Eventually, she lets out a loud sigh before announcing her retreat to bed. I toss the empty tea bag and place the empty mug inside the dishwasher.

I don't turn on another light after leaving the kitchen. Used to navigating the space in the dark, I shut the bathroom door behind me and undress. I don't stand underneath the water until the steam tells me it's hot enough to burn. I cup my hands around my breasts and squeeze. The smallest of whimpers escape. My body shivers beneath the heat. The wetness below still hasn't washed away. I dip my fingers between my thighs, gliding through the sticky mess left there before. I curl them up and release them again, spreading one layer of skin across another.

She was such a good girl tonight. The sound of her voice calling out to me was hard to ignore. My body reacted even when I didn't want it to. My eyes stayed glued to the mess she created between her thighs even when I told myself to look ahead, out the patio door.

I tried to ignore her. And she kept pushing my buttons. She kept demanding me to notice. So instead of wrapping my hands around her neck, I dug my nails into my fists. As badly as I want to touch her, I can't. It's what she wants, too.

When she screamed, I wanted to kiss her, if only to shut her up. There's a mole on the side of her neck I keep wanting to sink my teeth into. I'd lick it first, tasting her while pumping my fingers in and out of her with no mercy. Of course, she'd open as wide for me as she could and only mildly complain when I push her to go further. She'd thrash underneath me as if she's a helpless victim when we both know she's not.

And when they came to listen, even though it was what she wanted and what I needed for the night to be a success, I wanted to kill them. But I can't think about them right now. I can only think about her.

My fingers circle faster, creating more moisture, more need. My throat clogs around the word I struggle to say, but want so badly to scream. Breath catches in my chest. Muscles lock into place. I release.

My breath pushes against the steam billowing in the darkness. "Emmy."

Lately, it's always and only her. Sometimes I wish it wasn't. Every time my phone pings as a reminder of her existence, I do my best to dispel the myth of who she is becoming and who she can never be.

With my body clean and refreshed, I make my way to my bedroom, only to be interrupted by a familiar chime.

Emmy [1:32 a.m.]

Are you awake? You didn't say goodnight.

I never have. She's always the one who sends the pleasantries. I ignore them. Whatever story she tells herself is none of my business.

Daisy [1:33 a.m.]

You should be sleeping. Don't tell me I have to teach you how to do that, too.

Even if she needed it, she'd find some way to sabotage it for her benefit.

Emmy [1:33 a.m.]

I was asleep, but you woke me up.

I shake my head and type out my response.

Daisy [1:33 a.m.]

How?

Cold night air hits me once I swing open the bathroom door and head down the hall to my room.

Emmy [1:34 a.m.]

In my dreams.

She is not as she seems. She can't be. As silently as I can, I gather the clothes I need for the night and change. I slip in under my covers and take a glance at the other two beds. They're still sleeping.

Daisy [1:36 a.m.]

So you had a nightmare?

Emmy [1:36 a.m.]

Hmm. Now that you say that. Yeah, I guess I did.

I let out a breath of relief. Everything is as it seems. We both know what role we need to play.

Emmy [1:38 a.m.]

I missed you. I didn't realize how much I missed you until you were no longer touching me. I wish you had touched me tonight.

Missing each other is not a part of the plan. I stare at the screen and watch as small dots turn to small paragraphs.

Emmy [1:38 a.m.]

And not just like that. I don't want you to think it's just that.

Emmy [1:38 a.m.]

It's not.

Emmy [1:38 a.m.]

I miss touching you, too. I wish you'd let me do it more.

Every sentence sinks me deeper into where I promised not to go when we started this. The three dots blinking on the screen do not stop even though I refuse to respond.

Emmy [1:40 a.m.]

In my dream, I couldn't find you. You were there and then you would disappear. Crazy, right? I don't even know what you look like, but I could feel you. I knew it was you I was looking for.

It *is* crazy. A little. But I've been a passenger on her fantasy train for a few years now. After a while, her version of crazy became our normal.

Daisy [1:41 a.m.]

That doesn't sound scary. I thought you were going to say you dreamt of me chasing you in the woods somewhere.

She probably has. It fits in with what she really wants and is too afraid to say aloud.

Emmy [1:42 a.m.]

Why would that be scary? You could chase me anywhere.

Emmy [1:42 a.m.]

Just don't leave.

Without hesitation, my fingers glide across the keyboard. The words come easily even when my mind is having second thoughts.

Daisy [1:43 a.m.]

Don't worry. I'm not going anywhere.

There have been a few times when I've told myself it was time to leave, but each time never felt like the right time. This is not one of those moments. She's a perfect distraction from the chaos. Being her villain for a little while longer is the least I can do.

Chapter Ten
Gabriella

BONNIE WAS NOT EXAGGERATING when she said this event was going to be big. I did not expect this to be as popular as it is. Who voluntarily shows up to campus on their day off from classes? Thousands of losers, apparently. If I had any good sense, I wouldn't be here, but with the amount of work I had to do to help make this a success, I earned it. I sent too many emails for it not to be.

Sara and Taylor haven't rested since they arrived. They've filmed several introductory takes to be used in the university's promotional videos for years to come. Unsurprisingly, they're doing a good job pretending to like each other. Sara lovingly loops her arms around Taylor's while repeating her line about campus support and community; all the while, people run around and play games in the background.

The live band leaves much to be desired. But the good stuff is yet to come.

They've taken a photo with anyone who's asked. My social media feed is already blowing up with notifications about Sara. So far, Bonnie's plan to change the perception of her mentees' friendship is working. Taylor being close with Sara gives me better access to her, or at least makes me work less hard to gain it. She recently moved from her parents' house to an apartment in Santa

Monica with her best friend, Nicole. The exit of the building leads you right in the middle of the Third Street Promenade. There's a doorman, but no private entrance. She's still trying to look normal and relatable. If you can relate to a $ 15,000-a-month two-bedroom apartment, that's a five-minute walk from the beach and has a rooftop yoga studio.

I watch as the photographer chases after the fresh duo while they pop balloons with darts, throw colorful bean bags at mechanical clowns, and aim streams of water into tiny holes. A crowd of people has formed for each of them. Although Taylor's side *ohhhs*, when the bean bag Sara throws goes too far left and almost hits Taylor in the face, Taylor laughs and takes her turn like nothing happened. The story she weaves of camaraderie is almost convincing, except I know her too well. No one calls out when she accidentally steps on Sara's foot or when she uses the mallet to whack more than the little brown mole.

Sara doesn't make a big deal of it. There's no need.

My gaze follows Taylor from the carnival games to stand behind the stage. Sara's up first. She laughs and giggles at the appropriate times to the pre-approved questions.

"Do you stalk all the girls like this?" She notices me watching her, even though she's looking at the ground, twirling in place. No. The others were easier to deal with. The difficulty with Taylor has been that she and Sara are usually never in the same place at the same time. Usually, I'd strike on location, but Sara and Taylor are not currently competing for any roles since Taylor has announced her break from the business. And oddly enough, although Taylor has taken a step back, there are more eyes on her than usual given how interested some are in her *journey*.

"I saw you in the parking lot when I got here. You were standing under that tree while I talked to Bonnie. And then followed me to every game."

"How do you know I wasn't there for Sara?"

"You weren't looking at Sara. You were looking at me."

She doesn't flinch away when I move closer to her, forcing the edge of our almost identical white sneakers to touch. She looks nice in her light pink halter top and skirt. The shoes are a little unexpected, but very practical for today's duties.

"Maybe I was looking at you because you were with Sara."

She busies herself studying my outfit. Her eyes travel from my ponytail down to my shoulders.

"May I?" Unprepared for her touch, I try not to react when her hands run across my arms. Her short nails scrape against the inside of my elbow and down my wrist. She does it on both sides, silently nodding to herself as she goes.

"I don't have any tattoos." She doesn't either. She gave an interview once about feeling like she could express herself better through piercings. A small smirk plays across her lips.

"Don't tell me you're afraid of needles." I don't tell her anything. I sink my hands into the back pocket of my shorts, forcing her to release me.

"Does it surprise you I'm not afraid of you?"

"No, but you will be." The knife slices through the light fabric of her skirt with ease. Taylor's wide eyes are the only acknowledgment of anything being wrong. I should have left the blade up against her skin longer, allowing the fear to fill her eyes.

Her hands are the only thing available for protection. She squeezes what's left of the skirt together to shield herself from behind.

"You really will do anything for her." It's hard to decipher her expression. There's a bit of surprise, some disbelief, and a bit of what I think is anger. None of it means anything.

"Please welcome to the stage, my dear friend, Taylor Townes!" Sara's voice signals Taylor's entrance from the other side of the wall. Taylor moves without pause, stopping to peek around the edge of the backdrop. The crowd's cheers soften almost instantly. She braves the release of one hand, accepting the mic in the other. In the sweetest voice she can gather, she greets the crowd.

"I'm so excited to be here with you today. Classes only began a few weeks ago and because of all of you, campus already feels like home." She pauses for the whoops and cheers that follow. "Unfortunately, I've had a bit of an accident with my skirt and if I were to go on stage right now, I would be front page for all the wrong reasons. I know it is an extremely hot day outside, but does anyone have a shirt or jacket I can borrow?"

I step to the side of the stage in time to see several hands fly up. Taylor graciously accepts the button-up that clashes with her outfit but meets the only other requirement.

Even with her back to me, her voice carries over. Some of the sweetness from addressing the crowd earlier remains. "I've changed my mind, Brie. Looks like I'm exactly what you need." I catch her eye only for a second. It's enough time for the meaning behind her words to sink in. It's a shame we've only been paired together recently. I could've humbled her a long time ago.

She receives nothing short of adoration when she fully steps on stage. How delusional of them to think she's some kind of hero for overcoming something as small as a torn skirt. I could've done worse. I should've. I won't forget next time.

Sara and I share a glance once I move into the larger crowd. She's not happy. It's hard not to agree with some of what I know she's thinking. I should've gone at her harder. I should've torn that skirt to shreds and left it to lie at my feet. Taylor doesn't understand that by defying me, she's only pushing me to hurt her better the next time. She should submit to me before Sara becomes impatient. While my plan is always to divert and not destroy, Sara doesn't always see it that way.

The charade between the two of them continues with little suspicion. No one suspects anything when Sara announces a surprise. They don't bat an eyelash when four extra chairs are positioned on the stage. Taylor dutifully sits in the one Sara points to, her back facing away from the others.

"Now while I have been in an amazing relationship with my girlfriend of four years —"

"Everyone give it up for Brieeeee!" Taylor's public interruption shocks me. While our relationship is known, Sara has made sure we have never been the center of attention. Not together, anyway. My feet move begrudgingly to the end of the stage. Sara's kiss is the first I've allowed in weeks. Complicated feelings swirl in my stomach. I've been pushing some of them away for months. Others, for years. The only reason I'm being bothered by them now is because of Taylor.

She'll pay for this.

The flinch from the blindfold is barely noticeable. I saw the way her shoulders twitched and the dark gleam in Sara's eyes. Still, Taylor maintains her demeanor, basking in her triumphant glow. It's to my detriment for now, but that will change soon.

"As someone who has known Taylor for a long time. I am highly invested in her dating journey. Which is why today, I want to give it a little jumpstart. Who here would like their chance to go on a date with Taylor?"

A sea of hands fly up. Taylor's shoes tap against the stage floor. Her hands grip the edge of her seat. *Good*.

"Taylor, you've been pretty vocal about wanting to only date the ladies, but you are bi. Tell us, will you be giving any of the men here tonight a shot?"

Taylor takes several seconds to consider the question. "Like Sara said, I have been very vocal about my dating journey, including the fact that I am looking forward to going on a date with a woman. To give myself the best possible chance of success, I'm sticking to that."

Not bad. The question was a tricky one on purpose. She made the answer about herself and not about rejecting men. It'll save her from some criticism, but not all. If she had said she was open, people would've judged her for that, too.

Sara makes her three selections from the crowd. I can't tell if they're totally random. She only floated this idea to me this morning. I had hoped Taylor's wardrobe malfunction would have been enough to send her home early. I'm learning she has another knack; not knowing when to quit.

The three contestants sit in a row of seats behind Taylor. None of them look terrible, so it's hard to know what Sara's angle is here. Sara takes the blindfold off before placing a stack of cards in Taylor's hands.

"Contestant number one, tell us who you are and what your major is."

"My name is Missy. I'm a junior and I'm majoring in art."

"Oh, we love an older woman, right Taylor?" Taylor allows the crowd to see her laugh at Sara joking about a woman who, at most, is a few months to a year older than she is.

"Contestant number two?"

"Hi. I'm Celia. I'm a business major and a sophomore."

"Number three?"

"My name is Catie with a "C" and my major is currently undecided." More than a few groans go off in the audience. Catie recoils from the reaction.

"Take your time, Catie with a 'C.' No one's timeline is as important as yours." Taylor's support for Catie earns her whoops from the crowd. Catie places an appreciative hand over her heart at Taylor's words. The mood in the audience shifts to one of approval.

"And if all else fails," Sara begins. "Dating an award-winning actor would be a good backup. Taylor, what's your first question?"

"Contestant number one, you brought me home real late from our first date. Where were we?"

Taylor looks into the crowd as she waits. Bonnie arrives on the side of the stage, joined by the photographer from earlier and a few others.

Contestant number one steadies the mic to her lips. "For our first date, we went back to my place where I cooked us dinner, and then afterward we got so lost in each other's eyes we lost track of time."

Oh, please.

By their reaction, the crowd appears to approve of the response.

"Contestant number three, same question."

"To make up for my lack of talent in the kitchen, we went out to eat and then out dancing until closing. We had such an amazing time, we didn't want to say goodnight. Instead, we drove to Griffith Park to watch the sunrise, but instead of looking at the sun, I was looking at you."

Taylor let out an exaggerated giggle. If I didn't know any better—and I do — I'd think it was authentic. "Woah contestant number two. I don't know if you can top that." Contestant number two shakes her head in a panic with her mic sitting on her lap.

The crowd disapproves. Some people shout words of encouragement, while others give signs to Taylor that contestant number two is a waste of time.

"No?" Taylor asks into the mic. "Going once. Going twice. Ok, next question." She shuffles through the cards until she finds one she likes. "Contestant number three. I once said in an interview that yellow was my favorite color. Tell me why." She was eight when she gave that interview. They had grouped her with some other child actors on a talk show for comedic relief. Taylor wasn't on every night, but you could catch her at least once a week. Sara was also on a few times. I even think they might've been on together, both sitting on a big red couch, entertaining the live audience with their inherent cuteness. I remember those segments clearly. Just like I remember the answer to this question.

Contestant number three takes a while to answer, killing whatever momentum she earned after answering the first question. "Hmm, because it's the color of your favorite flower?"

"Oh, no. Sorry. I don't have a favorite flower, though maybe I should." Taylor looks thoughtful, as if considering her own suggestion. Contestant number two doesn't respond again when she's called upon. The crowd boos. "Aw come on, everyone. Cut her some slack. Being on stage is hard. I'm impressed she's still sitting here. Contestant number one, your response, please."

Contestant number one looks deep in thought. Her legs cross and then uncross. Her head shifts from side to side. "I don't have the best memory, but I think it had something to do with awards."

"Wow! That's right. I said my favorite color was yellow because the Emmy award — which is the one you win for television — is yellow." Contestant number one looks pleased with herself. Taylor doesn't explain that the Emmy award is gold and not yellow. It was an acceptable answer when she was eight that I haven't heard her repeat since.

Sara stands to the side, watching it all unfold. Her eyes narrow each time Taylor flips through the cards. She taps her foot during the answer portion and surveys the crowd for their response. From where I'm standing, the audience is unswayed. Even when a fact about her is revealed that is supposed to make her look vapid and out of touch, they dismiss it. They're thoroughly entertained by her charade.

"Contestant number one. You notice I'm a little tight. How do you help me loosen up?" Each question after this is more risqué. She most likely skipped through them in the beginning, but now they're the only ones remaining. And the crowd hangs on to every word.

Contestant number one gives the obvious answer of a sensual massage that no one is impressed with.

"Contestant number two. What do you do to make sure my throat stays...moist?"

Oh shit.

I'm not the one who says it aloud. Several people whisper to each other around me. Sara's foot is no longer tapping. While her arms are crossed, her eyes are dark and hungry. She's been waiting for this.

The riskier the questions have become, the more contestant number two has come out of her shell. Her response is simple and expected. "I would give you a tall glass of Celia." She emphasizes the accent in her name, moving her hips in her chair.

Taylor bites her lip at the next card. Her eyes briefly flick to Sara and then down again. Nerves drip into the pit of my stomach. "Contestant number one, how many times can you make me come?" Taylor slowly lets out the breath she was holding. It reminds me to release my own. An audible gasp rips through the audience with a few noticeable giggles. Of course, they would want to watch Taylor's reaction to this, hoping they learn something new about her, something forbidden.

Without notice, contestant number one stands. She confidently struts across the stage, Taylor her only goal. In one swift movement, she bends to whisper into her ear. Taylor stays poised in her seat. If contestant number one makes an impression, I can't tell.

"Contestant number three, same question." Contestant number three follows the example left by contestant number one, except this time, she lowers herself to her knees in front of Taylor, revealing her identity. Her mossy brown hair sweeps to the side when she leans forward, pushing Taylor's knees apart with her hands. Taylor pushes back against her shoulders. "Oh, no no no!" Contestant number three is relentless in her attempt to wedge her head underneath the borrowed sweatshirt.

"Someone help her!" Sara glares at the audience member. More people chime in to express their outrage. Taylor continues to push back the rapid contestant. This is fucking embarrassing. And why I always tell Sara to leave everything up to me. She'll never live down a sexual assault allegation if anyone figures out she hired contestant number three. To be honest, I thought contestant number one was the saboteur of the whole thing, but number three has her beat.

It's Bonnie who ushers a few staff members on stage to drag contestant number three away. Sara runs to Taylor's aid; fixing her hair and smoothing out her clothes, lightly lifting the sweatshirt in the process. Taylor's hands clamp down on the raised hem.

"I'm so sorry!" Taylor only nods at Sara's apology.

"Well, that was quite the experience!" Sara calms the crowd enough to settle them. Taylor has regained her composure. Her ever-present smile is back plastered onto her face, her white teeth shining. "Taylor, I think we've heard enough. Which lucky contestant would you like to take out on a date?"

"While it was a hard choice," Taylor chuckles along with the audience. "Contestant number one, would you like to go on a date with me?" I'm mildly surprised. I would have thought contestant number two's shyness would've made her a magnet for Taylor's faux affection.

The crowd agrees with her. They shout and whoop at their embrace, only quieting when Sara announces additional food truck options.

"Can you fucking believe these people?"

I find Sara stewing at the side of the stage. Taylor is lost in photo-op heaven with her new date, who's probably going to serve her burnt steak and potatoes for dinner.

"Well, you did have Taylor assaulted on stage, in public." It'll be one hell of a headline if something else isn't deemed more interesting. There's a chance it may not come out at all, given Taylor's aggravating ability to handle it with grace. Her freaking out and attacking contestant number three would make a bigger story.

Not that contestant number three didn't deserve it. She did. And one day, karma may come back to bite her.

Sara sucks her teeth at me. "That wasn't assault! She's fine! She's just putting on a show, so all these people think of her as a helpless victim." It's no use arguing with her. Sara never responds well when things don't go her way.

"Missy better hope she does better than Catie if she wants to get paid."

"You hired both of them?"

"I had to. No one ever seems like they can do their job anymore." Sara wraps her arms around my waist, resting her head on my shoulder. "I'm tired. What time are we going home?"

Chapter Eleven
Taylor

**TAYLOR TOWNES
OPENS UP ABOUT
SEX AS A COLLEGE
STUDENT**

THE NEWS THAT COMES out isn't too bad. It's also not entirely accurate, but clickbait titles never are. It's odd to think of my date with Missy as my first proper date with a woman since Daisy and I have been doing *something*. Last night was a continuation of that, but without her saying much of anything, I worry *something* is wrong.

To Daisy, I had framed the dating game as if three different women randomly asked me out.

Daisy [6:37 p.m.]

What were you doing?

I know I earned every ounce of her suspicion. Nothing is ever as it seems with us. I'm not who she thinks I am, and she is more than I bargained for. We learn from each other with every new experience. This was just one more.

Emmy [6:37 p.m.]

> *Nothing. I was just there. It was a huge event.*

It was a bigger event than I expected. I had planned to take photos and answer some questions about my new life as a college student. The dating show was a surprise sprung up on me that morning by Sara. Bonnie loved the idea, of course. I used the opportunity to my advantage — with Daisy.

Daisy [6:42 p m.]

> *Sure.*

Her response did not surprise me. She rarely gave anything away.

I'd sent her pictures of my outfit and asked if she thought it was too much. She didn't respond. The lack of response made me anxious. I never know quite how far to push her. I think she likes it when I'm not one hundred percent agreeable. It makes things more exciting between us. Isn't that the point of all of this? To have a new experience?

I'd changed into a different skirt before driving to Missy's apartment. Separate from the three requests I have already mentioned, I'd told Daisy about an opportunity from an acquaintance to taste some of the food she's preparing for culinary school. I probably overdid it. Missy didn't specify which type of art she studies. Culinary art should at least be considered career-adjacent.

I'd gone on the date with Missy as planned and looked for

reasons to text Daisy a play-by-play of what was going on.

Missy was nice. She had an easygoingness to her that helped ease my guilt about anticipating my time with Daisy. I soaked up enough information about her to use with Daisy, later. Throughout the date, I snapped a few pictures, both for Missy's benefit and mine. She had to receive something from this other than interesting dinner conversation.

Missy was in a different outfit as well. The short shorts and fishnets were a surprise to see, but they worked great in the photos next to my skirt. I'd strategically placed the plate of food she made, a steak and loaded baked potato, in the same shot, and then sent it to Daisy. The response I received was unexpected.

Daisy [8:03 p.m.]

You better be home by 9.

The time had ticked away out of my control. I couldn't come up with a good enough reason to tell Missy that I had to leave her apartment in the middle of dinner. The lie of needing to leave because of an emergency got caught in my throat the few times I tried. She grabbed my wrist so hard I had no choice but to sit back down. In the end, I stayed, continuing to send photos of the meal Missy made and the strawberries we dipped in chocolate.

Finally, I'd snapped a picture of me in my car - an image of my hands placed on the steering wheel - well past nine.

Emmy [10:13 p.m.]

Sorry. Didn't see your message. On my way home.

Her only response was a screenshot of our text thread, proving I had read the message as soon as she sent it.

Damn it. I need to turn that off.

I'd driven my car home through the busy Santa Monica streets and squirmed in my seat in anticipation. Excitement surged through me at the possibilities.

She was going to make me pay.

I worried about Nicole being home. Instead of spending the weekend with her boyfriend, she stayed to attend the back-to-campus event to support my new partnership with Sara. While I appreciated her following through on her duties as a best friend, it disappointed me she stayed for the weekend.

Daisy hasn't taught me how to be quiet, yet.

Daisy [10:53 p.m.]

> *Shower. Now. I want her off you.*

Missy barely touched me. Perhaps our shoulders bumped or our knees knocked together, but nothing significant. Nothing like what she was implying.

It took a few rings for our call to connect. I didn't bother apologizing. It wouldn't change anything. The black spiral staircase that leads to my bedroom did its job of concealing my presence. There was no evidence of Nicole wanting to chat about my date or talk about anything else that happened, like my unexpected wardrobe malfunction or my sudden ability to talk about sex with a large crowd of strangers, though I guess that last one wasn't so entirely sudden.

The digital seconds turning into minutes were the only way

I knew my call with Daisy was still connected. She's always unusually quiet over the phone. I guess we both would be if I wasn't the one always forced to make my presence known in an assortment of ways, usually with my hands between my thighs and my inability to keep my mouth shut and my breath stifled. I've never heard what Daisy sounds like when she's feeling too good to breathe.

I want to.

One day.

I'd made a strategic choice not to turn on my bathroom lights. If Nicole came investigating, I wanted her to think I was too tired to converse with. I lit the candle on the counter instead.

The hot water fell from the shower head almost instantly. That's something Daisy seemed to be good at. Patience. She demanded that I complete whatever she had in store for me, but she never rushed me into it. With every article of clothing I removed, I imagined her watching me as the pieces fell to the floor.

I placed the phone in the spot that's usually reserved for beauty products, keeping it protected from the water necessary to absolve me of my misdeeds.

Daisy [11:12 p.m.]

Use the shower head.

There was enough heat from the steam in the bathroom to keep me warm. To maintain a little disobedience, no matter how unnoticed, I took my time cleaning my body before complying. The sharp breath I inhaled at the pressure applied to my clit was enough for me to use the wall to keep me steady.

Daisy [11:17 p.m.]

Good girl.

The boost of confidence I continue to receive from those two words keeps shocking me. I dream of them spilling from her lips no matter what position I'm in. I want her to whisper them from behind me, underneath me, or on top of me. In whatever way she pleases, I'd do anything.

The messages of encouragement followed me from the shower to the bedroom. I lie in bed naked, not bothering to put on any night clothes. I knew she wouldn't allow it.

That night was a true test. I screamed into my pillow until she took it away from me. One finger turned into two and I bit down on my lip until I drew blood. That had never happened before. I couldn't take the risk of Nicole knowing something was going on. Daisy cared enough about my injury to use it against me. She forced me to pack my mouth with my underwear instead. The ones with the center, still sticky from my earlier anticipation. The ones I rocked against in my car after she caught me in my lie.

I tasted myself for the first time.

I had no choice. She forced me.

And then she was quiet again, like she was every night. My goodbyes go unanswered until the next time I have a complaint, a confession, or a self-initiated emergency.

Today, I have to stare at a headline with half-truths. I opened up about sex, but not with who they think.

Joke's on them.

I ignore the feelings of frustration and annoyance while I gather the box of tulle, rhinestone-wrapped headbands, and other small accessories.

We've been doing this enough weekends for us to develop a seamless routine. I drive from my apartment and pretend I don't see Sara's girlfriend behind me. The routine is always the same. She follows me to the rescue center, parks three rows down and waits for me during my entire shift. I didn't notice her at first. I'm not sure what salacious behavior she expects to learn from my time volunteering at an animal adoption center, but whatever it is, she's dedicated.

Debra greets me, holding open the door the same as always. The indoor rabbit space is one I've helped design and redesign over the years. I started volunteering at the rescue when I was a kid. I couldn't have a pet because of my work schedule. My parents let me come here one day during a cuddle event and I've loved it ever since.

I've moved around the rescue a few times, servicing different animal homes. Rabbits are by far my favorite. They're not loud like dogs or suspiciously independent like cats. Rabbits are indifferent and free. They just want to eat and run around.

"Hey, Amber." Amber looks up from the hay she's scattering around the artificial grass. The rabbits sit and eat around her, not caring she's currently in their space. Her red braids glow against her dark brown skin. I've always been envious of that. Sometimes I wish I was bold enough to do something as daring as to dye my hair. Amber colors and cuts without a second thought. I've seen her change her hair color halfway through the day.

"Is that what I think it is?"

"It sure is."

I've been responsible for making the adoption accessories for years now. Crafting is the only hobby I have. For a long time, it was hard for me to watch TV without critiquing myself. Watching crafting videos is a lot less stressful. I mostly make bandanas, hats and collars of various simplicity and fancifulness for each event.

"I hope they find someone to run it before next weekend."

"What do you mean? What happened to Michelle?"

Amber's eye roll is the only answer I need. Drama. Michelle's days are filled with drama. Either she's sick, someone's sick, someone died, her grandma died, or something. It's always something with Michelle.

"Hold on. I'll be back."

The car is parked in the same spot it was in when I saw it. I hesitate to knock when I notice the empty front seat. The seats are clean. The floors are free from random things. Very unlike my car. It's not disgustingly dirty, but sometimes, I lose the encouragement to bring everything I brought outside, back inside.

And then I see her, barely clothed and sweaty, asleep in the back seat. Her clothes balled underneath the side of her face for cushion. She has on the tiniest pair of stretchy black shorts. In this heat, she has to be burning up. It somewhat explains the location. Out of all the space in the parking lot, she's parked underneath a tree. Most people would hate the idea of the leaves falling onto their car.

I tap my knuckles against the glass a few times. The more still she remains, the more I panic inside. I tap harder while watching the beads of sweat roll from her stomach to her side.

"Hey! Wake up!" My fists pound against the surface. She pops up, presses a button on her key fob and pushes open the back door.

"What?!"

"Oh, excuse me for saving your life. You could've died in there. How are you yelling at me right now?"

"I wasn't going to die. I'm yelling at you because you're bothering me."

"You're not even supposed to be here. You stalk me, but I'm bothering you?"

"Yes! You volunteer here for six hours, which means I get six hours to myself to do whatever I please. Today, I chose to sleep and now you're bothering me five and a half hours before schedule."

"Wow!"

She nods at me as if she's happy I finally get the point. She's insane. Sara's insane. They deserve each other.

"You need to come with me." She moves to close the door and I latch onto the handle. We push and pull, all the while screaming at each other from our respective sides.

"Let go of the door!"

"Get out of the car!"

If anyone were to come into the parking lot, they would see me as unhinged as I have ever been. It would be the perfect picture of everything Sara has always wanted me to be. And I don't care.

Her back legs brace against the back of the driver's seat for strength. My feet plant firm on the hot asphalt for stability. I haven't lost to her, yet. I don't plan to start now. The door swings back and forth between the two of us. When it slams shut, I pull back before she can lock it. When I swing it open, she refuses to budge.

"If you come out, I won't call the police," I say with as serious of an expression as I can muster, despite my exhaustion.

Her laugh is disrespectful and oozes with meaning I know too well to be true. She knows I would never call the police unless the circumstances were truly dire and even then, I would hesitate.

"Fine!" I say it through gritted teeth. My neck and forehead are caked in sweat. I can feel the sheen on my back becoming heavier and heavier with each burning ray of the sun. I'm dying to return to the cool air-conditioned animal sanctuary formerly of my imagination.

I let go.

The door slams shut. The lock clicks. I turn to leave, only to remember why I ventured out into the parking lot in the first place. Brie lies on her back with her eyes closed. Her hair piled onto the top of her head.

"I need your help." She makes me repeat it more than once before she gives me her attention. She jumps to the front, turns the keys in the ignition and rolls down her front window.

"Come to my office." I can't tell if keeping myself from laughter is slowly killing me, or if I'm slowly dying because she dares to be funny.

Still dressed in nothing but a sports bra and tiny shorts, she stares at me. I take my time observing her for what feels like the hundredth time. Her arms are free from markings. No bruises. No scars. No birthmarks. Her skin has a golden tan.

"We have an adoption event next weekend and the person who usually runs the show dropped out."

"What does that have to do with me?"

"You're a future showrunner, right? Well, I have a show for you to run. Everything is mostly set-up. You just need to approve some final choices and make sure everything goes according to plan. I'll vouch for you."

Vouching for her will be the simple part. Throughout the years, I've had a few friends stroll through the rescue center for photo ops. It almost always brings publicity to the center and more pets are adopted because of it. Working with Brie on this would be a win-win for both of us. It's a community adoption event, not an award ceremony. There's no way she can fuck this up.

"You think I can slap *animal adoption event coordinator* on my CV and get hired in someone's writing room?"

"No, but you can do the show, invite your girlfriend to take photos and maybe feel less like a bitch." She doesn't look convinced. I try again, squelching down the fire of hatred I feel in the pit of my stomach. "It will be an opportunity for you to showcase your versatility. Humans are hard enough to manage, but animals? If you can make it here, you can make it anywhere." The corners of her lips twitch.

Her wrist flicks to shoo me backward. I oblige without complaint, leaving all insults crowded in my brain. She finally exits from her vehicle and heads to the back. Her trunk is as neatly organized as the inside of her car. She rushes ahead of me after redressing, only allowing me in front to open the front door and unlock the volunteer area with my badge.

Debra is happy to see a new face. She's been a receptionist at the center since my first visit. She's one of those naturally nice people with a welcoming spirit. Not even Sara's girlfriend can change that. Debra greets her the same as everyone, completely oblivious to the nastiness that lies beneath. It makes me chuckle, honestly. I know what she's capable of. I've heard the stories for years, but I'm more intrigued than fearful. Cutting my skirt was unfortunate and forcing me to discuss sex in public—something I've never done—was uncomfortable. But, I don't know. It's not that I enjoy having a stalker. At least I don't think so.

"Debra, this is Brie–"

"My name is Gabriella." She holds her hand out to Debra, who waves them off and leans in for a hug instead. Gabriella accepts it. For cleansing purposes, I imagine whatever conjoined dark spirit Sara and Gabriella share seeps out of her. As if she's aware of my thoughts, she glares at me over Debra's shoulder, only to adjust her expression once the two separate.

"Gabriella has agreed to help us with the show. I'm hoping she can take over for Michelle." Debra gives me a knowing look of gratitude. Everyone's tired of Michelle.

Gabriella is silent on the tour. I take her to where the dogs, cats, and small reptiles are housed, ending with the rabbits.

"We need to get started on the photos, so people already know who they're adopting before the show. The goal is to make them want to come in sooner."

I empty the bag of accessories I brought with me. First, I grab a black rabbit with a trail of white fur underneath. "This is Oreo." Oreo sits dutifully for me to tighten the hat around his head. I'm careful to not make it too tight and to run and get his partner before he grows too annoyed with me. "And this is Cookie." Cookie's light brown. She is less agreeable to me disturbing her, but calms after I hold her close to my chest, careful to keep her legs pressed close against her. After Cookie's hat is attached, I set them both in front of the mini backdrop decorated with artificial vines I put together last week.

"You want them adopted out together to get rid of them quicker?"

"Yes and no. The rescue always needs the space, but rabbits do much better when paired with other rabbits. People don't understand how social rabbits are. They groom each other, play, eat and sleep together. We want to send the message early that they should be adopted in pairs for the best possible chance of success."

I continue the task with Mario and Luigi, Velma and Daphne, Apple and Banana, Honey and Bee, Mary and Jane, Salt and Pepper and Pooh and Tigger. Finally, I grab the last pair. I place the pink crown on one, "Princess Peach and..."–I place the white crown on the other– "...Princess Daisy."

Amber and I go over our ideas for the show.

"We can have some rabbits come out of tunnels, like Mario and Luigi."

"The princesses can knock over a foam castle."

"Salt and Pepper in a small play kitchen."

Gabriella listens intently but doesn't offer any feedback, positive or negative.

We walk out together at the end of my shift, which - given the day's events - has become our shift.

"How'd your date go?" I'm surprised to see her standing at my car door after I turn the ignition. I fully expected her to walk past my car with no acknowledgment we had just spent hours working together.

"Fine."

"Did she cook?"

"Yeah."

"Was it good?"

"Eh."

Her lips twitch. It's a natural occurrence I'm starting to expect. The mere possibility of a smile is averse to her.

"Are you going to see her again?"

"I don't think so." I haven't spoken to Missy since last night and hadn't thought of her until this moment. "Do you have an opinion about who you thought was the better choice?" Of course, she does. Sara is the type to have an opinion about everything and there's no reason that wouldn't extend to the girl she's been dating for years.

"She wasn't up there."

"Who?"

"The girl you were looking for. She wasn't on stage that day."

"How do you know that?" She shrugs her shoulders, moving past my car on the way to her own. Her voice carries low enough to force me to strain my ears to hear.

"I see more than you think."

Chapter Twelve
Daisy

I'M PAYING FOR A room I shouldn't be paying for in a city I technically don't even live in. It's the most I've spent on her for us to spend time together, and I haven't even asked her if she can or if she's willing. She's never turned me down before. This could be different.

Earlier she sent me pictures of her at a theme park. I saw enough articles of the clothing she's wearing to piece together that she has on light blue jeans, a white t-shirt and a rainbow L.A. snapback. She's not wearing a snapback like I would, but I know she looks cute regardless.

The photos were nice to look at. One of her random, unexpected spurts of communication outside of our usual hours that have only grown more frequent. It wasn't the pictures, though, that had me slowing down at work and concocting this idea in my head. It was the words attached to them.

"Someday. One day?" An invitation I think for a future we're not supposed to have. Not together at least. There is no us after this. I still haven't responded. I stare at the words on the screen repeatedly and try to move my fingers to form sentences. The one I choose is completely irrelevant, but if I'm honest, sometimes I miss her when she's quiet.

Daisy [6:13 p.m.]

What's your favorite dessert?

Her response comes quicker than I expect.

Emmy [6:13 p.m.]

You're right on time.

The next photo she sends is one of her holding a churro that's almost the size of her arm. I get the dumbest idea and that idea forces me to spew out a lie I know will only pull me deeper into a place I'm not supposed to be at in the first place.

Daisy [6:15 p.m.]

Do me a favor. Send it to me in a voice message. The picture isn't coming through.

She does exactly as I ask. I play the message on repeat, cringing every other time my thumb presses the button. All the other times, I smile. Emmy's terrible pronunciation isn't a shock, but it's something that needs to be fixed.

Tonight.

I send a voice message back with corrections. She obediently responds, still butchering my first language. This is unacceptable. Such a failure of the American education system requires in-person lessons. It's exactly what I should do given I've already secured our space. The amusement park will close by 8:00 p.m. She'll probably make it back to the city by 9:00 p.m.

I could look at this as a sign that I know her so well I

preemptively booked a room for her to learn a new lesson. A crucial one. Though it shouldn't be. Whether or not Emmy learns to speak Spanish shouldn't matter to me. There is no us. There can't be.

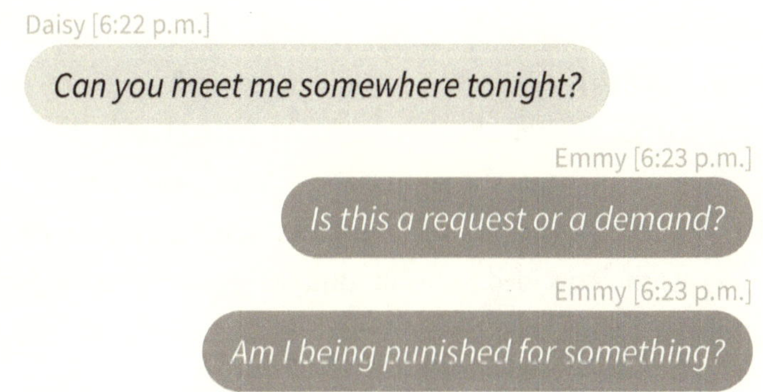

I breathe a sigh of relief. She gets it. She knows this can only go one way.

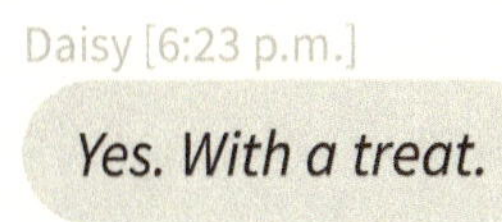

I stand in the bathroom and watch the light from the hotel room door spill across the floor. My heart is beating faster than it should. This means nothing. This is nothing. Act normal. Everything is as it always is.

Except her feet move faster across the carpet than they should. I listen to the small puff of breath she lets out when her eyes land on what I left on the bed, illuminated by the lamp on the nightstand. I shouldn't have done it. One would've been enough. Half a dozen is entirely too much.

I peek around the doorframe and see her sitting on the edge of the bed cradling the ridiculous churro bouquet that I should've stopped myself from making. She probably likes the ribbon. It's colorful and sparkly and while I would hate it if she got something like that for me, I can tell by the fact that she hasn't looked up once and turned to spot me, she appreciates my craft store run.

The blindfold is laid out on the pillows. She hasn't put it on yet. If it's a rule she's decided to break tonight, I have enough material to punish her with.

I step out of view when she stands to place the bouquet on the desk near the window. I listen to the sound of clothes hitting the floor and the mattress creaking. I wonder if she'll click the light off. Usually we do this in the dark for reasons never stated, but always somehow understood.

The glow of the light still shines on the white walls two minutes later and I know there's no need for me to wait any longer.

I exit the bathroom and follow her earlier path.

"Did I ever tell you I was homeschooled?" My heart nearly jumps out of my chest at the sound of her voice. In relief, I stifle a laugh. Only she would offer a random fact while half-naked in the middle of a bed.

I shake my head knowing I shouldn't answer her. It will only encourage her to keep misbehaving and while those are sometimes the parts that I like, we can't be here all night. She continues anyway.

"My mama was a teacher. Technically still is, I guess." I dump my clothes on the same pile as hers, not seeing a need to separate them.

I run my hands over her thighs and feel her shudder. She rolls her hips and I know it's because of the picture she's painting on the other side of that blindfold.

"I don't have a favorite food." Her breath hitches when I move my fingers from the tops of her thighs to in-between. "Sometimes I say I do, but then I eat something and it changes." She rushes out the words, desperately trying to conceal her panic. Her thighs spread further and further apart the closer my hand gets to her panties. I know they're already damp. I can tell by the way she bites down on her bottom lip and twists the blankets into her fists.

She's more than ready.

My hand sweeps across her smooth skin and I watch her head dig into the pillow, her long coils a halo around her face. Her breasts rise and fall in her bra, pushing the lace to its limits.

I kneel where I stood, never leaving the warm touch of her skin. The soles of her feet dig into the mattress as her knees rise up. There's enough space for me to lie in between them. I rest my hand where I would my lips and watch her groan and pleasure and whisper in desperation.

"Please..." She whimpers when I abandon her warm middle. A small wet circle is already visible there. I shake off the temptation to see the source covered by her lace underwear. Now is not the time.

She lets out a long breath when I step away from her. I move across the carpeted flooring, backwards, knowing exactly where I need to go. The paper around the churro bouquet crinkles in my grip. Emmy's chin lifts higher toward the ceiling and I wonder what she's expecting. Her glossy lips part and I no longer have to guess.

I rip a piece of the treat and place it on her bottom lip. She sweeps it inside with her tongue. Traces of sugary spice stick to her skin. My tongue sweeps across and gathers the tiny specks and her moans fill the room.

"Churro," I say with my lips pressed near hers, wanting her to feel the vibration of the trill of my tongue.

She swallows and takes a breath. Her lips form into a pucker and her eyebrows scrunch up close and then separate.

"Choo-row," she attempts to repeat with a giggle. I suppress the smile that threatens to form on my face. It doesn't matter that she can't see me. She shouldn't be rewarded for misbehaving. It's the principle. She barely tried.

My first instinct is to punish her. I contemplate landing a heavy slap on one of her breasts or far deeper to where I'm not supposed to go. Still, I do what I shouldn't -- lean forward and capture her lips. They're still covered in sweet and savory churro dust. The sharp edges of the crumbs prick our tongues when they meet.

Emmy's feet dig into the mattress again. Her hands claw up my arms in an attempt to lower me or in insistence to allow her to rise. I'm not sure which. I do know I'm not supposed to be enjoying this. We were never meant to kiss. Especially not like this.

She would taste this sweet even without the sugar. Her skin has already proven to be addicting. I wouldn't be here if it wasn't. Somehow one in-person meeting has sprawled into this; me hunched over a naked girl who's desperately trying to hold on to something that was never supposed to be.

Emmy exhales a breath when our lips part and our tongues no longer tangle their lies together. My teeth clamp down on her bottom lip before she gets too far.

"Sorry," she whispers after I tug it free. "I'll try again."

She does. Her face scrunches the same as it did before. She puckers her lips and then relaxes them. I try not to kiss them again. Even though they're now only stained with the blended color of her lip gloss, they're still beautiful.

Just like her.

"Chul-low," she rolls out, holding her tongue in the incorrect position. As wrong as she could possibly get.

I sigh and run my hand down her stomach to the place I've tried the hardest to not go myself. Emmy's thighs part further than necessary and her hips tilt upward. My touch against her lips is light. Just enough for a few sticky strands of her to attach to my finger. Her twitch is faint. Her gasp is light and airy.

"Try again." I bring the glistening blend to my lips and taste her for the first time. She tastes just as forbidden as I knew she would. My mouth waters with a new craving that will never be satisfied. This first time has to also be our last.

Better make the best of it.

Emmy mumbles to herself while more cinnamon-sugar sprinkles splatter onto her skin. She accepts tiny pieces in an attempt to please me. The goal is purely personal. She has nothing to gain from learning one Spanish word correctly, but I'll relish the fact that she did it because of me. Whether she knows it or not. Whether they know it or not. Her pronunciation was mine to produce. No one else could have done it. Not this way. Not with her squirming under scrutiny while equally yearning for a punishment...or a reward. She's not picky about which.

Usually I sway in one direction. The punishment used to be enough. Something else is seeping into our dynamic, but I can adapt.

Rewards can be just as deadly. I round the corner of the bed to the end. The middle of her is covered in her wetness, thick, shiny...and delicious. When I touch her thigh where her body curves at the base of her ass she shivers. As badly as I want to believe it's fear, I know it's not. I do it, too. She'll never know it, but at times when she infiltrates my mind, I feel a jolt zap through me that takes me a while to shake off. Eventually, I do, but sometimes it takes a while.

Since I'll be taking my time with her tonight, it'll be longer than a few minutes. I've already broken the rules. Might as well stay for a few hours.

Her shaking increases the closer my face gets to her pussy. I inhale her scent, flip out my tongue and with the tip take one long swipe up in between her lips.

Emmy squirms. She scratches at the bed spread and belts out a pleasurable groan.

"Please," she whispers and raises and lowers her hips so my tongue continues to taste her. I laugh at how predictable she is. Pleading for mercy has never crossed her mind. Pleading for pleasure is always first on her list of priorities.

"Churro," I break away from her and repeat the word from my position between her thighs.

She sighs and turns her head from side to side on the hotel's stark white pillows. "Choo-dough," she butchers. Her attempt is shorter this time, but delivery is equally as inaccurate.

That won't do.

The spices from the churro scratch against her skin as my fingers trill up her stomach to cup her breasts. Light brown specks stick to her erect nipples. Emmy places her hand on top of mine and forces me to squeeze her breasts into the palm of her hand.

She'll blame me for it later. She'll say that I forced her to do it, but we'll both know the truth. I gave her an opportunity and she went after what she wanted because she didn't know how to ask for it herself.

I can't complain. The act causes her to arch her back and press her chest forward. Her hips rise, too. In my new position, my thigh settles in between hers, but not close enough for her to use the placement to her advantage. She would love, too, but I can't. That's one rule that I won't be breaking tonight.

"Churro," I repeat for the third time tonight. Instead of my thigh, I reach one hand down and melt my fingers through the slick wetness that covers her sex. I don't press forward, even though I want to. I don't glide one finger down her middle and watch her squirm in ecstasy, even though I would enjoy the sight of her at my mercy.

I wait.

I trap the freed nipple between my lips and suck.

She gasps and this time her *please* is quieter. My teeth scrape against her nipple and Emmy's hands reach up and pull at her hair in frustration.

"Why does it matter how I say it? Everyone knows what I mean," she whines through labored breaths. Her breathing slows. I can't see her eyes behind the blindfold, but I imagine them fluttered closed in frustration. She's not getting what she wants from me. Not completely, but she's not in charge here. This isn't Emmy's fantasy.

It's mine.

"Churro," I say against her lips, putting an end to her squirming. Emmy hands untangle from her strands and slide against the side of my face. I repeat the word again and feel her copying me, readjusting her tongue over and over until she's successful. It's a small success -- a low trill that ends in a giggle.

"That kind of tickles," she says. Her hands leave mine and she rolls them across her jaw and lips, ending our enriching kiss. My lips trail down her throat and past her collarbone. She squirms again. I feel the strands of my hair tug in her grip. The tension does nothing to deter me. I'm no fool. I know she's not a fragile little thing scared to feel my touch or fully experience what it will be like to be my evening treat. I've deprived myself of her long enough. It's a reward, really. A testament of how good of a job I've done keeping her in line.

"Oh, fuck," She breathes, not being able to withstand the second time my tongue makes contact with her. I place a steady hand on her stomach to steady her hips and stop them from rising. The ring of her belly button presses against my hand. I fight the urge to tug at it and instead, think of all of the other things I could punish her for.

How many people did she talk to at the amusement park? Did she flirt with anyone? Bend over a little too far or get her t-shirt too wet on purpose, so others would notice? If she did she hasn't told me about it yet, which means she's probably saving it for another time to entice me back into bed with her.

I press in a finger at the thought. She gasps and tugs a little harder, mumbling words I don't bother to strain myself to hear. The cinnamon sugar is still glittering against her wetness. I can taste the sweetness and feel the crunch brush against the inside of my cheek. Emmy's breathing grows more erratic the more I move inside of her, teasing her clit with my tongue as I go.

"Please, I can't take it." Of course, she can. She thinks this is a punishment. It can be. I could torture her all night like this. Even when my tongue grows tired, I could suck at her lips and kiss her clit until her body grows still and there's no movement left in her except for small twitches of defeat. A breath exhales from her chest, but is abruptly cut off at the long swipe of my tongue. "Fuck!" she curses down at me.

My chin swishes against what I'm unable to drink up in my position. My face is a mess. It glides across the stickiness against her thighs with ease.

"How do you say please in Spanish?!" Her desperate tone rings through the room even as her hips buck against me, aiding in her own downfall. "My brain isn't working. I can't think! This isn't fair. Please..."

Fair. She's never thought about fair before. Not during those years before we ever touched each other's skin, when it was her fantasies we were playing out from a distance. Fair didn't seem to matter then. Lucky for her I learned my lesson with fairness a long time ago. It's not fairness that has sustained our arrangement for all these years. It's vengeance. Her cravings to incite and then enjoy her punishments is what brought us here. I am only fulfilling my duty as her accomplice.

All she can do is sigh when I refuse to heed. Her fingers untangle from my hair and her nails claw at her skin. I shake any thoughts of me kissing away whatever wounds she leaves behind.

"Churro," she rolls out perfectly. I smile despite myself. Pride keeps my finger in place, exiting slowly and twirling just a little to her splatter of breaths. She repeats the word with her breasts smashed together in her hands. I dip my tongue in the same place as my finger and don't stop my movements until I feel the spasm of her muscles and her body convulse against the bed. When she's done, her hips aren't bucking anymore, though they still wind up in front of my slathered face.

Her thighs collapse from around me and she lets out a long breath. "I thought you were trying to kill me," she says. I smile and wipe my face with the back of my hand. The bed creaks and the mattress sinks with my exit.

"Please," she calls out. "Can you stay with me?"

The request halts my movement against the soft carpeting, reminding me that I've paid a lot more money than I ever have before. Not that she's ever commented on the difference.

She's taken her punishments wherever I've deemed fit, never preoccupied with the contrast. I look back at her. Her eyes are still covered by the blindfold.

"Could you hand me my scarf? I dropped it on my pile."

I do as she asks. The head scarf is folded neatly on top of her clothes. It's mostly black with colored flowers and a few flying bees. She sits up and turns when I approach the bed. I unsnap the back of the blindfold and tie on the scarf to her instructions. She likes it tight so it won't slip off. The knot has to stay on the edge of her hair, so as not to leave a mark. I know this, but I do as she says anyway.

Blindly, she pulls back the covers and slips inside.

She moves over and makes room for me and I carefully slide in behind her. The spot is warm from her earlier body heat. Probably all the thrashing she was doing. I feel her hand search for mine underneath the covers. When she finds it, she laces our fingers together.

"Is it okay if I talk about myself? I'd rather learn more about you, but I'm okay with waiting." I hesitate and consider her question. I have nothing to lose from hearing her talk. She likes to. It was that way before we met in person as well. That's not what's changed. It's the feeling that accompanies her words I try not to focus too much on. Why do I want to know more about her? More than I already know. It will be useless information. Nothing that will make a difference in the long run.

My hand squeezes hers in confirmation. "I love the idea of staying in a cabin in the winter, but I hate the cold. My favorite thing to do is sleep. My mama would always make fun of me for taking a nap in the middle of the school day."

She strings more words together to give me a picture of her life. I contribute nothing to the conversation, but she doesn't seem to mind. "I have one sister. I wish we were closer, but it just feels like we've lived two separate lives. Sometimes, I'm not sure if she really gets me. My best friend usually plays that role. We've been tight since we were babies. Maybe you'll be able to meet her one day."

Someday, one day.

I squeeze her tight around the middle in response.

"You feel so warm," she says as she snuggles closer, scooting her body against me. "Thank you for inviting me. I know it wasn't easy for you."

It was fucking hard. I thought about it so many times. I changed my mind. Canceled a reservation. Then I made another one. Every day with her messages and every night I spend in her presence makes everything so much harder than it was ever supposed to be.

And somehow with all that contemplation, need and regret, tonight, this is the only place I want to be.

Chapter Thirteen
Gabriella

THE WORST THING ABOUT having to work with Taylor at the rescue is enduring her presence. Sara insists on it. She was less than thrilled about Taylor catching me tailing her, but lightened up at the opportunity for publicity.

I've been following Taylor to the rescue for months now. She has a history of posting photos with various animals on social media, but she never tagged the rescue. I don't even think she's ever formally hosted any of the adoption events. There is not one article I remember reading where she declares her love for crafts or animals.

And yet, here she is. She dresses them, walks them, feeds them and cleans them. Although her current leadership role is with the rabbits, she seems to spend an equal amount of time in all the animal houses. Even a surprising amount of time with the rats. 'They're very misunderstood, you know.'

She does that a lot. All around the rescue, every day we come in to volunteer, she spouts out some animal care fact I swear she thinks is going to blow my mind.

Before, I may have argued that Taylor was only single because she was picky, stuck-up, self-centered and controlling. Any of those would work. I could never lie and say she isn't beautiful. Everyone knows that, especially me, who has had the displeasure of listening to Sara rant about Taylor's physical appearance for years.

While the other options could very much be true, it has amazed me how good she is at missing the obvious. For weeks now I've had to watch the resident dog groomer gawk at her from across the room, finding every excuse she can to travel from her grooming studio to the rabbit house.

Taylor has her usual pleasant demeanor when speaking and waving to her, but it's nothing special. I can tell. She hasn't realized that when the ol' girl asks her what she's doing on the weekend, she's asking her out on a date. She's oblivious to her constant presence, her ridiculous jokes, and my least favorite—running her fingers through her hair for inspiration.

It's sick.

I delete all photos I take of them to send to Sara.

Taylor's been involved with the organization for a long time. I can tell they like and respect her, but I can also see the cracks. Another casualty of her obliviousness.

She's been more preoccupied than usual this week—staring off into space, and checking her phone, only to look disappointed afterward. I hesitate to assume she's dating someone when I have seen no evidence of that myself. I wouldn't want to get Sara too excited over nothing.

"You know what I find weird about your relationship with Sara?"

Today's the first time we've been alone since our parking lot tug-of-war. With time ticking away to the start of the adoption event, they suggested I help Taylor with the props she created for the show. And now my hands are covered in acrylic paint and glitter.

While they've been great at pretending to be friends in front of the cameras, neither Taylor nor Sara have made any effort to speak to one another outside of Bonnie's assignments. Tomorrow will be their latest friendship charade for a magazine spread. Sara has high hopes that she, alone, will grace the cover.

"Are you asking me because you think I care?"

"No. I just think it's weird how people would talk about you, but also not talk about you, you know? Like, only talk about you as Sara's girlfriend, but never as Gabriella."

"I'm not important on set."

"Unless you're ruining someone's life." She looks me square in the face. "But that's what I mean. When the rumors first started, everyone said it was Sara. It wasn't until later—Jessica Matthews, maybe—that people started saying it was Sara's girlfriend who was responsible."

Jessica Matthews was an actor I locked in a crew van and drove offset. The day had been filled with technical delays and poor Jessica went to take a nap. I didn't drive it too far away, just far enough for people to look for her for a short amount of time before deciding she must've abandoned filming. No one batted an eye since she was a few years older than us. She only had one scene with Sara, but Sara didn't want to share it with anyone. She didn't like Jessica because she was taller and believed the producers had made a mistake in casting her.

Sara never left the set. It was only logical someone else had driven Jessica away. Still, no one ever said anything to us about it directly.

"How is Jessica these days?"

"I heard she moved back to New Jersey."

"Pity. Some people just can't hack it."

My chalkboard bunny rabbit painting looks pretty good. I push it over to Taylor knowing she's about to ruin it with Mod Podge and glitter. It doesn't matter. They'll mysteriously get lost before the show and never see the light of day.

"I know it's you who keeps leaking stories to the press."

Leaking stories to the press is stupid and tedious. You have to have relationships with people to do that and I don't like any of the vloggers enough to talk to them.

Missy has been giving several interviews about her date with Taylor. Her allegations aren't terrible. She talks in circles, not revealing much of anything. At least until a few nights ago, when she referred to Taylor while squirting water into her mouth with a water gun.

"Give it a rest. People already know you have a vagina." I try in vain to fluff the stubborn glitter off my sweatshirt.

"Gabriella, my parents have to see that shit." She huffs, almost sounding defeated.

"Just tell them it's not true."

"I will not talk to my parents about my sex life."

She's modest even when she's angry. The article insinuated Taylor had a certain talent in the bedroom. A streaming, wet one.

"If it's not true, just have your people put out a statement calling her a liar."

"You know I can't do that." I know. And Sara does, too.

She stares at me without blinking a few beats too long. It must be so hard trying to always pretend you have it all together. It makes little sense for her to worry about the article. She'll be fine. She always complains about something being unfair and eventually comes out on top. Anything for attention, I guess.

"You could also just move. What actor in L.A. retires in L.A.? You look so unserious."

"I should be able to live wherever I want. My job doesn't give people the right to bother me." She dips the paintbrush into the bottle of Modge Podge and smears it across the chalkboard bunny's face.

I cringe. "Who bothers you? Your 24-hour concierge? The masseuse they have on standby for you downstairs? Your trainer? You have a butler that delivers your packages to you and a rooftop park with a farm. Do you hear yourself right now? You live in a $15,000-a-month fortress and you're acting like the world's biggest victim."

"It's 9.5k." She talks down to the bunny rabbit while covering his body in gold glitter.

"What?"

"This apartment with my *three* rooftop parks, car wash and detail service, and private surf lessons costs $9,500 a month. The three bedrooms start at $13,000, but alas, there's only two of us." A noise sounds off downstairs in the living room and although I can't see her, I know Nicole's responsible for it.

"How many lectures do you give Sara about living in *Brentwood* in a house worth millions? I didn't realize you were her bodyguard and her accountant."

I toss the stupid package of bows she handed me earlier to decorate a sign with. "Why did you invite me here? If you just wanted to argue, you could've sent a text."

"I don't want to argue with you. I want you to understand that what you and Sara do has real-life consequences. I'm a person, Gabriella. I'm not a character on a TV show."

"That's where you're wrong." The fierce look she summons during her speech drains from her face. "You're whatever I want you to be."

The air is still warm when I walk outside. Taylor graciously provided me with a visitor's parking pass to save me the drama of having to find parking on the streets of Santa Monica. I bide my time walking around the lot, craning my neck and straining my ears to hear the beep of my alarm, lightly tapping the button that's supposed to produce some kind of sound alerting me to my car's location.

I venture back up the walkway into the shiny glass building and press the only button familiar to me. It's Nicole who answers the door this time, having decided I had been gone long enough for her to escape her bedroom.

"Did you forget something?" Her smile isn't as sugary sweet as the one Taylor preserves for pleasantries. She's supposed to be the nice one. Genuinely. Her parents are pastors or something. I've never met them and before today, I've only heard good things about Nicole. You can't believe everything you hear.

"My car won't start." She sighs and then reaches for a pair of keys looped on the hook nailed to the wall.

"I can give you a jump." I hold up a hand and shake my head.

"It's not the battery." She stops with her keys grasped in her hand.

"How do you know that?"

"I just had a new one put in two days ago."

Lies. They're all lies. Nicole allows her grip on the keys to loosen and her arm to fall. She reaches into her back pocket and slides out her cell phone.

"I'll call the car service."

"I went by the desk. They're closed." I passed by the desk on the way upstairs. They're not closed.

"Ok. Are you going to call Sara to pick you up?" She searches around me, presumably looking for the cell phone she expects me to already be using.

"I tried. She didn't pick up."

"Did you call an Uber?"

My mouth falls open at the suggestion. "You expect me to ride with a stranger? At this time of night?" Nicole glances behind her toward the kitchen.

"Is this your way of asking for a ride?"

"Not at all." I cross the threshold, shouldering my way through the small opening. Her shoulders stiffen against me before she steps to the side. My feet slide out of the sneakers I barely tightened on my way out. "I figured since Taylor and I are going to the same place tomorrow, I can just ride with her."

"And where exactly do you plan to sleep?" As if summoned from a dark abyss, Taylor appears at the top of her ridiculous spiral staircase, dressed in a long t-shirt with her hair tied up in a scarf. I throw my backpack on the floor in front of the couch. The view is impressive. I stare out the glass windows into the lights of the Santa Monica pier.

"This is fine. I'm not a stranger to sleeping on the floor." Sleeping on the couch is bad manners. It ruins the cushions and shortens the lifespan of the furniture. "Helps with my back." I tap my lower back gently, bending slightly for dramatics. The lines on Taylor's face smooth over. Nicole's arms remain crossed.

The rug greets my back with praise for tonight's accomplishment. It's one of those soft shaggy ones. Boldly white.

The click of the kitchen light is faint. Doors open and close in the distance. My body feels the late hour tick by. My eyes flutter closed for a few seconds before I stretch them out again. I used to not be able to sleep when there was any type of light nearby, but after sleeping in a variety of places over time, you adjust.

The sound of footsteps comes from up the iron stairs. Slowly. As if she has all the time to give tonight. The pillow she drops makes a soft sound next to me.

"The rug is wool, so it should keep you warm tonight, but here's a blanket, just in case." The blanket she sits on the couch. A sideways glance tells me there are two blankets. One thinner and lighter, just in case the wool rug does its job and one thicker, just in case the wool fails.

"Thanks." I turn my attention back to the view of the Ferris wheel. She stands there for a while, minutes too long, presence too stifling. I won't sleep much at all tonight, but I certainly can't with her standing here, watching me. Finally, she leaves. Her departure sounds slower than her arrival, with each step increasing the rhythm of my heart rate.

I wasn't always like this. I don't think. Sometimes it's hard to remember. In the early days, when I would go with Sara to her acting classes, there wasn't anyone for me to be with. I'm not an actor. And I've never wanted to be one. It would have been nice to be left at home to do whatever I wanted instead of sitting at the back of Sara's classes, watching them improvise with exercises I could never tease Sara about after.

There was a girl. Once. She complained along with me about the wait. Her twin sister was the actor. She was normal. I had just stopped going to school that year after switching to independent study for Sara's benefit. I did not know how much I would miss it until this girl came along to complain about it.

The girl told too many stories. They were fun stories I told to Sara, who I thought was never truly listening by the way she would nod and sometimes interrupt me with unrelated statements or observations.

That girl hated everyone and everything. Every dance theme. Every student council candidate. Her teachers were all out to get her and her friends were constantly mad at each other about something. Every day. I liked her. She was someone who talked a lot, but was also great at telling a story. Conversations feel easier when the other person is doing all the work.

One day, I said something interesting enough to catch Sara's attention. The next day was the first I had ever heard that girl's sister cry. I never saw the girl again after that.

I allow an hour to pass by before I lift myself from the warm rug. The stairs make no noise under the weight of my footsteps. There's a small room right before Taylor's bedroom where she keeps the exercise equipment she most likely never uses. No light comes from underneath the door. The handle turns without resistance. The moon illuminates my path to her nightstand.

She's one of those quiet sleepers who barely makes a sound. No snoring or rolling around. No talking or whispering or weird positioning. She sleeps on her side with one hand tucked underneath her pillow. Her expression is calm.

Her phone slips from the nightstand into my grip, quietly. It asks me for a password I don't need. The screen displays a photo of Taylor and her family in the background. The light dims on their faces with a press of a button. I toss the phone in the hamper on the way out.

"Sweet dreams, Princess." As expected, my whisper goes unanswered.

It's an easy trek to Nicole's room. Her door also opens easily. Her phone is more difficult to find. After my eyes don't find it where I think it should be, I search for it beneath the blankets where I find it on the empty side of the bed. I place Nicole's phone on the shelf in the laundry room. With all the privileges that come with living here, I doubt they use it. I drop their keys in the tea-labeled canister in the kitchen.

My car engine turns smoothly. I only have a few hours to sleep before I have to be at the photoshoot with Sara. While any other night I would resist it, I pull onto the street I've never felt like I belonged, even though it was the place I slept and ate at more often than my own. Sara's asleep when I get upstairs. Her room is pitch black and still. I try my best not to wake her. It's too late to engage in her preferred planning and schemes. I'm feeling more emotions tonight than I should.

Tomorrow won't have a big impact on Taylor. Not like she thinks it will. She's gotten over a lot of things. She'll get over this, too.

I successfully take off my outside clothing before getting into bed. Sara's eyes flutter open and then close again. Her hands graze over my now half-naked skin. She pulls herself closer to me. The soft kiss she lands on my shoulder scatters my thoughts and deepens the twisted feeling knotting its way through my belly.

"Finally," she whispers, sliding her body over mine.

She takes barely any effort to finish undressing me. This is usually how it goes. In the past, I've used stored memories to get me through these moments and to prepare me for the slight physical pain.

I'm used to the emotional scarring in times like this when she needs me to provide her with a different type of release. Except this time, I don't need the visuals. Taylor has already unwittingly provided me with everything I require.

I feel it every time she throws me a look or an insult. For each second she takes her time inspecting my body, always starting at the same places. From my neck to my arms to my wrist. She does it at every meeting. No matter how many people are around or who's paying attention. She notices me.

I have never seen Sara angry. Not really. Not in the way people would think. That someone else could replace her is a dream that has haunted her before she ever stepped into my life.

She gives me a few minutes after closing my eyes to touch me. It used to be shorter, but Sara has grown more patient over the years. I don't ask what sparked this one. I learned a long time ago it didn't matter what made her upset. The results are always the same.

"You understand, right, Brie?" I give her the nod she's looking for, knowing it's true. I *am* the only one who understands. Her fingers sink into me at the same time the blade makes its first lick. It doesn't burn nearly as bad as it did the first time. Each slice gets easier. Each mark against my skin heals faster than the one before.

I have been a shield for Sara for many things. Through me, she expresses her emotions without consequence. I make it possible for her to be good enough. No matter what it costs me. The darkness that covers my name and smokes out my reputation is irrelevant. The more she suffocates me, the easier it is for her to breathe.

Chapter Fourteen
Taylor

NO SUN SHOULD RISE at five-thirty in the morning. Not during the months of summer, and especially not when you forget to close the curtains at night. I bury my face under my pillow, willing the sun to go away again. If it wasn't for Gabriella, this would have never happened. Fighting with her last night forced me to start my nighttime routine later than usual. And then she came back, which made me forget to close my curtains, blinding me hours before I'm scheduled to get up. Not looking at your phone is key in times like this. Knowing the damage of how many hours of sleep have been stolen from you is the worst feeling. Instead, I roll out of bed, pull the curtain panels together and snuggle under my blankets once again.

I can hear the swoosh of cars passing through the Santa Monica traffic, with people traveling to the beach on a Saturday morning. Oddly enough, I'm not an avid beach person. It's the sand. I hate it. It gets everywhere it shouldn't and it takes forever to make it go away. I run as fast from the waves as a surfer swims toward them. The safest place for me at the beach is in the parking lot.

My hand smacks against the wood surface where my phone should be. I search around, pounding my palm on random spots, waiting until it lands on exactly what I need. My hand bangs against the tissue box, the TV remote, and my emergency nighttime lip balm, before my fingers catch hold of the lightweight charger cord.

I finally peer over. At some point last night, my phone must've fallen to the floor. I lean my upper body over the side of the bed but see nothing. It didn't bounce underneath the bed, either, and I didn't leave it on the bathroom counter.

I check behind my nightstand, on top of my crafting desk. Nothing. I remember flipping through social media right before bed. I check all the places it shouldn't be. The living room is free of Gabriella. The blankets look to be in the same spot I left them in with the pillow I let her borrow sitting on top of the pile. I check the couch cushions and then underneath the couch. The kitchen counter is free from clutter, and pristinely wiped down before bed, which is how Nicole likes it.

I glance up at the time on the microwave and realize—

"Shit!"

It's 9:03 a.m. I was supposed to leave for my interview with Sara at 8:30 a.m.

I run into Nicole's bedroom for her phone. Her nightstand is empty.

"Nicole." My soft, but urgent whisper does nothing to wake her. I shake her, adding more pressure with each second that passes without her opening her eyes.

"Nicole, I need to borrow your phone. I can't find mine. I'm late for the interview." With eyes still closed, she reaches her hand under her pillow and swipes at the smooth surface. Nothing. She tosses the pillow to the side. It rolls before falling to the floor. Still nothing. She tosses the other one. The comforter goes first. Then the sheets. Each layer we strip from the mattress reveals nothing new.

"I don't understand," Nicole mumbles to herself.

I do.

"She really will do anything for her." The realization of my words reaches Nicole's slow-waking brain in waves. The lines Nicole's face produces remain stuck in disbelief.

"No way."

My laptop is right where it should be. My app won't sync because my phone is off and its last location was right here in my home. I know Gabriella didn't take the phones to steal them. She'll never admit to taking them at all.

"We should just go. I'll drive you. You can get dressed in the car." Nicole paces around my room in frustration.

I already laid my clothes out. It's an old habit from childhood when my mama would get our clothes together for the week. I've never been late for an interview before. I've never been late for any job. Gabriella has made me look unprofessional and unreliable even while semi-retired. They could spin this in a million different ways. It's amazing how someone could twist your reputation to dismantle it, even when it's a good one.

"No, I don't think I should go. If I go, they win."

"No, if you don't go, they win." She lists everything they could say about me. "They'll say you're not really bisexual or you're only using the community for clout. They'll say you're trying to distance yourself or you don't want to be labeled. If you don't go, they'll call you a fake and a liar and you can't say 'Sorry everyone, Sara's girlfriend stole my phone.'"

She's right. No one would believe it and Sara would only spin it as me trying to pick a fight with her. She would win.

"But if I go, I look just as bad. They can still say all of those things and they'd feel justified because I was late. Suddenly, I'm lazy, unprepared and lack professionalism. Suddenly, I don't value other people's time. They still win."

Nicole huffs and sinks to the floor on my pile of blankets. I pull my laptop towards me again and do the only thing that makes the most sense.

> To: BSilvers@faculty.mail.com
> From: Ttownes@student.mail.com
> Subject: Sick
>
> ———————————————————————
>
> Hi Bonnie,
>
> I'm sorry to have to send this email late. I made a terrible dinner choice last night and ate leftover sushi right before bed (stupid, I know). I'm exhausted. Somehow the bathroom floor became my new resting place and I'm just now waking up. And to make it worse, I can't find my phone anywhere. I'm hoping I didn't accidentally flush it down the toilet during my many trips to the bathroom.
>
> When you have a chance, if you could please pass on the student association's email address to me, that would be great. I'd like to apologize to them directly.
>
> I hope all goes well with the interview and shoot today. I'm sure Sara will kill it.
>
> Hope to speak to you soon.
>
> Taylor

Nicole scrutinizes my email before making adjustments of her own. She squishes some words together, makes grammar mistakes where there were none, and rewrites a few sentences.

"What now?" I shrug, completely at a loss for words and strategy. There is no direct competition between Sara and me. I'm not actively auditioning or booking roles. I'm not attacking her in the press. Me being a threat to her career is a story of which she is the sole author.

"I don't know."

We find our keys hidden in a canister in the kitchen and our phones in places they shouldn't be. Even if we wanted to, we couldn't deny Gabriella's involvement. It's my fault she was here. It's my fault that I will have to work with her at the center, and it may even be my fault that she's targeting me at all. Though if that's the case, I don't regret a single thing.

Emmy [4:52 p.m.]

This might sound weird but, can I take you out on a date?

I need a pick-me-up and a reprieve from Sara and her girlfriend trying to ruin my life. Bonnie responded favorably to my email only a few minutes later, attaching her images of Sara sitting next to the interviewer. Her message was simple enough: "Don't worry. Get well soon. I'll talk to them about rescheduling."

Minutes tick by without a response from Daisy. My request is not all thanks to Gabriella and her meddling. I've been thinking about this for a while, even before I asked Daisy to stay the night with me at the hotel.

Emmy [5:07 p.m.]

We could go to the movies. One of us can come in after the lights go down and just not look at each other.

It sounds silly in my head. Going on a blind date—well, blind. I'm the reason the rules were ever in place and now Daisy won't break them.

Daisy [5:10 p.m.]

Ok.

I scroll through the current movie selections and hit send on my response.

Emmy [5:16 p.m.]

Rom-Com? Drama? Oscar bait war movie?

I bypass the latest horror movie since it's clear I won't be able to cower against her. It's amazing to me that after two years, we've never had this conversation. We did everything backward.

Daisy [5:17 p.m.]

Comedy?

Shit. I hate comedy. Most comedies depicted in movies aren't my kind of comedy. They're either too crass or too freaking weird. Still, even though I won't be able to see her laugh, I'd at least know what her laugh sounds like.

Emmy [5:18 p.m.]

Sure. 7?

Seven o'clock seems like a respectable time to meet with a girl you may or may not have already had sex with.

Daisy [5:18 p.m.]

8ish. I'm just getting off work.

Daisy's job is a mystery to me. She never seems to work on the same days at the same times. I could visit her there. If it's at a coffee shop, I can sit and read or do homework.

I calm the ache in my heart with a slice of cinnamon toast. The secret to good cinnamon toast is making sure the butter is still hot when the cinnamon goes on, forcing it to sink into the bread. Anyone who disagrees with that can argue with their mama. They're wrong.

It only takes a few clicks of a button to purchase the tickets, select the seats and pre-order the food. I'm three cinnamon toasts deep when Nicole finds me laid out on the couch. Moving in together was a natural decision, and I have no regrets. For one, Nicole is barely home on the weekends. While I've been on my dating journey, she's been working to nudge her boyfriend toward wedding bells.

"Do you want me to cook tonight?" She eyes the crumbs on my plate with amusement playing across her lips. I open my mouth to respond, only to remember I haven't told Nicole anything about Daisy. Our relationship was never supposed to go on this long. We're well past summer and entering the fall. I never imagined I'd still be seeing Daisy and contemplating the beginning of other things.

"Oh. Hm...you should sit."

Stunned, Nicole makes a slow decline onto the coffee table behind her. She watches me silently debate on how best to start.

"I met a girl."

Nicole is up and off the table before I can continue. The dance she does around the room is a mixture of something too difficult to describe. "I knew it! It was the shoes!" she says while spanking the air with her palm.

Nicole gifted me a pair of rainbow stilettos weeks ago. I posted a photo of them online and received plenty of compliments and sure—some direct flirty messages. Direct messages are a sure way for people to expose your personal business on the internet. I never respond to them.

"I've actually known her for a few months now."

"Oh. That's okay. Tell me about her." Nicole resumes her seat, looking less enthused than before, but still attentive.

"Her name is Daisy. We met up a few times and I think I want to pursue something more between us."

Nicole clamps her hand over her mouth and squeals.

"You wanna have sex with her?" she whispers.

Oh shit. Nicole and I both hadn't had sex for very different reasons. Me, because I hadn't found someone I liked enough, until Daisy, and Nicole because, well, Jesus.

"No...yes...no...I–"

"You had sex and didn't tell me?"

"I didn't know how." I couldn't quite put *Hey Nicole, I'm thinking about going to have sex with this stranger* into a coherent sentence. One that wouldn't encourage her to lock me in my room, or worse, tell my parents.

Nicole takes in slow breaths and pushes the air from her lungs at an even slower rate. I wait until she's done, fully aware that I've been a bad best friend by withholding so much from her these past few months.

"I feel like you don't tell me anything anymore."

"Nicole, I–"

"No. You've kept your relationship with this girl a secret and you didn't tell me anything about what Sara and her girlfriend did at the festival. I was right there. You know I would've never let them get away with that."

I throw my hands up in surrender. "You're right. I'll start from the beginning, but please don't trip out on me. Everything I'm about to tell you is a little unconventional."

The movie theater is empty when I arrive. When the food is delivered, I set it up on the armrest between us with Daisy's selections on her side, so she won't have to reach across. My stomach hasn't stopped churning and I have to sit on my hands to stop them from shaking. This is ridiculous. We've been together plenty of times in more intimate situations. I tried to spare Nicole those details, only telling her I thought Daisy was just going to be a hookup, someone to help me release my feelings in private. She gawked at the idea that I'd never laid eyes on her directly. *"I'm sure she's figured it out, but is keeping it a secret until you're ready. Isn't that a good sign?"*

Since slacking on my disguise, I've been suspicious she already knows who I am. She has mentioned nothing about it and Nicole's right—our arrangement hasn't gotten out to the press. Maybe she doesn't care at all.

Mini explosions go off in my heart each time someone new walks in. My eyes stay glued to the dimmed phone screen until the danger passes. When the lights darken and the trailers start to roll, I panic in a different way. What if Daisy doesn't show? What if I'm left here like a complete idiot on a movie date alone?

I watch scene after scene of upcoming action, animated and thrillers. Some people find it strange that being in a blockbuster has never been a dream of mine. I enjoy working in television. I like long-term relationships and predictable schedules. As exhausting as growing up in front of the camera can be, on the flip side, you get to watch your character grow up, too.

I spent hours in guitar lessons, so when Dream Daniels got her solo on the show, people believed it. She had grown from a scared, timid kid to a badass musician. The network even included a scene at the end of the show of me performing the song live. And although Piper Paige was always a confident, young detective, throughout the show she learns to think less about her reputation and care more about the surrounding people. Sure, they could have shown all of that in two and a half hours, but it feels more meaningful when you, as the actor, are going through similar struggles. I was just as insecure as Dream, but when I nailed that solo, I felt like a pop star.

The seat reclining next to me pops me out of my thoughts. I remember not to turn my head at the last second, only glimpsing the bucket of popcorn lifting from the armrest. The muscles in my chest loosen a bit more. To offer protection, I placed my purse - which I hardly ever wear - between us. I shove it out of the way just a little, feeling the cool leather on my face.

I'm surprised to see she's wearing shorts. Mostly because I cover up at the movie theater as if I'm preparing for a winter trip to Big Bear. The movies are always freezing. Even now, in a hoodie and jeans, my knees are folded up to keep me warm. I swat away at the mental images of using my body to warm hers. She's usually the one in charge of our intimacy, even when the fantasy belongs to me. I haven't even had the privilege of touching her like that, softly. We skipped so many steps.

A small chuckle rolls through her throat, pulling an easy smile from my lips. Too focused on her skin, I missed whatever joke had encouraged her reaction. Her hand fills the spot where the bucket of popcorn, now crammed between her knees, is supposed to be.

Too many thoughts slink in and out of my mind, each with their images attached to what could be or should be. My hopes and my fears. Her fingers loosen enough to allow mine to slide into place. When she squeezes, firmly pressing our skin together, I breathe.

We stay like this. Only releasing our grip when one shifts, and quickly reconnecting again. It's hard to imagine her soft hands previously being so forceful and rough. They're usually so demanding and relentless. Now, her hand sits calmly against my own. Her thumb grazes across mine in a circular pattern.

It tickles.

I love it.

The credits roll without either of us moving. The mid-credit scene only buys us an additional few seconds. It's not very long and pretty unnecessary. I know if I stay, I risk breaking my promise. The lights will come up and there will be no cover for Daisy to maintain her privacy. Maybe she doesn't want to be seen with me. I hadn't thought about it until now. Maybe Daisy knows who I am and she's embarrassed by me. When we first met, she admitted she wasn't a fan of Taylor's—mine. Maybe the reason she has leaked nothing about us is that she's ashamed. She can't even walk out of a movie with me.

My new realization is crushing. My hand slinks out of Daisy's grip. I stand to leave, careful to not look in her direction, grabbing my purse blind. I trust her to take care of the empty food trays on her own.

Daisy [10:33 p.m.]

> *You didn't say good night. I might have to punish you for that.*

Lost breath rushes out of me too quickly. I'm not sure if my shivering spine is reacting to the promise of what's always been or to the promise of more.

Emmy [10:34 p.m.]

> *Come home with me.*

The request feels rash and borderline stupid. When I ran it by Nicole earlier, she said, "Well, she hasn't killed you yet and she's had plenty of opportunities." Exactly! This is fine. This is way more cost-effective than renting a hotel room for the night. I want to be with her again. I want her to be with me. I ... I want to keep her.

Impatient with no response, I send a voice message detailing my plan on how we can make this work until she's ready. The walk home is quiet. The movie theater is less than a block from my apartment on the promenade. Any of the faces I pass on the way home can be hers. I push the volume button on my phone to ensure its ringing capabilities, only to turn the volume down seconds later. Vibration is better. I might miss the ringtone, but I won't miss the buzzing in my hand.

I dim the lights on my way up the stairs, leaving a clear path for

Daisy. In my room, I light a candle on the nightstand and one in the bathroom. My usual spot on the bed is the one furthest from the door. I won't see her come in and I can close my eyes if she needs to go to the bathroom. Once I'm asleep, it won't matter, anyway. Nothing will.

The silence of my cell phone and the still night air is the only thing I can trust for an answer. She's not coming. I've pushed too far. My hopes are too big for what Daisy is prepared to offer me.

A single tear of surprise rolls from my eyes, across the bridge of my nose and into my pillow. I didn't expect this. Maybe I should've. A shallow quake in my heart follows. I did this all wrong. I permit myself to cry for fucking up so badly. There is no coming back from this.

With the full force of my strength, I wipe the tear away. It's stupid to be crying right now. Over this. Over her. I barely know her. She's kept everything from me, even as I've revealed more about myself during our time together. I don't care if she knows who I am.

At least, I didn't.

Chapter Fifteen
Daisy

UNTANGLING MYSELF FROM HER before the sun comes up may be harder than I expected. She pulled me to her last night almost as soon as I slid underneath the covers. She still hasn't let go. I fell asleep with her back pressed against me, with no guidance on what to do next. And she's still here. A small smile plays on her lips while she dreams.

I knew it.

This was only supposed to happen once. After the first time, I showed up again and again. We went from hotels to cars to movie dates and now, sleepovers. She went from hiding herself to laying next to me fully exposed.

What the hell are we thinking?

I should leave before her roommate gets home. I waited as long as I could to make sure it was just the two of us. There was no sign of anyone else in the apartment when I arrived.

Foolishly, I kiss the back of her neck. I allow the guilt and shame to rest inside of me for as long as my lips remain against her skin. She grinds against me in response. I've been on my best behavior. I have stoically positioned my hand on her stomach, over her belly button. I may have brushed against it a few times, but I stayed centimeters above where I shouldn't. I may have even played with the ring she has pierced to her skin there.

But in true Emmy fashion, she's pushing it.

We've never been this exposed by the sun. It's when her faint smile pulls into a full grin that I know she's awake. A slight panic courses through me, but her eyes remain closed.

"You came. I thought you were a dream."

She easily climbs over me, settling on the top of my thighs. Instead of her eyes, her fingers roam. One finger trails across my waistband. Another glides across my breasts. She rises a little, shakes, and then settles again.

"You rarely let me touch you."

It's not on purpose. At the start of this whole thing, I was never the focus. She's always been the reason for everything. And touching her has always felt like enough. I kiss the tips of her fingers in response when she finds her way to my lips. She inches closer after each kiss until her lips land on mine. I want to kiss her every time I see her. I savor every sound we make together, every move of her hips above me. They'll fuel me later when I have to make hard decisions I know will be for the best, eventually.

Her lips leave mine to trail over my jaw. A giggle erupts from my throat when she pinches the skin there with her teeth. Bold. I'll remember that for next time. When her hands tug at my bra, I'm grateful her eyes are closed. Now would not be a good time to explain why my breasts aren't the perfect image she expects them to be.

Her mouth covers one nipple. She makes a sound that vibrates through my skin and sends a response to the place right underneath her. I hate how much I love this. I hate how I keep coming back rule change after rule change.

She was only supposed to be a moment, an insignificant amount of time. Maybe in the future I would've looked back at our time as a rash judgment, a misstep... a regret. Except, I don't know if that will happen anymore.

"I knew I wanted to be with you when you were the only one I could imagine doing this with."

My words hide behind my teeth. I want to say everything and nothing all at once. Blindly, she lifts my waistband and swoops her hand inside. My breath catches in my throat. A pained look crosses her face. The elastic snaps back into place when she pulls her hand free. My lap feels empty and cold when she leaves it to sit back on her side of the bed. The pain eases from her face and is replaced with a more neutral expression.

"I don't want this to be like the other times. I should ask you first. Is it okay if I touch you? Even if it's not, you don't have to leave - unless you want to. I - I want you to stay no matter what. God, this sounds so bad."

I'm sure she means to keep that last part to herself. Her hands sit in her lap like a patient, obedient student. That probably has less to do with me and more to do with her parents. A few strands of hair escaped from her scarf overnight. I take the end of one and run it across her nose. It twitches, but she keeps it together. In hindsight, it's a foolish decision. She could open her eyes at this moment and it would all be over. I'll lose everything. Even her.

I do the hard part for her. My shorts make a sound against the wall they slam into. Placing her hand in mine, I guide her to the exact place she had meant to go minutes before.

We breathe together, with both of us on our knees and our thighs pressed against each other. I slow her pace when she goes too fast. She's always so eager to get the prize. I've waited a long time for her. She can wait a few more minutes for this and maybe a few more weeks for everything else to pass.

That's what I focus on when she buries herself deeper into me and I pull her closer than I ever thought possible. I lay on my back to grant her more access to me. Access she was never supposed to be permitted to have.

I've broken all the rules, even the ones I wrote myself in secret. I'll have to fix it after today before I damage anything beyond repair. For now, I steady her hand and teach her the rhythm I need her to match against me. Today, I keep my thoughts to myself and enjoy how it feels to have her wrapped around me.

When I'm able to put some distance between us, everything will go back to normal. She'll go back to being a deviant goody two shoes and I'll go back to being her escape.

Next time.

"Someone stayed out all night, again." Krystal's the only one sitting in the living room when I arrive. She's still dressed in her pajamas, an extremely modest short set. My usual pillow and blankets are tucked in a corner out of sight. Krystal eyes my stuffed backpack with last night's clothes. My surplus of extra clothes in the trunk of my car came in handy. Spending the night with Emmy was not their intended use, but, hey.

My decision to move in with Krystal and Chasity was last minute. Sara expected me to move into the apartment she rented close to campus, but I knew if I did, she'd misread my intention. I needed a place to stay. I didn't need an overlord.

"Chasity's worried about you, you know." Krystal's teasing smile tells me she doesn't share the same sentiment. Chasity and I have been friends since preschool. Krystal joined our duo in third grade. We've been inseparable ever since. Well, almost. Sara took over my life for a long time. Chasity doesn't like to let me forget it.

"She thinks you're back with Sara and you just aren't telling us." She takes a bite out of the apple she's holding.

"Do we even want to talk about what Chasity thinks about you?"

Krystal slows her chews to think of a response. When we're all together, we pretend there's not an elephant standing in between the two of them. Since Chasity isn't here, that gives me free rein to ask whatever I want.

"I think it's clear Chasity isn't interested in me at all."

Liar.

"Sure." Whatever's going on between them isn't a problem. They're not trying to kill each other and no one has gone missing.

"So, is it Sara?"

"What if I told you it was?"

"I'd fucking cry." She pokes her bottom lip out. "I probably shouldn't be telling you this, but we've talked about asking Carmen to help you." I don't know too much about Carmen other than she comes from a family with a lot of money. While money is something I need, I have no interest in being indebted to another person.

"Don't. I've got it covered."

"You have a terrible habit of not letting people help you."

"It's not about letting people help me. I don't need help. I've got a plan."

"Fine. If it's not Sara, that only leaves one other person."

Krystal's eyes follow me around the kitchen. I busy myself with the rice I pour from the bag into the strainer.

"I'm thinking of chicken teriyaki and rice tonight. What do you think?"

"I think you're in serious trouble."

"I have a plan," I say to her again while she tosses her apple into the trash can. Krystal takes a breath and blows it out, slowly.

"I'll steam the veggies and you can tell me all about this plan of yours. And then we can come up with the emergency plan together. Just so you know, it'll involve ice cream and a road trip. Once this is all over, we'll probably all need comfort and a vacation."

Chapter Sixteen
Gabriella

TAYLOR HAS BEEN ABSENT from class for the last few days. I have to admit; her plan worked. Before coming up with her excuse, several people, including Bonnie, were running around trying to find her. Bonnie even asked me to stand at the school entrance and call her when I saw Taylor's car enter the parking lot. I took a nap on the couch in her office instead.

I woke up to several messages about Taylor being sick. I've never seen so many people happy that someone had food poisoning. Sara is happy. There's not enough time to shoot them both for the cover, especially since Taylor is doing such a good job playing ill.

Nicole walked into the only class we all shared, with immediate apologies on Taylor's behalf. By the end, the professor was offering to send food to the house. Nicole assured him that Taylor was being taken care of by her parents.

They even posted pictures of Taylor tucked underneath her covers. An outcry of support from her fans followed. 'Get better soon. We love you!'

Sara didn't care about the charade. She only focused on the results. Her face will be the one on the magazine cover with her interview smack dab in the center. Not Taylor's.

I'm more than certain she's sitting at home hot gluing elf ears to headbands, getting ready for whatever she has planned for those rabbits for the winter adoption event. She probably already has a list of names written down, like Mr. and Mrs. Claus and Jack and Sally.

And it will all be for nothing.

"We are so excited about what you've planned for the adoption event. Almost as soon as we ended our conversation last week, our phone rang non-stop. At this rate, we might not even have any animals left." Sara beams at the acknowledgment from Linda, the owner of the organization. The plan for Sara to take over the event formed almost as soon as Taylor presented the idea of me becoming a part of the team.

I have no interest in animal welfare. Don't hurt animals is a pretty simple rule to follow and beyond that is someone else's job. This project is a joke. Something for Taylor to preoccupy her time away from the cameras. I can honestly understand why she hasn't made a big show of it, but it was a mistake. Sara will now deliver on everything Taylor has never promised - visibility.

"This is where the pet whisperer is going to go. I've already received so many comments about how excited people are to see her in person." The pet whisperer is some woman on the internet who gained notoriety for successfully matching people with pets that best fit their personality, and sometimes even matched their appearance.

"And Reggie has agreed to offer his pet grooming services for free for a year." Reggie - no known last name - is an award-winning dog groomer. He styles dogs to look like lions and giraffes, using color I'm not exactly sure is even safe to use on animals, but they're pretty and they look good. And best of all, he's agreed to participate in the event for the amount of money Sara offered him.

Linda and her staff express their gratitude over and over. Never once do they mention Taylor. They don't talk about how disappointed she'll be when she sees her designs and hours of hard work sitting in the dumpster. A professional shoot will replace the photos on the website. No cute, small hat or bandana will be in sight. She spent years here, and they forgot about her in seconds.

Taylor walks in with her hands full with drinks and small dessert packages. Her eyes slowly roam from me to Sara. The smile remains on her face with each smoothie deposit she places in their awaiting hands. She laughs away the concerns about her illness, shaking the green juice in its cup.

"I'm doing my best to stay healthy now," she says without an ounce of light in her eyes. I've grown so used to seeing it, I immediately miss it. Linda casually asks to speak with her in the office. Nothing about Linda's demeanor has changed. Everyone moves the same. They don't understand what they're about to take away from her.

Sara coordinates the changes. Taylor's backdrop is removed.

"Should we be doing this right now?" Sara doesn't address Amber's question. From the few weeks I've been here, I got the sense that Amber considers Taylor a friend. They're nowhere near as close as Taylor is to Nicole, but their relationship seems genuine.

Amber packs up the things Sara's team tosses to the side. She places them in their boxes neatly, judgment oozing from her eyes in my direction. I don't bother avoiding her gaze. We both know what I did. Taylor emerges from Linda's office, steady, her face void of any emotion. She scoops up one box as she passes them. Amber follows behind with the other. Sara watches her leave, a smirk clear on her lips.

"Wow, you move fast." Linda marvels at the quick changes. One of Sara's men is already tearing up the artificial grass to make way for Sara's new design.

"We're eager to get started. I hope Taylor's okay with the new plan."

"Oh, she was fine. She's always so good about these types of things." I turn my back on Linda's continued compliments. Amber passes me on her way back in. I swerve in time to keep her body from slamming into me. Even if I deserve it, she's not the one who gets to discipline me for it.

I find Taylor sitting in the open space of the hatchback, her boxes crammed inside. Taylor's tears run freely down her face. I ignore the pain in my gut. *She'll be fine.* I need Sara to be happy long enough to forget me. She needs to feel like she can fly high enough to set me free. Taylor is a casualty of my escape. One day she'll get it. Until then, she'll adapt.

"Did she ever tell you why she hates me?" Her question surprises me. She shouldn't care about what Sara thinks or what she believes. Her time at the center is over. She should go home and enjoy her retirement. Ditching Bonnie as a mentor also wouldn't be a bad idea. I miss the defiant look on her face, how she smiles even when she's pissed. I need her to be okay.

Shrugging my shoulders is bound to upset her. Feigning nonchalance and dismissing her should be what she needs to get back to normal.

"Do you even care? Are you just attacking me on autopilot because your girlfriend told you so?"

"Yes." It's the right response. The only one that matters. Yes, I don't care about you. Yes, I love her. Yes, she's terrible and yes, I'm selfish. All the right responses and yet, only two of them are true.

Taylor can do anything she wants. She can find new bunny rabbits to home and start her own organization with its own silly name. Linda didn't deserve her. In the end, everyone is always out for themselves. The time and energy she's spent in this place meant nothing once Sara walked in promising promotion and money. If

I have learned anything from Sara, it's that everyone has a price, even your parents.

"Shouldn't this be a good thing for you? You've been playing around with the idea of retiring, without ever doing it. Now's your chance."

"Now's my chance? The only reason I haven't been able to live my life how I want is because of you, isn't it? You didn't just magically become Bonnie's intern, only for Bonnie to request me to be placed under her wing, did you?"

I shift my feet against the pavement. My plan was different. None of that matters now because my plan failed. Sara was the only one between the two of us who kept her head on straight long enough for us to complete our goal.

"Sara uses you to do her dirty work because she can't handle not getting everything she wants." She leans close enough for my eyes to catch the scatter of fine glitter that has made its way to her cheeks. "And you don't give a shit about taking that photo because you know she fucks every girl that comes walking her way. The reason people don't notice you isn't because you're easy to miss, it's because of how easily she replaces you."

"Wow." I'm surprised the words come rolling out. They sting. It's not what she says that's hurtful. It's the fact that she's the one saying it. "Congratulations. You finally said something you really mean."

"Are you going to answer that?"

The first notification comes after I drive out of the parking lot of the center, leaving Taylor, teary-eyed and angry, sitting in the back of her car. There is no reason for me to go back inside. Sara won. I almost drive back home to San Diego, but it's the wrong day of the week and the wrong time of day to face traffic. Sara's house is where I end up.

I instinctively start organizing things. She never does it herself and she never allows the housekeeper to do it. Her shirts are folded wrong and her pants are incorrectly hung. Usually, her shoes are lined up for easy access, not thrown in the pile she has them in right now. It's a miracle she's been able to get dressed at all.

"No," I say confidently, not letting on that I've been dying to check my messages for hours. The phone sits in my back pocket, buzzing away, loudly reminding me how badly I've fucked this one up.

"Do you want to see the new press announcement about the event?"

"No." My tone doesn't change. A simple social media post about the event will suffice. A grand notice about Taylor being replaced as a non-profit volunteer feels petty, and I don't think it'll be as effective as Sara is hoping it will be.

"Did you see my message about Lisa Perry?" The gloat in Sara's voice is evident. Unlike Taylor, who walks around pretending everyone is equally important, Sara has never had an issue with name-dropping.

I peek out from the closet to see Sara on the bed, flipping through her beloved notebook. "What about her?"

"I heard she was looking for some help with a new show she's producing and I got you in." Lisa Perry is a very well-known and respected showrunner. She started as a writer, like me, and then began producing her own television shows and now she's unstoppable. She's everything I want to be.

"What's the price?" There are caveats and consequences to this. With Sara, there always are. There's no way I'm getting an opportunity with Lisa Perry without there being some advantage for Sara.

She shrugs, dismissing my concern. "Just tell me you love me." She says it in a playful tone with an unbeatable smile. You don't joke with Sara. With Sara, jokes have hidden meanings woven into a trickier message. "Just tell me you love me" really means "I can feel you leaving me."

And she's right.

"I made you a promise and I plan to keep it." Sara's smile drops. It's a memory forged in my brain from years before that serves as a lesson on what happens when you dare to love someone who doesn't know how to love you back. I not only made a promise to Sara that day, but to myself as well.

"And I'm telling you to break it. Brie, tell me you love me."

There's no way she has ever loved me. Not after all this time. Not when everyone can see how imbalanced we are.

I shake my head, knowing that with each passing second my opportunity with Lisa Perry slips further and further away. Staying used to seem easy. On the outside looking in, traveling with a famous girlfriend would seem fun and exciting. No one would expect it to be all-consuming.

Everything is always about Sara.

"You first." I turn the shirt in my hand inside out and fold it properly. I pick another shirt out of the pile and pretend I don't hear her approach.

"Do you think I'm running around negotiating positions for anyone else? You're the only one I care about." I imagine her face red with anger, talking over me. I refuse to look at her. She doesn't deserve my full attention.

"Should we go down the list of times when that wasn't true?"

"It's always been true. I chose you for a reason. There were hundreds of girls in that school and I chose you."

"That doesn't make me feel any better." I used to sit and try to figure out why fate chose me. Sometimes I decided it was for my family. Other times, I thought it was for Sara. I've never settled on an answer, but so far, it's been more of a cruelty than a benefit.

The row of shoes I organized tumbles back down to the floor. Hangers clang together as the clothes fall to the ground. Energy spent. Time wasted. All for nothing. I abandon the continuously growing pile of Sara's bullshit and head for the door. Her screams follow me as I go.

Chapter Seventeen
Taylor

DAISY HAS ANSWERED NONE of my messages. Nicole was almost as shocked as I was about what happened at the center. She graciously didn't go into a tangent about my boneheaded decision to bring Gabriella into the program. How was I supposed to know that Sara was interested in more than entertainment stardom? What fame does she expect to gain from hosting an adoption event? The whole thing is maddening and to top it all off, the person I think I need isn't responding to me. Nicole offered to come back home for the weekend, but I assured her I'd be okay.

I thought about shopping, but dressing incognito is just as exhausting as pretending I'm not being recognized at all. "Excuse me, are you Taylor Townes? No, but I get that a lot. Is she super famous or something?"

No, thank you.

The rooftop terrace attached to our balcony is busy with other neighbors mingling about. That's what I should be doing. Maybe my focus should've been on living my life as a normal person instead of girls. They really do ruin your life.

Since Nicole isn't home to join me, I busy myself with the giant Connect Four game. Beating myself again and again becomes monotonous after a while. Mini golf isn't much better. I'm tied 0-0 for the third time. The stupid white ball circles the hole before bouncing off the side.

"A little too much force with that one."

He's cute.

His dark brown skin glows underneath the terrace's bright lights. He gently takes the putter from my hand and bends slightly to push the stubborn ball into the hole. His smile tells me he appreciates my small clap.

My reputation, although mostly scandal-free, is not without its rumors. When I was 12, I was supposed to be dating Malik Johnson. Malik was nice, but our relationship never grew past friendship. He quit the business sometime back. I haven't seen him since. Then there was Shane. Photos of us at Universal Studios were posted online and people automatically assumed we were dating. There were about eight other kids on the outing that day, all orchestrated by our publicists. In the photo, we were standing in line for a ride. I don't even know his last name.

And then there was, of course, the guy I was supposed to be dating when I came out as bisexual, who was severely heartbroken by my revelation. It was a story written by some international tabloid known for their lack of credibility. I had never even met the guy whose picture they published next to mine. Truthfully, I have less experience with men than I do with women.

Daisy was the first of many things, including apparently my mistakes. If there was some kind of homework meant to prepare me for unwittingly falling for a girl I barely knew, I missed it. I opened up to her too quickly and trusted her too soon. Online life was so consistent, but since our relationship has moved off the internet, it's been one juggling act after another.

I try not to think about her too much during my lesson. The ball cooperates this time, apparently less bored with me no longer playing a solo game. He introduces himself as Daze, which makes me laugh with skepticism I can't deny. He doesn't take offense, instead chooses the moment to explain his full name is Dayshawn and that his mama would not appreciate me laughing at his name when I meet her, which makes me stop laughing and sends me into a tailspin of other thoughts.

"You're quick, Daze. To be fair, I was laughing at Daze and not Dayshawn. I knew your mama didn't name you Daze." I say the words with my full attention on the putter that isn't so stubborn anymore. Daze hasn't stepped away from me since he arrived. My elbow pokes his hard abs. He doesn't flinch. I try not to notice.

"A real man knows when to be decisive. Meeting a beautiful woman isn't the time to play around."

Shit. Maybe I have been doing this all wrong. Buzzing in my back pocket gives me the distraction I need to not look too impressed.

Daisy [9:17 p.m.]

Where are you?

I continue my conversation with Daze as we follow the markers on the track. He's much taller than I am. Conversation with him is easy. He's an L.A. native like me, a few years older. His cousin is the one who lives here. An aspiring rapper whose music I have heard before. I don't tell him that, not wanting it to be used as leverage later, if there is a later. He points out his cousin with his group of friends seated around the fireplace.

"You should come over and chill." I'm not naïve enough to pretend to not know there are multiple meanings behind the word *chill* that extend beyond *to relax*. Chilling with a rapper's cousin and with this rapper cousin's friends would be one hell of an experience.

Daisy [9:26 p.m.]

Get in here. Now.

I'm much farther away from my patio than when I started. A glance around Daze's tall frame tells me someone is standing behind the patio door, slightly shielded by the sheer curtain meant to provide small amounts of sunlight separate from the heavier set. *Oh shit.*

Daze looks too, searching for the interruption in his proposition. I don't need any more problems and before starting something with someone else, I should probably deal with the headache I already have.

"Sorry. It's my roommate. She needs help bringing up the groceries." He nods and takes the handle of the putter.

"No worries. You can slide through with her later." He points to the balcony doors right above my own.

"I'll talk to her about it. She's got this thing with–" I lean close, pushing myself up by the tips of my toes. Daze meets me halfway, offering me a shoulder to rest my hand on. "–Jesus."

"Damn, alright. We don't wanna disrespect the man upstairs." His laughter makes it easier for me to escape with a small promise I'll hit him up some other time. The words *I'm sorry my possessive not-girlfriend is demanding I come inside* never quite emerge from my lips. With a fresh new phone number stored in my contacts, I ignore the incessant buzzing.

The form behind the curtain disappears the closer I get to the patio. This should be it. I can tell her we're done tonight. It was never supposed to be what it has turned into. After dealing with Sara and her girlfriend, I need a break.

Daisy [9:29 p.m.]

Where are you going?

She's no longer standing where she was before, and I'm not sure if that's a good thing. The apartment looks empty. True to my upbringing, I turned off every goddamn light, and they remain off. We'll have to talk about her arriving at my apartment unannounced and uninvited. Yes, I gave her the code to the door after the movies, but that doesn't mean she can just use it at her discretion. Another mistake.

Daisy [9:29 p.m.]

Who is that?

She was watching me. She invited herself into my home, searched for me and found me with someone else. She must've been furious when I didn't answer her messages. I didn't even glance at my phone.

I was busy.

Daisy [9:29 p.m.]

Why are you still talking to him?

Her anger fuels the energy that propels me through the game area and across the gravel. I slow my pace just a little and imagine her watching me from her new position, pissed.

Daisy [9:29 p.m.]

Emmy, I swear.

She swears what, exactly? That she'll punish me? That she'll make me regret the day I responded to her message in the first place? She already has, and I already do.

Daisy [9:30 p.m.]

You're driving me insane.

Or she was already insane, and I missed every sign possible because I was too busy trying to live my best life.

Daisy [9:31 p.m.]

If you go anywhere with him, we're done.

The gravel crunches underneath my feet as I continue to scroll past her words.

Daisy [9:31 p.m.]

Fuck that.

That was fast. I try to remember what Daze and I were doing to influence such a swift change in someone so confident and demanding. My mind comes up blank. It doesn't matter anymore.

Daisy [9:31 p.m.]

Don't make me come after you.

Daisy chasing me across the rooftop while everyone's watching would be a sight to see. She won't though. Us being seen in public together, especially in that way, is against the rules.

Her loss.

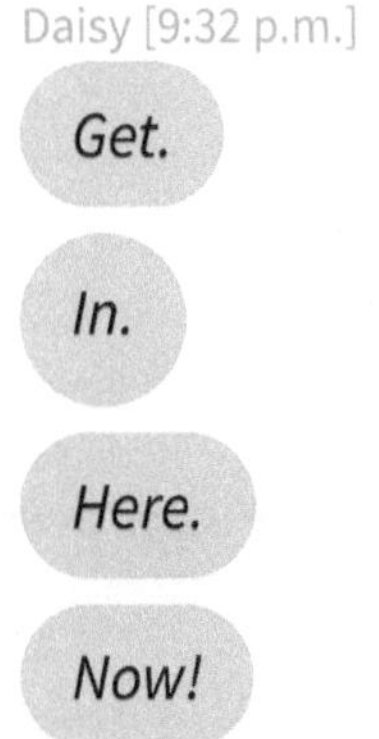

I move from the gravel to the manicured lawn when there are no messages left to read. I'm less annoyed now than I was when I said goodbye to Daze, who's now becoming a distant memory with each step I take toward the glass patio doors.

Something's wrong. I should be terrified, questioning all of my life's choices and plotting my escape. The heat pulsating between my thighs should not be happening. It started when she sent the first text. I tried to ignore it, using Daze as a diversion, but each follow-up text continues to suck air from my lungs to feed the growing flame of control. I shouldn't like it when she talks to me like that.

My feet carry me up the stairs instead of to the nearest exit. Away from Daisy and her inconsistencies. Away from the drama my body has craved since the first night we spent together. I miss her and loathe her at the same time.

Nicole, if you can hear me. It's me. Your best friend. Send help.

The bedroom is empty. The bathroom is untouched. Everything is in place exactly the way it should be. My crafting desk is neat. My clothes are put away. The sheets on my bed are firmly tucked and the pillows fluffed.

She's not here.

Nicole's room is the same. Not a thing out of place. Daisy was either tired of waiting for me or was done with threatening me.

A few people walk by the patio. There are fewer people on the terrace now, but enough for me to join a new group or meet with Daze and his cousin. I shouldn't be presumptuous about what his plans are. He could just be an extremely nice guy looking to have robust conversations. Or he could be planning to bend me over the kitchen table while his cousin and his friends watch. Maybe his cousin shouldn't watch. On second thought, he's not *my* cousin. The images of how the night might progress are unhelpful to my distant attempts to douse the flame left burning by Daisy.

Daisy.

She would hate what I'm thinking about right now. I could be with someone else. Daisy is not my only option.

A vivid illustration plays out before me. Daze standing behind me. My hair wrapped tightly around his fist. A wave of pure ecstasy courses through me as my body responds to my imagination. My nails scratch against the warm patio doors. My breath leaves fog traces behind on the clear surface.

Daisy.

She finds us there. Pissed. She's so pissed. True to her word, she snatches me from Daze, but not by my hair. Her hand squeezes my neck. With my back arched and thighs opened wide, she punishes me from behind, slapping her hand against the place no one else should have ever been. My body makes the sound I've only ever produced for her. I say the words she tells me to say. The whimpers escape my lips only when she allows them to. And I don't look at them. She banishes them from the room, forbidding them to look at me. They can hear me, she says. Her name is the only one she permits me to breathe.

Daisy.

I barely feel the cold blade wedge between my bra and sweat-covered skin. It tears through the band and slices through my shirt. My gasp is cut short, swallowed by my skipped heartbeat at the feel of her hands jamming inside my shorts. Shorts she doesn't approve of. Shorts she watched Daze stand directly behind while I pretended to not notice what was poking in between us.

I know better than to apologize without approval. I stand there and take it, working my hips through the rubbing of her fingers against my panties. They're already soaked. They work in unison to steal the air from my lungs, forcing scattered breaths through strained muscles. I struggle to keep my eyes open and alert. The terrace is almost empty, but anyone passing under the bright lights next to us could see us.

Not that she cares.

Daisy continues to punish me with two hellish fingers. The blade she used to partially undress me now tilted to the side, waiting for its next instructions. I already know what they will be. She steadies her hand against my rocking hips. I stifle the curse word trying to force its way through from the pressure. She removes herself from me, smacking my thighs closed. My shorts fall to my ankles. Rips made to loosen them stare up at me mockingly. Daisy's hands grip the edges of blue panties. I feel the weight of them fall away with each fresh slice. She cuts the rest away from me. My bra, barely used, falls in tatters and the shirt, comfortably worn, falls, too.

Clear defiance reflects on my face in my reflection. Maybe I knew that was going to happen at some point. I place more weight into my palms and wait. Two fingers push through my slick entrance.

"Oh Fu–," I almost sink to my knees.

It takes a second to adjust to her. My feet slip against the floor. I try to remain steady against the glass, opening my thighs wider for her to continue her assault. Like a good girl. Flashes of her fall out of my reflected view as she drives her fingers into me in rhythm, digging deeper when my hips push back. Her knees settle on the floor in between mine. The feeling of her tongue swiping against my clit intensifies with the visual of her movements. One tender lick, then two each.

Please. Please. Please.

Please stop.

Please don't.

Please, more.

She stands and her fingers dance where her tongue once played. Small kisses rain on my lower back, my cheeks my–

"Ah..." My outburst earns me the loss of her fingers and a smack on the ass before they slip back inside. The message is simple.

I am hers.

And she can do whatever she wants to me.

I agree.

I agree so much that when she empties of me and pushes the small of my back to force me to settle on my knees, I comply. She pushes up against me, still dressed in her intact jeans. One hand covers my eyes. The other returns to the emptied space. Teeth bite my shoulder and graze other parts of my skin.

She pulls away.

My eyes remain shut as commanded. The unmistakable popping sound of a well-received treat vibrates through my ear. She's tasting me. With a small push, I turn on my back. The swoosh of the patio doors causes me to jump. Warm air comes rushing in, battling back the electric breeze. Firm lips cover mine at the same time my scalp burns with pressure.

Then she drags me.

My back scrapes over the stainless steel track. There'll be a mark there tomorrow. She releases me when my breasts cross the threshold, keeping the lower half of me waiting on the other side. My eyes open then. I stare up at the bottom of the top patio, exactly where Daze said his cousin and his cousin's friends will be spending time tonight.

Anyone can see me out here. Any moment now, someone can walk by. Daisy pushes my legs into a position that's almost too uncomfortable, except the picture painted in my mind is of how she looks at me, exposed. Without ever being spoken to, I've bent to her will time and time again.

Even now, spread to her desire, her hair flipped over and sweeping across my stomach. I tug at the ends of the silky strands wrapped around my fingers. It's the only way I can communicate the way I feel when she locks my voice away to conceal my secret. Our secret, now. My hands in her hair are the only way I know how to scream now. She grips me tighter in response, bringing her face closer, burying her tongue deeper.

I almost want to scamper away. This level of pleasure used to be too much for me to handle on my own. She taught me differently. Now I grind back into her, welcoming the surge of tension and immediate release, rising and then falling again.

It's just like us. We rise and then we fall. I obey and then I run.

And she chases me every time.

It's the wrong time to say everything I feel. She licks away the memory of the pain caused by her silence and absence. Her tongue strums to the rhythm I've grown accustomed to rocking my hips to. And her lips. I want them all over me. All the time.

The more I shiver, the more my breasts tremble under the patio lights. There's nothing I can do to stop them. My hands are full of the only piece of Daisy I'm allowed to hold. I keep them free and imagine the sight of me someone will see when they glance over their balcony; a halo of black coily hair, glistening brown skin and dark nipples.

You're welcome.

I grip tighter when my hips rise. She hasn't stopped feasting on me. Each ascent places me in a different position. Whether she pushes one knee back toward my belly or slung over her shoulder, she eats. I scream in silence, knowing there's nothing I can do to save myself.

Please. Please. Please.

Please don't let go.

Please don't leave.

Please stay with me.

Laughter echoes in the distance. Someone shouts in another direction. A window opens. A shadow looms in the corner of my eye. This is exactly what I asked for many months and messages ago. I'm on display for all of them. She made sure of it.

A pair of bright yellow tennis shoes comes around the row of hedges. I stare directly at her to catch the moment she notices me panting with fluttering eyes. Her face is lit up by the display of her cell phone. A sharp gasp pushes through me. The girl pauses, then turns. Her eyes land on every place it shouldn't. Nothing is exciting around us. Manicured lawns, trimmed hedges and expensive water features couldn't produce the feeling racing through my body right now.

Look at me.

Look what she did to me.

Look how far I've come.

Before the girl can correct her mistake, someone calls out in the distance. I watch her go back the way she came, never knowing what she left behind.

I release Daisy to feel my skin. My hands cup my abandoned breasts. Daisy's lips on my clit propel me to squeeze my nipples between my fingers. My hips buck against the kisses, both small and tortuous, landing on the perfect spot.

"Ah!" I call out. The pressure building in my belly is too high for me to keep locked in. The flat of her tongue washes away the sting of the smack.

"Fuck!" I do not attempt to be silent. She grips my thighs harder in warning. The next swipe is slower, traveling at an agonizingly slow pace. My breath lodges in my chest, then flutters out as she leans her face forward, grazing the most sensitive spot.

"Yes!" The patio door above me flies open.

"Yo, did you hear that?"

My hands drop to my side, leaving my breasts in full view. This is it. The moment I've been dreaming of. The aftershock of Daisy's work rolls through me. I've been discarded by her now and left for someone else to enjoy. Not like her. There will not be another Daisy. Never again.

The light dims as they file out onto the patio. They look around in the distance, still laughing at one another about what they think they heard. Daze is the first to check over the balcony. Our eyes lock. My heart thuds in my chest. One hand of his smacks the back of another. The rest of the group turns. My eyes scan over them in a flash. I manage to lift my head to avoid the track. The patio door slams shut. The thick curtains drape us in darkness.

Chapter Eighteen
Daisy

"I'm sorry." She whispers the words repeatedly. Every few minutes she stops to breathe, thinks and then says it again. I don't even think she knows what she's apologizing for. My fault, probably. Things usually are in situations like this. I do my best to reassure her. I'm lying in her arms tonight. The chilly air keeps us bundled underneath the covers. Outside I know it's still warm. People are probably still moving about even with the stores closed and the street vendors packed to go home.

Hours.

I made her say my name for hours. I had half the mind to let them hear her. It was a terrible idea that would've backfired on me. And not because of who she is to the world, but of who she is to me.

No one else can know.

"I'm sorry." I squeeze her fingers clasped in mine in reassurance. I like this part more than I thought I would. If she had asked before she changed the rules, I would've said no. Now I can't imagine her without this. And I want no one else to have it or her.

What have I done?

She's sucked me into a world I'm not supposed to be in. I went from freeing myself from one girl and falling into the arms of another. This was not a part of the plan. Look what she's already done to me. I'm possessive, angry and vengeful. She had the absolute gall to stand and talk to another person in front of me. Maybe she didn't know I was there, but she knew I was coming. How could I not? I had to show her she couldn't replace me so easily. That pattern can't repeat itself.

"I'm sorry about today. I didn't mean to hurt you."

I forget the moment she stopped trying to conceal her voice. And I'm glad. I love hearing it. We haven't spoken about last night. There's no way for me to explain what I was feeling, even if she asked.

"I'm sorry, Daisy."

I know. Me too.

"Well, look who the cat dragged in." Tonight's welcome is a lot like that. With a busy school and work schedule, I have had little time to work at Diego's. My check from my fancy restaurant job looks way better than the checks I earned from working at Norma's. Still, sometimes you miss what you don't have.

"I missed you too, Star. Did you get a little nicer while I was away?" I accompany my words with two kisses on her cheeks. Star's expression doesn't change. Her eyes still narrow behind her brown eyeliner and thick false lashes.

"You think you can just walk in here after not so much as a phone call?" The code to my locker still works. I throw my bag and shoes inside. My ripped jeans are extra tight today to earn Luis' approval after so much time away. I even slip on a pair of heels after checking to make sure I stuffed my tennis shoes in my backpack.

"Star, what do they need me for when they've got you?"

My shrug earns me a vigorous nod from her. "I know that's right. I wish everyone would pay me the same amount of respect around here." I agree with her on the way out, sidestepping Roxie with her phone pressed to her ear.

I'm barely through the threshold of Luis' office when he spots me. "You look good enough to help at the bar." His attention is back on the stack of papers in front of him. I ease out of the way I came to turn the corner that leads me to the floor. It's as busy as any night. I take drink orders from raised hands and frustrated expressions. I leave my white jacket service behind for tonight. There's no place for that here.

I dance around questions about my age. Both men and women ask me what time I'm going home. My response to them is the same. "As soon as my girlfriend tells me." It's partially true. I've made a habit of spending the night at Emmy's during the week, and on weekends when I can't stay, we talk on the phone instead. Well, she talks. I laugh reluctantly and text my responses. Who falls asleep first remains debatable.

As for the title I bestow on her to strangers, I haven't asked her. For obvious reasons. I know the rules, even when she breaks them. There are parameters here that I can work with.

"Johnny, how are you?" I realize Johnny is the real reason Luis sent me out to the bar tonight. The girls don't like him. If you ask Roxy, she says, "he's just got that vibe." Jade shudders. London walks the other way.

Johnny gives me a nod without speaking and accepts the beer from me without looking in my direction. His eyes scan around the club. His leg bounces in place, uncontrollably.

"Do you need me to get you anything else?" He offers me a small shake of his head. As long as he stays on the floor, there's nothing for me to worry about. Security has been told to not allow him in the private rooms. If Johnny asks, they're full.

"I need to talk to you." Sara isn't supposed to be here. There's no way no one noticed her glammed up in this club, dressed like she came to upstage the dancers instead of enjoying the show. It technically should be against her image, anyway. No matter which way you slice it, a teen actor, most known as the lead singer of a middle school band, should never be in a place like this.

"What are you doing here?"

"You won't answer my calls."

"Because I don't need to." Our lives together were over months ago. Although I pulled away to make sense of all of it, I've only recently accepted it. I've teetered every time a new girl became more helpful.

"Your mom told me where to find you. Everyone else seems to understand us except for you."

"Why did you go see her?"

"Relax. I was looking for you. She was very nice about it. Maricela, on the other hand." She rolls her eyes at the tenacious spirit of my younger sister. Their history together was brief, but impactful. I'm sure Sara is slightly wrong about my mom, though. She doesn't like her, but tolerates her because of the help she provides.

"You know what? It's fine. I need to talk to you anyway." Something sparks in her eyes. I'm not sure if I've ever seen it before. "Are you staying in town all weekend?"

"Are you planning on coming over?"

"Yes. To talk."

I cross my arms over my chest for good measure. It's supposed to send a message about how serious I am, but it only makes her eyes focus where she doesn't have the privilege to look anymore.

That access has been granted to someone else.

Sara gives me a face that I probably once thought was adorable, until I got to know her better.

"Never mind. We'll talk here."

She bends her thumb back and directs my eyesight toward a nearby table. Daley and Michelle sit there. Daley is a reality TV star who became famous after a stint on a dating show. Her big moment was throwing up on her date and then falling down the stairs. She didn't make it home with a fiancé, but gained one hell of a social media following. Michelle is a quintessential mean girl. She was never on reality TV, but has made her living reporting on the lives of trashy reality TV stars and hawking shitty products to her viewership.

"Where did you find them?"

The Sara I know is a loner. She never lets people hang around. Our relationship has been a back and forth with me being replaced at the most unexpected times.

Sara's acrylics dig into my forearm before trailing down to my wrist. They'll leave a mark that'll disappear in a few hours.

"We'll talk here and I'll see you later." I watch her walk back over to her new group of friends. They're too busy taking photos of their drinks to notice her return. This is typical Sara—concealing personal motives as goodwill gestures. Later, she'll either tell me she helped provide promotion for the club or tell the girls she was helping them gain more exposure.

"Hey. You're needed in the back. Room 5." I give the waiter a nod in acknowledgment and allow my eyes to wander away from Sara and her guests. We reserve some rooms for special clientele. Room 5 isn't one of them. The hallway to the private rooms is much emptier than the main room. I put on my best welcoming face while passing customers. *Nothing you've done in there is scandalous at all.*

Without knocking, I open the door to Room 5 and see Doll, a short and puffy-faced dancer with her arms crossed over her chest. Only her thong and heels remain on. She stares at an older couple sitting on the couch. Perhaps in their late 40s.

"What's the problem?"

"They're trying to rescue me."

"Oh, no." I hold back my laugh. The sight of Doll looking at the couple with pouty disapproval is enough for anyone to lose their professionalism.

"You should both be ashamed of yourselves." She wags her finger in their faces. "I'm a beautiful woman." She steps back and turns to allow them a full view. "I like to show it off." The woman becomes more angry with each turn. The man tries to look away. Doll walks to the door, still swaying her hips to the beat of the song that was supposed to add to the private dance experience. She stops at the threshold, giving them the perfect view of her barely covered backside.

"I'll get you someone else, I promise." Satisfied with my response, she leaves. I approach the couple next. The woman still has a sour look on her face. The man keeps wiping at the sweat that drips from his hairline.

"I assure both of you, Diego's has ethical practices as far as our dancers are concerned. No one is here because they don't want to be. We have a very strict termination policy for dancers who feel they are being forced into employment. Life is too short to be dealing with unnecessary drama, don't you think?"

I pull two complimentary drink cards from my back pocket. The woman eyes them warily and then slides them from my grip. She tucks them into her bra and then leaves. The man's walk to the door is much slower.

"See you next week, Earl," I whisper as he passes.

Sara and her friends are still at the same table as before, but this time crowded by a group of men. Sara looks at them as one would expect a beautiful woman to look at a man wearing a shirt too tight with intention. But inside, I know her heart is cold and her panties are dry. Neither is their fault. She was born that way.

"Any chance your friends want a private dance tonight?"

Sara glances back at me. My elbows rest on the back of the booth she's sitting in. I dodge the hand that attempts to touch my hair.

"I don't usually share my girlfriends." *Well then, it's a good thing you don't have one.*

The more people in the room, the more money Doll will make. Daley was half-gay in at least one episode of that show she was on. The men will spend the money because they can't stand being outshined by any of the women.

I have no idea what Michelle's sexual orientation is, but it doesn't matter. At worst, she's straight, but is terrified of being left at the table alone. At best, she's a closeted lesbian, bisexual, bi-curious or subscribes to the idea of a man finding her more desirable if she's capable of having sex with another woman.

There are no losers here. Only opportunities.

Sara leans into the ear of the nearest guy and the news goes around the table like a perfect game of telephone. I step away to prepare Doll for her new guests. I'm thrilled to find that she took a break after her run-in with Earl and his wife. I lead the group to a waiting Doll, who's dressed in a new outfit and ready to perform.

The cheers and whoops follow me out the door. But so does Sara. "You're not gonna give me the spiel about not touching the merchandise?" *Shit. I did forget to do that.*

"If there's a problem, Doll will call me."

"And what about me? Am I gonna hear from you later?"

There's no music coming from the door behind me. I ease it open and flick on the light. My first instinct is to stand, but exhaustion seeps into my muscles at that moment. I sit. Sara lays out on the couch and rests her head on my lap.

"We haven't had a quiet moment in a while."

I wonder what she would count as quiet. I can't recall, anyway. Every time she replaced me, I got a new job or worked longer hours. There was never any rest on my end.

"I have the money." Her eyes slowly turn up to reach mine. Sara from earlier, with the spark of hope that flashed across her face, is officially gone.

"Is that why you've been doing all of this? You've spent all this time away from me to leave me?"

"You don't need me. You have her—"

"She means nothing to me. How many times do I have to tell you that? What the fuck do you want me to do? Write it on a fucking billboard?"

She'd never do that. Sara Aguilar gives a shit about someone? No way.

"I can't get over it." I'm not sure I ever tried. It's not like I didn't think she was capable of it. At some point, I told myself it was part of dating someone famous. Famous people cheating on their partners is an unspoken assumption. They can have anyone in the world. Why would they only pick you?

Sara has shown me many times that I'm never going to be her first choice. Eventually, I had to believe her.

"I have the money that I owe you. I can pay you tomorrow. And then after that, there's no reason for us to see each other again."

She sits up on the couch with her elbows resting on her bare knees and her chin balanced on her knuckles. Her pissed-off expression hasn't changed.

"You think all you need to do to get rid of me is pay out your contract? You promised to be there for me whenever I need you, and you can't cancel that with a check."

"You don't need me."

"Of course I do. You think too much about them. You give them too much credit and make them more significant than what they are. She serves a purpose. They all do. But none of them are you." Her heels dig into the carpet with each step she takes to the door. She's never been good with confrontation. The hand, with the watch identical to one I used to own, pauses on the door handle.

"If I asked you to stop, would you?"

"In time. It's not time now. I need you to be patient."

I shake my head. "We've run out of time, Sara."

She turns to me, her hand still clutched around the knob that will keep me trapped in the endless loop of our lifeless romance.

"Then reset the fucking clock, Brie."

Chapter Nineteen
Gabriella

SARA'S NEVER BEEN GOOD at hearing the word 'no' and I'm finding Bonnie to not be any different. She has it in her head that as her intern for the theater department, I am also her personal assistant.

No, I'm not.

I leave Bonnie's dog's food on the porch of her Burbank home instead of lugging it into the house. It's bad enough I had to drive to the Valley to deliver it. Sara promised it would be the last errand for Bonnie that I would ever do. Her takeover of Taylor's adoption event has been a tremendous success. Several billboards up the 5 freeway adorn her face next to some random, fluffy pooch with a ridiculous haircut.

Sara has mentioned Taylor's expected absence at the event on podcasts, in comments, and even on a morning show interview, where she showcased a few of the freshly groomed pets that were supposed to be available for adoption day.

They were adopted live on air.

Bonnie is in the dark about Sara's plans to ditch her. Sara will frame it as a professional mismatch and claim she and Bonnie differed in their vision for her career. While Bonnie might be a little shortsighted, the truth is Sara has no idea where to go from here.

My last act of servitude for Bonnie before Sara gives her the boot is to book her honeymoon surprise for her wife. A few mouse button clicks aren't much of a sacrifice. If I were Mrs. Silvers, I would want to leave the city altogether. Old Hollywood money should vacation in some foreign country on a remote island with a private chef and fancy cheese. The Four Seasons in Beverly Hills is nice, but come on, it's practically down the street.

I bet it's something Taylor would like to do. She'd say international travel was too much of a fuss, even though she'd be doing it in business class with those comfy lounge seats in a semi-private space. She'd probably start off pretending to not know the proper pronunciation for said cheese and then would clap in glee when she nails it. On the second try.

She's bound to release Bonnie as her mentor shortly after Sara does, if she hasn't already. There was never any benefit to her having a mentor. It's just another example of what happens when you strive to please too many people.

The Four Seasons is synonymous with luxury. Bonnie's suitcase glides across the waxed marble flooring. I shouldn't have it at all, except somehow she left it behind in her office.

"What are you doing here?"

I've never met the people Sara is sandwiched in between. They look around our age. The guy is trying hard to belong in his skintight jeans, designer glasses and scarf tied around his neck. His accomplice is dressed in black. Her brown hair is cut in a bob with bangs far too short.

"Waiting for you." Sara's kiss misses and lands on my cheek. She leads me to a corner bench partially covered by a green plant. "Bonnie left a spare key right under there." *There* is a giant vase of roses sitting on a table that's probably an antique.

"Why the hell would she do that?"

"Because I told her to." Sara casually looks side to side as if waiting for someone else to arrive. According to the itinerary I had to put together, the Silvers should arrive back from their couples' massage soon. "Ah, there she is. Right on time."

Taylor saunters through the lobby. She's ditched the relatable persona and stands out as a Hollywood someone. Instead of a suitcase, she carries a bag with straps settled at her elbow. The dark sunglasses scream, "Bitch, I'm famous. Don't bother me." She bypasses reception and rounds the large table before walking up the grand staircase. I barely notice her swiping the key.

"I can't believe she and Bonnie have been seeing each other this entire time. It all makes sense now. Bonnie was so eager to get her hands on her. She talked about it with everyone. No one ever suspected the truth." I stare blankly at the last spot Taylor stood before disappearing from view.

"It was a small mix-up. Bonnie sent the wrong message to the wrong person. Taylor thinks they're celebrating them tonight. She's brought everything Bonnie asked for. The rope. The handcuffs. The knife."

My grip falls from Bonnie's luggage handle. I turn to Sara to see her looking directly at me. "I'm not mad. It's probably a good thing you got it out of your system. Now we can go back to normal and you can stop hanging history over my head. I'll even forget all about that photo."

History was yesterday and it repeats every week. I wasn't in Sara's bed last night, and I know she wasn't sleeping in it alone. I also don't care. Sara's head falls on my shoulder. Her brown curls drape over me and clash with my much darker and tighter ones.

"Bonnie's wife will realize what she's been up to all these months. Can you imagine? Taylor, the mistress. She found freedom in a broken home." Sara wraps her arms around me.

"You've already won."

"Perhaps. You didn't tell me the cost of winning would be you."
One last deed. One last sacrifice.

"Sara, I was never yours." We've always been on borrowed time. As soon as I had Taylor, there was no way I could ever let her go. I just hope she forgives me for it.

Sara flashes the second keycard in my face. "If you do this, I will take your entire family down." I've been preparing for this. I've worked independently of Sara for over a year in hopes I can afford to take on whatever challenge she throws at me.

"Goodbye Sara." The keycard struggles out of her grip and into mine. A small glimpse of a much smaller piece of Sara shows on her face, briefly. It's replaced quickly by her usual defiant expression. She's banking on me failing. I either won't get to Taylor in time or she won't believe me. I have to try.

The suitcase slows on the carpeted wing where the rooms are. I follow the numbers hung on the side of each door to the one I have memorized in my head. After a flashing light and a few clicks, the door to the room unlocks. Taylor lies flat in the middle of the bed, covered in rose petals. Naked.

Fuck.

"Taylor, get up."

Her upper body pops up like she's auditioning to become an extra in the latest zombie movie.

"What are you doing here?" Suspicion gleams in her eyes. The petals fall one by one, exposing her body to me. While the sight and feel of her has made my mouth water, thighs clench and heart skip a beat many times before, we can't afford for this time to be one of them.

"Get dressed. Bonnie is on her way with her wife."

"I don't know what you're talking about. You need to leave. Now!"

"God! Sara is setting you up, okay? If you get caught here, she's gonna tell everyone and their mother that you are having an affair with Bonnie. Or maybe even her wife."

Or both.

What a headline that would be: *Taylor Townes Caught In Lovers Quarrel With Hollywood Couple!*

There's no way she could spin that into something positive. Who knows what evidence Sara has cooked up to trap Bonnie in her latest attempt at a scandal. Bonnie's not the type to look out for cunning con women like Sara and me. She gave me unlimited access to her private life with just one request from Sara, and Sara always takes full advantage.

I push the suitcase into the corner and do my best to spread out the rose petals. I try not to stare at her getting dressed. The glow from the candles isn't helping. They only make her skin appear soft like velvet instead of smooth silk, which is something I shouldn't even know.

"How do I know this isn't a trick? Am I going to step out of this room to a horde of paparazzi?"

She pretends she doesn't see them any other time. Today shouldn't be any different.

"If you see them, then just keep walking. We can leave something here for Bonnie and say you were dropping off an anniversary gift or something and you asked for my help. As long as you're fully dressed and everything looks normal, you should be fine."

She grabs the bag I saw her walk through the hotel with and removes the clothing she stuffed inside. Her sunglasses are now clipped to her shirt. She works in silence, gathering everything she prepared; the small speaker playing the soft music, a box of strawberries covered in dark and white chocolate, a small black box, the handcuffs and the rope.

She knew Daisy would have the knife.

I'm sorry.

"Good thing I kept the box." She places one unlit candle back into its white packaging and ties the black ribbon into a bow. "You think it's enough? It costs over $500."

"I'm sure it's fine."

It's so on-brand for her to be thinking about the quality of her impromptu gift at a time like this. When she's gathered everything and the room looks as close as it probably did before Taylor added her touches to it, I pull open the door handle and look out. The hallway is empty from every direction.

I steer Taylor with one hand on her hip in the opposite direction from where I left Sara. Brightly colored exotic cars and turned-up noses fill the back of the Four Seasons. I hop into Taylor's passenger seat after the valet brings her car around.

I make the mistake of thinking she could get herself in. She takes forever. She slides one foot in and then out again. When she sits, she glances around the parking lot, never moving from the valet drop-off point. Her hands clutch and release the steering wheel.

"What are you doing?"

Her eyes close and her face scrunches up into what I can only describe as agony.

"I can't leave. I...I have to wait."

Small, wet droplets attach to her closed lashes.

"She's not coming."

Pushing the words out empties all the air from my lungs. Her crying makes it worse. Tears run down her cheeks and drip from her skin, splattering over her chest.

And somehow she's even more beautiful.

"I don't understand."

The words quake out from her throat and force more water

to flow. Tears spread like glitter, sharpened by the rays that peek through the windshield. The crying continues as I remove her from her seat. It's a slow walk to the other side with every step, feeling like she's pulling free from quicksand. She snaps in her seatbelt, leaving traces of her sadness on the back of her hand.

I'm sorry.

It wasn't supposed to happen like this. Fifteen years of longing overshadowed Daisy's purpose. I thought I had dealt with and dismissed it. Taylor Townes was supposed to be a self-involved, superficial Hollywood snob who only pretended not to be a bitch because it was contradictory to her image.

I told myself that for years.

We broke her.

Sara's dreams have finally come true. I'm free at a higher cost than I meant to bargain for, never considering I could regret all of it. And I don't. Taylor will recover from this as she always has. We'll go home. She'll sleep. Everything that happened with Daisy will become a distant memory. I'll fix it. We all serve a purpose.

Taylor is mine.

Chapter Twenty
Taylor

I HATE NATURE. ALL of it. Birds shouldn't be allowed to chirp in the daytime. They all need to feel how dead I feel inside. How sad and hopeless. There's nothing to chirp about after you learn the last two years of your life have been a lie.

Daisy lied.

Sara...is evil. Twisted. Disgusting. In the past, the thought of Sara may have elicited an eye roll. Now, I want to throw-up. The thought that she could have ever touched me. Tasted me.

I...I touched her. I spread her legs and buried my fingers in her flesh. One by one. I'm covered in Sara. I hate that for me. She slowly corrupted my personal and professional life. She tainted my career. Her scent and her memory contaminate the bed I sleep in. There are so many memories. Memories of us tangled and twisted with my body underneath her. Our breathing clashed together. Her hands locked in my hair.

I craved her. I wanted her.

She broke me.

My head slides from the toilet seat and rests on the cold tile floor. I'm clammy and feverish at the same time. My feet rub against the sheet Gabriella placed over me last night. She tried to get me to stand up, but I refused.

I wish she'd go away. She didn't care about me when she was

helping Sara to destroy me.

Speaking takes more energy than I can gather. Last night, I swatted at her and shooed her away into my bedroom. She still sits on the floor in the doorway. I think she slept there. There are hazy memories of her placing her hand over my forehead. I think she brought me water once.

She tied her hair up in a knot very similar to mine. I remember that one. I couldn't push her away and throw-up at the same time. She won that round. They both did.

"I ordered you Menudo. It'll help your stomach."

I raise my head just enough to look at her. She has that stupid notebook again. The alcohol I drank sits empty beside her. The girl across the hall courteously gave me half a tequila bottle. Gabriella sneered at her, but I grabbed it before she could take it away. My parents don't drink. I've never had alcohol in my house to sneak. It tasted disgusting, but I deserved the relief it was supposed to bring me. Now look at me. It ruined me. That and my broken heart.

"I've never had Menudo." I've heard of Menudo, sure. My family has our assortment of soups; chili beans with cornbread (I like mine separately. Daddy likes his mixed in), chicken and dumplings, gumbo and jambalaya. Chitlins are eaten twice a year, on Thanksgiving and Christmas. New Year is for Black-Eyed Peas. Since I've made myself sick from grief and heartache, chicken noodle soup will do just fine. Mama's neck bones and rice would be nice, but I've never learned how to make it myself and if I ask, she'll want to know what's wrong.

I got played, Mama.

"That's fine. You'll get used to it."

I hate how confident she sounds. Who is she to walk in here and tell me what to eat?

"Shouldn't you be leaving?" She should go back to her

girlfriend. They should be celebrating what they've done to me.

"No."

"Isn't Sara expecting you?"

"No," she repeats, not moving an inch.

"You're a terrible girlfriend. No wonder she cheats on you." My heart pangs a little at my words. The same thing happened the first time I said it, too, back at the center's parking lot. It's not her fault Sara's a terrible person. Gabriella may have been different before she met her. She's making me into a terrible person, too.

"I'm sorry," I say, filling the quiet between us.

"It's okay. I used to think the same thing." Damn. "We broke up almost a year ago, so no, she's not expecting me."

"What?" Suddenly, my stomach doesn't feel as weak as it did. This makes no sense. I saw them kiss on stage. In front of everyone.

Gabriella shrugs. "Sara likes to keep up with appearances." That can't be it.

"Why did you break up?" There's a slight pain in my stomach when I bend my body to see her properly. The distraction is worth it. I've spent an insane amount of hours in absolute agony. They owe me this relief.

She tosses her notebook to the side. The bottle tumbles to the floor when she stands. Her hand extends out to me. I take it and ignore the nauseating roll of my stomach. Apparently, the elixir I needed was not tequila, but gossip. Gabriella leads the way through my bedroom and down the stairs. It's like she owns the place now after taking up residence in my brief stint of incapacity.

Nicole must not be home. I groan at the thought of telling her everything with Daisy was a lie after I gushed about her weeks ago.

I follow Gabriella out of my bedroom and into the kitchen. Everything's already set up. I must've had more blackout moments than I remember for her to have had time to put this together.

The Menudo's red broth stains the white styrofoam bowl it sits in. "You don't know how to make it yourself?" I don't mean it as an insult. At least I don't think so.

Gabriella doesn't seem to take it that way. "It takes longer to make than it looks." I take a spoonful.

"Are you going to tell me?" It's her business, but she helped orchestrate my heartbreak, so I should be entitled to hers. God, I'm sure Sara shared every intimate detail about us. Not us. There was no us.

Gabriella places a napkin stacked with tortillas next to my bowl. "It started with Savannah Logan." I know her. She was slated to be a big deal at one point. Got her start in a small indie movie that took off. She was everywhere. The next big movie star. She's maybe a year or two older than us. Haven't heard her name in a long time. Her star never rose as high as everyone expected.

"What did you do to her?"

"Nothing. Maybe I should've beat her ass, though. It's not like she didn't know. Everyone knew. They just didn't care."

They didn't care because Sara didn't care. I don't say it even though the words roll across my mind with certainty.

"Sara swore it didn't mean anything. She was a 'means to an end.' The rumor was she was up for a big role. Some queer awakening flick. I don't even know if she was really queer. Anyway, Sara slept with her. Said she needed to build up their chemistry for the test."

Chemistry tests during the casting process aren't uncommon, but it never involves sex. It's an opportunity for the producers and the director to watch the actors interact together before anyone needs to film.

"After that there was Danica. Then Ebony. I finally broke up with her when I found her in bed with her neighbor's daughter.

They moved from New York. We watched her dad flirt with her from the balcony. I left for the weekend to visit my parents. When I got back, I didn't even need to go upstairs to hear them. Sara was making a point."

If by Danica she means Danica Christ, I remember her. She guest starred on *Sunny and the Dreamers* as a musical guest. In the show, she was competing against us for a record deal. As a rising country music star, who was Chinese American and not white, she fit in perfectly with the message of the show. In person, she was a sweetheart. Gabriella wasn't around then, which means Danica somehow crossed paths with Sara years later.

Ebony Shaw is a model. Ebony Jackson is another actor mostly known for her amazing comedic timing. Neither is known to be queer. It's hard to say with Sara. Hell, Gabriella could very well be talking about my own cousin.

"What was the point?"

"It's complicated. Her family—they don't communicate. Passive aggression is their love language. Sara felt disrespected by her dad, so she fucked her dad's new weekly interest and made sure he could hear it. While Sara was sexing his new potential mistress, he was sitting in his office with the door open, drinking Scotch."

"Why'd you stay so long?"

"It's complicated."

"Why'd you do her dirty work? She hurt you, so you needed to hurt other people?"

"That's complicated, too."

Her sadness is the only thing keeping me from expressing my frustration. Everything is complicated. Sara weaves her way through life by making simple things into confusing puzzles.

There's a change to Gabriella's usual indifference. I can tell she disapproves of my final slurp. She cleans it up anyway, giving me the freedom to make a new home for myself on the couch. The television clicks on a random channel. I'm aware the other side of the couch being occupied means she hasn't left. I guess we can be sad together. A contrast to the bright Santa Monica streets below us.

"Where do you live?" Her sock-clad feet slightly scratch against my thigh.

"Culver City."

"Oh. Not too far."

She shakes her head in agreement. Nothing changes. She doesn't make an excuse to leave or claim to be too tired. She doesn't ask if there's anything else I need before slipping on her shoes and out the door. Her body stays in place. Her eyes stare at the screen. I could tell her to go. She's not a friend and I don't know in what universe someone befriends their rival's exes. Sara broke her heart more times than she ever broke mine. She spent years looking the other way for a reason I cannot understand.

"Come here." Fingers latch around my wrist and pull me over. I go willingly, my body tired, my stomach filled with soup. My eyes have drooped closed a few times. She noticed. My head rests right underneath her breasts. I tuck my hands underneath the small space between her back and the couch pillow. Her thighs open wide enough for me to settle in between them. She feels good. It's hard to fight the tingling that erupts from my scalp when she runs her fingers through my hair.

She has no choice but to stay now.

The window in Bonnie's office overlooks the orange grove on campus. I walked by it once and read the plaque. It's supposed to commemorate the area's past farming history, now replaced by concrete buildings and asphalt. Having lunch there has been on my to-do list since school started, but other things keep getting in the way.

Bonnie's words barely register. Her lips are moving, but I can't tell you a damn thing she's saying. Nothing she says is important. If it wasn't for Gabriella, I wouldn't even be here. I slept through most of the day yesterday, only waking when she forced me to eat. She refused to leave me in my bed this morning. I lost count of the many times I pulled the covers around me, only for her to snatch them away. Dressing me was equally challenging, but she managed it.

"You'll be fine," she kept repeating. *I know, but it still sucks.*

I can't even blame Sara for what happened. It's my fault. It was my declaration that placed me in her line of fire. She knew exactly what to do to cage me in. I loaded the arrow she shot me with—right after she dipped it in poison.

"I'm retired." Bonnie stops speaking. I look directly at her for the first time this morning. She looks refreshed. The usual amount of makeup still layers on her skin, but she looks brighter and more youthful. The weekend with her wife did as much good as it did damage.

"Taylor?" There's an edge of concern in Bonnie's voice I can appreciate, even in my depressed state. Perhaps in another professional capacity, we'll be able to work together again one day. The timing is terrible, and the company isn't any better.

"I told the world I was taking a break."

"No one's forcing you to be here." I've purposely ignored Sara all morning. She and Gabriella shared a brief exchange I didn't bother to stick around for. After spending even more time with Gabriella, I don't understand them.

I take a deep breath, maintaining eye contact with Bonnie. "When I accepted this mentorship, I didn't realize how much it would feel like working, even though it was on a smaller scale. Sure I'm not on set, but I just haven't had the rest that I thought I was going to have when I stepped away for a while."

"Wow. Maybe try showing a little more appreciation to Bonnie with what she's done for us–"

"I would appreciate you shutting the fuck up!" The sound of her voice reminds me of too many almosts that would never come true. "You're a terrible person. Toxic to your fucking core. I don't want to breathe the same air as you, let alone sit in the same room as you. I hate you."

It all comes pouring out. Sara's eyes swell with tears. She looks at Gabriella, who's looking at me with the same concerned expression she's had on her face since yesterday. Tears drip from Sara's eyes. She wipes them away before they can fully wet her cheeks.

"Don't you see?" Her gaze lands on Bonnie. "I told you. She's not okay." I'm out of my seat before I have a chance to compose myself. Gabriella's hand on my arm is the only thing that stops me. I want to drag Sara across this table and beat her. For so long, she's gotten away with hurting people. It's not fair. Not for me. Not for any of the other girls. And not for Gabriella.

"Bonnie, she's done." Gabriella's tone commands a finality. I had no idea I would feel relief from someone having my back. There've been so many secrets and secrets limit the amount of support you're allowed.

Bonnie's response to Gabriella doesn't reach my ears. I'm so tired. I want my apartment, my bed, my sleep.

Gabriella leads me around campus from class to class with her arm hooked around mine. She sits me next to Nicole in the one class we all share before returning to her usual seat.

"What's going on?" Nicole watches Gabriella depart wearily. "Did she do something to you?" With a shake of my head, I lean forward to rest my head on my folded arms. It's impossible to fall asleep here. The professor more than once asks Nicole about my well-being. Her response is always cheery, "She's not feeling well today, but she really wanted to be here." No, I didn't. My ex-costar's ex-girlfriend forced me here.

Nicole is not so cheerful when Gabriella shows up at the end of class to retrieve me. She ignores Nicole's questions, gathers my things, and leads me out of class again. How she knows the exact location of all of my classes, I do not know. But she's there at the end of each one. She answers my phone when Nicole calls to meet for lunch.

"She's *my* best friend. I don't need a chaperone. I can take care of her on my own."

The intense stare they give each other over the lunch table reminds me of my earlier stand down with Sara. No one asks me what my opinion is. Gabriella orders me an Oreo cookie shake and a bacon cheeseburger. Which, I have to say, is a good choice. Nicole drops the Kale salad with parmesan cheese and almonds on the table next to it. Some of the Kale splashes from the bowl onto the tabletop.

"If she's not feeling well, she should eat this and not grease and cheese."

I'm not sick. Just heartbroken. And embarrassed. I shudder at the thought of having to tell Nicole the truth about Daisy one day.

"She's not sick. She'll be fine. She just needs time."

"Time? What did you do to her?" Nicole's hands cup my face. She examines every part of me she can see. "What did they do to you?" *Nothing. Everything.*

I don't have an answer. Sara played with my emotions and tricked me into *something*.

"I'm fine," I mumble through pinched cheeks. Nicole continues to glare at Gabriella while simultaneously lowering herself in the seat across from me. Gabriella does the same beside me. She tears off the paper covering of the milkshake straw. I drink when she places it to my lips.

"Taylor!" Nicole shouts at me. She snatches the milkshake from Gabriella and places it in my hand. "She said she's fine."

Undeterred by Nicole's stance, Gabriella reclaims the milkshake, offers me another sip and places it back in between the two of us. She then cuts my burger in half to make it easier for me to eat. I take a few bites of the salad in between to promote unity.

Throughout lunch, I learn Gabriella's two friends are not named Quiet One and Too Arched Eyebrows. Krystal is the quiet one and Chasity's eyebrows are now acceptable. They're roommates and I gather they're who Gabriella lives with.

Chasity hasn't glared at me once today, though I catch her giving Nicole a few nasty looks.

Lunch wraps up with the same routine. Even with Nicole close by, Gabriella walks me to and from class. She drives me home, too, regardless of Nicole's insistence she be the one to take care of me.

And for some reason, I follow.

Chapter Twenty-One
Gabriella

THE DOOR TO SARA'S dad's house is unlocked. It's usually left that way. When I first moved in with them, I would sneak and lock it at night before bed. I couldn't stand the thought of someone walking in and murdering us all. Now that I no longer do, they can do whatever they please.

"Hola Señora. ¿Como estas?"

Lupe is the only housekeeper Sara has ever had. It's an accomplishment considering how many nannies Sara's dad employed throughout the years. Some of them traveled with us, but they always got lost along the way.

Lupe tolerates Sara, in that she mostly ignores her.

"Muy bien. ¿Como estas?"

"¿Está el diablito aquí?"

Lupe started calling Sara a little devil after one of her many tantrums. During this incident, Sara destroyed her dad's office, which Lupe had just finished tidying up.

Lupe rolls her eyes and flicks them towards the ceiling. I left Taylor in her bedroom, completing a homework assignment. When I told her I needed to leave, she only asked when I was coming back. Not if, but when. Not where are you going, but when am I going to see you again. I explained anyway. I didn't tell her I was coming to see Sara. I told her I needed to run an errand.

She's mostly back to normal, as I predicted.

She's always fine.

I walk the familiar path up the staircase to Sara's room. Sara's home has none of the warmth one would picture in a home right out of a Hollywood movie. It has a winding staircase, expensive statues and paintings, marble flooring, and even custom furniture, but no warmth. Family photos don't line the walls of the hallway here. No portrait hangs above the fireplace or in the dining room. The long table that seats ten sits empty every night.

Sara's bedroom door is open. Her floor is a mess with random knick-knacks I know have assigned places. I step over what's in the way, fitting my shoes into unoccupied spaces. Sara sits in her window overlooking the pool. I hated that view for a long time. I used to fight the urge to sit and stare out of it, watching the inevitable happen before my very eyes.

"I hope you're not coming to beg for forgiveness." She doesn't turn to look at me. In an ideal world, I could walk away with no repercussions, but that's not reality.

"Name your price." She turns, her eyes lit with a familiar fire. I've never been afraid of Sara. She needed me for something she couldn't get from anyone else. I accepted that for a long time. Not anymore.

"You can't be serious." It's the reason I've been working so hard. Why I've never stopped. Whenever I had a break from her and didn't need to work for her, I worked for myself. Hoping someday I could buy my way out.

"How much?"

"You think she's gonna choose you? She wouldn't have looked at you if you weren't standing next to me."

"I have her." *And you tried to take her from me.* That's what the night at the hotel with Bonnie was really about. Sara couldn't stand the idea of there being someone else who could want me. Even when they, themselves, didn't know it, yet.

"Let's see how long you'll keep her."

The sneer on Sara's face does nothing to convince me I may have made a mistake. I've planned a lifetime. There was a point when I thought Taylor was unattainable. Even Sara, so close in proximity to her, couldn't touch her.

"It all makes sense. I should have seen what was happening." The bookcase she is sitting next to rocks when she pushes it. She doesn't have enough strength to knock it over with everything she has weighing it down.

Taylor was another assignment. My last one. I was supposed to slay her greatest enemy and then walk away. Except, I couldn't.

"I'll really do it," she says with her voice low. Her favorite threat comes out a few times a year. Threatening suicide was the first tactic she used when her dad spread his attention elsewhere. When that stopped working, she started sleeping with his prospects instead. Tainting them. Taking them. That didn't work either, but her body is the only thing she has in her control.

I bend to pick up the pillows and toss them on the bed. In another life, I would have fixed them exactly the way she likes. Not after Taylor. She used to be another face on TV. Until she wasn't.

It was at San Diego Comic-Con. Sara booked a spot on a panel to promote her new show.

The Paige Society's popularity was in full effect. People dressed like Piper Paige or other characters—mostly ghosts. Taylor signed autographs and took photos, all with a smile on her face. It was hard to ignore her only a few booths down.

I wasn't allowed to sit with Sara, so instead I walked around with Maricela. Their equal dislike for each other, and Maricela's tendency to use the death glare as her main combat skill, made keeping the peace between the two challenging.

Maricela was a huge fan of Taylor's—and still is. She watched *Sunny and the Dreamers* religiously. The last episode would end and then she'd rewatch the entire series as if it had just been released the day before. It was maddening. She complained that Sara's character wasn't a loyal friend. And when the series ended with her going solo, and leaving her two group members behind, Maricela's hatred was solidified. Sometimes, she skips that episode entirely.

Almost as soon as *Sunny and the Dreamers* ended, Piper Paige debuted and Taylor went from co-star to the lead. Her face was everywhere. She downplays it now, pretending to be incognito when everyone in the room is staring at her.

Maricela was just as enthralled. Because of her, we kept passing by Taylor's booth, weaving ourselves through the extensive line. Hers was one of the few that required a ticket, and those tickets sold out within the first hour. So, as Maricela walked along the line she couldn't join, I strolled beside her.

She was still standing there when I left her to check in with Sara. I remember the look on Sara's face when I peeked around the marquee. That was when I was getting used to the idea of us. I can't count the number of times I told myself Sara wasn't *that* bad. I'm still unsure. People are who they are for a reason. Shit happens. Life sucks. Sara isn't an exception to that.

When I got back to Maricela, she wasn't there. I ran up and down the line, looking for her. I screamed her name inside the nearest restroom and checked the concession stand. She was nowhere to be found.

"Are you okay?" I turned too quickly. I remember that thought coming to me only after my hair slapped Taylor across the face. Instead of being angry, she laughed. She barely had any makeup on. They always presented Piper Paige as a normal small-town girl, only aware of the existence of lip gloss and eyeliner.

"I'm fine. I'm just looking for someone."

"Dressed like Nikki?"

"Wh- what?"

"Who you're looking for. Is she dressed like a ghost named Nikki?" Nikki was beloved on the show. Any respectable Paige Society trivia would include a question about Nikki's origin. How did Ghost Nikki get her name? Answer: She was named after the real-life best friend of Taylor Townes, Nicole King.

"Yes. Did you see her?" I looked around, hoping to spot the top of Maricela's head nearby.

"I have her!" I remember her face lighting up with pride, as if she had just discovered the biggest treasure. She clasped her hands together and stood on her tippy toes. I knew to follow her, although she never told me to. She led me back to her booth, where people still patiently waited. And there, sitting on the ground at the base of Taylor's chair, was Maricela. She had taken up the job of sorting through photographs for Taylor to sign, keeping her well stocked.

"Your friend is back for you." Taylor pointed to the person behind her. "I think Camden is done with his break now. Thanks for all your help." Taylor enveloped Maricela in a hug and then released her. Maricela couldn't stop beaming. She skipped around the rest of the convention with her signed Taylor Townes photograph. Sara was livid when she saw it. Maricela did not hide it. I was too late to prevent Sara from ripping it. She tore it at the corners before I grabbed it. It was no longer in its pristine condition.

That was a night of many firsts.

It was the first time that we argued. The first time I tried to leave. It was the first time she threatened to kill herself if I did it, showing me the proof of her other attempts. Or what I thought were attempts. It wasn't the first time that we had sex. That had happened long before. But it was the first time that sex included a knife and blood and pain. And throughout the pain, I thought of one face and one name.

Taylor's.

"Tell me how much." I feel like I've asked a million times. Over the years, I've learned it's never good to feed the beast. Her threats become bigger the moment you give them any validity.

Sara stomps around her room, knocking more things to the ground. Her screeching fills the four walls. I imagine Lupe, downstairs, rolling her eyes at the performance. It's always the same. Instinctively, I grab the remote before she flings it at the mounted television. She's broken the screen of more than a few and while they're not expensive, Lupe will suffer more if Sara doesn't have something to distract herself. Although she has other means.

At my interference, Sara throws a once-forgotten coffee mug at the wall instead. The empty mug breaks. Its pieces shoot in different directions. "You're not going anywhere!" She stands in front of the door, banging the back of her head against the wood frame. She does it again, belting out a scream every time she makes contact. I make myself comfortable on the bed. I had hoped that after meeting with Bonnie this morning, Sara would be pissed off enough to let me walk away. I was wrong.

"This isn't about her. There's no way you would leave me for Taylor." She says her name like she just spit poison from her lips. "You're still mad about what happened. Why can't you just get over it?!"

"I did!" I yell back. It's not that I believed her when she said she had to sleep with Savannah Logan. I didn't. But I believed she thought she had to sleep with Savannah Logan. And that was enough. Until it happened again. I could rationalize it when it was for a job, but Sara didn't have sex with her neighbor for a role.

I would be lying if I said that Taylor also didn't scare me. They were different, but also the same. Both successful and sought after. Both skilled in keeping up appearances and pretenses, even to their detriment. But Taylor met with a girl she barely knew, secretly, in a hotel room for months and when they were together, she made her feel like she was the only one that mattered.

Except once.

And that won't ever happen again.

"I forgave the first time, but you're right, I couldn't get over the others."

"You didn't even try." I know the tears streaming down her face are real. She's mastered not crying in front of her parents, no matter how much they disappoint her. She's never hidden them in front of me. Her knees buckle, pulling her down the white wall. She crawls to me then, using my stable knees to support her weight.

Sara is very pretty both on and off-screen. She has eyelashes that always remain curled, teeth that have never needed braces, and one dimple. It was her trademark for a while, though as she got older, she shied away from it more.

She pulls herself up enough to stand. Her knees settle on both sides of me until she's perfectly seated in my lap. My arms remain slack when hers wraps around me in a hold that temporarily restricts my breathing. She lets out a deep breath as her head falls to my shoulder. She wiggles a bit, scooting closer, fully entrapping me. No more tears run down her cheeks. Her voice is calm as she says, "You can try harder. I'll help you."

Chapter Twenty-Two
Taylor

GABRIELLA HASN'T COME HOME. I know that sounds silly. She's been here for two days and I've already gotten used to her. I figured she must've gone to work after she finished running whatever errands she had.

I made dinner from the leftovers in the fridge after declining Nicole's offer to cook. She would have been upset if she had come home and I had already eaten. But as the minutes tick by and the hours round up, I know she isn't coming. Her side of the bed feels cold every time I run my hands across the sheets.

In all my crankiness, I must've missed something. Maybe I hurt her feelings more than she let on when I asked questions about her and Sara. And not to mention what I said to her; *no wonder Sara cheats on you*. The thought of it sends a punch to my gut. What a terrible thing to say.

The story she told me made sense for Sara—a selfish, self-centered brat. Sara would think it was perfectly fine to cheat on her girlfriend, with no consequences. I just don't understand why. Gabriella looks tough and unforgiving. Why would she allow Sara to mistreat her so blatantly?

I scroll through my contacts for an answer. Someone has to know something more that I missed. My thoughts race with the names of people who have been on set with Sara within the last few years, and maybe met Gabriella along the way. My fingers pause on the newest entry in my contacts. When I click it, an old photo I nearly forgot about pops into view. I type away. The first message is long. The second is vague. I settle on the third one and hit send.

Taylor [10:53 p.m.]

I'm sorry about what I said yesterday. I hope you're doing okay.

My phone only has time to hover over the nightstand before I feel it vibrate in my hand.

Gabriella [10:53 p.m.]

What did you say?

Her question gives me pause. Either she doesn't remember how terrible I was to her, or this is a trick. I reflect on my words. Even if this is a trick, it's the right thing to do.

Taylor [10:55 p.m.]

Your history with Sara is none of my business. I am truly sorry for what I said.

The small dots pop up immediately after I hit send.

Gabriella [10:55 p.m.]

It didn't hurt my feelings.

I breathe a sigh of relief, even though I worry about how truthful she's being. When you're in a relationship with someone like Sara, you have to become a professional at downplaying your feelings.

Taylor [10:55 p.m.]

Regardless, I shouldn't have said that. With the way you've been treating me lately, you're the best girlfriend I've ever had LOL.

I wait for her response. When she's quiet, I read and re-read my message. And then send another one.

Taylor [10:58 p.m.]

I guess what I'm trying to say is, thank you.

Gabriella [10:58 p.m.]

You're welcome.

Crisis averted. Mission successful. I change the subject to something more neutral.

Taylor [11:01 p.m.]

What are you doing?

My nails tap against the screen while I wait. The dots don't pop up as quickly as they did before.

Gabriella [11:02 p.m.]

Leaving work.

Taylor [11:02 p.m.]

Are you on your way?

I pull up my navigation app in preparation to calculate how long it'll take for her to get here and switch back to the messenger app after I realize I don't know where she works. I position my fingers to type out the question when her response to my earlier one comes through.

Gabriella [11:03 p.m.]

If you want me to be.

Her response is confusing. Earlier, she said she was coming back. I was fine with that. Her uncertainty makes me feel anxious. Maybe she doesn't want to come back here. She could be tired of me. I've never been so needy. I practically called her my girlfriend a few minutes ago. She needs space, and I need to get my shit together. The most upsetting part about all this is how much I want her to be on her way.

I miss her.

I miss the way she makes me eat even when I complain. I even miss the way she ignores my complaints. Gabriella does what she wants and I like that. Even though I'm not supposed to like her.

Taylor [11:11 p.m.]

I just realized what time it is. I'm going to bed. Drive safe. Goodnight.

There's a feeling I can't quite place swirling around in my chest. It's a massive mix of pain and stupidity. It seems I'm destined to fall for women I shouldn't. In my mind, Gabriella has just become a replacement for Daisy, without the secrets, the punishments, and the sex. Shame on me for not learning my lessons.

My bed should be empty. I should be grateful for cold, unruffled sheets. I curse in the darkness, tossing and turning and willing myself to stop thinking long enough to fall asleep. I'll regret it in the morning when the sun starts to rise and tiredness only begins to set in.

I resort to listening to a sleep meditation that prompts me to place my thoughts into balloons and watch them float away. The exercise is easy enough. I have to send the churros more than once. They look awkward in the first balloon I place them in. I focus too much on making them fit, and the damned thing pops. I try again with a blue balloon, willing my mind to shrink the sizes of the churros, like Daisy shrunk the size of my heart. When that balloon drifts away, I stuff her into the next one. She fights me more than the churros. I summon the hot-air balloon stored in the back of my consciousness somewhere and watch her tumble over the wicker basket. I'm not one hundred percent sure hot air balloons have wicker baskets, but they do here.

Faceless Daisy tries to scramble out, but is too high up to be successful. She doesn't look like Sara to me. Her hair is darker, her face fuller, and her body a little thicker. I want her so badly to be someone else. The higher up she goes, the smaller she becomes and the less weight I feel in my chest.

Goodbye, Daisy.

"What are you doing?" My newly featherweight heart jumps out of my chest. Gabriella stands over me with curly, clumped, wet hair and a towel wrapped around her body. I can barely make out the steam streaming across the ceiling from the bathroom. I didn't even hear her come in. She has that same concerned, but amused, look on her face again.

"What?" I take a while to calm myself. The serene woman's voice still drones in the background.

"You were waving in your sleep." Gabriella moves to her side of the bed. Her clothes for the night are already laid out there.

She completes her entire routine in front of me, only turning when it's time for her to put on her sports bra. I clasp my hand over my eyes when I realize it's time for her to put on her underwear. She laughs when I do it. I hope it appears more playful than shameful. The truth is, my mouth is watering at the prospect and my mind is getting careless with uninvited images.

I'm going to need more hot air balloons.

"Are you going to make me listen to that all night?" She leans over me to shut off my meditation guide before I have a chance to respond. I set it to repeat in case I needed more time than I thought.

I'm a work in progress, after all.

My body moves with Gabriella's adjustments. First, she moves my pillows over towards the center and fluffs them. Then she grabs my thighs and slides me down. I'm shocked at how easily she does it. She never asks me questions or considers my preferences.

And it's fine.

I stay on my side as placed and wait for her arms to wrap around me, pulling me in closer. Somehow I know it's coming.

"Thank goodness I came home when I did. I was almost out of a job." I can tell by her smile against my back that *goodness* is not a word usually in her vocabulary.

"You didn't need to come." She ignores me at the same time

I attempt to ignore the feeling of her fingers playing at the band of my shorts. My attempt is weakened by the rotation of my hips against her.

Shit.

Shit.

Shit.

I'm going to need to set fire to that hot-air balloon. Every movement of her fingers lights my skin ablaze. She moves from my waist up my stomach to the barrier of my bra and back again. Each sweep becomes lighter. My breathing becomes shorter and my panties — well, they were dry when I got into bed earlier.

Turning around is a better idea. She won't be able to feel how badly I lack control of my hips this way.

She doesn't stop me from moving. The hand that played with the front of my shorts now slides to the back. My hand glides down her arm, trying to gain control of this situation. My pounding heart is a direct contrast to Gabriella's calm expression. Though her fingers move slightly on my lower back, her eyes are closed and her face rests. The skin I touch is soft.

Maybe Sara did change.

"I thought you were going to sleep." Her eyes don't open when her lips move. I try not to panic when her hand moves down my shorts, around my ass and hooks underneath my knee, pulling me closer with my thigh now draped across her hip.

"I am. You interrupted me." There's a slight moment where I worry she might take offense. The corners of her lips twitch.

"If you want, I can leave." She says it with a slight chuckle that bounces between us.

I dismiss her comment. "You're already here. I might as well keep you." Instead of placing my thoughts inside balloons and watching them blow away, I listen to the sound of Gabriella breathing while counting the number of tiny freckles splattered underneath her eyes and across her nose. Funny, I never really notice them during the day when her mood takes over. I count them on my way to sleep, stroking her arm in the same rhythm as my breaths release.

The bed is empty when I wake up. During the night, I turned onto my belly and rolled to my side. My phone vibrating on the nightstand wakes me.

The insistent rattling is hard to ignore. I have no plans today other than to sleep and sulk. Napping has become my coping strategy. I'm good at it when Gabriella isn't commanding me into action. It takes a while for my eyes to focus against the bright light.

Sara Aguilar Sparks Fans Concerns With New Social Media Video

If nothing else, you have to admire Sara's consistency.

Sara's face is plastered on every article I click on. The black and white still image of Sara ugly crying online sends the correct message. I scroll down to read the comments and then stop myself. I click on the email icon instead. Zara's email is marked as important and sits at the top although I can tell from the time, it was the first one I received after the video dropped.

From:Zarajamesmngmt@mail.com
To: Ttownes@mail.com
Subject: DO NOT RESPOND TO THE VIDEO!

———————————

I know I don't have to tell you not to do this, but just in

case. DO NOT RESPOND!

Except for the small snippets I'm able to read without clicking, the text messages remain unread. I should've chosen vacation over temporary retirement. A cool ocean breeze would've made me immune to Sara's wickedness instead of sucked into her tentacles.

Poor Gabriella.

The phone keeps buzzing in my hand while I roll out of the bed. Her things are on the side, tucked neatly in the corner. The curtains are drawn downstairs. A faint mumbling voice wafts through the air, making me cringe inside. I groan at Nicole, sitting on the couch eating a grilled cheese sandwich with Sara's face in her palm.

"I guess it's too early for popcorn," I say as I round the corner to the kitchen. There's already an omelet warming in a skillet.

"Sara's girlfriend left that for you." Nicole's eyes and mine meet from across the room. Her usual playful tone is lost. I grab the knife set beside the stove, slide the omelet onto a plate, and take a seat across from her.

"She's not her girlfriend. They broke up a while ago."

"Oh? That's not what her girlfriend says." Sara's voice pauses momentarily while Nicole rewinds the video with her index finger. I try not to roll my eyes at Nicole's reaction to Sara's latest stunt.

The video starts with her sniffling. Tears are already streaming down her face while she wipes away a visible row of snot. "I never wanted to make a video like this. I know so many of you understand what it has been like for me these last couple of years, being constantly betrayed by people who claim to love me. Tonight was bad. I got into a huge fight with my girlfriend. We both said things I know we didn't mean. This year has been hard for both of us, but we used to support each other without interference from outsiders. And I'm not blaming Taylor–" *Bitch*. "I just think that sometimes, even when you have the best intentions, you need to be aware enough to know when your presence is causing someone else pain."

"And you're buying this?" I cut into the omelet and grab the first piece with my fork.

Nicole pauses the video. "Of course, I'm not buying *this*. *You're* buying it. Do you really think she isn't in on this? I bet she's pretending to be heartbroken by Sara to pull you in, only to stab you in the back afterward. Open your eyes, Taylor!"

"She's never said Sara broke her heart." She doesn't talk about her at all. If I didn't ask, you'd think Sara never existed.

"Then why'd they break up?"

"You know why." Nicole heard the rumors as loudly as I had. It pains me to think that everyone knew what was going on, but no one thought to say anything, including me. Gabriella was insignificant in the grand scheme of things. As the talent, Sara was the priority.

Nicole presses play on the video once again. Sara's whimpering continues. "Brie, if you see this, please come home. I know we can fix it. I know we can make it right. I lo–"

The sound of the patio door sliding open causes me to jump. Gabriella walks through the crack with clear eyes and dry cheeks. She ignores Nicole, who hasn't bothered to press pause on Sara's latest manipulation tactic.

"Do you wanna go on a drive with me?"

There's nothing on her face that reveals her current mood. She looks the same as she always does. I instantly nod, shoving the rest of the omelet in my mouth. Getting dressed is quick and independent. It feels like a long time ago when she was shoving me through my clothes. Though it was only yesterday. I already know she's driving and don't bother to pocket my keys on the way out the door.

Her walk is the same. She still slightly bumps into me as though she can't be bothered to make enough room for me on the sidewalk. Her usual don't-talk- to -me- if- you're-breathing expression is there. The peace from last night is gone. I cradle her arm in my elbow the next time she swings my way. She's not wearing a hoodie like I am. Despite the heat, when the sun reaches midday, it gets chilly by the beach.

Her bare skin feels warmer the more I touch her. My fingers loop around her wrist, then back up again. This side is just as smooth as the other.

"There's not a lot of people out right now." I want to reassure her she's safe here. No one knows that she's with me. Sara will probably look for her in San Diego or harass Chasity and Krystal about where she is. As much as I'm not the biggest fan of theirs—Chasity in particular — I doubt they'd give her up.

I let go of her long enough for us to claim our places in the car. She places one hand on my thigh while she drives. If my destination is local in Santa Monica, I'd rather walk. In traffic, it can take you half an hour to drive a few blocks.

The donut shop she stops in front of is nearby. It's a local, smaller one and not one of the fancy ones, which always has a line wrapped around the block.

I take one glance at the display cases, turn to Gabriella and say, "I don't want anything. I'll get us a seat." This place is sparsely populated. I can tell it attracts more of an older crowd who desire quiet and not social media clout for breakfast photos. Gabriella joins me a few minutes later.

"Here." The cup she sets in front of me is warm. I feel the usual guilt that springs up whenever anyone buys me coffee. Out of politeness, I bring it to my lips and take a delicate sip, hoping I don't scald my tongue. A familiar sweetness greets me instead of the bitterness I expect.

"This is hot chocolate."

Her eyebrow rises at my astonishment. "You don't drink coffee."

"I know that. How do *you* know that?" A silly image of her and Sara lording over a notebook filled with facts about me appears in my mind. I brush it away, not wanting Sara to infect the moment. Gabriella looks content now, drinking her drink and biting into her croissant.

"You said it in an interview once. You like hot chocolate with milk and water. You have a favorite recipe, but you botch it every time you try to make it yourself. And you lied at the festival about your favorite color being yellow because the Emmy is gold. Your favorite color is purple. You do want to win an Emmy one day and agree with most people that they robbed you of your nomination last year, which is the real reason you stepped away from acting."

I clutch the warm drink in my hand. "I didn't say that last part in an interview."

"I know."

I'd been on the shortlist. I had been told about it multiple times. Journalists had written articles about it. I would have been the youngest to win for Best Actress in a Drama Series, had I won. But when they announced the nominees, I wasn't there.

"You refused to campaign for it."

"I didn't refuse." Not exactly. I wanted it on merit. I didn't want my win to be based on a popularity contest. I had worked my ass off as Piper Paige. We were number one in our demographics, the most-watched show on Thursday nights.

The show won.

And I wasn't even nominated.

I am not Emmy Award-Winning Actress, Taylor Townes. After the Paige Society, I struggled to give my all to another role. I needed a break. The writers always knew the show would end after season four. It was perfect timing, and Sara's attacks gave me an even better excuse to walk away.

The man who previously stood behind the counter interrupts the memory of my career-high disappointment. He places a chocolate-stained bag on the table. Gabriella thanks him in Spanish (who doesn't know what gracias means?) and he walks away.

She looks into the bag before slipping two fingers inside. "You also only eat donuts with sprinkles on them." The icing on the chocolate-sprinkled-covered donut is still moist. The case was empty of them when we walked in earlier.

She takes a piece between her fingers. "Ven aquí." I know that one, too. I lean forward as expected, opening my mouth wide enough to accept the treat. When her fingers touch my lips, other things explode inside me. I go in for another bite and hope lifting my hips helps stave off the building heat.

It's just a donut.

And Gabriella is just a friend. A new friend who knows what it's like to feel sad and heartbroken. I shouldn't think of anything or anyone else when she commands me in another language.

She's not Daisy.

I fight the inexplicable urge to lick the chocolate from her fingers. It would be a terrible thing to do in public. Completely inappropriate.

"Are you ready to go?" Gabriella looks at me expectedly, unaware of the role she's currently playing in my thoughts.

I nod without speaking and follow her out the door with my hot chocolate in hand. It's a little warmer outside than it was when we first came. In the car, my hands stay locked to the styrofoam cup. Her hand finds its place back in my lap. She glances at me once in question. I maintain my cool. Only a few blocks left to go.

She unlocks the front door when I can't. Nicole isn't in the same place that we left her. I'm slightly disappointed at not having a distraction to keep myself from thinking about the past. I was sure she would wait inside to chastise me about going out in public with Gabriella. I'm not sure which one of us is the bigger target at the moment. Sara has sent her message. Her dogs will attack.

Gabriella sits on the ottoman across from the couch. The windows behind her make for a perfect backdrop. Anyone could see us inside here. When I moved into this apartment with Nicole, I thought nothing about the windows or the access it would give others to me. The location of our apartment and its proximity to the terrace make it more expensive, yes. We can easily afford it.

We thought about morning brunches on the patio and late-night walks over the city lights below us. I didn't imagine my outside view might become the portal to my secrets. And Gabriella has no idea.

If I press my fingers any deeper into the cup, the hot chocolate will spill all over me. She'll undress me, I'm sure of it. She'll do it without thinking, without realizing she's exposing me to everyone lucky enough to take a walk outside.

And I won't say a thing.

I'll lift my arms when she tells me to and stand in place while she checks me over for burns. I'd test her patience by turning too slowly to take off my pants. My hips will sway in assistance. I mean to help. I'm trying hard to be obedient. Promise. She didn't touch my panties at all last night, but she will here. She'll grow frustrated with my slow movements and do the only thing she thinks she can do. She'll rip them. Of course, she doesn't mean to, but it'll be too late to go back.

Gabriella doesn't admit to mistakes and she doesn't make apologies. Her hand will slide around my waist and dip into the space she has uncovered. And when my hips move against her, soaking her skin underneath, my eyes will stare through the glass and into the sunlight.

She does not know what she's done.

"Taylor." I focus my eyesight to stare at her face that's now a few inches from mine. I didn't even hear her rise. My empty hands are outstretched before me. My hot chocolate is missing. A glance spots it sitting on the coffee table in front of me.

"Yeah?"

"What's going on with you?" She looks at me with her head tilted to the side.

"What do you mean?"

"You've been quiet since the donut shop." Her hands cup my face softly. Embarrassing tickles soar down my spine. "You not only deserved to be nominated, you deserved to win, Emmy."

She doesn't recognize her own mistake. Her eyes still look into mine, unmoving, even though I swear I stop breathing a few seconds before slowing the words to calm me. It's an easy slip of the tongue when your brain is processing too fast.

"I deserved to win *an* Emmy."

"Of course you did." She does the same as she always does and lays out on the couch cushions. And I follow her as I always do. My body fits in between her thighs easily. My eyes drift closed with every slight tug of my hair strands that elicit the warm tingling through my scalp.

She's the perfect distraction from my earlier fantasy. It was never meant to be. Gabriella, in her moodiness and dark history, feels more real to me now than Daisy ever did.

Chapter Twenty-Three
Gabriella

THE INSULTS COME FAST. My profiles have always been private. I'm not friends with people on social media that I don't know in real life. When they can't get to me, they go for them. Krystal ignores it. Chasity has fun with it. She almost looks to be in a trance, with a crazed look on her face, when replying to them all.

An overuse of the casket emoji litters almost every comment. It's both a callback to a popular song Sara sang on *Sunny and the Dreamers* and a threat. I remember sitting through an interview of hers when she claimed to write the song about her girlfriend. It was around the time that she came out and announced our relationship. Her fans went crazy over her false confession, even petitioning for a reboot of the series. To my knowledge, Taylor didn't publicly comment on the possibility of the show returning. What Sara's fans failed to realize was we weren't even together.

Sara lied.

She lies about everything.

This is no different.

I haven't watched the video. I don't need to. Leaving was never going to be easy. I knew that and did it, anyway.

For Taylor.

I walk right past her and Nicole on the way into the classroom. Nicole is more than happy to pull at Taylor's backpack when she tries to stop me. I'm mildly grateful for it. Since the release of Sara's video, Taylor has become quite clingy. Her check-ins throughout the day have become more frequent, which has only increased Nicole's annoyance. Nicole is going to be a problem, but she's not my problem. She'll get in line, eventually.

Sara's already here. I'm certain the people surrounding our desks are not students in this class. They scowl at me. I sit in my usual seat next to Sara. There's no need for me to change it. All the others are taken, and if anyone can ignore Sara, it's me. A few of them look away when I meet their gaze. Sara turns to face me in silence. Her face is bare with red cheeks, not from makeup. She nods toward the door, giving the group permission to leave. One mumbles something incoherent as they walk past. I let it slide.

"It's not too late." I stare into her red-rimmed eyes and contemplate her words. Our relationship has always been complicated. I had to learn to love Sara. It was only after I finally did that I realized love wasn't what she wanted. She wanted control.

"Did you even watch my video?" She sent it to me before she posted it online. I saw it for what it was–a threat. She was hoping I would give in to protect Taylor. I didn't and I won't. No matter what, I know Taylor will be okay.

She's always fine.

I shift away from her pleading eyes. "I was clear the first time." The rest of the class suddenly files in. There will be no viral videos for them to devour today, though I'm sure by the time they leave, this moment will be shared for all to see on the internet.

A white paper bag lands softly on my notebook. Taylor stands at my desk with a smile on her face. "This one's freshly made from scratch. No preservatives." The vanilla glazed confetti sprinkled doughnut is almost as cute as she is. "How are you doing?" She lowers her voice slightly above a whisper, though I can tell Sara can still hear her.

"I'm fine." I see the lens of the cameras she always pretends to not notice poking out over people's textbooks and backpacks. Some don't hide them at all. It will only fuel Sara's claims that Taylor got in between us. She's wrong. Taylor was first in line.

"Am I going to see you tonight?" Taylor's gaze flicks to Sara quickly and back to me again. Sara's eyes narrow, but she makes no other movement. She's never been confronted head-on like this. I'm usually the one who attacks from behind while she smiles in people's faces.

"I'll let you know." I'm unprepared for the look that crosses her face. If I didn't know any better, I'd think I'd hurt her feelings.

"What does that mean?" Her eyebrows push together in an uncharacteristic frown.

"I don't know if I'm coming over. I'll let you know before I go to work."

"How do you not know?" The more she argues with me, the more quiet it gets around us.

"I might go home afterward."

"Why? You have plenty of clothes at my place." Someone sucks in a breath in the stillness. It's the last thing I wanted her to say here.

"You've been staying with her?" The scraping of chairs accompanies Sara's raised voice. People are out of their seats. Their cameras are no longer hiding.

"Why wouldn't she? She's my friend." An innocence I know doesn't exist laces Taylor's words. The thoughts that roam through my mind when we're in her bed are less than innocent. Severely. She addresses Sara, her shoulders squared and her back straight. It's the self-righteous stance Sara has always despised.

"My girlfriend is not a friend of yours," Sara says, her nails scratching against the smooth surface.

"She's not your girlfriend."

"I'm not your girlfriend." We say it at the same time. Nicole, who stands behind Taylor, smacks a hand to her face and groans. She tugs Taylor to their usual seats. Taylor goes, but stares at me and Sara the whole way.

The professor walks through the door warily. He's twenty minutes past the tardy rule. No one noticed the opportunity for a free morning. Fewer cameras point in our direction as the class continues. Sara's head lies on her desk in my direct view. Now and then a tear rolls from her eyes, across her nose, and melts into the single piece of paper beneath her.

Everyone seems to linger at the end of class to prepare for the next show. I get up after Nicole leads Taylor to the door. Taylor gives me a questioning look without pausing.

"You know what will happen if you don't come home." Sara's change in position makes her look even more pathetic. She can barely hold her head up while she clings to my desk. One tear is pushed over the edge and glides down her cheek. I wipe it away instinctively and then pull my wrist back. I hear the shutter sound of a camera going off in the background.

My phone vibrates and the screen lights up.

Taylor [10:20 a.m.]

You better be at home tonight. MY home.

It's *our* home. Even if she doesn't know it. I gather my things and take one last look at Sara. There's a big part of me that wants to provide her with some relief.

I'm leaving, but...

Taking care of Sara was my job for a long time. While Taylor will always be fine. Sara might crumble. And that's no longer my responsibility. "Goodbye, Sara."

The buzzing from my cell phone is non-stop. The apron absorbs most of it, which helps me focus during my shift instead of worrying about what the world is saying about Taylor.

Someone posts the video shortly after class ends. I watched it even though I shouldn't have. Hundreds of comments with irrelevant and uninformed opinions had already materialized.

I toss my apron into the hamper on the way out the door for my break, as trained. My phone continues to vibrate in my hand through my short trek. I press the message belonging to the only face I care to see at the moment.

Taylor [9:13 p.m.]

What time are you getting off work?

I'm the last person she'd call if she was scared. This isn't that. She's been here with Sara before. I'm sure her team has an entire protocol in place. Not that I wouldn't protect her. If anyone ever tried to physically harm her in my presence, things would get bad. Fans can be downright neurotic when they obsess over their *"fave."*

Taylor has always had the emotional part down. She engages

with her fandom only when necessary and disappears when she needs to. Like now.

I read her next message and smile to myself.

Taylor [9:16 p.m.]

When are you coming home?

Home.

Taylor [9:20 p.m.]

Do you need me to pick you up?

I type out a response to that one to save her the trip. Yes, I'll be home and no, I don't need a ride.

I'm fine.

It's been busy at Craft. I take my place underneath the trees lit with small lights. It's always quiet out here at night. By this time, the office spaces nearby are closed and the Century City Mall is just far enough away to not be near the traffic.

I cycle through the many messages that have come through during my shift. Taylor has nothing to worry about. I'll be home tonight.

I've never pegged her for the possessive type, but maybe this has more to do with Sara than with me. Sara's mob is scorching through social media on a Taunt (short for Taylor haunt) and she doesn't seem to care. Her page has remained silent. No snarky remarks. No subliminal messages or photos. And no statement.

Sara is spiraling. Her messages differ from the ones posted. I only read a few. Each one blends in familiarity. I've heard it all before.

I've had more responsibility over Sara's life than her parents, and even herself. It shouldn't be up to me whether Sara lives. I have to preserve my life. And I choose to spend it with Taylor.

It takes a while for my thumb to press the block button and for me to confirm that I mean what I feel. I'm done. The comments I read underneath Taylor's very public page only affirm it for me.

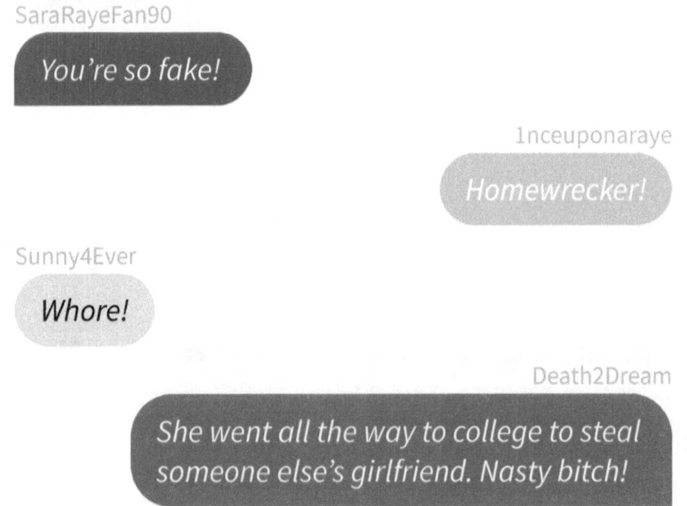

This is what I hate about fan culture. Everyone thinks they know you when they don't know shit.

My phone vibrates in my hand and the face of my mom pops up. "I don't have a lot of time, Mom."

"Aye. Who taught you to answer the phone like that?" I hold back my smart remark. No matter how I feel about my family sometimes, I have to be respectful.

"Good evening, Mother. How may I help you?"

"You're such a smart ass. I tell your dad all the time. You get it from him. Neither one of you listens to anything I say." I let her go on her rant for as long as she needs. If I try to interrupt, she'll just talk for longer. "Why haven't you called me yet? I shouldn't have to hear about my daughter from strangers on the internet."

"Are the girls okay?"

"They're fine. Mari wants to throw a party." I chuckle a bit at that. She would. She'd have no problem making a banner and hanging it over our front porch. "So, did you?"

"Break up with Sara? Yeah, it's over. I think it'll be okay. I got a lot of tips today and as long as I keep working, we should be able to cover the penalty."

I hear my grandma in the background yelling in Spanish. Her words are a threat meant for any future attorneys coming to knock on my parents' door.

My mom's voice overtakes hers. "Forget about that. Is it true you left her for Taylor?" I've never told my family what being in a relationship with Sara was really like. They didn't know when I broke up with her. They only have a little more information than the anonymous people on the internet. And only because they were there first.

"Yeah. It's true."

Mom hushes the noise that goes off around her. If I had to guess, I'd say Mari was huddled up close to hear confirmation of the news. I'll be receiving a call from her next.

"You know I support you, Mija. I'll talk to your dad about it. Don't worry."

I'm not worried. I haven't been worried in months. It doesn't matter to me how my family comes to terms with my decision. I've done all I can and I'll do more if I have to.

I end the call with my mom and return to work. Closing time comes quickly and I walk away with thousands of dollars in tips. Most of it will go into my bank account for a potential rainy day or thunderstorm. I'm not sure yet which one will hit first.

Once in my car, my phone rattles against its holder. And I'm sure it's Taylor, again, checking to see if I'm on my way or not. I got too distracted and forgot to message her back. I wait until I stop at the red light to read the first message from Chasity. It's a simple link.

Sara Aguilar Enters Rehab. Struggles with Mental Health After Break-Up

Shit.

Chapter Twenty-Four
Taylor

I NOD OCCASIONALLY, THOUGH Zara's words stopped registering in my brain some time ago. Zara summoned me to her office after I stopped responding to her emails and text messages. Once Mama called me, I knew there was no avoiding it. I did as I was told and arrived at Zara's office fifteen minutes before scheduled. They were already waiting. The questions started immediately with photographic proof of all their concerns.

"Taylor, do you understand where we're coming from?" Zara has asked me that question multiple times.

"Nothing is going on. She's my friend." My very attractive and newly single friend, who I left in my bed this morning. It's completely normal. And totally fine. I've actually been proud of how well I've been able to not allow my brain-filled fantasies to overtake my physical capabilities to control myself.

Daisy always made me feel out of control. Sara will do that to you.

Of course, I can't say this to any of them. I can barely explain what happened. Building a friendship with Gabriella should be the least of their worries.

"Have you seen these articles? Are you paying attention?" Since I was little, Mama always liked to say that I was lost in 'Tinsel Town.' It started after I booked that Christmas play that I didn't enjoy. It was a local hit driven by a review in the newspaper. Many schools used it as their holiday field trip before winter break. My face was on the front page of the events section. When Mama showed me, I glanced at it and then went back to whisking together the eggs I needed for the batch of cookies I was baking with Daddy. She walked away muttering about me being lost in 'Tinsel Town.'

"Yes, Mama. I see them. They're gonna say what they wanna say no matter what I do. If I hadn't been standing there, they would've said I was being a terrible friend to Sara, regardless. They don't need an excuse."

"That doesn't mean that you help them fan the flames. It's better to have words without pictures." Zara's disapproving face matches her tone. Nothing like this has ever happened before. My years of being Zara's easiest client are gone.

"I don't think you're listening to Zara. You'll need to come back to your career one day. Let's make sure you have a career to come back to."

I can't stop the whine from exploding out of me quickly enough. "Mama!" I hate when they say that. Being able to say that acting is something I wanted to do and not something my parents forced me into has always been something I said with pride. I used to feel like I could walk away at any moment. After Sara's first stunt, which forced me out of my proverbial closet, the energy changed from opportunistic fun to necessary survival.

My dad reaches around her to squeeze my shoulder. He's always been the supportive observer, only speaking when necessary.

"I met a girl." The words come out as deflated as I feel. I think carefully, separating the necessary information from what's not. They don't need to know everything. Zara and Mama exchange a glance. Daddy squeezes a little tighter.

"I thought it was going somewhere. It only lasted for a while.

When it ended, Gabriella was there to help me. And now I wanna help her, too."

"Why didn't you tell me?" Mama sounds almost betrayed. I've always considered myself close to both of my parents, but telling them I was secretly meeting up with a girl in a hotel room for sex was never an option.

"I didn't want there to be a lot of pressure on us. She was already weirded out by the whole dating-a-celebrity thing. And I was right. She couldn't handle it. Said I didn't have enough time for her with everything I was doing with Bonnie."

Pity replaces the disappointment previously etched on Zara's features. I continue with confidence. "Gabriella was there for me. I don't think Sara knew. That's probably why she got so freaked out when she saw us together."

Mama's reassuring knee pat accompanies Daddy's comforting squeeze. She lets out a sigh. "Ok. If you say the two of you are friends, then I believe you." I revel in the warm hug she gives me.

Daddy follows me out of the office, leaving Mama and Zara to talk about upcoming projects.

Without asking, he wrangles the keys from my hand, unlocks my car and pops the hood with the press of the button. "You need to take your car in for an oil change." He reminds me with his head tucked underneath the hood.

I whine in protest. "It takes too long." Before I moved out, Daddy handled the car maintenance. Now, I'm on my own.

"So, just a friend, huh?" He wipes off the oil from the dipstick with a napkin he finds in my cup holder and replaces it. A sly smile spreads across his lips. I try to stop mine from forming.

"That's what I said."

"For how long?" I shrug my shoulders. I moved too fast with Daisy and I'm not exactly sure what I want with Gabriella. I like how her arms feel wrapped around me and how warm my bed feels with her in it.

"She's cute though, right?" The laugh shakes out of his chest so loudly that I practically feel it vibrate through me. As my original wingman, he's had a longer time listening to me obsess about the women I've found attractive.

"It's the hair, I bet. You've always had a thing for dark, curly hair." I'm not sure if I've ever categorized it as a preference, but Daddy knows best. I get the same warm hug from him I got from Mama before driving away. It's all Daddy's fault when I can't stop imagining Gabriella's hair wrapped around my fingers.

Something smells good. Gabriella was asleep when I left this morning and she hadn't messaged me at all. She must not be upset if she plans to feed me.

The apartment is bright and spotless when I open the door. Gabriella stands in the kitchen at the stove, as predicted. Nicole sits on the couch, peering over the edge of her textbooks.

"Good morning," I sing out. On their own accord, my lips pucker out and a kiss lands on Gabriella's jaw. "Muah!" I exaggerate the gesture to cover up my eagerness.

"Good morning," she responds coolly, not letting on if anything I did was weird or inappropriate. A look at Nicole's half-hidden face and sharp gaze is all the confirmation I need.

I pluck one piece of pastrami out of the skillet and toss it from one hand to the next to cool. Gabriella smacks my hand away when I go for the second piece. "Ow! Mommy." My laugh evaporates into silence. "I...uh...didn't mean it that way." I slink out in horror through the living room and out onto the balcony, avoiding Nicole's gaze as I walk by. A mere second passes by before I hear the unmistakable sound of the patio doors sliding open and shut again.

Nicole follows me to the patio chairs. "Is there anything you want to say to me?"

"The apartment looks good." Nicole and I are both neat people, but now and then Nicole goes the extra mile and does things like wash the curtains and clean the windows. Those sprints usually happen in the early mornings and I can tell by how the sun gleams through the apartment that today was one of those days.

"Thank you. Now tell me the truth about you and her." There's something about the way Nicole refuses to say her name that bothers me. Gabriella hasn't done anything to Nicole to be treated this way.

"Please be nice to her?"

"Because you're dating her?"

"Because I love you." Nicole lets out a breath and I watch her shoulders fall. "Don't let Sara turn you into someone you're not. She's good at it."

"I just keep feeling like I'm missing something. Like you're lying to me. And the only thing different is her. *You've* been different since her." I've been different since Sara. Nicole is right. I am lying to her. She doesn't know the truth about Daisy or Sara. As selfish as it may seem, I want to keep it this way.

"I talked a lot with her about how Sara treated her. How we know Sara treated her." Nicole and I exchange a knowing glance.

"So it's true?"

"Yeah, and more than we knew, apparently." She glances back at our apartment. From our view, we can't see Gabriella standing in the kitchen.

"I guess she's not that bad. I barely know she's here most of the time. She cleans up after herself and she cooks."

I swat at her accusation. "I cook."

"You cook cereal and cheese toast." Nicole relaxes more into her laugh. I lie my head on her rested shoulder and wrap my arms around her elbow.

"We're not dating. I don't know what we are."

"No, but you want to."

"Isn't that what you wanted for me?" I shake my wrist and watch the sun's rays shine on the gold, rainbow-colored bracelet.

"I want you to be happy with someone who's gonna treat you well. I worry she's too much like Sara." A thoughtful expression crosses over Nicole's face. "She doesn't have any scars?"

"Nuh-uh. I checked."

"Well, that's good. Maybe she's less damaged than I thought." She yips when I pinch her thigh.

I've felt a growing protectiveness for Gabriella these last few weeks and it's getting harder to ignore.

Nicole leaves after lunch. To my surprise, she thanks Gabriella for cooking. A sentiment Gabriella reciprocates in gratitude. I take over Nicole's former spot on the couch and flick on the television. Gabriella reappears from upstairs with a stuffed bag.

"What time do you have to go to work today?"

"I'm off tonight. I have a paper to write. Do you want me to pick you up in the morning or drive separately?"

"You don't plan on coming back?" I relax my facial muscles into a more neutral expression.

"I can if you want me to," she suspiciously responds, peering at me from across the room.

"Please do." I only offer an exaggerated smile when in reality my heart is racing in anticipation of a decision I wasn't sure I was going to make until this very moment, when the thought of her leaving is too much.

Chapter Twenty-Five
Gabriella

MAYBE THIS WAS A mistake. The paper I silently boasted would write itself sits on the screen, blank. I have no words to feed it while Taylor occupies my thoughts. I woke up this morning without her beside me. Breakfast was made in preparation for an arrival that didn't come. I made lunch with hope and reminded myself how silly it was that I was even thinking about her not coming back to her apartment.

Meetings like that rarely go in my favor. Whenever Sara was pulled into one, either someone new got dropped on my plate or a new expectation was set. Taylor didn't need me in the same way Sara did. I figured they would tell her she needed to get rid of me and that I was too much of a liability.

My, how things change.

The door to Chasity's bedroom opens with a slight squeak. We share the same surprised look on account that we each thought the other would spend the day elsewhere.

"Have you seen Krystal?" Chasity slowly looks around the bedroom before stepping inside.

"I'm pretty sure she's at work." Chasity is my best friend. I will never judge her for any decision that she makes about her life. Not that I disagree with what she's doing now, but she should be honest with Krystal about it.

"Why are you here instead of your girlfriend's place?" She makes mocking, kissy faces at me.

"Why are you here instead of at work?"

"I got the day off." I eye her suspiciously and wait for the rest of the story.

"After working overtime last night?" I push the laptop further away from me. My paper will have to wait.

Chasity flings herself on the bed and lies on the pillow beside mine. We both stare up at the ceiling. "Of course not. But let's not talk about me. How's everything going with your *new* actress?"

"I hate when you say it like I'm pursuing back lots for girlfriends."

"I think at this point, it's clear you have a type."

"I didn't choose this game."

"The game chose me," we say in unison, laughing.

"You finally broke free." The sincerity in her words is as clear as it can be. I truly believe that even when we aren't getting along, Chasity wants what's best for me.

"Yeah," I confirm in response. My friends don't know a lot about my relationship with Sara. They know they hate her and they know it took me a while to accept our relationship.

"Taylor seems okay. A little pretentious, but I guess she's earned the right to be snobby."

"That's what's funny about her. She doesn't even talk about acting unless she's asked. The business was Sara's entire personality. Every day was a strategy about how to navigate through it for the best possible outcome. Taylor just...is." The truth doesn't do much to soothe me. This feeling is unfamiliar. "I keep waiting for her to tell me to go away. She had to leave this morning. No one ever leaves that early for no reason. It had to be about me."

"She didn't say anything?"

"Nope. She came home as if nothing had happened. And when I was leaving, she asked if I was coming back."

From my peripheral vision, I can see Chasity's face turn in my direction. "Why is that weird?"

"With Sara, especially in the beginning, every second I wasn't with her had to be accounted for. If I was home, I had to be home and with my parents. If I was going to the store, I was on a timer. It feels weird that Taylor doesn't care about the specifics. 'You're going out? Great, have fun.'"

"Wow. She sounds...normal." I hear the smirk in Chasity's voice rather than see it for myself.

"She could hurt me." It's one thought I've been trying to push out of my mind all day.

"Don't stress about it too much. You've been through way worse things than dating a paranormal detective." She barely gets through the last word before she laughs.

"I know," I say, laughing along with her. Taylor's reputation is the reason Sara hates her. So much goodness without cause. So much gained without struggle. She shouldn't be this perfect.

But she is.

Chapter Twenty-Six
Taylor

THE BATHROOM IS CLEAN, with enough space for Gabriella to keep her things on the counter and in the shower. I pat myself on the back for picking the apartment with double sinks, even though Daddy said it was unnecessary for one person. Past me knew I was going to meet a girl in a coffee shop and bring her home with me. And although that's not our actual story, that's the one we'll tell everyone who asks. *We locked eyes over the head of a barista*. I'm sure Nicole will play along and invent some monologue about how she encouraged us to date.

I do the same in the closet. Lucky for us, I've never grown too attached to items I couldn't part with. I make space in the drawers for things Gabriella doesn't want to hang up and sort hangers to the side that I don't need.

I stroll down to a sushi restaurant and a flower stall. I grip the petal of a white daisy and pull. Not all of it breaks away from the center. The piece that does falls to the ground at my feet. Daisies are more prevalent than I thought. Never having had the opportunity to buy flowers for a girl, I paid little attention to them. One bouquet, combined with an assortment of pinks and reds, catches my eye. Gabriella doesn't seem like a lover of pink. The red is questionable. But there is something about the combination that feels like us. I wrap them in my arms, listen intently to the care instructions given to me by the florist, and then carry them home.

The hours tick by. My phone remains silent. I set the dining table Nicole and I have barely used for two. Placing candles in the center feels like overkill. Plus, I don't have those cute, white, long-stemmed ones with the crystal candle stick holders.

The terrace isn't busy tonight. My skin drinks up the sun, something I always feel is both good and bad. I'm terrible at wearing sunscreen, but if I try to hide in the shade, my body feels cold and neglected. I compromise by sitting in a shady spot next to a sunny location.

Sitting alone in public is quite a challenge. In my escape, I forgot to grab my phone, a puzzle, a book, or anything to entertain myself. In the past, I would message Daisy, but that's all over and done with. Now I have to wait for Gabriella to deem me worthy of her time.

"Hey, how you doin'?" Daze's voice carries to me from out in the distance. He doesn't wait for a response to start his walk over. Memories of the night I last saw him flood my brain. I will never forget the look on his face in those brief moments when his eyes locked on mine. It's not the same look now. Maybe my mind imagined it like it imagined my feelings for Daisy growing. It's hard to think about wanting someone who only wants to hurt you.

"Hey. What's up?" My hand shades over my eyes, although I can see him enough. My shady spot is doing its job well.

"Nothin' much just chillin'." When he reaches me, he shoves his hands into his pockets and leans back, balancing his new position with the heels of his feet.

"That's good," is all I say in the empty space.

"Yeah. Uh…what happened to you the other night? I was hoping you were gonna drop by." His eyes roam over me at the same time his tongue rolls over his bottom lip.

"Oh, yeah. Hmm." A good lie doesn't float to me fast enough. I shouldn't have to lie. I don't even know if I said I would hang out with him and his cousin that night. "Can I just be honest with you?"

He takes his time, considering my request. It's almost funny and a little cute how he does it: pacing back and forth with his fingers rubbing his chin. "Yeah, I think so."

I take a deep breath, contemplating my confession. "I was hooking up with this girl that night and I completely forgot about it." Daze's eyes grow wide. His reaction is a shock to me since I'm fairly sure Daze knows exactly who I am and, therefore, is aware of my sexuality.

"Is that right?" I nod in confirmation. "Is she coming over tonight?" His question is unexpected. I teeter on the answer, unsure of where this is taking us. Daze's demeanor changes from playful to confident. He steps into my sunny space and then moves closer to join me in the shade.

"Taylor, what are you doing out here?" There's an edge in Gabriella's question that feels dark and possessive. It starts from the way she draws out my name. Clearly she can see I'm having a conversation with my neighbor's cousin. Daze's eyes bounce between her and me. I can't help the smile that spreads across my face. It's nice to see her show emotion toward me, especially in front of someone else. I curl up my knees and swing them around to the other side of Daze.

"Yeah, she is," I shout my farewell to Daze on the move. Gabriella's eyes aren't on me at all as I approach. When I look back, Daze is returning her gaze. I don't like it. Despite the feeling that quakes below me at this silent, but intense battle, he's no one to challenge her like that.

I pull Gabriella through the glass doors and shut them behind me. "I thought you would text me first." Gabriella doesn't respond as I lead her around the apartment. My mind scrambles to recover and salvage my plan. I feel her impatience grow with every false step. I place her in the kitchen before changing my mind and ushering her back into the living room. She sits on the couch.

"Stay here." I run upstairs and grab the blindfold I haven't used in weeks. I secure it over her questioning eyes and say, "When I knock on the door. Answer it." I dash to the kitchen where I sat the flowers she hopefully did not notice or didn't think twice about. A quick stop to the bathroom tells me my hair is fine. I step out into the hallway and close the door behind me. The jitters in my belly are all too familiar. They come at the start of every shoot and then dissipate with every action. That won't change tonight.

It's showtime.

My knuckles tap against the door three times. I wait with the flower bouquet held behind my back. Gabriella's face appears fully. She's beautiful. I knew that before, but somehow seeing her from this perspective at the start of my plan and our new beginning hits deeper.

"Hi. Gabriella?" She nods slowly and slightly tilts her head to the side with a ghost of a smile in the background. By the end of the night, I will have earned the real one.

I present her with the bouquet; reclaimed red daisies, red and pink roses and pink lilies. Stunned, she takes them from me. She smells each flower while cradling it to her chest. She may not know why I need her to love them, but I do.

"May I come in?" Her expression changes from startled to confused to flustered. It's cute.

"Oh, yeah! Sure...of course." She steps back and swings the door open to allow me space to enter. I follow her to the kitchen, where she spots the vase already filled with water. Her eyes look up at me.

Her lips spread a little wider.

"Are you okay with sushi?"

"Yeah. It's one of my favorites."

"Wonderful!" I lean against the island and shift my eyes toward the oven behind her. Gabriella stares at me. I repeat the gesture. "We can eat here, if you want. There might be a long wait if we try to leave the apartment."

Gabriella turns and pulls open the oven door, reaches in and retrieves the plate of baked sushi rolls I had stashed in there earlier to keep warm.

"Sounds good to me." She sets them on the table.

I take my seat. "Mind if we share?"

"No. Not at all." She begins to take her seat, but then pauses while surveying the table.

"I hope you don't mind. I think I only have water." After filling the glasses, she returns to the table. "May I?" She places one sushi roll into my mouth and slowly slides out the chopsticks. My closed lips gently press down onto the smooth wood. When the chopsticks are fully free, they open. Gabriella's alert gaze never wavers from my face. Her ghost of a smile is now upturned into a smirk. Her empty chopsticks, free of me and free of sushi, disappear behind her grin. She glides them out slowly, ending in a moan.

"Delicious. I think you're my new favorite flavor." She uses her tongue to lick the corners of her mouth and roll across her top lip. She does it slowly. And softly. And...deliberately.

I hadn't thought of what her tongue could feel like until then. All moist. And strong. And...willing.

I hope my attempts to clear my mind of dirty images are not obvious by the way the glass of water shakes in my grip. "Uh, have you lived here for a long time?"

"No. I moved in a few weeks ago."

"Really? It seems built for entertainment. Do you like your neighbors? Do you hang out with them on the terrace?"

Gabriella takes a sip of her water. Her eyes shift to the windows facing the rooftop and back to me again. "Most are fine. I have one annoying neighbor I might have to speak with soon."

"Why would you wanna talk to someone who annoys you?" I take a bite of my sushi and watch the shadow return to Gabriella's face.

"Because he needs to learn to stop trying to claim things that don't belong to him." I gulp down the tiny pieces of rice and seaweed that had been resting in the back of my throat.

"You don't like to share."

"Oh, I can share." Her chopsticks clatter against the plate when she stands. She walks over to me, slowly. The legs of my chair scrape against the floor as she pulls it away from the table. My hands automatically fall to her waist as soon as her legs settle on the sides of me. "I've been very patient with you. It's taken you entirely too long."

"I-I just got here."

"Who did you speak to on the way up?" Her hands caress my neck, igniting a flurry of invisible sparks against my skin.

"W-What?" My breath comes out more shallow than I intend it to.

"Before you came to see me. You had a conversation with someone without my permission, didn't you? Who was it?" Gabriella's eyes bores into me, shrouded by darkness with intent to instill fear. I did something wrong. And she wants me to know it. I wrack my brain for the correct answer.

"Your neighbor. I didn't know I wasn't supposed to talk to him. I was just being nice. He asked me what my plans were for tonight and–"

"And what did you tell him?"

"I didn't...I didn't know what to say."

"You don't say anything. The only word I want coming out of your mouth tonight is my name. Do you understand?"

I pull back the breath that almost utters the word and nod instead.

"Good Girl."

I feel the breeze in the room kiss my skin when the fabric of my shirt is sliced open and my breasts fall free from their supports. The scream empties from my throat at the same time her mouth sucks one inside. No apology lies behind her eyes. The blade of the knife circles around the nipple of the other. I watch it intently. Heat rises beneath me with each round it takes.

Light continues to pour in from the outside. If anyone is watching, they'd be able to see us from the back with a clear view of Gabriella straddling me. The wall that separates the dining room from the outside is solid, with no windows to put us on display.

I bite my lip to keep myself from saying anything. All I can do is breathe. And watch. I watch her mouth move to the other side, leaving a trail of kisses behind. The knife tickles the sides of my stomach, making it difficult to concentrate.

In one quick movement, she pulls to turn me until she presses the front of me against the back of the chair. My once-covered breasts fit perfectly in the space intended for aesthetic pleasure and not for sexual ones.

"See. I do know how to share." I hear the rattle of something dropping onto the table and feel her hand snake around my hips. They move instinctually backward and rock against her body. The disapproving tisk she makes taunts me. "Don't try to run now. There's so much you need to learn tonight. I hope no one's expecting you home."

I shake my head and she presses me forward until I spread my thighs as wide as the edges of the chair will allow. With both hands, she undoes the buttons of my jeans. As she frees each one, the space between her hand and my source of arousal shrinks. Her fingers glide against my silk panties with very little effort.

My hands grip the back of the chair to steady me against the movement. She strokes and I rock. I'm careful to stifle the words that try to escape through my throat. Only sounds replace them. The desire to beg her for more with no permission to speak only serves to feed me. She whispers things in my ear I've never dared to say aloud.

I answer her questions in silence.

Yes, that feels good.

No, please, don't stop.

I'm sorry I was a bad girl, but I'm not sorry I got caught.

"Who does she belong to?"

"Gabriella." Her name pours out of me like the wetness she coaxed into a flood for her fingers to enjoy.

"Do you see that?" My eyes focus straight ahead on the group of people walking toward us on the other side of the glass. Panic sets in and intertwines with the chase of the buildup caused by our friction. If she wants them to watch her destroy me, they've come at the perfect time.

My head leans back to rest on her shoulder. My breasts are pulled from their display case, giving my hips room to move quicker with longer strokes. Gabriella applies more pressure to the soaking wet fabric as it glides against me. My heart skips as many breaths as I forget to take until I mumble out, "Fuck."

The dark, crippling feeling of defeat consumes me when her hand snatches away from me, severing our connection.

"You're a terrible listener," she says while moving from behind me. My back feels as cold without her presence as my jeans feel empty and incomplete. "That mouth of yours really does get you into trouble."

I watch the group walk by without glancing into the apartment.

"Get up and go upstairs." I grip the back of the chair in defiance. If she wants me to move, she'll have to move me herself. I watch her sock-clad feet disappear from the corner of my eye. The sharpness of the tip of the blade pokes at the base of my spine. "I don't think you understand what's happening here. This is my house. You do as I say."

Chapter Twenty-Seven
Gabriella

SHE RISES FROM HER seat gradually. I'm sure she's afraid of how far I may go, while internally gushing about how exciting it all is. She has everything that she wants: sex mixed in with a bit of danger. She always wants to be right on the edge without dipping in too far.

I withdraw the knife when her feet are at the bottom of the staircase. She comes to a complete stop once in the bedroom. I pull the torn shirt and ruined bra through her arms and say nothing while I remove her jeans. She does the same, looking down instead of directly at me.

She trembles when I touch her. I take that as my cue to continue. I slice through the silk panties as well. Although the nude covering blends perfectly with her skin, they're the wrong color.

Her eyes only shift to me when my clothes hit the floor. Once I'm only covered by my bra and panties, I give her one more command. "Get on the bed." She moves one inch until her muscles harden and her body steels. "Or I can take you on the floor. Your choice."

Her climb up is agonizing, with her hips hiked into the air. The missing presence of dark curls makes it hard to hide the mess she forced me to create downstairs. And now she's going to help me clean it up.

Her feet rise and fall against the comforter, displaying a sense of boredom. She's always so bold in her challenges, knowing I can't help but give her exactly what she wants, my way.

I capture her feet in my hands and press them forward, pushing them down into the softness of her ass as far as I can. She lets out a moan as she opens wider, her knees sliding against the sheets to make room for me. "If you aren't already flexible, you will be by the end of the night." She grinds against my knee as it settles into the new space.

Unable to continue to deny my pool of wetness, I ride the bent leg I hold down beneath me. Her fingernails scratch against the sheet with each moan I allow to empty from her as her hips rise and fall. My eyes close as the intensity inside of me increases. Her sounds fuel me. I revel in the responsibility of their creation. No one will ever make her sound like that. Beg like that. Hate and love it all at once, like I do.

"Make sure ..." her words cut off as her eyes flutter closed and her breathing becomes more rigid. "... you say my ... name... when you come."

Her ass is the only thing I can reach. My hand smacks down between her lower cheeks and the bottom of her soaking pussy. She yelps on one hand and pushes back at another, looking for the solid force of her pleasure that I took from her.

"See what happens when I try to be nice to you?" Two fingers sink into her without resistance. They stroke with welcomed gasps. I retract them. They emerge glistening with her rebellion. My fingers trace around her lips from behind. "Lesson number one: I will do as my girlfriend says." I feel her hips rise a little before settling again. Her mouth opens to form a small gap that I slide my fingers through. She sucks my skin and cleans them of every drop. I repeat the process again and again. Each time she opens quicker and wider and without complaint. She licks and sucks in gratitude, always reluctant to free me until the next serving.

"That's a good girl."

I barely touch her and she rolls to her back. Her eyes fill with unsatisfied hunger. I position her exactly where I want her. My panties drop from my thighs and fall to the floor in silence. Her eyes roam from my newly revealed skin to my breasts. I know what the narrowing of her eyes means before she has time to raise her hand and add to her punishment.

I kiss the wrist captured in the palm of my hand. "Lesson number two: I will eat only when given permission." I push her legs back until her knees nearly touch her shoulders. Scissoring isn't a myth. It's a puzzle.

Despite her attempts to mask her excitement, she forgets to not bite her lip and restrict her hands from reaching toward my hips when I settle on top. We create the perfect friction together. One small movement forward and her mouth falls open and her hands grip my thighs. I hold on to her ankles, using them to anchor my slow movement backward and forward. Her hands fly all over the place. They grip the pillow over her head, cover her eyes and pinch at her skin. She bites her fingers to keep from screaming, but it's too late. She belts out more curse words than I've ever heard her say.

I'll teach her more later.

Her hands scramble back to my waist and she holds me while I ride her, my hips sailing through the mess we make between us. Her eyes can barely stay open. Mine never leave her face. My breath is ragged as I try to keep up with the intense pleasure. She's all I ever wanted. I feel it more and more with each stroke. My pace quickens and our clits meet in a stimulating kiss repeatedly.

The neighbors can surely hear her now, though they'll never be able to make out the noises she makes underneath me, completely overtaken and out of control.

"You see what happens when you disobey?"

There's not enough breath for her to form a sassy remark. Instead, she grits her teeth and yells out in pleasure.

I lift one leg completely and let the other one fall flat. My hand grips the base of her neck. It's just enough pressure to remind her how we got here. I'm in control. She belongs to me now. The pressure builds between us with each swipe of our moistened lips sliding together. My clit throbs in a demanding release. I rock quicker and never let up on my promise.

"Lesson number three: Her name is the only one I will ever say again."

"Gabby."

She chokes out immediately, with as little breath as her lungs will allow to keep her chest from exploding. I empty my lungs and we create music together with just a small bit of her fantasy mixed in. I can handle that.

It's official.

She's mine.

Forever.

"Can I ask you a question?" It's been hours since the walls heard her scream my name. And since then, we have spent the time in a comfortable silence with a few kisses traded in between.

"Hmm," I say with my eyes closed.

"I don't want this to get too confusing. That's why I'm asking."

I open my eyes fully and stare at the side of her face. Being hesitant isn't like her. "When you called me Emmy..." I suck in a breath. "Were you making fun of me for not winning?"

"What? No. I told you they should've nominated you. If they had, you definitely would've won."

"But I didn't get a nomination, and I thought maybe you and Sara—"

"No," I say, quickly.

"Seems like something she'd be happy to gloat about." Sara hoped Taylor didn't get a nomination. If she had, her moniker would have forever changed. She would always be Emmy Nominated Actress, Taylor Townes. No one could ever take that away from her.

Once the nominations were announced and Taylor was absent from the list, Sara moved on to her next plan of attack.

"If it's not that, then why do you call me Emmy?" I tug at a loose strand of curl that peeks out from her scarf.

"Consider me your oracle. You're going to win it one day. I know it." She smiles.

"I hope the voters will be as confident as you are."

"If you want, I may be able to convince them." She laughs.

"No, thanks. I don't want it if it's not honest."

I shrug my shoulders at her conclusion. "Doesn't matter how you get it as long as it's there."

"Have you always believed that?" she asks.

"Maybe."

Sometimes it's hard to remember life before I was dragged into the entertainment industry. Winning was never on my radar until I met Sara. Before her, I was just living.

"What do you keep in your notebooks?"

"Scripts."

"Really? Can I read one?" I shake my head. "No one's ever read them before. I revise them the more I learn, but the stories stay stuck in my head." Her teeth gnaw at her bottom lip in thought.

"What?"

"It's invasive. I shouldn't ask you."

"Well, you kind of have to now."

"Did you ever write one for Sara?" It's a fair question to ask. Most people would expect that level of dedication between two people who were supposed to be in love.

"Never."

"I'm sorry."

"Don't be."

"But I am really sorry. Sorry enough that I can make it up to you."

She's still completely naked from the night before. Her lips press down on mine. We tenderly part and then meet again with each reunion lasting longer than the previous one.

"May I have permission to eat?" The burst of anticipatory flame passes when her fingers scale over my bra strap. "They're so beautiful. My mouth is watering just thinking about them. Will you let me taste them?" It's the most obedient she's ever been. I arch my back in approval and she takes no time unclasping the strap and pulling it from my arms. Her tongue swipes at one pointed nipple, then another. With my knee settled on her hip, she dives a hand in between us, eliciting a moan from me that only grows louder.

She mumbles to herself, lapping away at my breasts and nibbling my skin with her teeth. I coat the hand stroking me, easily. The added moisture does nothing but aid in her goal of atonement. I turn to my back for space and time. It's a move that upsets her. She uncharacteristically growls at the change, but never releases me.

Her tongue licks from the connecting skin from my right breast to my left. She stops. "Who did this to you?" I cringe. The level of concern in her voice makes me uncomfortable.

"It's fine. It doesn't hurt." *Not anymore.*

"Did you do this? When was the last time? Do your parents know? Are you seeing someone? Is there anything you need me to do?"

An increasing amount of dread drops into the pit of my stomach with each new question. I remove the hand she has placed on my skin and stand. Her arms fling around my waist and she struggles to pull me back down.

"I don't want you to leave. I only wanna know you're okay."

"I don't need you to feel sorry for me."

"I don't!" Her shout is enough to wake the neighbors into the early morning. "I've tried hard to not think about what you've done in the past. I care about you. And I will not let go until you tell me you're okay."

I may be imagining the stream of tears that drip down my back while she holds me. I could be making up the amount of strength she's using to keep me in place. And maybe I do want to leave, even though my heart is telling me to stay.

"I'm okay, now." I take a deep breath. "I've been okay since I met this girl in a coffee shop." I allow myself to smile. Her arms relax against me. The tremble in her voice is less. Her words, softer.

"The two of us locked eyes over the head of a barista." I trap the smile between my puckered lips. My eyes had locked on hers long before then.

"You're stuck with me now."

"Good." Her arms tighten back around me, cloaked in warmth and comfort instead of mad desperation. "Because you're stuck with me, too."

Chapter Twenty-Eight
Gabriella

THE FRONT DOOR OF my parents' house swings open before we plant our feet in the driveway. It's been two months since our first official date and my family decided a welcome wagon was necessary for Taylor's first visit.

Inflatable Christmas decorations litter the yard, complete with Santa's sleigh sitting on the roof. It's the one holiday my dad will decorate for. There's something about Christmas that brings him to life.

Grandma peers her head around the corner of the wooden doorframe. I see her clutch her chest when Taylor steps out. Mom tries to push her out of view, but she's swatted away. I ignore all of it and pray Taylor hasn't noticed their behavior.

Taylor bounds up the porch steps in confidence, with her carry-on suitcase rolling behind her.

"Hi, I'm Taylor. It's nice to meet you." She extends her hand out to my mom, whose eyes follow her every movement.

"Good Morning, Taylor. I'm Isabell–"

"And I'm Claudia." Grandma takes Taylor's hand from Mom, who frowns at her intrusion. Grandma looks at Taylor with clouded eyes and a smile that barely shows what teeth she has left. She cradles Taylor's chin in one hand and shakes it from side to side.

"Muy bonita," she says as she nods in approval. A giggle sets off inside Taylor as she's ushered inside the home with Grandma's hand on her back.

"It took you a lot longer than I thought," Mom says, taking a bag from me.

"It took the same time it always does when there's no traffic on the freeway."

"Regardless, I'm glad Taylor could clear her schedule for us." The hidden message in her words is clear to me. I didn't always come home for Christmas before. Or birthdays, Mother's Day and Father's Day, when my availability heavily depended on someone else's calendar.

I swallow down the apology that threatens to expose itself. I follow my mom to my bedroom, passing Araceli on the way. She's sitting at Taylor's feet, listening to whatever my grandma is telling her. Taylor diligently nods at every word. Pepe, Grandma's chihuahua, sits in Araceli's lap emitting a low growl. He doesn't like to feel replaced.

The couch they're seated on looks new. I do a double-take at the change. The large navy sectional takes up much more space than the previous gray sofa.

Maricela is sitting on the bedroom floor in front of the mirror propped up against the wall. She screams when she spots me and then aggressively brushes her hair back into a ponytail while mumbling to herself.

"Oh, no. She's here!" The hair tie tucked between her teeth is stretched, twisted and put into place. "Why didn't you call me and tell me you were close?" I roll my eyes at the instructions I was never given.

"Why are you getting all dressed up? She's literally in leggings right now." Taylor called them her traveling clothes when we were leaving her apartment.

Mari stands and smooths out her red dress. Mom helps untangle her curly ponytail by raking her fingers through the length of it.

"She can wear whatever she wants. She's gorgeous." Maricela eyes me up and down and turns up her nose, dismissively. "Do better," she whispers as she passes, raising her chin a little higher in the air. Mom follows her, sparing me no glance.

Catching the hints Taylor was dropping about spending the holidays with my family, I made room for her things in my dresser a few weeks ago. In my mind, there's no reason to unpack when we'll be leaving in two days, but at least she has the space, if she wants it.

I can tell Mom has cleaned. The comforter on the bed smells fresh and the sheets are crisp and tucked. It's rare, but each time she does it, I notice.

The bathroom is spotless and smells like pine. The carpet has those fancy lines in it you usually only see in hotel rooms. I've certainly never seen them in *this* house.

She already cooked breakfast; chorizo and chilaquiles. Mom also set aside eggs and pancakes, covered to stay warm, just in case Taylor desires something else to eat.

With the way they're crowded around her in the living room, breakfast may go untouched.

"You were my favorite little kid on *The Loved & The Wicked*. When you lost those two front teeth, I lost my mind. You were so adorable." If Taylor finds Grandma's attempt at a baby voice as annoying as I do, she doesn't show it.

"Those two teeth almost got me fired."

"No!" My family joined in unison.

"Yup. There was one exec that did not like that both my two front teeth fell out at the same time. He said I looked hideous and they needed to find another kid to replace me." The outrage Grandma expresses with her mouth hung open could win her an Academy Award.

"David and Michelle — my TV parents — fought for me to stay, and then my catchphrase went viral and there was nothing they could do about it."

"I can't believe them. If I had known, I would've found every single one of them and gave them a piece of my mind. How dare they!" Taylor gingerly pats Grandma's knee in comfort.

"And he never even apologized for being so rude. He said all those negative things right in front of me." It's Araceli's turn to offer reassurance by patting Taylor's shoe one-handed.

"Was anyone mean to you on the set of *The Paige Society*?" Maricela's hopeful expression is ready for information about her favorite show.

"No. Everyone was nice. They always threw me a party when we filmed on my birthday." She's their shiny new Christmas present, straight out of the package, batteries included with no installation required.

She walked through the door, perfect.

Maricela clears her throat a few times to get everyone's attention. Grandma shoots a sharp eye at Mom, not thrilled that Maricela interrupted her time with Taylor.

Maricela pulls a single piece of paper out of its sheet protector and hands it to Taylor. Everyone else leans in and peers over Taylor's shoulders.

"Oh, I remember this!" The glossy photograph has torn edges beside her signature. "When'd you get this?"

"Comic Con, right before season two premiered."

With her finger, Taylor follows the tear from beginning to end. "It's ripped. Do you want a new one?"

Maricela squeals and runs from the room. She returns seconds later, holding her cell phone. She squeezes herself in between Taylor and Grandma, knocking her shoulder against the ones of our elder. Grandma does it back, but while grinning at Taylor as if it's all perfectly normal.

I step out of the frame and towards the tree. My elementary-school-aged face stares back at me from the crafted ornament. It was the last one I ever made.

The group changes from pose to pose with slight shifts in their body's position. Araceli sits on the other side of Taylor, snuggled up close. Mom settles with her elbow on the couch, sometimes alternating which arm she lifts and which wrist she rests underneath her chin.

It feels like they take hundreds of them when Mom says, "OK. It's time we let Taylor eat. We know Gabby woke her up early to get here." Remarkably, they all shoot me a stare as if I'd done something unusually cruel.

"Oh, don't worry. She fed me on the way here." I can't help the feeling that arises when she walks over to the corner I placed myself in. She studies the tree closely and spots the little face on the red-painted wood ornament.

"Aww. You look so cute." She presses her face close to mine. Her lips land on my chin. She whispers, "Am I allowed to kiss you in front of your family?"

Yes, is the only response that matters.

Taylor sticks close to me as the day wears on. Never once does she show frustration with Maricela and her millions of questions about the show. She answers with "Hm, I'm not sure if I can tell you that" but welcomes more questions and more theories about Piper Paige.

When Dad arrives and offers her a handshake, she uses both

hands. He doesn't sit and crowd around the couch with her or pay her any amount of compliments. It's typical of him. He and Mom barely look at each other before he leaves out the back door.

"Are you hungry, Mija?" I turn to Mom, whose eyes are set on Taylor. "I can make you a snack if you're hungry before the food is done." Mom started making dinner shortly after we all ate breakfast. To my count, it's the fourth time she's asked Taylor since.

"She's fine, Mom." I push the words through my teeth. I can tell from my mom's face that she doesn't appreciate my tone.

Taylor's hand grips my thigh and for the first time tonight, there's not a smile on her face.

"Can you show me your room? I haven't seen it yet." I nod and wait until she's standing next to me to move. I can feel everyone's eyes on our backs as we walk away. Taylor walks around the bedroom and observes every detail. She studies the photos taped to the wall above my bed, Araceli's enormous teddy bear collection and Maricela's extensive makeup collection crowded on the top of the dresser.

"Don't be mean to your mom." Even though she says it while looking directly at a perfume bottle, I know she's talking to me.

"I'm not being mean. You're a big girl. You can tell her when you're hungry."

Her eyes shift from the perfume to the nail polish. "You do the same thing, except you don't ask. You make me food and then tell me to eat it."

I do not.

She leaves the dresser to stand in front of me. The look she gives me suggests she's suddenly gained the ability to mind read.

"Feeding me is how you show you care about me. I know that. If I had to guess, I think it's the same for your mom, too."

The smirk on her face both irritates and calms me. "I feed you because if I didn't, you would starve." I accept the kiss that falls directly on my lips. Her arms wrap around my waist with a tight squeeze. I pull her closer. A slight groan escapes from me at the feeling of her face nuzzling against my neck.

"That's where you're wrong. My concierge would never."

Taylor slips into my family and takes space that feels like it was always reserved for her. When my cousins arrive, they try their best not to look too excited to see her. Most of them never met Sara unless they were over at the same time as her; completely unexpected and unintentional.

They laugh at Taylor and with her. They congratulate her when she stops including the hard *Th* in Tia and Tio, and pronounces it correctly. I make a mental note to congratulate her when we're back in her bed and not living out of our suitcases. When they refer to her as their *prima*, she walks around as if they've clipped the title to the front of her shirt.

It's adorable.

I've caught Grandma making requests for Taylor to say her favorite lines from that soap opera. I've kept our silent promise to be nice and not intervene on Taylor's behalf. Not that she ever needs my help. She happily obliges and makes a few jokes about not looking nearly as cute as she used to. They all disagree.

If they hadn't, we wouldn't be family.

I know she's drained when she retreats to sit next to me. She's emptied at least one basket of warm tortillas by herself. Her hair retired to its ponytail long ago. It's warm in the house compared to the cooler temperatures outside. That doesn't stop my dad, uncles and cousins from traveling in and out to smoke cigarettes and drink.

"Your sister's a good dancer," she mumbles. Araceli twirls around in the center of the room and sways her hips to the beat of the song.

"You're getting sleepy." My cheek touches the top of her head that's resting on my shoulder.

Taylor shakes her head with her eyelids half concealing her vision. We still have a few hours left until everyone settles down to open presents as close to midnight as we can stand.

"I'll be okay. Just need to rest a little."

"This'll help wake you up, prima." My cousin Jr. pushes a can of beer across the table. I catch it in the palm of my hand and push it back. Jr. laughs at the sight of my glare. "Hey. This is better than that weak shit they serve at your job. Every time I go there, I complain."

"Then stop going."

"I would. But I think I'm in love with Jade. Her dancing does something to me." I don't bother reminding Jr of his girlfriend and their three kids as a reason he should spend less time at Diego's and more time at home. I'm sure Yesenia has already told him that. More than once.

Taylor tilts her head back to look at me. "They dance at the restaurant you work at?"

Jr. chokes on the gulp of beer that was meant to slide down his throat.

Taylor's eyes flutter closed a few times. I rub the side of her face to wake her. Her features scrunch together in response. "Come on. Let me put you to bed."

Her groans accompany her protests as she follows behind me. She sits obediently at the edge of the mattress while I shift through her suitcase to find the pajama set she insists she sleeps in. "There's a matching set in there for you, too."

The red and black flannel is soft. I breathe a sigh of relief it's not a onesie or a handmade crafting project. I dress her, shifting her to the side and pulling up her hips when needed.

"Are you going to put yours on now?" Her hopeful expression is hard to resist. Against my better judgment, I toss my worn clothes into the corner near my suitcase and pull the pajamas over me.

I'll be teased relentlessly once I walk out this door and back into the fray of music. But her smile, now, is all that matters.

"Wake me before they open the gifts. I don't wanna be rude." I smother the words I know she wouldn't appreciate hearing from me after this morning's admonishment.

"I will." And then I kiss her like I haven't been able to kiss her all day.

Mom isn't too happy when she realizes Taylor is gone. She berates me in rapid Spanish and English, cosigned by Grandma for not telling her how tired Taylor was.

"You woke her up too early. You should've let her sleep in more. We would've waited."

Sure.

They each shuffle into the bedroom and stand over her soundly sleeping body. After silently staring at each other for a solution, they come back out into the living room. Grandmother turns down the music. Mom shushes everyone she thinks is talking too loud. My cousins and I, who all grew up with an expectation of learning to fall asleep under some of the loudest conditions, balk at the accommodation.

"Now we'll have to wait to give her time to recover." Mom stares at me as if it's my fault Taylor became exhausted from socializing. I wasn't the one asking her questions I could easily look up on the internet. It wasn't my camera she smiled for, or my friends I begged her to say hi to on the phone.

Everyone listens as Mom barks orders for the next hour. They make plates for others to take to go. They package and put away the food, clean up the house and prepare piles of presents for each person.

Mom removes the pillows and cushions from the couch and extends the new bed. She grabs the sheets and pillow she set aside for Taylor and fits them onto the mattress. Pepe is shooed away when he tries to claim the space for himself.

I rouse Taylor once I'm given the go-ahead from Mom. It's hard not to react to the sound she makes when she stretches and arches her back. She does it on purpose. Her favorite game is pretending to be clueless, but having all the cards.

To my surprise, Taylor bounces out of the house and to my car to retrieve a bag from the backseat that I somehow missed. She places a gift covered in festive wrapping paper in Maricela and Araceli's piles first. She doesn't have time to drop Grandma's gift on her pile before she's squeezed into a hug. Mom gives her a gentle smile when accepting her gift and Dad looks as surprised as I feel.

The multi-heart Tiffany bracelets Araceli and Maricela unwrap are the same. They shake their wrists at each other in glee. Smart to not give them something to fight or argue over. Both Mom and Grandma pull out a set of earrings, equally expensive as the bracelets, if not more.

I look at Dad to find bewilderment etched on his usually stoic face, but it's not whatever pricey item Taylor has stored in the small box in front of him that leaves him speechless. It's the card. Mom has one, too. She kisses it and tucks it away in her bra. When she catches me watching, she shakes her head at me and takes a swipe at her eyes.

Taylor's present to me sits between us. It's bigger than the others. For a moment, I think about rejecting it. I could say I want to open it in the morning and then come up with an excuse why I want to wait until we get back to the apartment when it's just us, alone. The rustling of wrapping paper being torn and discarded plays like background music to my thoughts.

Taylor opens my family's gifts one by one with the same smile she reserves for everything. She sprays and sniffs the perfume Maricela picked out for her. She marvels at how soft the scarf Grandma chose is. "Did you make this yourself?" No, she hadn't. Grandma has tried for years to learn to knit, but has never gotten the technique down. Araceli painted Taylor a mug from one of those pottery stores. And Mom and Dad – well, Mom, with Dad's name scribbled below hers – splurged on a nice jacket. It doesn't cost nearly as much as even the gifts she bought, but it's more than they would have normally spent.

Her attention turns to me once she finishes and runs out of gratitude to spread around. She extends the same happiness to me as everyone else.

"Aren't you gonna open it?" Her eyes sparkle and her lips twitch mockingly. I rip the top of the perfectly taped present to reveal a new iPad. "For your drawings. I've only seen you draw on paper, but I thought this would be nice. You don't have to. You can use it for whatever you want."

My hand brushes against the white, manufactured box. I thought about buying one more than a few times. The risk was never worth it. It couldn't be. There was always too much at stake.

Still is.

Taylor's face contorts into a concerned expression at my delayed response. The words, "Thank you, I love it", smooth over the lines that were forming.

I slide the small bag from behind my back and into her waiting hands. She giggles a little to herself at the sight of it. It calms me. Her hand disappears inside the small bag to pull out the small box.

Everyone goes quiet.

I've envisioned this very day in my mind countless times before making this trip. And yet, it never went quite like this.

"Is it okay if I open it?" At my nod, she closes one eye and pulls back the top of the lid. "Oh. Aw."

Her sigh of relief is joined by the faint laughter of everyone who thought I was going to propose to the girl I have only been dating for two months.

Not yet.

I fit the gold, open-heart ring onto the middle finger of her left hand. It gleams in the twinkling Christmas tree lights.

"No rainbows," I tease, referencing the gold bracelet on her wrist and the ring on her other hand.

She rotates the heart on her finger with her thumb, lifts her eyes to look up at mine and says, "What do I need rainbows for when I have you?"

Chapter Twenty-Nine
Taylor

Traveling from Gabriella's house to mine on Christmas morning is a breeze. There's hardly anyone on the road, freeway or otherwise.

"Do you think we'll do this every year? Or alternate?"

"Do what every year?"

"Drive down to spend Christmas Eve with your family and then in the morning, drive up to spend Christmas with mine?"

It's a nice idea. I've never thought about how holidays would look with my partner and their family. It never crossed my mind that we would make long-distance plans. It wasn't bad. With the right planning, we could make it work.

The question seems to catch her off guard. "Whatever you wanna do."

"I like your family. I'd be sad if I didn't see them every year."

"You spent less than two days with them."

"So?" She sighs.

"If you wanna drive down every year, we will."

"Good."

I feel like I've won a battle I didn't expect to fight. Something shifted with Gabriella that first night. For a moment in time, she felt far away. Her mood improved as more people left and the house quieted. Eventually, I convinced her to share the sleep sofa with me.

The mattress was nice. And next to her, I slept like a dream.

We ride in comfortable silence for the duration of the drive. The house is decorated solely with lights. Mama always uses the same multicolored ones she's had for years. She keeps them stored in the garage until the correct time rolls around. It was always our duty as kids to spend the hours needed to untangle them. That's one perk of no longer living in your parents' house.

The warmth from the heat of the oven greets me at the door. The inside of our home smells exactly like I expect. Depending on who you talk to, you either hate or love the smell of chitlins. Mama cleans her chitlins to meticulous perfection. They smell of bay leaf and vinegar. The smell of nutmeg and cinnamon is from the half dozen sweet potato pies laid out on the table, ready for consumption. Sometimes she'll make something extra like a peach cobbler or apple pie, but sweet potato is always a staple.

This is not a pumpkin pie household.

"Mama, Taylor's home!" My sister Eryn's face is the first one I see. She hugs me before she pushes me, sending me tumbling to the ground.

"Mama! Eryn pushed me!" I plant my body on the floor with my arms spread out and my legs twisted in an odd position.

"Cut it out, you two." Mama's voice hails from the kitchen. She has no time to entertain my theatrics while making her finishing touches. I roll over and push myself up on all fours.

There is no scheduled time to eat during Christmas. Mama cooks all the food in the early morning and we eat as we wish. Throughout the day, multiple relatives will stop by and gather plates to go. We'll ignore their complaints about their blood pressure while also filling their bowl with chitlins. To our family's credit, turkey has replaced most of the pork products throughout the years. There's turkey in the greens now instead of hog maw. And we eat turkey legs instead of ham, though I miss the roasted pineapple that used to bake on top of it.

The only pork we consume on holidays is the chitlins. Once or twice a year never killed anyone. At least, I don't think it has.

Eryn rolls my carry-on through the front door behind Gabriella, who stops in front of me with a concerned look plastered on her face. I allow my wrists and knees, which had been in the process of pushing me up to stand, to slide from underneath me.

"Baby, she attacked me," I say, with one strong index finger pointing at Eryn. Eryn mocks me inaudibly, twisting her face and churning her lips repeatedly. She rolls my carry-on to the base of the stairs and leaves it.

"If that's how it's gonna be. Carry yo' own damn luggage."

She walks back to the living room and plops down next to her boyfriend, Marcus. I roll back onto my knees and stand. "Your training sucks, Marcus. Do better!" I hear them both laugh while Gabriella smirks. I kiss her. It's quick, but meaningful. She's almost back to normal.

Gabriella follows me up the stairs and into my bedroom. I rush to remember how it looked from the last time I was home. I think it's clean. And if it wasn't, I'm sure Mama made sure it would be presentable for guests. Since the door is wide open, I know I'm correct. If it had been an absolute disaster, she would've pulled it closed.

Gabriella rolls her suitcase next to the side of the bed that's closest to the door. It's the same side she sleeps on at home. It was different at her parents' house because I wanted to sleep next to the Christmas tree.

"Are you hungry?" There's no traditional Christmas breakfast in the Townes household. She's more than welcome to get started on the mac and cheese, baked beans or turkey legs.

"Are you offering?" The electric jolt that penetrates through my body tells me I should be. We've gone longer than this without touching each other since we weren't blessed with the cycle-syncing perk.

Having sex with Gabriella at her parents' house while sleeping in their living room was on a level of naughty I was unwilling to experience. Here, though, in my bedroom behind a locked door - it's possible. She hasn't taught me how to be quiet. Now might be the perfect time to practice.

She cups my jaw in her hand and gives it a gentle squeeze. "I'm teasing you. The last thing I need is for your parents to think I've corrupted their daughter. After all, my reputation precedes me."

"I don't think that's something you need to worry about." The gossip around her last relationship has practically diminished. No one thinks or talks about them anymore. And no one has seen her in months. I contemplate telling her about the picture of us I sent my parents a few days after we started dating.

"Don't tell Eryn she's now your third favorite daughter." They both laughed and mustered up the technological knowledge required to send the appropriate memes and GIFs. After that, messages that would normally read, "*What did you do today?*" read, "*What did you and Gabriella do today?*"

Eryn occupies the lounger next to me, overlooking the pool. It's warmer here in L.A. than it was in San Diego. "You know, it's rude to leave your guests unattended."

"I didn't have anywhere to sit," I explain before emptying a slice of sweet potato pie in my mouth. Gabriella's formal introduction to my parents went well. I sat next to her at the kitchen island with my arms wrapped around her waist and my head on her shoulder.

Daddy interrupted Gabriella's conversation with Mama several times to ask her if she could breathe with all my smothering. Gabriella separated from me to follow Mama from the stove to the oven to the fridge. When it became clear she didn't need me anymore, I cut into the pie with the most golden crust and slipped out the back door.

"Daddy has her in there eating cookies," Eryn informs me, stretching out her legs. He'll want to know which one she thinks is the best; his or the ones he bought from the grocery store. It's a test I didn't prepare her for. She risks losing her spot as the second favorite daughter if she guesses wrong.

Before I have time to contemplate returning to the kitchen and knocking all the cookies to the floor, Eryn continues. "I have to admit, she doesn't look like an escaped victim of a psychopath."

"What exactly were you expecting?"

"I did my due diligence and snooped on her social media. There's not much out there about her. Now, her friend, the one that's always arguing with people online, she's *loud*."

It doesn't take me long to think of who she's talking about. It's become somewhat of a routine for us to spend at least one night hanging with Gabriella's friends. They're important to her, which means they're important to me, too.

"Hmm, Chasity."

"Yeah. Her."

I know by *loud* Eryn is referring to Chasity's tendency to flaunt her designer goods. She used to be more subtle about the labels, but lately, she's been more expressive.

"What do her parents do?"

"I do not know."

Eryn's focus of questioning is validating for me. I have asked myself these same questions over the last few months. I know Chasity has a job, like Gabriella, but even Gabriella's job perplexes me.

"What are you thinking about?"

I shift in my lounge chair and concentrate on savoring the last of the crust. The back door opens behind us and Nicole emerges with two plates of food in her hand. She hands me an extra slice of pie, unintentionally motivating me to finish my pie crust, and sits on the opposite side of me.

"Did you come alone?" Eryn asks, craning her neck to see Nicole fully.

"No. My parents are inside."

Eryn's family doesn't always join us on Christmas, but I can count on one hand the few times they haven't.

"No Josh?"

Nicole shakes her head but does not explain. Eryn reaches over and smacks my shoulder with her palm.

"You're not off the hook, Taylor. Tell me what you were thinking about."

"I don't want you to use it against her."

"Who? Gabriella? Your parents seem to like her." I catch Eryn rolling her eyes at Nicole's observation.

"And I want it to stay that way."

Eryn lets out an exaggerated sound and throws her hand over her shoulders to grip the back of the chair. "I can promise nothing, but I'll try my best."

I mentally review all the evidence in my brain to validate my concerns. "She has money. Like, a lot of money. And I don't know how."

She works at Craft, which caters to higher-income diners. It could just be the tips. I've heard stories about how much money a waiter could make when serving that kind of clientele, but a few months ago, Gabriella was practically homeless, though she didn't need to be.

"If she's smart, she stockpiled whatever money Sara gave her. How many stories have we heard about a girl being dumped by some famous person and not having anything to show for it except for bags and shoes? They were together for how long? Four years? She should have a down payment for a house by now."

"Come on, Eryn," Nicole chimes in. "Sara wasn't making that much. She hadn't had a successful show since *Sunny and the Dreamers*. And I doubt her dad was paying her girlfriend." We all grow silent. "Was he?"

It was a joke we all used to say back then; Sara's parents bought her friends. I guess it couldn't be unreasonable that they would buy her a girlfriend as well.

"I don't like this. Let's talk about something else." The thought of Gabriella being used in that way, and being hurt by Sara, is upsetting.

"My news might cheer you up." Nicole's pie remains untouched in her lap. She added whipped cream to the top of it, something I've never cared to do. "I'm moving out."

"What? Why?"

"Joshua needs me right now. I called management and they have a one-bedroom available. We can still hang out. We just won't be sharing the same kitchen."

"So you're moving downstairs? Do your parents know?" While the Kings decided that being Christian didn't bar Nicole from being friends with me, there are other things in life they did not agree with.

"They do and they're not happy about it. I had to listen to an entire lecture about temptation and sin. It was confusing. On one hand, they kept telling me it was wrong to live together before we're married, but then kept stressing about how important it is that I take care of him."

"Do you wanna marry him?"

Nicole and her boyfriend have been together since we were kids. They met on the set of *Sunny and the Dreamers*. He was the drummer of our rival band. Everyone thought they were a cute match: two quiet, good kids. Her parents didn't bat an eye at the two of them spending time together. Her boyfriend's parents are also very conservative. Their first date was attending church together, for God's sake.

"Of course. One day." Nicole's eyes cast down at her pie for the first time.

"Sounds like you have some explaining to do." Eryn doesn't say it to be helpful. With Nicole gone, it'll just be Gabriella and me. While my parents were fine with Gabriella spending the night, her moving in may be a different conversation entirely.

The group of us crowd around the Christmas tree. It's only mid-day with plenty of sunshine left outside, but the first time since the morning that there aren't any additional visitors. Mama hands out the presents. When we were little, Eryn and I would always try to figure out whose present was whose. We'd search all over for any sign and could never discover her method. Even now that we're older, Mama refuses to let us in on her secret.

Every attempt I make to sit in Gabriella's lap is thwarted. By her. "You were nicer to me at your parents' house," I whisper so only she can hear. Her hand holds mine in response. I land a kiss on her cheek. There's something cute about her wanting to make a good impression on my parents. It's very different from the Gabriella I thought I knew before.

"Don't let Taylor get you into trouble, Gabriella. You know she's homeschooled." Dad's remark causes everyone to erupt into laughter. Everyone except me.

"Excuse me? What's that supposed to mean?"

"It means our pampered princess knows nothing about the real world," Eryn answers with her back up against the wall. Marcus sits beside her.

"That's not true. Mama, aren't you going to defend me as my teacher?"

"Taylor, I'm not paying them any attention, so why are you?"

"Did you go to school, Gabriella?" Eryn looks disinterested in the answer, but there's nothing Sara-related that Eryn doesn't have an interest in. We spent a lot of time apart as kids. I was always on set and she was always at home, but whenever there was trouble, she had no problem showing up, and Sara was always trouble.

"I left halfway through sophomore year and went back senior year," Gabriella answers very matter-of-factly.

"You left school to sit with your girlfriend on set? How'd your parents react when you told them?"

I feel like we're traveling into dangerous territory. No one's laughing anymore. And the look Gabriella has trained on Eryn is...different. One wrong question from Eryn and I'm afraid which way this will go.

"I didn't. They told me."

Eryn takes a sharp breath and opens her mouth to speak. I beat her to it.

"At least you got to go to prom," I pout. "I didn't even graduate." You don't understand all the life experiences you choose to give up when you have a career as an actor from an early age. I decided not to return for senior year when filming switched to a summer schedule. It was too awkward.

Nicole gasps and places a hand over her chest. "How dare you say that? Our graduation party was amazing. We went to Barcelona!"

"See. Pampered, homeschooled princess," Eryn singsongs.

"That's not the same thing. We didn't have the events leading up to graduation. There was no yearbook. No cap and gown."

"Someone sounds like they could use a little more gratitude."

"Eryn, cut it out," Mama interjects with an elevated tone and a raised brow. She hands me my stack of presents, her face softening.

No one knows the sacrifices of living my life like I do. The only friends I had were the ones I worked with. Anyone outside of that was suspicious. Everyone wants something, even if it only lasts fifteen minutes.

I was lucky because my parents were always there for me. At least one of them was a presence on set or a voice in a meeting. I was never alone.

Gabriella's hands move to my lower back. I try to focus more on her touch and less on my sour mood. I unwrap the pajama set Mama gifts each one of us, including Gabriella.

It's not the same style as the one I got her. Mine was more subtle. I didn't think she'd like walking around in a reindeer onesie.

Gabriella places another small box, identical to the one she gave me on Christmas Eve, in my lap. I look up in surprise. "You gave me my gift already."

"That was your Christmas Eve gift. This is your Christmas gift."

"That's not how that works." Shame fills my chest. "I can't take it. I don't have a second gift for you."

"I don't need a second gift. It wouldn't have mattered if you didn't give me a gift. I got this for you." A glance tells me everyone is watching us. I swallow down the words that threaten to explode from my lips.

The open-heart gold ring is like the last one, but different enough to set it apart. While the first one swirled around my finger, this band is solid.

"Thank you. I love it." I save my kisses for later. She removes it from the box and places it on my index finger.

At Mama's insistence, everyone changes into their pajamas for the annual family photo. I alternate keeping my head resting on her shoulder or my legs in her lap.

I giggle at the view of her tail wagging in front of me on the way up the stairs. We place our gift bags in the corner of my bedroom. Although I'm happy my girlfriend has been getting along well with my family, I'm grateful for the quiet.

"How hard is it gonna be for me to convince you to take off that onesie?"

She stretches out on her side of the bed. The lazy look she gives me is one of contentment. Here, she's less annoyed and less on her guard. "I don't know. It's comfy and it has pockets."

I resume my usual position between her thighs, with my head right underneath her breasts. It feels as good as it always has. "Nicole's moving out."

"Why?"

"Something is going on with Josh."

I ask the question I've been thinking about since Nicole delivered the news hours ago. "How do you feel about moving in with me? Is it too soon?"

"Sooner than I already live there?" she asks. I laugh.

"Well, yes, unofficially, but now you'll have your own space. You can escape from me anytime you want." I wait for her reaction to my joke. Of course, it's a joke. She's never gonna be away from me again. "I think you can use your room as storage and use my bed for sleep. Do you accept my proposal?" I look up to see her face half concealed with a hood that has two antlers attached to the top.

A rare smile spreads across her lips.

"I do."

Chapter Thirty
Taylor

"Is it good?" I keep my eyes on Gabriella's face instead of the churro in her hands. She came home with two in a styrofoam container. I keep my distance on the other side of the couch and try not to balk at her using the caramel dipping sauce.

Churros need no assistance. I'm sure they're cold by now and everyone knows churros are the best when they're warm.

Sure, Taylor. Go on. Tell the Mexican girl how to eat a churro properly.

I would never do that. And not because this Mexican girl is my girlfriend, who I've been happily living with for the past five months, but also because if I did, she'd have no choice but to punish me. And I'd have to explain why I like it.

"Mmm," Gabriella moans in between chews. She tears off the top piece of the churro and stretches her arm out to me.

"Oh no. It's fine. Messy." I wipe the invisible cinnamon sugar crumbs off the throw blanket that covers my lap.

Her eyes narrow low to the level of annoyance I know will soon get me into trouble. I haven't seen it since the night I frantically banged on our front door for her to save me. It was a thought that came to mind while returning from Nicole's apartment a few floors down.

I'd had no clue where it would go. It could've very well been a hallmark-inspired sweet romance that ended with us making love to candlelight, but no. Once Gabriella realized I was in character, she was pissed.

The night ended with her revealing herself as my attacker. My punishment for trying to escape? A mouth-watering strap-on. My first. I've never spent so much time on my knees begging for forgiveness. It was a night that resulted in a tired jaw and sore thigh muscles.

I don't regret it.

I lean in and take a small bite between my teeth.

"Good girl."

I do my best to clamp down on the excitement that rolls up from my vagina to my heart.

I love when she praises me. The looks she gives me now, with empty fingers covered in spice, is dangerous. Keeping my fantasies in check has been a struggle. Gabriella has said nothing about it, but after our stalker-murderer incident, I think it's safe to say sometimes I go too far. Of course, it all worked out in the end with mutual satisfaction, but I scared her. I know that now.

I use a napkin to wipe away the light brown dust. She laughs while I do. Something else I love.

"Come here, Emmy."

She tugs the edge of my sweatshirt, and I go willingly into her lap. My underwear is all I'm wearing underneath. The base of them soaks up the response she elicits from me automatically.

"What's this called?" she asks after testing my resolve with the amount of kisses she plants on my neck. The churro in her hand is already coating her fingers in sweet goodness and dropping its crumbs onto the couch.

Scaling back on role play has increased the opportunity for personal Spanish lessons. I attached sticky notes to most things around the house. I don't get a reward every time I say a word correctly, but saying something correctly at the right time - one similar to this - can lead to significant benefits.

"Churro," I say perfectly. I mastered trilling my Rs after several practice sessions that involved me moving the tip of my tongue rapidly against her while she gasped for breath. Another thing I love. With each passing moment we share, she lets me see her and touch her more.

Theoretically, we spend less time together now than we did before. We have no classes together this semester. And we no longer travel to and from campus together. After the premature end of her work with Bonnie, she started working at the school library instead. She likes it much better. Less drama. She's only home for a few hours before she leaves for work at the restaurant during the week.

"Muy bien."

I use my tongue to roll the cinnamon sugar from her lips into my mouth.

"I'm gonna miss you." It's Saturday, which means she'll be leaving to go to San Diego. It's only for one night. Her sister, Maricela, texts me when she gets there and when she leaves on Sunday morning. It's a nice gesture, but I don't need it.

I know she's coming home.

"You won't miss me. You'll get Nicole to take my place."

"That's not true. Besides, there are things I can do with you I can't do with Nicole." I have dinner with Nicole on Saturdays when Gabriella isn't home, but that doesn't mean I won't miss her. "I think about you all the time."

She kisses the ring on my thumb. It's the third she's given me since Christmas Eve. She slid the box into my view during our Valentine's Day dinner in Malibu. Knowing I wanted to make it special for her, I asked her not to plan anything for that day. She listened. While I didn't give her any guidance or details, I watched her dress up in the tightest, shiniest dress I had ever had the privilege of watching her walk in. She straightened her curls. Her nails were done. And I was the luckiest girl in the world. Still am.

"Why?"

I stare into her dark brown eyes that sparkle with amusement. "Because I love being next to you. When you're gone, I want you close to me and when you're here, I never want you too far away. You're probably tired of me by now. The only reason I haven't smothered you in real life is because I spend all night wrapped around you in my dreams."

Gabriella doesn't join me in my slight chuckle. Her hands untangle from underneath my sweatshirt and busy themselves in my hair. My eyes flutter in reaction to her attention.

"Is that why you only say it at night?"

"Hmmm, say what?"

"You love me."

Everything stops. The tingling sensation she was coaxing from my scalp is no longer in existence. My vision becomes shrouded in darkness once my eyelids clamp shut and refuse to open. My brain forgets how to process the English language. And for a moment, I forget to breathe.

It takes a minute to realize my brain hasn't stopped working. I can still hear the TV in the background and the distant chatter of those outside on the terrace.

Trying to come up with something lame about loving her, but not *really* loving her, seems pointless. It's all in her face. She knows. "You say it every night when you think I'm asleep."

I do. I have for months now. I remember the moment that it hit me. There was no big declaration or grand gesture. We were here, sitting on the same couch we're on now. I just...looked at her. I looked at her and my heart felt like it was too big for my chest.

And I knew what it meant.

It felt safer to say it when I thought she couldn't hear me. I told myself I would work up to the grand gesture. She deserved a parade filled with floats of I love yous. Except she hadn't had the time, so I kept whispering my secret in the darkness. "It's too soon. You don't have to say it back."

"Emmy. I'm a lesbian. You're five months too late, babe."

"Doesn't that mean you were supposed to tell me first?"

"Who says I didn't? Maybe I've loved you before you ever knew my name."

I move from her lap to the space next to her. She leaves the living room for her bedroom, then returns after a few minutes with a notebook and the iPad in her hand. Until now, I've only seen the notebooks in passing. Lately, she's been using the iPad. I keep my curiosity to myself. Whatever she's writing or drawing is important to her. I don't want to overstep.

My expression remains calm as she turns the pages. "I've been redrawing some of my older ones." She flips through the notebook and swipes the drawings on the iPad simultaneously.

"Is that me?" The face looks familiar. Her hair is like mine, but longer with a looser curl. She also looks older. She could be my big sister if Eryn had taken after Mama more than Daddy.

"Inspired." She makes the statement sound like a question.

"How long have you been drawing her?"

"A few years now." I hold back my next thought.

"Do you wanna read it while I'm gone? It'll keep you company."

I grab the notebook out of her hands before she has the chance to change her mind. There's a drawing of the girl every few pages.

Sometimes she's on set or in a dressing room. She always looks determined. Never frightened or shy.

"What's her name?" I stop at a different drawing. This girl reminds me of Gabriella. Again, she looks a little older. Her hair is longer. Her face is more cruel.

"Adriana. Try not to tell me what you think until you're done." I seal my promise with a kiss and place the notebook on the coffee table. I'm dying to read it. If I look too eager, she may regret allowing me access to it. It's best to remain calm.

Gabriella glances at the time on her cell phone and turns to me. "Can you go with me to my appointment?"

"What's wrong? Are you sick?" I place the back of my hand on her forehead. She feels fine.

I watch her lips slowly lift into a smile. "No. It's for moral support."

With no further questions, I leave for my bedroom to put shorts on. If banging on the door got me into trouble, imagine what would happen if I tried to pass the threshold half-naked. Gabriella's standing at the entryway with keys in hand by the time I'm back downstairs. I pass the coffee table with the notebook in place and pause.

"Mind if I read it in the car?"

"If you want."

The slight shrug she gives suggests neutrality. I gather the book in my arms and follow her to the elevator. I don't flip to the first page until she drives. The appropriate amount of silence goes by before I decide it's safe to read.

I'm not aware when we've reached our destination until Gabriella attempts to slide the notebook from my hands. I clench down on it with the full strength of my fingertips. She releases it once I pull the door handle and let myself out.

It takes no time to recognize where we are. I'd know Venice anywhere. I keep the notebook grasped in my left hand and hold Gabriella's hand with my right. We sidestep the many skateboards and shirtless men on the way down the block, closer to the beach.

Gabriella makes an abrupt turn into a shop I can't catch the name of. It's obvious, once we enter, exactly where we've gone. A heavily tattooed woman at the desk greets us. I walk over to the wall covered in framed art. Some say you can learn any skill. I've never tried to become a good drawer, but I know I'm a terrible one.

"Did you get your last piercing at a tattoo shop?" Gabriella asks before sitting on the couch after check-in. It surprises me how bright this shop is. I always think of them as dark and gritty places. Having ample lighting makes sense when you're permanently etching ink into someone's skin.

I have six piercings in each ear along with my belly button. Lucky for me, I've never been afraid of needles. I give blood like a champ.

"No, I got them done at a piercing shop." I expected more fight from my parents, but Daddy took me to get my belly button pierced without complaint. Twelve piercings followed that. I turn away from the artwork and take a seat next to her. "I'm surprised you don't have any other ones." None other than the common two earlobe piercings.

"Never cared enough, I guess."

"Are you getting your septum pierced? People might question whether or not you're a real lesbian," I tease.

She smiles at me. "Does it matter? I'm gonna be with you for the rest of my life." My heart has the same feeling it did that night when I looked at her and knew I loved her. She has a way of expressing her feelings in a very matter-of-fact way, displaying no emotion. It's maddening and overwhelming. I clutch the notebook to my chest.

"Hi. I'm Cynthia. Do you want to come over and talk with me about what you're looking for?" The woman who approaches Gabriella doesn't have as many tattoos as the woman at the front desk. She has a half sleeve of an array of colors. It looks pretty. Something I think looks good on other people, but never on me.

I stay in my seat and decide to devour more of Gabriella's work in progress before her meeting ends. Cynthia approaches again with a few sheets of paper and a pen. "Can you write your name in cursive?" Of course, I can. Cursive writing is a lost art that Mama insisted on. She studied calligraphy for a time and at some point, hoped one of us would take it on. We didn't, but I try to remind her I was at least a good handwriting student.

When I think my writing looks acceptable, I hand it back to Cynthia. I watch her go into a back room that is separate from where other people are getting their work done. The buzzing from the machines is indistinct from one another. There's probably some rule about performing piercings separate from tattoos for contamination protocols. That makes sense.

As time ticks by, I worry Cynthia hasn't come back. Gabriella, even with all her toughness and nonchalance, could very well be afraid of needles. She asked me to come for moral support. I'm supposed to be with her.

My eyes shift around to see if anyone will notice me going somewhere I shouldn't. I close the notebook once again and make my way down the path I saw Cynthia travel. Many eyes meet mine. No one says a word. I reach the door at the same time Cynthia opens it. Her smile fades from view when I notice Gabriella down on the table with one arm out of her t-shirt. One breast is exposed with the nipple covered with white tape.

"Gabby." I inch inside. Her eyes move down to me in

acknowledgment. "What are you doing?"

"Getting a tattoo."

"You are?!" I rush from the doorway to Gabriella's side.

Her face scrunches up in confusion. "Why did you think we were here?"

"I thought you were getting a new piercing."

"No, Emmy."

I have no choice but to move when Cynthia comes to take the place next to her sterilized equipment. She asks, "Was the placement okay?" Gabriella nods in confirmation. I realize I missed the black sketch underneath her breast, right over her scars.

"What does it say?" I rise from the small stool I placed myself on and attempt to look over Gabriella's body. Cynthia casts her eyes up at me. I imagine it to be some kind of uplifting and motivating statement or symbol.

"Taylor," Gabriella speaks with her eyes closed. Cynthia hasn't turned on the machine yet. I wrap my hand around hers and ease back down.

"I'm serious. I can't read it from here."

"I'm serious, too. That's what it says. Taylor."

"No, it doesn't." I shake my head with the power to change words. Cynthia's machine starts. She dips the tip into black ink with her full attention on Gabriella.

"Taylor."

I look up into my girlfriend's face. She doesn't look like she's afraid of needles. She looks exactly like the girl I locked eyes with in a coffee shop many whispered words ago. The one who likes cookies and cream ice cream and learned to make my favorite hot chocolate recipe so I wouldn't have to go without it anymore. She always feels like she knows everything about me.

A fantasy turned into a dream.

A fairytale into reality.

The explosion in my chest only increases with her words. They're so simple. They land perfectly in my heart and instead of pressure, my chest finally calms in completion.

"I love you, too."

Chapter Thirty-One
Gabriella

THE DRESSING ROOM AT Diego's is a mess. I step over unmatched pairs of stilettos, forgotten and discarded tubes of mascara and makeup pigment smeared on the linoleum floor.

"Hey! What the hell happened here?" They're all too busy yelling at each other to answer me.

"You need to respect everyone's space, Roxie. This ain't yo house."

"I've been here for 10 years. This is my house! I don't give a shit how many of you little bitches they bring in here." Roxie swats at the opened nail polish on the vanity. Blue polish smears on the floor and walls.

"Roxie, clean that shit up!" I repeat myself when she doesn't react to my instructions. "Either leave for good or clean it up, now!" Roxie slowly drops to her knees to retrieve the fallen glass bottle, luckily still intact.

"Someone tell me what the hell is going on."

Doll huffs. "Luis hired a new girl, but there's nowhere for the new girl to go. She sat her things on Roxie's station and well..." She waves her hand around the room.

There is some locker space available, but the vanities are usually always occupied. We'll have to figure something else out. "Ok. I'll handle the new girl. Doll, can you please pick up the new girl's stuff for me?" Doll does it without complaint. "Roxie, I'll let Benny know you'll be the last to go on tonight. You'll have plenty of time to clean up."

Her silent eye roll bounces off my back while I exit the room. The hallway to Luis' office is dark as usual. He hasn't sent me out to recruit any new dancers in a while. Not since Coco. And Luis doesn't just hire anyone.

Diego's has an excellent reputation with our employees and an extremely high retention rate. That says a lot for a strip club.

Luis' voice answers my door knock. My eyes blink rapidly to adjust to the visual of Taylor sitting in Luis' office. She looks a little different with her trademark curls hidden beneath a wig. She has on more makeup than I've ever seen her wear. It's not bad. She looks as glamorous as any dancer at an upscale establishment.

"Ah, Gabriella. Meet our new dancer. Today's her first day." Taylor and Luis are all smiles. I try to cover my shock, though I'm unsure if my jaw picks up fast enough.

"Luis, we aren't hiring anyone right now."

Luis laughs. "Excuse Gabriella. She's not here as much as she used to be since starting school. I'll be sure to update her."

Taylor walks past me on her way out. I try not to look at her and let Luis know I know exactly who she is.

"I don't think this is a good idea," I say once the door closes behind her. "The girls –"

"–Will get over it. Make her as comfortable as possible. You've been talking about updating the girls' room. Now's a good time to make it happen."

Now? After years of complaints from the women who work here and the countless times I've advocated for updated facilities, Taylor comes along and suddenly anything is possible.

"What are you getting out of this?"

I've always admired Luis for being the owner of a place like this without all the seedier qualities. He never made passes at any of the women or ever tried to take advantage of me. They respect him even when they don't agree with him.

"Is she...paying you?"

"Why can't you just accept when something good happens?" Because everyone has their price. Nothing comes to anyone for free. I know that firsthand. "Keep her happy. Make sure the girls are nice to her and that the customers respect her. She only plans to come on days when you're working. No need to brief anyone else on this."

Fantastic.

There are no lesbian strip clubs in San Diego, or much of anywhere in California. Some clubs have nights designated for lesbians or other members of the LGBTQ+ community, but it's not commonly the focus.

Diego's is trying a different model, where some dancers are assigned to only serve women. It's been difficult to manage, since, unexpectedly, the dancers overwhelmingly prefer dancing more for women than for men, regardless of their sexual orientation.

Women are less aggressive, tip better and they're more likely to return for consistent service, instead of each new visit feeling like an escalation to the inevitable.

I ignore every pair of eyes that try to meet mine on the way to find Taylor. I can't believe she's here. After years of hiding Diego's from her, she walked right through the door.

The locker room is in better condition when I return, but there's no sign of our newest dancer. I grab what I think I might need to contain her tonight. If she won't listen and go willingly, there are other measures I might have to use.

I take a while to find her on the floor, bent over, talking to a group of women who visit frequently. Thankfully, she's wearing extremely tiny shorts and not the G-string I imagined.

These people are unaware of the gift they've been given. Or that it's mine.

She catches my eye and excuses herself. I do nothing to dampen the anger present on my face. Admittedly, it's difficult. Too many people have noticed her. Diego's thrives on consistency. They see the new treat. And they want her.

She extends a hand to me. Confidence and cockiness ooze from her lopsided grin. "Hi. I'm Emerald. You're Adriana, right?"

Fuck.

Tiana Edwards is an award-winning actress with an addiction to the spotlight. She's done everything from commercials to film, even hosting a few reality TV show competitions. She has several TV shows in syndication and is named one of the top actors of her generation, even so, it's not enough.

One day, she gets an idea to feed her addiction by unconventional means and convinces a local strip club owner to allow her to dance there in disguise. She adopts the name Emerald for her *new* stage, explaining to the owner her latest hobby was necessary for research. He agrees to keep her secret at a price Tiana is more than willing to pay.

That is until she meets the floor manager at the club, a beautiful and stoically silent Adriana. Adriana is placed in charge of Tiana's safety, though she doesn't know why. At first, she's resentful of the new dancer's privileges, but as her feelings for Tiana grow and change, her anger shifts from resentment to possessiveness, and pretty soon, watching Emerald dance with strange customers becomes too much.

Will Adriana find the courage to claim the woman she loves? Can Emerald contain her hunger for admiration for the sake of her relationship with Adriana?

I don't know. I haven't finished writing the script.

Taylor has mentioned nothing about it since I gave it to her months ago. It's a work in progress. I have had little time to complete it.

Emerald is not based on her completely. She is as beautiful as Taylor, but also a lot more stubborn.

"Would you happen to know what time I go on? I didn't see my name on the list and the DJ said he didn't have my song ready."

"New dancers don't start their first day on stage. Floor duty first. You satisfy your customers long enough, then maybe you'll get a performance slot."

That won't happen.

She won't be here that long.

I'll make sure of it.

She shifts her weight to one side, sweeps her hair behind her shoulder, and crosses her arms. "That's too bad. I was hoping to show off tonight."

"Yeah, well. Some singers never make it outta the shower."

"Are there any dancers here who've never touched the pole?"

"Yeah. And at least one who never will."

I attach the pink band to her wrist in one swift movement. She looks surprised at her new accessory. "Women Only. No men." The dark gleam in her eyes tells me there may be some resistance to this I'll have to look out for.

I still have a job to do and won't be able to follow her around the club for the next four hours. My best bet is to contain her. Taylor likes to make up her own rules and discard the ones that no longer please her. That's the difference between her and Emerald. Emerald would know them and play by them.

All actors interpret their characters differently. From the looks of it, Taylor plans to continue to harness Emerald's boldness, which only means trouble for me. Emerald takes care of herself. She never cares about what Adriana thinks.

"Isn't there some kind of scrapbook or something you should be putting together?" She laughs at my question mockingly while pulling her hand away.

"Don't worry. I'll throw plenty of confetti on your grave." She also plans to channel Emerald's ruthlessness.

She backs away from me and surveys the entire floor. Plenty of eyes are watching her. It's amazing to see their energy fuel her. With each pair of eyes she locks with, her back becomes a little straighter, her eyes darker, and her grin more dangerous.

"Nice chat, Dree. I can call you Dree, right?"

"No!" My voice is void of the playfulness that's present in hers. The urge to drag her away from the table she's walking toward is strong.

She sits in an empty chair and leans forward with her elbows resting on the table and her hand supporting her chin. Her eyelashes are longer than usual. She flutters the hell out of them.

My eyes stay planted on her all the way to the DJ booth. I check the setlist to make sure the name Emerald is nowhere to be found.

"Hey, Benny. Did you see the new dancer?" Benny shakes his head with one ear still covered by his headphones. I point Taylor out to him. She still sits at the table, but now her chair is closer to one woman whose face I recognize, but whose name I can't recall. Taylor's hair is swooped to one side while the woman whispers something into her ear. The money she's holding between her fingers travels up and down Taylor's exposed thighs.

"Make sure she doesn't set foot on stage. If she tries and you can't find me, stop the music." Benny looks at me as though I've gone more than a little crazy. Admittedly, my eyes haven't stopped following that trail of money scratching against her skin.

She's gone beyond role play. Now she's trying to get someone murdered.

Taylor waves over Jamal. I like Jamal. We've been working here for the same amount of time. He's funny and reliable. I hope I don't have to kill him tonight.

Whatever Taylor says to him prompts him to tug on his earpiece and speak into our shared channel. "J to Gabby. J to Gabby. Emerald is requesting a private room. She's gonna need a big one."

Six women are sitting at the table with her. They order more drinks from the bar to be delivered to their room.

"Copy that, J. I'm on my way."

Taylor's eyes find me when I'm halfway across the floor. Her head cocks to the side. Her hands roam down her buttery, moisturized skin. She glows in the brightly covered club lights. Every single one of her fingers is naked. My rings are missing. It's not her biggest mistake, but she will pay for it.

I paint a smile on my face and look directly at the group. "Excuse me, ladies. I need to speak to Emerald really quickly. I'll come and get you once your room is ready."

A chorus of understanding follows me as I walk behind the black curtain, into the private hallway. I don't pause for Taylor to follow. She'll intend to take her time and I intend to teach her why that isn't a good idea. I detour into the storage room where we keep our specialty items reserved for customers who show great financial promise. Only a select few dancers have access to this room.

I leave the door to the biggest private room we offer open. Unlike the others, it has a mini stage, complete with a pole. I settle on the couch and wait. This is what she wants. And it'll make me feel better.

Her shorts look even smaller by the time she walks in and I swear the shirt she wears hangs not much higher than just beyond her breasts.

"Close the door behind you."

She kicks it closed with her stiletto. "Did I do something wrong?" She walks across the room to stand in place in front of me.

"Of course not. We're all about opportunities here at Diego's. You wanted to dance. Now's your chance."

She leans forward. Her face is less than an inch from mine. If I look down, I know I'll see her round breasts peeking out from her tiny scrap of a t-shirt. "You wouldn't be trying to get me into trouble, now, would you, Dree?"

"I told you not to call me that."

"I know." Her tongue runs over her top lip, wetting mine. "But I like it."

The heel of her platform dips into the shag carpet. The bottom of her ass cheeks spills out the stretched denim. With one hand placed on the shiny, gold pole, she walks around in a circle. The thickness of her platform heels thump against the hardwood.

"No music?" It's the first time she drops the cocky act and replaces it with puppy dog eyes and a pout.

"Music? I thought you were looking forward to putting on a show?" I lean back against the couch and cross my legs in disinterest.

The pout spreads into a smirk. Those eyes...those beautiful dark brown eyes that I would give my soul to look into for the rest of my life, grow sharp.

"I guess I won't be needing these, then." She uses the pole as leverage to support her back while slipping off her shorts and kicking them to the floor. She has to shake her hips a few times before they give way. A movement that sends my heart beating down into my lower core. The once-hidden G-string is red. Another foul. She giggles when my eyes land on the strand of fabric. The unnecessary cloth once barely covering her breasts lands in my lap.

"How's this for a show?" She's not giggling anymore. Her eyes fix on me, waiting for my reaction.

My eyes grow wide at the shiny barbells pierced through her nipples. Those weren't there this morning. The gold heart-shaped rings complete with devil horns match perfectly with her new gold belly button jewelry. The stone on the belly ring matches the red G-string.

"Are you sure I'm not breaking any rules?" My eyes follow her hand down the front to the only part of her body that remains covered. She tugs at the small piece of underwear. Her mouth drops open and her hips move forward. She does it again and again, each time the sliding becomes easier and her moans become louder.

She stops to rub the flat of her fingers over her clit with one hand holding onto the pole. "If you wanted me all to yourself, all you had to do was say so."

The shirt falls to the floor when I stand. She does not stop what she's doing. Her tiny gasps for breath fill the room. She watches me watch her. My hand grazes her stomach and then moves up to cup her breast. "Are these for me?"

She shakes her head. "No?"

She shakes her head again. My thumb rolls over her nipple. She grits her teeth and sucks in a breath.

"The rules say you need to ask permission before proceeding with any procedure that alters the appearance of one's body. That includes piercings." I hold the second breast in my other hand. Her hand slows down its pursuit of pleasure in anticipation of my next attack. I lower my head to the side of her nipple, capture the shiny ring between my teeth and pull.

"Fuck! Fuck! Fuck!" she screams louder than any music could play.

"Did you ask me for permission?"

"No." She grits through her teeth.

"And why not? Do you think you're too good for rules? Do you think you're better than the other dancers here?"

"I am better," she sneers. "And I didn't ask my manager's permission because I asked my boss." Her eyes lock onto mine with twisted defiance and malice. "Luis helped me pick out the jewelry. And you know what else?" My hand wraps around her throat in response. Hers wraps around my wrist. "My pussy's next."

Emerald's a bitch. And she deserves everything Adriana has planned for her tonight.

She slides down the pole and falls to her knees when I release her. My trip back to the couch is a blur. I'm not aware of what I'm doing until she gags on the tip of the glass instrument I wasn't sure until this moment would be used to inflict her punishment.

She closes her lips around it and adds the right amount of pressure. Like a pro. She's had plenty of practice since the last time she played her little game. Clearly, she didn't learn her lesson. I'll have to do better this time. She sucks with bravado and a piercing glare, challenging me.

The toy releases from her lips with a loud pop. I push her onto her back before she has a chance to act out whatever rebellious plan appears in her mind. I shove the dark red triangle shielding her from me and rub the tip of the toy against her entrance.

She lets out a breath and then a moan. Of their own volition, her thighs stretch out as far as their constraints will let them go.

"Whose pussy did you say it was, again?" My new weapon slips past a bit of resistance. The glass glides against her flooding walls. I rub her clit at the same time I thrust inside her.

"Yours, Dree! Yes, oh fuck yes!"

Every time she yells out, her eyes fly to the door she never locked after she kicked it closed with her stiletto.

"No one's ever taught you how to be a good girl, huh?" The sounds of her dripping out and covering my hands in pleasure mix with her shouts. "After tonight, you're going to be a good fucking girl. Do you hear me, Emerald?"

"Yes!" she screams out, banging her heels against the wood flooring.

"Yes, who?"

I slow the circular attack. She bites her bottom lip. Her eyes are no longer filled with defiance.

"Yes, Adriana."

The glass empties of her to a protest that I ignore. My clothing falls to the ground. I make sure she watches me walk to the door. I twist the lock and listen as it clicks into place. A spark of rebellion returns to her eyes. But I don't care. The sight of her naked, waiting, and wet is all I need to feel triumphant. That, and something else.

"Good girls never reveal their secrets." I shake my head at her in disappointment. I sit in a position where our pussies almost meet. She pushes forward in response. I hold up the double dildo I swiped off the couch on the way back.

I slide in the side I've designated for myself and groan at the welcomed pressure. Taylor's eyes fixate on me. I know what she looks like when she's hungry. Her mouth is watering at the anticipation of something more. Something she's never done before.

"Are you a good girl, Emerald?"

She nods slowly. On her hands and knees, she crawls. Her neck drops over the exposed side and she captures it into her mouth. When she's satisfied, she leans over to kiss me, first on the lips and then on the side of my breast that bears her name, while hovering her hips over the toy. She lowers and we both gasp at the same time. She doesn't scream out as loud as she did before and her eyes never glance at the door. We rock together in rhythm, creating our music and performing our dance.

I meet every "I love you" with the same words. And I mean every syllable. I always have.

"Gabby, I–" The words get lost in her orgasm and can only be communicated through her tight muscles and bucking hips.

I hold her through her shudders and quake through my own. The rug underneath greets us when we fall flat on our backs. I squeeze the hand that slides into mine and make a mental note to replace every single ring.

"Emmy."

"Yes?"

She rolls over to kiss my shoulder. A glance tells me her eyes are shut. She looks exhausted and at peace. Nothing like a determined Hollywood starlet on a secret mission.

"You're fired."

She sighs. Her face scrunches up, then relaxes again. "I figured."

Chapter Thirty-Two
Gabriella

I SEND THE CALL lighting up on my screen to voicemail. It's a number I don't recognize.

The sun beats down steady rays on the grass outside the kitchen window. I watch Taylor with my dad while he tends to his rose bushes. It's a mystery to me what they talk about when they're together. I never ask and she never offers.

"How are things going with the two of you?" I look back at Mom sitting at the kitchen table, peeling potatoes. It's finally summer again, and this is the third weekend I'm leaving Taylor alone with my family to go to work. With no classes to attend, my schedule has shifted. I work at Craft from Mondays to Thursdays and leave Friday mornings to drive down to work all weekend at Diego's.

Taylor staying at our apartment through the weekend is not an option. I considered having her stay with her parents instead, but as soon as I heard her telling her dad how great a drive down to San Diego would be, I nixed that idea. Who knows what trouble she was planning to get into. She would probably convince them to go to a fancy dinner and then ditch them once stuffed and sleepy.

No. That wasn't going to work.

"We're good, Mom."

"Yeah? Then why are you watching her like you're afraid she's gonna disappear?"

She taps the space on the table next to her with her elbow. I take one last look at Taylor with the watering hose in her hand and sit as instructed.

"I like Taylor. But if I need to be worried about her, I need you to tell me."

"I don't know what that means." I shake my head in annoyance, aware that my muscles are tensing.

My family has had continuous conversations with Taylor since Christmas Eve last year, separate from me. They have their private jokes and send each other photos I've never seen.

"It means I like Taylor for you. She's a sweet girl. Unlike the other one. But if you're not happy, it's okay for you to let go."

"I'm happy. Why would you say that?"

I place the scattered peels into the plastic grocery bag in front of her. I grab the skinless potatoes from the bucket of water they sit in, grab the knife, and cut them into smaller pieces.

Not looking directly at my mom is a strategy for both her and me. If she's implying that there's something wrong with my relationship with Taylor, that'll piss me off.

"Your face says otherwise."

"What does my face say, Mom?"

"That you're scared!" She brings her fist down on the dining room table. A few of the potatoes roll to the floor. I pick them up and place them back in the pile.

She continues in my silence. "That city is rife with devils dressed in nice clothes with beautiful faces and pretty hair. If she's one of those devils, then you need to tell us."

I steady my balled fists on the table, but I'm unable to steady my voice. "She's not a devil and I'm not afraid of her." I pause and then push out the truth. "I'm afraid of losing her."

My mom's face softens. Her brows remain furrowed, but something in her eyes changes and her lips turn down into a frown. "Why would you be afraid of that? You look happy together. Mom's always sending your pictures to everyone. I get all these messages every day that the family needs new photos of Gabriella and her girlfriend."

This, I know to be true. Taylor has randomly stopped us enough times throughout the day for random photo opportunities that never end up on social media, blogs, or magazines. She's freed my hair from its ponytail more times than I've liked by simply stating, "'Your grandma likes it better this way'" before the mock sound of a lens shuttering goes off on her cell phone.

"Not Dad's side."

I side-eye my mother, who shakes her head and shrugs. "They don't matter."

My parents were teenagers when they met, already living in San Diego. They grew up in this same neighborhood and hung out with the same group of friends. Their views differ from our relatives who still live in Mexico in a lot of ways. It's one of Mom's favorite complaints.

"Did you think I was good enough for Sara?"

Mom snaps her head back in shock. "That girl didn't know how to do anything for herself. You did her homework. You took her shopping. When you got your license, you drove her around the city. It was ridiculous. I don't know what you ever saw in her."

I saw nothing in her. I didn't even see her coming. There was no way to predict my life was about to change on the first day she walked into my class.

"Has anyone called you?" She denies it with a shake of her head. "Come by?" Same response.

Maricela rounds the corner with her phone clutched tightly in her hand. She takes a peek through the window I was standing in front of just a few minutes ago and groans.

"Man, she's not done yet? How long is she gonna be out there with Dad?"

"No idea. What do you want with her?"

"She promised she'd do a live with me. I've already posted about it to my followers." She says it to me as though this is information I should already have. I barely keep up with my own social media account. Surely she doesn't expect me to pay attention to hers.

These days the only pictures Taylor posts are of us together. Sometimes it's us walking down the promenade. She takes photos of me cooking and her eating. We've been together for almost a year. While people have short attention spans, they don't lose access to their memories. Whatever comments she continues to get about us, she doesn't share.

"What are you going live for?" I ask. Mom has returned to peeling the potatoes. She looks unconcerned with Maricela's announcement.

Maricela lifts her chin high in the air. "I'm teaching her how to speak Spanish."

"No, you're not!"

"Yes, I am. The lives are the perfect place for them. She reads the comments aloud in Spanish—after I approve them, of course. She gets to practice with native speakers from all over the world."

"Um, hello. I'm a native speaker!" I say, unnecessarily pointing to my chest.

"Yeah, but you're never home. She says you're always working."

Mom interjects, "Why are you so upset, Mija? She goes to the store. She asks for things in Spanish. If she needs help, we help her."

"That's not the point."

Not that I could ever fully explain the point. I love that Taylor has committed to learning my first language. She takes it very seriously. It's honestly cute how she greets people, especially older Latinos, whom she insists on opening the door for. She señors and señoras them to death.

Taylor walks through the back door first, much to the delight of Maricela. "Finally!"

Maricela runs to grab her hand, but I get there first.

"We need to talk." My words sound more urgent than I mean them to. I can't help it. It feels like I'm losing something I didn't realize was available to be stolen from me.

Taylor looks mildly alarmed. She follows me from the kitchen to the bedroom. At the sight of Grandma down the hall, I reach to grab Taylor's arm and pull her into the bathroom, ignoring Grandma's shout of "Margarita!", before shutting the door.

Taylor stands in the middle of the room with her lips turned down in a frown. We have more to talk about than her opinions about my family relationships. I tell myself to be calm and open to her explanation. There might be a good reason for this.

"What is this I hear about my family teaching you Spanish?"

She shrugs nonchalantly. "I needed to put my sentences together better, and I called your mom one day and she helped me." She places her hand over her chest and smiles at me. "Are you jealous?" I deny it by swatting away her attempts at a hug. "Ah, don't be jealous, babe. They'll never be as good of a teacher as you."

When I relent, she wraps her arms around me, pinning mine to my side.

"There was one time when I made the mistake of calling your grandma, *abuela*, and I think she thought real hard about throwing her shoe at me."

I pull myself free from her. She makes a whiny noise that

reminds me how cute she can be. I'm not mad at her. I don't know how to be.

"Don't listen to Araceli. She wouldn't have thrown anything at you, but she does hate *abuela*. She thinks it makes her sound old."

Taylor interlocks our fingers together. I'm unsuccessful at keeping her from swinging our hands from side to side. "After tonight, I won't do it anymore if you don't want me to."

"I don't want you to."

"Fine. It's settled. This is my last Spanish lesson in the Flores household."

"In *this* Flores household," I correct her. I feel the movement of her laugh through our kiss. "Thank you."

The only good place to take a break at Diego's is out back near the employee entrance. It's the furthest from the club where the bass of the music isn't thumping in your eardrums.

I click play on the nagging voicemail notification, with one finger hovering over the trash icon. The voice that comes through isn't that of a robot. It doesn't ask me to confirm my identity or press any buttons. It's a voice I don't know, but a name I recognize.

"Good afternoon, Gabriella. This is Lisa Perry calling. I got your name a while back from a mutual acquaintance of ours. I'm sorry it has taken me so long to contact you. If you're interested, I have an opportunity I'd like to discuss. Please call me back at your earliest convenience."

Lisa Perry called me. I stare at the phone number listed on my caller ID. It's too late to call her back now. When I can't find Sara's number in my contacts, I remember I blocked her. And for good reason. If she's the one who called Lisa, I would like to know why. I click through the necessary buttons to get to my block list. Her name is the only one there.

Sara has never read anything I've written. She's never even shown an interest, unlike with my drawings, mostly because she liked to look at her own face. Taylor hasn't asked me to draw her, and I've given her permission to read through as many of the notebooks as she wants. She always brings up the couples at the most random of times. 'Do you think Diana would own a restaurant like this?' Sometimes it feels like she thinks about my characters as much as I think about her.

It's best not to wake a sleeping dragon.

I slip my cell phone into my pocket and make my way back inside.

Diego's is under construction.

Clear plastic blocks an unfinished section of the dressing room. The dust is at a minimum, which has been nice. Each dancer now has their assigned area over the dark hardwood flooring. We've replaced the steel lockers with white closet space attached to glass doors. The girls can see their items clearly, and I make sure everything looks clean and organized.

Bambi hasn't stopped gushing about the new chairs with their names embroidered on the back. The last thing I need is a fight because of swapped chairs. I asked Jade for her opinion on the new kid area that is next on the list. It'll have a space for games and lounging and cots for sleeping.

The women have all agreed to take turns on babysitting duty until I can convince Luis to hire someone for the job. The renovation has come with rules, like committing to use the updated bathrooms to change into their outfits and a robe area directly on the outside of the dressing room, so the women are decent enough to enter when there might be nosey faces present.

The new area is much more glamorous than what it looked like before. The girls are grateful, and I'm strangely proud. Taylor hasn't been back to see the progress, but I've taken plenty of pictures. She had ideas for wallpaper that I only nodded at. I've been wrestling with the decision to allow her to come back to the club, but as herself. Having my girlfriend here as a dancer will only distract me. If we're lucky, no one will recognize her as the one who disappeared a few months ago.

The night goes by smoothly, with no conflict between the ladies and patrons who remain compliant as soon as they walk through the door.

Taylor is asleep on the sofa once I arrive back at my parents' house. In the beginning, she always tried to stay up for me, but I told her it was best that she slept. Otherwise, she'd sleep on the drive home. She remains asleep even after I dip in behind her. I haven't heard that annoying meditation lady in a while. It's a good thing, I think. I hate the idea of her feeling restless.

Taylor sleeps soundly beside me as time ticks by. I try not to check my phone and only stare at the speckled ceiling. My eyes shut when Maricela exits the room to go to the bathroom. It's still dark out. I hear her footsteps make a detour into the living room and feel her standing over us. I open my eyes again when I hear the door click shut.

First, the sunrise glows through the closed blinds. Then, I hear cars drive by. By the time Taylor's eyes meet mine, Grandma has entered the kitchen to start breakfast, and my eyes are drooping closed.

I shake it off and accept the cup of coffee I'm offered. When I feel like I have a little more energy, I excuse myself to go outside.

The inside of the car is freezing. In my escape, I didn't consider what the weather would feel like compared to the warmth of my girlfriend.

My eyes stay trained on the front door just in case someone comes out to see what's taking me so long. The sound of the phone ringing is the only noise I'm able to hear. I can feel my heart thumping in my chest and my foot jiggling in anticipation, but nothing alerts my sense of hearing quite like the abrupt stop to the ringtone.

"Hello?"

"Hi. May I please speak with Lisa Perry? This is Gabriella Flores returning her call."

Chapter Thirty-Three
Taylor

Zara's office has too many people inside of it. Technically, my parents don't need to be here. I'm an adult capable of making my own career choices. They know that, but they came anyway because it was Lisa Perry calling.

Lisa Perry is a legend. Her name was whispered behind the scenes before there was ever an article written about her. Now she writes and produces some of the biggest television shows.

And she requested a meeting with me.

Gabriella sits next to Lisa. Technically, she's here in an official capacity as a writer and not as my girlfriend. I look at her anyway and test her ability to ignore me. She hasn't turned away.

That pesky eyebrow of hers raises. She shifts her eyes to the side several times. While I refuse to lose this game, I decide it might be wise to listen to what Lisa Perry has to say.

"The show I have in mind fits Taylor to a tee. It's nothing she's ever done before and that's the good part. People are so used to seeing Taylor as the heroine. She's always the underdog and then the good guy." She turns to me, forcing me to break eye contact with Gabriella. I watch the smirk grow on her face while trying to keep mine blank. "Everyone thinks they know what you're capable of. Let's see what happens when you're the villain."

"The villain?"

"Yes. We don't have all the details yet. Just know you're no angel in this role. How bad you're willing to become for the sake of your character will be an ongoing discussion. We want everyone to be comfortable."

I glance around at the faces of Zara and my parents. They remain calm and smiling. Gabriella does as well.

"I have to admit, you're making me a little nervous." I don't think there's an actor alive who wouldn't like to push the envelope and showcase their skills. If by villain, she means serial killer, I can do that. If by villain she means serial killer of unsuspecting children, then I'd have to decline. It's not always worth it to be different. Becoming someone unfamiliar to your audience can sometimes be detrimental.

"Don't be. I'm assuming you trust Gabriella to know what your limits are. She's my confidant on this project." I never imagined my girlfriend playing a big part in my career. I knew we'd work in the same industry, but never did I think it would be this close. I'd always imagined us supporting each other on our projects. Now, I wonder if Gabriella ever thought the same.

"Taylor isn't a child anymore, and she has no interest in playing teenage roles forever. We've discussed her trajectory plenty of times. We'd need to discuss if this role is indeed the right fit. What is it, exactly?" Zara asks with a pleasant expression on her face.

"It's the story of a young woman who struggles with addiction, a myriad of abuses, and the measures she's forced to take to survive. She's got a bone to pick with many people."

"Why do you think that'll push my limits?" Lisa has my full attention now. The great Lisa Perry coming to me at this stage feels premature. Producers approached me for *The Paige Society* when Piper Paige was just an idea, but everything moved rather quickly after that. This sounds like Lisa went to sleep last night, had a dream, and decided to create a TV show.

"I don't know. Sometimes we can never be sure about these things until we try them out."

I nod in agreement. I think she's right in some circumstances, but not in others. There are plenty of roles I know I have no interest in taking on. There's something fun about the prospect of being a bank robber involved in a very sophisticated heist. A spy would be cool, and learning to speak several languages and accents would be a challenge worthy of an accomplished and dedicated actor.

The meeting ends with me agreeing to read whatever comes my way from this project and Lisa gushing about our future partnership.

I wave to Gabriella as her car backs out of the parking spot at Zara's office. We barely spoke since my parents also took up some of her time. She and Daddy have been swapping cookies for months now. I've been Gabriella's personal taste tester and the cookies are good, but I still haven't quite figured out the purpose of the new tradition.

"I'm so glad Sara called me about her. She has great ideas. And she knows you very well." Lisa Perry stands beside me staring at the same spot Gabriella's car once was before shifting her focus to me.

"Sara? Sara Aguilar?"

"Yeah. She contacted me a while back, asking if there was space available for a young writer on one of my projects. I've been out of the loop a bit and didn't realize it was for her ex-girlfriend. You two are fine now, right?"

I do my best to not allow any animosity to show in my face or seep through my voice. I don't know where I stand with Sara.

"We're not best friends, but I don't think we'll ever be."

"Yeah. That's what she said. I hope you consider it. You'd be great."

Gabriella is home when I get there. The stack of notebooks filled with Tiana and Adriana's story sits on the floor of her closet. She emerges from the bathroom in a fresh set of clothing, surprised to see me lounging on her bed.

"I thought you were gonna stay with your family longer."

"We had breakfast together before the meeting." I knew she wouldn't be able to attend. She's barely home now. With working at the restaurant, the club, and now with Lisa, she has no time for me. "Are you planning to drop out of school?" There's no way she can keep this up once classes start again.

"No, I can't do that. I probably have to quit Craft, work with Lisa during the day, and have classes at night. I can still do Diego's on the weekend."

"Or you can quit Diego's and work weekend shifts at Craft. The commute is way shorter."

She gives me the look that means she doesn't want to argue with me. It's how she shows me she's being patient, but becoming frustrated.

"There are other things I need to do in San Diego. It's not just because of Diego's." My teeth clamp down on the fat of my inner cheek. Sara is there. Sara, who spoke with Lisa to promote my girlfriend's career.

"If you didn't work at Diego's, we'd have more time together."

"We'll spend more time together once you start the show."

She puts her hair into a sleek ponytail, changes her mind, and snaps the hair tie back on her wrist. I hate how final her words sound. We've had one meeting, and suddenly the direction of my career has changed.

"It could take years for that show to start production and we still won't see each other. Screenwriters aren't usually on set for filming."

She lets out a breath in aggravation. I cross my arms in defense. "Taylor, is this about the time we spend together or you not being able to go to Diego's?"

"I don't have a problem with you working at a strip club. I'm upset that you're trying to orchestrate a deal so that my career fits into your schedule."

"What career? You haven't worked in over a year."

Shock pierces through my chest and renders me speechless. Gabriella fills her bag with new clothing and tosses the rest in the hamper. It's a few days until she's scheduled to leave again. I've never realized how eager she is to go.

"I'm not apologizing for taking time off to live my life out from behind a camera. It sucks that you don't value the time we have together as much as I do. I understand you feel like you have to work, but you don't have to work as much as you do. Working three to four different jobs is a choice you've made. And you can't keep trying to punish me for your decisions or downplay my success."

I stand from her bed and meet nothing but silence. We hardly ever fight. Standing before me is everything I love about her: her strength, her determination, and her independence. Her ability to move with confidence, no matter the opinion of the critics, is admirable. But in her eyes, I'm the critic and she doesn't give a shit about what I have to say.

"And if I don't have a career, then why are you using me to get a job with Lisa Perry?" Her eyes grow big at my accusation. I hold up my hand to keep her from speaking. "I'll let Zara know to tell Lisa I'm too underqualified to be on her show."

I angrily walk to the patio doors, open and then close them again. It's too sunny outside. My heart craves an environment that better matches my mood.

The walk upstairs is a blur. I strip out of my clothes, leaving only my bra and panties on, and curl underneath my blanket instead. Each teardrop falls for different reasons.

Gabriella doesn't care about spending time with me.

She's using me to further her career.

My heart hurts.

"Go away!" I scream out through garbled speech from the small space I created to allow me to breathe under the weight of the covers. The sound of the door creaking open is unmistakable.

I wrap the covers tighter around my body when the mattress dips behind me, anyway.

"I love you."

"Liar!" I snap back. It feels wrong. The tears fall out quicker at the contrarian feeling.

"I don't know how to fix this one, Emmy. Please help me." The pleading in her voice stuns me. She's never asked me for anything. Especially not for help.

"You don't want to hear what I have to say."

"I only care about what you have to say."

I roll over from my side to my back. My attention stays on the dresser across the room.

"Why did you wanna be with me?" If she asked me that question, I'd know the answer right away. She takes her time, tracing the edge of my jaw with her finger. It's a struggle to keep my body from both rejecting her touch and submitting to it.

"That's a complicated question." It's the wrong answer. The answer in my heart is simple. It's supposed to be completely absent from everything I fear. Nothing to do with Hollywood or TV or celebrity.

Please. I close my eyes in defeat. I feel the crook of her index finger trace my jawline to reassure me. It doesn't.

"For a long time, you were just this girl on TV, completely out of my reach, and then suddenly you weren't so far away."

"How'd you know I'd be in the coffee shop that day?"

She grimaces. "I followed you."

I shift my eyes to see the look of regret cross her face. "What was the plan?"

"You know the plan." The words come out in a hurry. It's unlike her. She's never flustered. Her anger doesn't look this defensive. I say what she doesn't to myself. *To ruin my life.* A chink in our fairytale never spoken about.

We locked eyes over the head of a barista, my ass. Our relationship now feels a lot like it did back in the beginning. Is Gabriella friend or foe? Is she my savior or my executioner? And if she's the latter, why haven't I built up enough sense to run?

"That means nothing now. That's not our story anymore. I love you." There's something in her eyes that feels desperate. They're saying the same thing as my heart. *Hold on.*

"I love you, too." It's the first time I feel a sharp pang as those words leave my throat.

She untangles me from the blanket and wraps her arms around me. "I called out sick tonight."

"You didn't have to do that."

"Yeah, I did. I'll think of a new plan, okay?"

I nod through damp cheeks and a heavy heart. Every touch between us that follows stings my skin and leaves behind invisible marks I'm unsure I'll be able to recover from.

She loves me.

I'm just suddenly not sure why.

If I'm going to be in a Lisa Perry production, I should probably get back to work. Committing to a months-long project sounds daunting. Most actors audition for guest roles hoping they will transition into a series regular. They hope the audience loves them enough to justify a recurrence or the writers frequently include their characters in scenes every week.

I don't want that.

I want to not get to the first day of filming whatever project my girlfriend is working on with Lisa Perry and look like I was just plucked from acting school.

A guest role would be perfect, but hosting a kids' crafting competition for a few weeks is fine, too.

"They still haven't decided on the kids yet. You're gonna shoot with one group first and then they'll switch them out with the second group."

I nod at Zara's words while also trying to focus on not losing an eye to the eyeliner the makeup artist applies. It's always my least favorite part. I catch Gabriella's smiling face in the mirror. It's so rare to see her like this in the company of other people. We've mostly recovered since our last disagreement, meaning we haven't talked about it.

Auditioning for this role is my way of offering a truce. I haven't decided yet if I even want to star in Lisa's new production. They have given me little to no details about the character or the plot. Still, this is Gabriella's dream and I'm trying to be supportive.

"Hey, girl." Small arms wrap around my shoulders in greeting. Whitney Grace's smiling face looks back at me with both dimples sunken deep into her cheeks.

"Hey, Whittle Whitney." I tease her with the same expression she greeted me with. "How have you been?"

"Good. Are you officially out of retirement?"

"Hmm. I'm easing in slowly."

"I must be your backup if you decide you're not ready to leave your life of leisure."

"Please." I wave her off and steady myself for the false eyelash application. I picked the smallest set. My face is not the place for fluffy caterpillars. "I'm the alternate, and you're the frontrunner. You're the only star standing in this room."

The Paige Society was my escape from teeny-bopper TV. Although Piper Paige was still a teenager, the show was a drama and not a comedy. We filmed it on a closed set and not in front of a studio audience with a laugh track.

Whitney Grace was the star of her show and the network wanted to keep her so badly that instead of canceling like they typically did after three or four seasons, they created a new one for her. Having someone who is currently relevant on a popular children's television program host a competition show geared toward children only makes sense.

"You're so sweet. I missed seeing you around. When you said you were taking a break from the business, you meant it."

It's been almost two years and I don't regret a single moment of it.

My makeup artist releases me with one last blast of matte setting spray. I always get the same speech about not wanting to look too shiny on television. Yes, I know.

"Let me introduce you to my girlfriend." I fan one hand to Gabriella, who remains sitting on the couch. "Gabriella, this is Whitney. Whitney, this is Gabriella."

"I've heard," Whitney responds with a wave. Gabriella wiggles her fingers slightly at Whitney, but says nothing back. "I see you got what you wanted."

"What do you mean?"

"The girl."

"Oh, yeah," I laugh. A knock on the door grabs our attention. Whitney's manager pokes her head in and signals for her to leave.

"It was good to see you, Taylor." She walks past the couch Gabriella sits on, takes another glance, and looks back at me. "I hope she's worth it." The flair of her identical dress, only a different color from mine, trails out the door.

I avoid Zara's gaze that has lifted from the phone in her hand, directly to Gabriella. There's enough room on the edge of the couch to fit right beside my beautiful girlfriend, whose deep brown eyes followed Whitney Grace from the moment she stepped in the room and still stays locked on the door she walked out of.

"Gabby." I turn her face by her chin when she doesn't look at me. "What did you do to Whitney?" I hold my breath for her response. I've heard plenty of stories, but none of them ever whispered the name Whitney Grace.

"Nothing, yet."

"Gabby."

"I think she just threatened you."

"She did not. Zara–" Zara tilts her head from one side to the other. Gabriella's face leaves mine and stares at the door again. "Gabby." She slowly turns to me with a fake smile spread across her lips. "Whitney is my friend. She would never threaten me."

"There are no friends in this business."

"That's not true. Nicole's my friend. My best friend."

"Nicole is your friend by default. You grew up together and your parents like each other. She secretly thinks she's better than you and quietly celebrates every mistake you make."

"That's not true!"

"It is true. It's why she keeps holding on to that shitty boyfriend of hers. When you were single, it made her look good. Now that you're in a relationship, she's in a longer one. It's a win-win for her."

Zara is no longer looking at us. Her eyes are downcast into her phone with her legs crossed at the ankles.

"Nicole has put in a lot of effort over the past year and a half to ensure that there is no conflict between the two of you. I'd like to keep it that way. Please, never say that again."

"Sure, dear." It's hard to describe the way her lips spread across her face. It's not a smile or a patronizing smirk. Whatever it is, I know it's fake.

I eye her suspiciously.

"Taylor, they're ready for you." Zara walks through the door the production assistant just vacated. I stand and make one last check in the mirror. I straightened my hair today instead of keeping it in its signature curls. Whitney always wears her hair straight, like Nicole, except hers is jet black, like mine.

"You stay here. I'll be back." Gabriella gives me that same fake, stretched smile she had before. "I mean it. You're not the only one who can dish out a punishment." I say the last part in a whisper. Her expression changes to genuine amusement.

I close the door to my trailer behind me and wish there was a key I could use to lock it or a boulder I could roll in front of it to barricade her inside.

Chapter Thirty-Four
Gabriella

Whitney Grace once barred Sara from her premiere party unprovoked. I know this because I had to listen to Sara rant about it for weeks. I never went to the parties. They were a place Sara would go to schmooze and mingle. She'd orchestrate her arrival with whatever It Girl was available and plan to have her picture taken by the paparazzi of her entering and exiting the venue. It was supposed to be one of those moments when fans would obsess about what other famous person their favorite famous person was hanging out with.

Except this time when Sara got to the venue, her name wasn't on the list. Imagine how embarrassed she was skulking away from the party after being rejected.

That night, Sara woke up the entire house by pulling every item out of the kitchen cabinets and flinging each one across the room. Poor Lupe had to refill the pantry from scratch. When she couldn't consume all the alcohol, she dumped bottles of it out into the pool.

None of that made it to the blogs. I suspect Sara's neighbors were used to her causing a ruckus, or her dad paid them well enough to keep them quiet.

To be clear, I'm not blaming Whitney for Sara's actions. Sara will always do what she wants. I'm blaming Whitney for being a liar.

Two weeks before the party, she came over to the house and invited Sara to that premiere. She invited her and then later gave a quote that while she admired Sara's work, she had never met her in person and therefore wouldn't have invited her to the party.

But I'm not doing this for Sara.

I'm doing this for Taylor.

Whitney will never have that opportunity again.

I wait long enough until I think Taylor has walked a short distance away. Whitney most likely would want to stay close to her competition. She won't be returning to her trailer anytime soon. She probably headed to set as soon as she finished talking to Taylor. She'll look more prepared that way.

"Look how dedicated she is to her craft," they'd say.

I exit the room Taylor intended to be my prison and walk. The laminated visitor badge shines brightly in the sun, gleaming at anyone who feels it necessary to glance at it.

There's more to dating a working actor than most people think. Everyone else has to support their partner by congratulating them when they earn promotions from work. I not only have to be supportive, I have to deliver the dream.

The door to Whitney's trailer is unlocked. They usually always are. Television stars have a habit of feeling too safe when on set, especially if they grew up with the lot being their only playground. Whitney's trailer is identical to Taylor's. It has the same white couch, vanity and bar. The artwork on the walls is different, but every mirror's placement is the same. A TV hangs over the counter, which holds the small fridge and microwave. It's modern with a neutral palette.

Do you know what happens when a star wrecks their trailer? No? Me neither.

The ornamental vase that once sat on the counter smashes to

the floor. The water runs in every direction. Some of it soaks into the rug laid out in the center of the room. Some of it remains in a puddle against the cabinet doors. I barely feel the white flowers crunch underneath my shoes.

The small bathroom, that's usually pretty empty, is filled with her products. She must've planned to stay for a while. The trail of her pink body wash follows me to the leather couch. I dump the tiny jar of gel into the sink and pile on the hair moisturizer and oil.

In the cabinets, I find a surprise, two bottles of Vodka. Tito's. One is already open. It soaks into the area of the rug that the water wasn't able to reach. Most of the second bottle dribbles onto the counter and drips onto the door to the microwave I leave propped open.

The reflection from the shiny black TV screen showcases my newest piece. It's been a while. I grip the bottle, pull back my arm, and ready my fingers to release and allow it to fly. It'll hit its target. Afterwards, I'll smash every mirror in sight.

"I don't need you to do this." Taylor's steps come at me fast. Before I know it, she twists her body around mine with her face in my neck.

The hand not prepared to launch the vodka bottle settles on her back. "This isn't the way to protect me. If I get this, we celebrate. If I don't, we eat ice cream and try again next time."

I hear her muffled words clearly, though I think my skin is wet. "She's a black girl from Atlanta. Her dad was murdered when she was three. Her mom died from cancer before she got to see her star in her own show. She was raised by her aunt and uncle, who went into debt so she could achieve her dream. If she wins, we all win."

Suddenly too heavy to hold, the bottle falls to my side. Taylor releases me and wipes at her face. "Let's clean this up as best as we can. I'll see if Zara can stall. Maybe she can take them to lunch or something." She types away on her phone and then eases it back into the pocket of her dress. I haven't told her yet that she looks beautiful in it. It's red—which isn't as great as yellow—but it glows on her skin. And now, I might not get the chance to.

Taylor finds towels she uses to soak up the liquid. "There's no way we're gonna be able to save this rug." She's mumbling more to herself than speaking to me.

I haven't moved. I've forgotten how to. The sight of her on her hands and knees cleaning up my mess conjures up an emotion I don't know if I've ever felt before.

Guilt.

Chapter Thirty-Five
Taylor

IF I HAD GONE to parties as a teenager, I would probably think this one is pretty lame. Lame seems rude. Tame is better. When Gabriella said that Chasity invited us to a party, my first thought was, *why*? I've been dating Gabriella for nearly two years and Chasity's never extended an olive branch. There have been no lunch invites. No requests for random hangouts. If Gabriella isn't there, Chasity is not interested.

Krystal at least asks me to go jogging with her, even though I always decline. One, I don't run. Two, sleep is better.

The music at this party is playing at a low volume. I don't know anyone here who isn't Gabriella or Chasity. Chasity talks to everyone and Gabriella ignores them. Krystal is missing. Every time the front door opens, I think it's her, but it never is.

"Is it true you used to date Kennedy Michaels?" I try not to look too disgusted. The girl who's sitting next to me has been hammering me with questions since we walked in. Kennedy Michaels is an asshole. His team hates him. His parents hate him. Hell, even his fans hate him. They dubbed him K-Drama after he had a meltdown at a fan event.

"No. I think you're thinking of Lauren Jacobs." No one likes her, either.

"Oh my God, yes. The two of you look so much alike."

No, we don't. Lauren Jacobs is a few inches taller than I am, a lot thinner and lighter skinned. We look nothing alike.

The girl keeps talking and I keep nodding as if everything she says is interesting. Though I catch Gabriella glancing at her a few times, she doesn't interject.

"Then, wait. Who are you dating?"

It takes my brain a while to bring her back into focus.

"Gabby." I point out Gabriella across the room. As soon as we walked through the door, Chasity put her in charge of drinks. It seemed kind of rude to me. Who invites someone to a party and then assigns them a task?

It takes the girl too long to process everything. Her mouth hangs open and then closes again. Odd. "Are you friends with Chasity?"

And do you know that she's gay? While I also find it unique that they had an entire friend group of queer people, girl, this is not that hard.

"Yeah, we work together." Her head keeps nodding and I follow her gesture in the awkward silence until I excuse myself and escape.

By the time I reach Gabriella, she's talking to someone else. The girl is darker than Gabriella, but Latina as well. She's very animated when telling her story. I catch a few of the phrases she throws out. Her anger is obvious even if you don't know what the word *puta* means or a *pinche pendejo*. Gabriella's grandma says that a lot.

When she notices me standing to the side, she rudely asks, "Can I help you?"

Now who's the puta?

"Cuida tu lenguaje."

The girl looks at me and then back at Gabriella. She clamps her hand over her mouth and then immediately apologizes. "My bad. I forgot."

I'm not exactly sure what she forgot, but Gabriella's warning was enough for her to correct herself. Gabriella looks at me with that crease in the middle of her forehead with her eyebrow raised.

"How long do we have to stay here?" It sounds bratty of me to ask, but Krystal is not here and Gabriella's too busy to entertain me. "What exactly is the purpose of this party?" It's not Chasity's birthday, I checked. Her birthday is at the beginning of next year.

Gabriella finishes stirring the jack and coke she just deposited into a plastic cup before handing it off. "She has some big announcement to make." Immediately, my mind jumps to the announcement I should have made weeks ago. We still haven't completely recovered from the Whitney Grace incident. Our lives together have become a thin film. We barely talk, barely touch and barely look at each other. Even now she focuses on the next guest and the next drink.

Still, I somehow know that if I tried to walk out of here with someone else, she'd suddenly be standing in the doorway.

I jump when the front door slams shut over the mellow music. Krystal stalks through the group, dressed in her uniform. Her name tag is still pinned to the front of her shirt.

"You motherfucker." Krystal's words are low and threatening. There's nothing on her face anyone could describe as aggressive. Out of the three of them, she's usually the one that's smiling. Her arms hang loosely to her side. Her eyes are trained on Chasity.

While the rest of us may be in the dark, Chasity looks like she knows exactly what Krystal is upset about. And that only angers her more.

"You selfish bitch!"

As Krystal moves closer to Chasity. Gabriella grabs onto the loop of her work pants to slow her pace. In true form, Chasity doesn't move from her position. Anyone else would have tried to run or plead their case. Not Queen Chasity.

Krystal continues to yell, and guests continue to watch the exchange. There's not a single ounce of regret on her face. Eventually tired of being restrained by Gabriella, she allows herself to be carried away out the front door. I hastily grab our things and prepare to follow them. Before my hand touches the knob of the door Gabriella has just slammed close, I turn to Chasity.

"I hope you live to regret whatever you did to hurt her." Her sneer is the only sign she gives that she even heard me.

By the time I make it downstairs to the parking lot, Krystal is sitting in the car's backseat bawling her eyes out.

"I am so stupid," she keeps repeating. Sobs turn into gasps for breaths and I worry she's having a panic attack. She clutches at her chest. Her long nails leave ragged marks along her neck. "I can't breathe! I can't breathe!"

"You can!" I probably shouldn't yell at her. "If you couldn't breathe, you wouldn't be able to speak." I look through Gabriella's glove department and find a pencil. I squat in front of Krystal's open door and raise it in the air. She's still sobbing and gasping, but not trying to tear her skin from her body.

"Follow the pencil. When it goes across the top, we're gonna breathe in. When I go down the sides we're gonna breathe out, slowly."

Krystal's tears swing from her chin with each nod of her head. I slowly draw the top of the invisible square and draw my breath in. Krystal follows along. I slowly empty the air from my chest while the pencil travels down. We follow the same pattern again and again. Gabriella waits to the side, patiently.

"Are you feeling better?" Krystal is visibly more stable. Her response is a few hiccups when words don't make it out.

I slide into the passenger seat, and Gabriella puts the key in the ignition to leave. The car ride becomes quiet, with fewer and fewer of Krystal's hiccups in between. Gabriella takes her to her bedroom. The slamming of drawers tells me she's looking for something for her to wear. I prepare a small snack and a glass of water and set it on the nightstand.

My bed is still empty after the completion of my night routine. Tonight my meditation involves leaves instead of balloons. *Notice each thought. Imagine placing it on a leaf and let it float down the river.*

I barely register the silence, but I'd know her touch anywhere. Gabriella slides underneath the covers behind me. The faint glow of my phone is the evidence I need to confront her.

"You turned my lady off."

It takes more effort than usual to push out the words through my sleepiness.

"Her voice is annoying."

Soft, thick lips land on my shoulder.

"She's soothing."

"She's full of shit."

An invisible force tugs my lips into a smile. "Since we didn't get to hear Chasity's news, wanna hear mine?"

I pause for her reaction. "Sure." She releases the word slowly.

"I got the call about the competition show." The muscles in the arm she laid across my waist tighten. "They changed their mind about wanting me to host. They asked me to be a judge instead." Her arm relaxes. She snuggles closer, clearly relieved at the outcome.

"When does filming start?"

"I don't know if I'm gonna take it."

"Why wouldn't you?"

"Because my meditation lady keeps trying to help me put your behavior on a tiny leaf, but it keeps sinking."

When she says nothing, I turn to face her. Wide eyes stare back at me. "I told you she was full of shit."

"Gabby, what were you thinking? You would've ruined your career before it even began." I don't think Whitney and her manager bought my excuse. Ironically, I'd pretended to have a panic attack and jumped into her shower fully clothed. I needed to explain the empty bottles of beauty products and the soaking wet floor.

I'd told them I must've been delirious and thought Whitney's trailer was my own. *"I drank the bottles of vodka, hoping to calm myself down. When that didn't work, I thought a cold shower would do it. I tripped and fell so badly that I toppled out of the shower. Gabriella heard the commotion and came to investigate."*

Lucky me.

I got the biggest tongue-lashing of my career from Zara. *"What were you thinking, insinuating you had a drinking problem?"* She demanded the real story, but I maintained the lie I told. The next day, Whitney sent me an email with the number for her psychiatrist.

It's what I deserved for acting like a maniac.

Am I insane? Well, why yes, I am. Insanely in love with the most frustrating woman I have ever known.

"I don't know. Old habits die hard, I guess." There's a hint of sadness in her eyes. I can't take the strange expression on her face, tainting her.

"I have other news." Her eyelashes flutter to help her eyes focus again. "I was asked to interview for a magazine."

"You don't sound too happy about it."

"I'm confused. It's for a magazine with a primarily Spanish-speaking audience. *The Paige Society* was just released in some new countries. It's nice that there are new fans, but I'm worried the interview will be in Spanish."

And while I've learned a lot of new words, I still have to slow my brain down to catch things from people who speak Spanish rapidly. Gabriella's family has become accustomed to talking slower for me and forcing me to practice.

"Ask them for the interview questions beforehand. We can go over them and then you can practice your answers. It's what Sara always did."

"Sara doesn't know Spanish?"

"No. We'd rehearse what she'd say, and she'd remember it. It's no different from remembering lines."

Gabriella's eyes drift close, and I keep the remaining questions to myself. I don't count her freckles tonight. Instead, I envision leaves drifting down a clear river toward a steep waterfall with all of them carrying the same flower.

Chapter Thirty-Six
Gabriella

It's that time of year in fall when it gets darker a lot sooner than it did in the summer. Every year, I try to remember which one I prefer. As a kid, I liked the long summer days and early mornings. As an adult, I curse at the first sign of sunrise, knowing that my time cuddled up with Taylor is nearly over.

I offer a reassuring smile to the waiter as they refill my water. It's mid-day and not busy enough for them to make me wait to be seated until the other member of my party is here. It's a nice restaurant with an ambiance I would expect in Playa Del Rey; casual, but expensive.

Eryn walks through the front doors with sunglasses pulled over her eyes and her curly hair perfectly fluffed. As the non-famous sibling, most people would assume that Eryn is more low-key, especially since she's older. That would be far from the truth. Her heels click against the floor with every step. Eryn always gives stay-away energy, which is the complete opposite of Taylor, who wants everyone to feel welcome.

Out of all the members of Taylor's family, Eryn is the hardest to read. Sometimes she gives off the vibe of the concerned older sister, but she can also be harsh. I haven't quite figured out for myself whether her behavior towards Taylor needs to be checked. Taylor always takes it in stride.

However, a good assessment is ongoing.

She follows the hostess to our table, looking straight ahead. I'm unsure if she's wearing a cape or one of those weird shirts that flare out on the sides for no reason. She places her small Chanel purse on the table behind the row of condiments. The waiter from earlier approaches and she orders a glass of wine.

"Thank you for coming," I greet her.

She pulls the shades up to rest on the top of her head. The curls provide the perfect cushion.

"Well, I'm curious to hear what you want to talk about so secretly."

"We should order first." I picked my selections earlier. Eryn takes the time she needs to order. When she's done and they remove our menus from the table, I dip into my bag and sit the two small boxes on top.

"I asked you here because I value your opinion." The top of the first ring box snaps back. The second does the same. "I can't decide which ring Taylor may say yes to." I've given her nine so far, all leading to this one moment.

The last ring.

And the rest of our lives.

Eryn's mouth drops open at the sight of the two heart-shaped engagement rings.

"Oh, my..."

She extracts both rings from their places. When she moves them, they sparkle. It has been a tough decision. Round cut or not. Traditional band or a band traced with round diamonds.

"Solitaire?" I ask her, almost impatiently. Eryn studies the more modern white gold, heart-shaped solitaire ring.

"I want to say yes. The simplicity of this one is stunning, but there's something about the way this one shines."

She slides each one onto her pinky finger. The only one they fit on. It was Nicole who tricked Taylor into having every single one of her fingers sized at my request. She did it begrudgingly, and only after I showed her some rings I wanted to buy. I don't know what excuse she gave Taylor, but it worked.

Eryn's eyes swing from the sparkle of the rings to the brown of mine. "Why do you love my sister? Really. And don't give me some bullshit about her being amazing. We fucking know."

"It's..." I pause to think about my answer. This moment has played out in my head before, but not with Eryn. I've expected this conversation to be with her parents and it still might one day. "It's not a reason." Eryn looks at me with narrow eyes and a twisted facial expression. "You know how some people will say that they love so-and-so because they make them feel special or they complete them?"

She nods her head slowly with her eyes still skeptically thin.

"I love Taylor not because of anything she's ever done, but because she's someone I've never been able to forget. Eryn, I saw her as a kid, and from the very first moment, there was this feeling that I couldn't explain other than knowing I had never felt that way about anyone. And never did again. Even when I was supposed to hate her. I love Taylor because I couldn't hate her. No matter how uncomfortable it was for me. No matter how hard. It should have been easy, but I thought of her and felt everything I wasn't supposed to feel."

Eryn's eyes fall to the rings in her hand.

"I know we've had a complicated and messy road. And I know I'm lucky. She's perfect. And I'm...work. I don't love her because she's perfect. I love her because somehow, all those years ago, I always knew she would be."

She secures each one back into its respective box. One box clicks shut. She turns the other toward me.

"This is the one."

Her eyes are no longer thin and although her smile doesn't resemble Taylor's, it's there.

"I think so, too."

I clutch the box in my hand. It's been so long. Almost two years of meticulous planning and waiting. The round-cut heart-shaped ring with the diamond-studded band had been my favorite, but I wanted to be sure.

Eryn removes her purse from its place and rumbles through it until she produces a notepad and pen.

"So, how many in the wedding party?"

Chapter Thirty-Seven
Taylor

THE MODEST ONE-STORY RANCH house looks nothing like what I imagined. I check and re-check the address on my phone for inaccuracies, but find none. The front yard of the home is well-manicured with nicely pruned rose bushes. This information I only know from my time with Gabriella's dad makes me smile.

My lips turn down in a frown once I remember where I am. Her home is too close for comfort. It should have taken me longer to get here, instead of the mere seven-minute drive.

They are the type of people who hang wind chimes and bird feeders on the porch. A custom doormat with a single initial greets me at the door. The birds chirp louder as I stand in place. They're either announcing my arrival, telling me to go away, or giving me good advice. *Run,* they probably say.

I knock anyway.

The woman who comes to the door looks almost exactly as I remember her. It's been fifteen years since I last saw her, but I'll never forget her face.

Sara's mother has always been beautiful.

"Good afternoon, Ms. Aguilar."

"Good afternoon, Taylor. It's been a while."

She opens the door wide to allow me space to enter. The furniture in the living room is older. There's a brown china cabinet filled with little figurines and floral patterned furniture.

"Can I get you anything to drink?"

"No, I'm okay."

She stares at me for a moment with a faint smile. Her eyes travel from my face down to my feet and back again. "You've grown up well." She nods in approval. "I wish the two of you would have gotten along better."

"Me too," I say it mostly because it's what she needs to hear from me at the moment. But I also say it because the plant-filled living room with vines traveling up the ceiling paints a different perspective of who I ever thought Sara could be.

"I'll see if she's ready for visitors." I watch Ms. Aguilar walk through the kitchen to the other side of the house. The kitchen looks just as traditional as the living room, with its brown wooden cabinets and white tiled countertops. Despite the age of everything, it all looks to be in good condition.

Older photographs of Sara hang on the walls. An outsider would easily mistake them for annual school portraits instead of headshots. Tucked in a corner of one is a wallet-sized photo of Sara and Gabriella in formal dresses. It's attached to the largest portrait and the only one that isn't a headshot - prom.

"Bold of you to come here." Sara looks the most casual I have ever seen her in a tank top and shorts. Her dark brown hair is thrown into a loose, messy bun. When she opens her palm in front of me, I notice the chips in her nail polish. I stare down at the house key she presents.

"What's that for?" She tilts her head from one side to the other.

"Brie didn't lock herself out of the house?" The ache in my chest sends shockwaves through my entire body.

"Uh, no. That's not why I'm here." Sara's fingers close around the key, protectively. She slides it into a pocket of her shorts and never breaks our gaze.

"Mom. We're going out back." Her mom yells back confirmation, and I follow Sara out the rear sliding door. Though smaller than the front yard, the back is immaculate. A variety of roses line the perimeter, meeting a water feature at the center. It's loud enough to produce the necessary effect for privacy on such a small property.

Sara sits on a swing bench and lightly pushes it with her feet. She notices me watching and stops it by burying her toes in the grass. I hesitantly stand in front of the vacant seat and claim the space once the bench comes swinging forward.

"It's hard to imagine now, but Brie loves to swing." The bench rocks back and forth from the weight of the two of us. "Did you know that?"

"No." There's no reason to lie. Every interaction with Sara is a test.

"Yeah. She'd go early in the morning before any of the kids got there to hog them all. That was before all the jobs, though. She's probably too tired now."

Listening to my girlfriend's ex-girlfriend talk about her as if she knows her the best is infuriating. I have spent my entire career denying I was ever jealous of Sara. I never cared about what she had or what role they offered her. I didn't care about her modeling contracts or her brand endorsements. None of that ever mattered.

What does matter are secrets.

"Tell me about Daisy." My request elicits a chuckle from her.

"She doesn't know you're here." There's a hint of pleasure in her voice. I can imagine what it's like for her to have me come to her with questions. She's tried to get my attention for a long time and now she has it.

Still, I maintain my silence. All I need from Sara is confirmation

I think I already have the answers to. If she won't give them to me, I'll go to the source. It'll hurt more coming from Gabriella. But sometimes pain is necessary.

Sara finally looks at me, her smile only slight. "What do you want to know?"

"Who is Daisy?"

"Me. Her. We took turns."

It's a truth I told myself I was ready for. I've been preparing for this moment for weeks. The more I loved Gabriella, the more I saw through her. Something was wrong.

"Why? You just thought it would be fun to play a two-year-long prank on me?"

"Pranks? Are we in kindergarten? The only thing I wanted was information. And you gave us plenty."

I shudder, thinking about the conversations we had. Daisy was the person I shared my secrets with. She knew about my fantasies about exhibitionism and role play. She made me feel like I was safe.

They lied.

"I was going to tell everyone about you." She leans close to me to whisper, though she doesn't have to. "Sweet, innocent Taylor wants the entire world to watch her come."

"Stop exaggerating. No one would have believed that."

"That's what my dad thought, too. He said you would just deny all the evidence. And because people loved you, they would believe you."

"What was the evidence?"

"Chat logs."

"Does Gabriella know?"

"About the logs? Of course. She stored all the evidence. There was so much I had to buy a bigger binder." I don't return the smirk she throws my way. An image of Gabriella saving, printing, and sorting my most intimate secrets together to carry out a conspiracy against me occupies my brain.

"Was any of it real?"

Sara lets out an exaggerated sigh.

"All of it was real. I *really* wanted to ruin you. You were *really* that fucking desperate and Brie, she was *really* done." She says the last part with a hint of sadness in her voice. I glance at her. She fixes her gaze on the water spilling out of the stone pot in the garden.

"If the binder is real, then Gabriella and I..." are based on a lie. "Is this a part of the plan?" Am I still a pawn in Sara's plot for revenge with my girlfriend as her accomplice?

"If it's a part of the plan, then I'm out of the loop. I don't know what you did to convince her to leave me, but it worked." Her shoulders give a slight shrug.

"You don't have to pretend you don't care about her." Sara's eyes shift from the fountain to the blades of grass she pulls between her toes. "No one keeps spare keys for people they don't love. That's something you have that I don't."

Sara twists up her face in confusion. When my words register, she shakes her head.

"Why do you need it? You already have her heart." Her words make everything even more confusing. "That's what I overlooked. We were both focused on you for two completely different reasons."

Sara is Daisy. And so is Gabriella.

"Did we have sex?" It's a thought that's plagued me the most since Daisy's disappearance. I've tried my best not to think about it too much.

"If we'd had sex, you'd know. It would be an experience you wouldn't be able to forget." It's amazing to me how unconcerned Sara can appear with all the damage she's done. With all the damage she tried to do to me.

"I didn't tell her about Lucy." Sara's shoulders lift, tighten, and then release. Lucy's name almost escaped my lips plenty of times. She was a fan, always hanging around near the studio lot with signs and cookies. Nicole and I always stopped on our way inside to greet her. Sara mostly ignored her. Until she needed her.

There was hope in the beginning that Sara had changed. Gabriella's arms and wrists were always free of marks. "I didn't think it would be helpful for her to know you used to slice open someone else's skin."

I follow Sara's gaze to the back door. It's empty. No one stands behind the glass looking out or listening in. "It wouldn't have changed anything if you had."

"Why not?"

"Because they're different." She casts a dark look in my direction. "Lucy served a purpose. Brie has a place."

My brain tries to untangle Sara's twisted logic. "I don't understand. Gabriella's scars were hidden, but Lucy's were the same."

Sara sighs and leans back on the bench with her legs stretched out. "You think Lucy is why I hate you." I nod. "Perhaps. Doesn't matter though. I would've dropped Lucy the moment I met Brie. If anything, I hate you more now than I did before."

I had hoped that by taking Lucy from Sara, I could prevent what happened to Gabriella. They described Lucy's injuries as superficial. Sara had cut deeper than she was supposed to, but not deep enough to cause any damage. The network couldn't afford to lose their star during the last season.

"So what now?" I ask. Technically, I've accomplished my mission. I came to Sara and found out the truth. Gabriella lied. The love of my life was my enemy. She gathered evidence about me to use against me, eventually. She infiltrated my family and manipulated her way into my home. My bed. My heart.

"Believe it or not, I think we can help each other." For the first time since coming outside, Sara looks directly at me. "You want your secrets. I want my girlfriend." I can't explain the territorial clench that constricts around my heart at her claim. I shake it off to process her proposal. Sara always has a plan. "If you break up with her, I'll give it all back. It's my only copy. You can do whatever you want with it."

"What if she doesn't go back?"

"That's not your problem. I overlooked the access I gave her to you. She knew everything about you. She thought she had a chance. But once you leave, she has nothing left. I'm her only option."

I hate how she talks about Gabriella, as if she depends on her for survival. She's stronger than most. Sara doesn't get to take credit for Gabriella being who she is. She's amazing despite her, not because of her.

"Are you even sorry for what you did?" I can't fathom hurting people how Sara does. She does it without thought or remorse and rarely is she held accountable for her actions.

And this won't be any different. There's nothing I can do about what happened all those years ago.

Sara displays no emotional reaction to my question. She leans back against the bench, her knees sway with the rhythm of the swing.

It sickens me how she sits through it all so peacefully. *Poor Gabriella.* "She owes you nothing." Even though I'm angry with her, I know that much.

Sara continues with her movement as if there was no interruption in our silence. "Tell me, Taylor. What did she lose by being with me?"

"Time. Love." Because when I told Gabriella I loved her, I meant it. Each word, every time I whispered them, was caked in truth. And when I could finally say it with no moon high in the sky and my voice low, I savored every moment. *We locked eyes over the head of a barista, you bitch.*

The rings on my left hand clink against the metal chain. There are nine with only one finger bare. The woman I love chose them all.

"Let me tell you about *my* girlfriend. She cares a lot about the people she loves. She's a very talented artist, whose work is beautiful and will someday be recognized without you. You don't get credit for being a shit partner and forcing her to walk away. She could've loved you, but you wouldn't let her. I love Gabriella. I used to complain that she barely smiled, but then I realized she was reserving her smile for me. I met my girlfriend in a coffee shop and thought she was the most beautiful woman sitting in the room. You're not a part of our story."

The chain of the bench swing rattles as I stand to leave. The short grass crinkles beneath my feet as I retrace the route that brought me here. I don't look up to see if Sara's mom is on the other side of the sliding door or standing in the kitchen as I pass.

It's time to leave.

I shut the door behind me and take each small step, one at a time, back to my car. I came here for the truth and I'm leaving with a dilemma.

It wasn't Sara's responsibility to tell me she lied. We have always had a strong dislike for each other. Sara has no loyalty to me. If given the opportunity, we'd leave one another locked in a burning building. Me, for self-preservation. Sara, for sport.

The moment Gabriella changed our relationship was the

moment she owed me an explanation. I never got it and now it may be too late.

Because there's something I didn't tell Sara about Gabriella; she gives with her whole heart and can shatter you with one breath.

Chapter Thirty-Eight
Gabriella

TAYLOR HASN'T COME HOME. We left for San Diego separately, understanding that she was going to spend some time with my family before heading back home. Before I could make it back, she texted to say she was going to be staying with her family for the rest of the weekend.

That was three days ago.

I sleep in my bedroom instead of ours. It's closer to the front. I want to hear when she comes home.

"Are you sure you didn't do anything?" Krystal watches me pace the entryway of the apartment from the living room. "It happens to the best of us." The possibility of living in an empty apartment, like Krystal now has to do without Chasity, is terrifying. My body isn't used to this. She's used to having a warm body asleep next to her. There's no humming between the walls. No random splatters of glitter on the floor.

It's lonely.

"I didn't do shit." At least nothing that I remember. And I've tried to recall every moment of our time together this past week. I've even asked.

Gabriella [12:34 a.m.]

Please tell me if I've done something wrong.

There was no answer. There hasn't been an answer in days. When I called her mom, she was in her usual bright spirits. She didn't sound angry at me. When she asked, *"Do you want me to put Taylor on the phone?"* my heart filled with hope. But when she left, no one ever came back. The line didn't go dead. It was just quiet.

I stayed on the line and watched the seconds turn to minutes and the minutes turn to hours.

"What do I do if she doesn't come home?"

"You stay in this fancy ass apartment for as long as you can and then you move in with me."

"That's not what I mean." I know how to survive. I've been doing it for a long time. "Maybe I should go get her myself."

"How? You think you're gonna walk into her parents' house and drag her out? They look like nice people, but I doubt they're that nice. And say you two get back together. They're not going to approve of you marrying her after that."

"We're not broken up."

"I meant broken up after she breaks up with you for storming into her mama's house."

"Then what am I supposed to do?!" My voice cracks with the anxiety that has been building up since I got the first text. She would've called me. She would've called and we would've talked. She would've told me she loved me after she said goodnight.

I've been whispering it alone, instead. After I've sent the messages that have remained unread.

"Do you think she's with someone else?"

"No, Krystal. She's...not like them." I had a place in Sara's life she refused to let me out of. Chasity refused to commit to Krystal because she thought she'd always be there. Taylor wouldn't cheat on me. I don't know how I know that, but I do. Even with her moments of make-believe, I was always the main character.

Always have been.

The sound of the private elevator arriving sends a shock to my heart. I wipe my eyes until my skin feels dry. I wait with labored breath, listen to the sound of the door unlock, and watch it swing open.

Nicole.

"What are you doing here?"

I didn't start disliking Nicole until I started dating Taylor. Before, she was a neutral non-factor and nothing to worry about. Since then, she has been a lingering pain in my ass. She's not externally combative. She doesn't start arguments or fights. Her dislike is clear on her face, like tainted sweetness.

I hate it.

"Be thankful it's me and not Eryn." She bends to the corner and stands to balance the two boxes in her hands. "You're supposed to be in class." I haven't been to class all week. I told my professors I was dealing with a death in the family. It was more like an assassination of my heart.

"Where do you think you're going?" I stand in the path that leads from the living room to Taylor's room. Our room.

"Look, Gabriella. Don't make this harder than it has to be. You had to know this was going to happen, eventually. I'm going to get what she needs and then the movers will be here this weekend. Make sure you're not. The apartment is paid for until the end of the year. I'm sure you'll figure something out after that. You're full of grand ideas."

If I hit her, Taylor will hate me.

I shake my head while staring straight at Nicole. The message is actually for Krystal, who silently moved from the couch to stand just a few feet behind my girlfriend's best friend.

Chasity would've hit her already.

"I'm not letting you up there."

"You can't stop this from happening. It either gets done today or this weekend. Regardless, it's over."

The whiplash across my face gives the same result, as if she raised her hand and slapped me.

"If it's over, Taylor can come and tell me that herself."

"You're not Sara. You don't get to make demands. You don't own Taylor like Sara owned you."

My arm rises and my hand connects with Nicole's cheek. It happens so quickly, Nicole is down on the ground before I have a chance to blink away the newest batch of tears. There's no holding them back now.

The boxes clatter to the floor and bang up against the window. It's dark outside. I kept the curtains open just in case I spotted Taylor wandering around.

Nicole kicks at me to keep me from getting on top of her. A raging bull with a split lip has replaced her usual kind expression. There's some redness beating under her brown skin. Krystal grabs hold of her neck and diverts her attention.

I can't think about the ramifications of our actions right now. Nicole's trying to take something away from me. Something I've wanted almost my whole life. I position my hips over Nicole's and pull back my fist.

"Gabby. Stop." I'd recognize that voice in my sleep. As if my arms are on autopilot, they slack at my side. Nicole is wrong. It's Taylor who owns me. Her arms wrap around me and she pulls me back. I stumble off of Nicole, who gasps for breath once Krystal releases her grip.

"Taylor, get out of here!" Nicole looks disheveled with wild eyes.

She tries to push herself up, but can't gather the strength.

"It's okay," Taylor says. Even if she's not talking to me, I allow her words to calm my anger.

She's home.

Everything *is* okay.

I turn over in her arms. I want to kiss her and apologize for every offense I don't remember committing. Whatever it is, she wants me to do. Whatever it is, she needs me to say. I'll do it. I'll apologize until I run out of breath.

My kiss lands on her chin. I keep it there and press my lips against her skin repeatedly.

"Taylor, don't." Nicole has gathered enough strength to get to her knees. She doesn't look so angry anymore. Her tear-filled eyes look back at Taylor. My lips soak in Taylor's tears that successfully escape from her own eyes.

"Emmy, don't cry."

She cries harder and grips me tighter. I try to kiss them all away.

Nicole sways when she stands. She picks up one of the fallen boxes and makes her way up the stairs one step at a time. I don't care what she takes with her. She won't be leaving here with Taylor.

I give Krystal the go-ahead to leave. She tentatively walks to the front door, looking from me to Taylor to up at the ceiling. I can hear Nicole filling the box with things that are insignificant.

Everything I need is right here.

We have a few moments of silence before she speaks again. The tears don't come down as quickly. Her breathing is steadier. Her grip is not as tight.

"We need to talk about Daisy." Her words come out slow and clear through the sniffling. My arms tighten around her. It's the last thing I want to hear.

"I'm so stupid. It was staring at me right in the face. You didn't even try to hide it." She's not stupid. I'm a good liar. I've been pretending my whole life. I know how to play the role of the good girlfriend as well as I know how to play the role of the good daughter. You give people what they need and they don't expect anything more.

With my parents, it's financial stability. With Sara, it was an emotional outlet. For Taylor it's space. I give her the room she needs to be herself in an industry determined to cage her.

It's not that I didn't try. I couldn't. Daisy is as part of me as Taylor is. That's why it worked so well.

The best lies are coated in truth.

I would have told her, eventually. After the wedding, maybe. When we were so far removed from it, it wouldn't matter anymore.

"What do you want to know?" I'll say anything to keep her. I'll sing like a traitorous pirate with her neck on the guillotine.

She looks down at me. Her hands caress my face for the first time in what feels like a long time.

"Your grandma calls you Margarita. For a while, I just thought she liked to drink. And then I realized Margarita is Spanish for Daisy. Sara doesn't know how to speak Spanish, but Daisy made me practice it once and then you continued it."

I can't deny it. I try to explain. "Emmy, I–"

"You never questioned anything I wanted to do. You just went along with it, even when it made you angry. I thought it was because you were used to a different type of relationship with Sara. I thought I had gotten lucky. My partner was so understanding and nonjudgmental. When really, I didn't need to explain anything to you that you already knew."

More tears trail from her eyes and drip down her chin. I trace my finger against her jaw in an attempt to collect them. Every one that escapes me, feels like it's mocking me.

I'm losing her.

"I understand. I know and love everything about you. It doesn't matter when I found out or what my name was or wasn't. I have always loved you."

"Love? You gathered an arsenal for her to use against me and you didn't even give me a heads up. There are pictures and voice messages and—"

"Sara doesn't have any of that."

"How do you know that?"

I grab her wrist and drag her to my bedroom. Leaving her in any room alone is too risky. The contents of the top drawer of my nightstand rattle when I pull it open. I slam the two cell phones on the table. One was gifted to me by Sara. The other, I purchased on my own.

"The moment Daisy went offline was the moment she lost all access. As far as Sara was concerned, Emmy and Daisy were done."

"Because she already had what she needed. You gave it to her!"

"Emmy–"

"Stop calling me that! That's not real. None of this was real!"

"It is real!"

The only thing I can do when she pulls away from me is drop to my knees and hang on. I wrap my arms around her thighs and bury my face in her jeans.

Please don't go.

Please don't leave.

Please stay with me.

Unable to free herself from me, Taylor collapses to the floor. All the tears I miss fall everywhere, except for in my hands. They're wet now. Along with my shirt and large patches on her jeans. My thighs are sleek with her sadness. The evidence of it drops just beyond the reach of my shorts.

"You broke my heart, Gabriella Margarita Flores." She says it perfectly. Not a syllable out of place. Not an accent missing. Even with the tears and the tightness in her chest that barely let any air in, she's perfect.

"If you love her, you'll let her go. You can't fix this," Nicole whispers the words in my ear while she stands over us. Taylor is wailing. She's not fighting me as much as she's trying to stop herself from falling apart.

I do, but it's hard. I can and I will.

Loosening my grip from around her waist is the hardest thing I have ever done. Watching Nicole drag her away, Taylor still heaving and gasping, shattered by the mistake I made, is the most heart-wrenching thing I have ever witnessed. My heart chips away into a thousand pieces with each step she takes from me.

I tell myself I will survive this moment. I will embed this image of her leaving into my brain until the point when we're meant to connect again. I'll do better next time. There'll be no more lies, no more tricks, and no goodbyes. I can't allow it. With time, she'll come to understand the truth. It took me a while to realize it at some point. She was never the girl I wanted. She's always been the girl I love.

She'll be fine.

Until then.

THE END

Are you sad? Me too. Don't worry though, the night Taylor explored her stalker fantasy is available now when you subscribe to my mailing list. Too soon? No worries. You can always read it tomorrow.

If you would like to keep following Taylor & Gabriella's story, Suite Enemy, the conclusion of the duology, is available here.

Goodies

If you would like to see what happens when Taylor encounters her biggest fan, the bonus scene is available here.

If you would like to continue to discuss the Intimate Beginnings of Taylor, join Lavender's Intimate Suite, a group for all readers of the series to come together.

If you would like to read ahead to the future books before they are polished and published, join me on REAM here.

Acknowledgements

I WANNA THANK MY MAMA for waking me up on Saturday mornings to oldies, dancing around the kitchen and singing out of tune. Most of all I want to thank you for always making sure I knew what love was and no matter how far I traveled, I could always come home. I love you.

To my husband, I love that you were able to support me when I told you about my dreams and the certainty that had cemented itself into my heart that I was indeed bisexual. Through Gabriella I express my love to you and the willingness you have shown to share with me your culture, hopes, fears and most of all your love. I have said it before and I'll say it again, I am so happy to be sharing my life with you. Te amo, mi esposo.

To Maritza, thank you for lending me your ear and beautiful mind to utilize when mine was stuck in the clouds and lost in the chaos. I greatly appreciate your help throughout this personal journey.

To Daddy, I miss you. I know you're proud of me every day. I don't need you to read this book to know that, so please, wherever you are in the universe, don't read it.

About the author

 **Lavender Quinn** is a lover of all things purple and sparkly. She's an avid believer of glitter when crafting, hot chocolate even when it's not cold out and eating ice cream when it's raining. She was born and raised in Los Angeles, CA in the same diverse community she strives to recreate and bring to life in her sapphic romance novels. When not writing about her daydreams and book wives, you may find her underneath the covers watching reality television in the dark, reading a love story, listening to music or silently dancing to the glow of candlelight.

www.Lavenderquinn.com

www.ingramcontent.com/pod-product-compliance
Lightning Source LLC
Chambersburg PA
CBHW020349010826
48973CB00005B/1334